THE PENGUIN CLASSICS

FOUNDER EDITOR (1944–64): E. V. RIEU

PAULINE MATARASSO read modern languages at Lady Margaret Hall, Oxford, and gained First Class Honours in 1950. She was awarded a Doctorat de l'Université de Paris in 1958. Her thesis, *Recherches historiques et littéraires sur 'Raoul de Cambrai'* was published in 1962.

THE QUEST
OF THE HOLY GRAIL

Translated with an Introduction by

P. M. MATARASSO

PENGUIN BOOKS

Penguin Books Ltd, Harmondsworth, Middlesex, England
Penguin Books Inc., 7110 Ambassador Road, Baltimore, Maryland 21207, U.S.A.
Penguin Books Australia Ltd, Ringwood, Victoria, Australia
Penguin Books Canada Ltd, 41 Steelcase Road West, Markham, Ontario, Canada
Penguin Books (N.Z.) Ltd, 182–190 Wairau Road, Auckland 10, New Zealand

—

This translation first published 1969
Reprinted 1971, 1973, 1975, 1976
Copyright © P. M. Matarasso, 1969

—

Made and printed in Great Britain by
Cox & Wyman Ltd,
London, Reading and Fakenham
Set in Linotype Pilgrim

Contents

Acknowledgements

I would like to thank Mrs D. R. Sutherland, Fellow of Lady Margaret Hall, who read a part of this translation in typescript and enabled me by her helpful criticism and suggestions to amend it in many particulars. She has also been most generous with her help in textual difficulties.

My grateful thanks are also due to Father Fabian Radcliffe O.P. who kindly agreed to vet the introduction and notes in case I had been guilty of any theological solecisms.

My gratitude goes out last but not least to my family, friends and acquaintances for all manner of succour and above all for their gift of listening without appearing bored.

PMM

Introduction

THE *Queste del Saint Graal* despite its Arthurian setting is not a romance, it is a spiritual fable. This may seem surprising in view of the fact that it forms part of a vast compilation known as the Prose *Lancelot*, which might justifiably be called the romance to end romances. It is less surprising however when one considers that it is the product of a period when things were rarely quite what they seemed, when the outward appearance was merely a garment in which to dress some inward truth, when the material world was but a veil through which the immutable could be sporadically glimpsed and perpetually reinterpreted. Most medieval literature can be read on more than one level, that of the story proper, and that of the meaning it served to illustrate, the famous combination of 'sens' and 'matière', so beloved of Chrétien de Troyes. The author of the *Quest* was not therefore doing anything exceptional in using his story to clothe and exemplify a meaning that transcended it; he merely did it with greater single-mindedness and took it to more logical conclusions. One can fairly say that he did not write a single paragraph for the pleasure of story-telling. It would be wrong however on that account to jump to the conclusion that his tale is boring. On the contrary, he tells it remarkably well, and the fact that every line is subordinated to his central theme enabled him to avoid the death-trap of prolixity into which his colleagues, responsible for the greater part of the *Lancelot* romance, so often fell.

The *Quest of the Holy Grail* has a place in the canon of spiritual literature, not among the theological treatises, but on the shelves reserved for works of popular appeal. This is a guide to the spiritual life aimed at the court rather than the cloister, and translated into what was then the most popular currency. It is hardly possible to overrate the vogue created in the latter part of the twelfth century by the unleashing of the first Arthurian stories on a society which they reflected in much the same measure as it imitated them. Some indication is provided by the pleasant story cited in 1220 by the Cistercian monk, Cesarius of Heisterbach, telling of how the abbot Gevardus, faced with a chapter full of dozing monks, exclaimed: 'Listen, brethren, listen! I have something new and wonderful to tell you: There once was a king, whose name was Arthur . . .' Here he broke off to point the obvious moral to rows of upturned and, one fears, crestfallen faces. The author of the *Quest* resorted to much the same means, but refrained from turning the carrot into a stick.

Given the dual nature of the work, two questions chiefly spring to mind: firstly, what were its sources? secondly, how did the author adapt them and how far was he successful? The first takes us on to ground as perilous as any of the forests in which Arthurian heroes lost their way. It is a problem of great complexity, bedevilled by conflicting theories, which considerations of space prevent my setting out. I shall therefore, treading warily through the maze, attempt at the risk of over-simplification to outline the subject as concisely as possible, referring the reader where necessary to works which examine the problems in greater depth.

THE LEGEND OF THE HOLY GRAIL

The 'matière de Bretagne' which formed the theme and incident of so much of medieval literature of the twelfth and early thirteenth centuries appears to hark back, at any rate in part, to a corpus of Celtic myth and legend preserved in Ireland, Wales, and to some degree in Cornwall, and cross-fertilized by constant contact between the indigenous populations. How the figure of Arthur came to be connected with this material is far from clear and this is not the moment to investigate his claims to a place in history as well as legend. It would seem however that at some stage legends woven round a hero of the British resistance to the Saxon hordes became incorporated in the older pagan heritage. Indeed these legends may have proved so resistant to time and change partly because they were the culture of a subject people.

The Saxons seem to have shown very little interest in these

stories sung or recited by Welsh bards, nor do we hear anything about them under the Norman kings, too busy establishing their grip on the conquered land. With the accession of the Plantagenets, however, things change: court life becomes more civilized, Eleanor of Aquitaine brings from France her poets and her minstrels, her love of life and letters. Perhaps, too, Henry II found it politic to foster past tales of British glory to rival the lustre which the legend of Charlemagne conferred on the kings of France.

Be that as it may, Geoffrey of Monmouth produced shortly after 1130 what a contemporary chronicler somewhat acidly described as 'the fables about Arthur which he took from the ancient fictions of the Britons and increased out of his own head'. He followed this up a little later by a book called the *Vita Merlini*. Most scholars no longer attribute to Geoffrey of Monmouth the prime role he was once thought to have had in the propagation of the Arthurian legends. Perhaps his Latin prose conferred a certain respectability on these 'ancient fictions'. Certainly the dates of his works are important, for before him there was nothing, and the trickle he started soon became a flood. In 1155 a Norman poet called Wace translated Geoffrey's Latin into French. Within the next thirty years the Tristan romances, the lais of Marie de France and the romances of Chrétien de Troyes had all seen the light of day.

Undoubtedly the Norman Conquest was a central factor in that it spread the French language and culture right across England to the marches of Wales and opened the gates of French courts first in Britain and then on the Continent to Welsh bards and story-tellers eager to peddle their wares. The same period saw the opening up of the routes to the East with the two-way traffic created by the Crusades. The courts of Northern France found themselves therefore at one of those crossroads of history where ideas, themes, subject-matter, much of it old but all of it novel, could intermingle and create fresh patterns, forming a new and exciting mould into which so much literary activity was to be poured.

But what of the Holy Grail itself? The legend as set out in the *Quest* represents the Grail as the dish in which Christ ate the paschal lamb with His apostles and which was brought to

Britain by Joseph of Arimathea, the first missionary to this island. The tradition attributing possession of this relic to Joseph of Arimathea goes back to the apocryphal Evangelium Nicodemi; the link between Joseph, the Grail vessel and an early Christian settlement at Glastonbury is found in a work composed around the year 1200 by a French knight called Robert de Boron, though where and how he came by the tale remains a mystery. The Grail vessel is also associated with a miraculous lance which the author of the *Quest*, along with certain of his predecessors, identifies with the lance known as the lance of Longinus, with which Christ's side was pierced on the cross.

Once these precious relics had come to Britain their custody devolved upon a line of Grail-keepers, known as the Fisher Kings, descendants of Joseph of Arimathea. The Grail was preserved in their Castle of Corbenic, enveloped in mystery and hidden from the sight of such adventurous knights as went in search of it. Here we come to the beginning of our story, which tells how Arthur's knights rode off in quest of the Holy Grail and accompanies some half dozen to their different journey's ends.

This brief account shows the Grail vessel in the light of a Christian relic. It seems however almost certain that its origins were very far from Christian. Chrétien de Troyes first introduced the legend into France with his *Conte del Graal*, written in 1190. Here we have a Grail Castle and a Grail-keeper, a large platter with mysterious attributes, a bleeding lance, and a question that must be asked in order to heal a wounded king and restore fertility to his land. There are indeed Christian overtones, in that this platter contains a host which is the sole food of the wounded king. Underneath, however, one can clearly discern the outlines of an ancient Celtic myth describing the visit of a mortal hero to an otherworldly palace. This myth in its different versions has certain constant elements: the maimed king who has usually been wounded with his own sacred sword or lance; the barren land (in primitive times it was popularly believed that the fertility of a domain was related to the potency of its ruler, and the maimed king is generally represented as wounded 'through the thighs'; traces of this belief still persisted in twelfth-century France); the extraordinary dangers to be surmounted in the quest for the palace; the question that must be asked in order to heal the king and loose his kingdom from its enchantments. Each of these factors, with the exception of the redeeming question (which is still an essential element in all the versions portraying Perceval as the hero of the quest), is present in our story, and it is quite clear that ancient legendary material has been reinterpreted to make it relevant to a society whose beliefs, philosophy and relationships were far removed from those of the ancient Celts.

The gods of the Irish sagas had also certain treasures or talismans which could on occasion be seized or won by heroic adventurers to the other world: there was the stone of sovereignty, in which it is possible to see the prototype of the Seat of Danger, the sword and the lance already mentioned, and which appear, though with a different history, in *The Quest of the Holy Grail*, and in the Welsh versions a platter or large shallow dish, apparently similar to Chrétien's 'graal', one of whose attributes was to furnish the feasting guests with whatever food they fancied.*

This reworking of old and doubtless disparate traditions which by the twelfth century had perhaps become, even to the Welsh bards, more hero-tale than myth, was not without its difficulties. Many incidents were obviously too well known, too firmly rooted to be jettisoned, yet their inclusion in stories of Christian inspiration laid traps for the unwary, and those who attempted this welding of the old and new were indeed at times unwary, or else prepared to tolerate a greater degree of internal contradiction and obscurity than we are today. Thus at the very heart of the Grail legend there lies a grave ambivalence in that the relics of the Last Supper and the Passion are made to appear responsible for the malefic enchantments and perils afflicting King Arthur's kingdom, while the sacred lance and the miraculous sword of King David, the 'sword of the spirit', appear at times in the light of weapons of vengeance and Nemesis. Underlying the Christian symbolism there flows a primitive current that occasionally threatens to perturb the smooth and limpid surface of the stream. To help towards a

---

*For a more detailed analysis of Celtic survivals in the Grail legend see Jean Marx: *La légende arthurienne et le Graal*, Paris, 1952.

better understanding of these different elements and the way in which they have been woven into the story I have where necessary supplied footnotes to the text. By relating these to the relevant passages and thus limiting their scope I have tried to reduce to manageable proportions problems which cannot for reasons of space be examined in their generality.

It is helpful to know something of the Celtic substratum of the *Quest*, interesting to be able to fill in the historical background; neither however is essential to the appreciation and understanding of the story and its meaning. Those for whom it was written knew nothing of Celtic myth; they were, however, not only well versed in the traditional teaching of the Church, they were also familiar with a vast range of symbols culled from the Bible, from bestiaries, from the works of the Fathers; these were their natural vocabulary, the intellectual framework within which they lived. It is this habit of mind we must acquire, these symbols we must learn to recognize if we are fully to appreciate the *Quest*. As it happens this is no esoteric work. The author's chief purpose being to edify and instruct and the delights of story-telling being but a means to that end, he has erected a liberal number of signposts along the way, ostensibly to guide his knights errant, but doubtless also to enable his readers to follow them on their pilgrimage.

His material and story-line were largely dictated to him by the previous books in the cycle which, with the exception of the *Estoire* relating the bringing of the Grail to Britain,* are entirely given over to the many adventures of Lancelot at King Arthur's court and to the tracing of his adulterous relationship with Guinevere, Arthur's queen. Arthurian literature celebrates that cult of the lady which was first hymned in the poetry of the early troubadours. The courtly ethos was based upon a conception of love to which marriage was largely extraneous, in which the lover was wholly subordinated to his lady who provided the inspiration which enabled him to excel in knightly skills, in combat, tournament and the virtues inherent to his way of life.

This paean to an adulterous passion hardly seems a suitable

* This, though chronologically the first, was in fact the last to be composed.

setting in which to integrate a work of spiritual edification which prizes virginity above all other virtues. The dichotomy, however, is more apparent than absolute. The *Lancelot* proper is interspersed with prophecies and warnings which make it clear that Lancelot's relations with the queen will debar him from the supreme adventure of the Grail, and which prepare the reader for the coming change in tone. Indeed this double standard gives to the whole a certain tragic grandeur, for it is plain that the architect* feels the attraction, even the nobility of that philosophy of love which he is soon uncompromisingly to condemn in the name of a higher and more exacting ideal. In the *Quest* itself the time for prophecy and veiled allusion is past. Here we have, if one may be permitted the term, an anti-romance. The stage is the same and so are the players, but all the accepted values are inverted. The *Quest* sets out to reveal the inadequacies and the dangers of the courtly ideal. By allowing his heroes to retain their traditional roles and character, the author is able to show how their much-vaunted attributes lead them to the outcome one would least have looked for; the last are perhaps not first, but he makes no bones about showing how the first are last. The concept of a quest was in itself traditional enough. The knights of the Round Table were forever setting out on quests, forever meeting with adventures of a more or less 'marvellous' nature, but by making it plain from the start that this Quest is to be something totally new and different the author is able to translate his whole story to another and symbolic plane.

The key that unlocks the door of the allegory is the meaning embodied in the Holy Grail. In this matter of interpretation I am much indebted to Étienne Gilson, author of an illuminating article on the Cistercian inspiration of the *Quest* which he sees as illustrating the Bernardine doctrine of grace and mystical union with God.† The Grail itself is the symbol of God's grace. At once the dish of the Last Supper, the vessel which received the effusion of Christ's blood when His side was pierced, and in the text both chalice and ciborium, its 'secrets' are the mystery of the Eucharist unveiled. Now whereas grace is freely given to

* See below, p. 26.
† Reprinted in his book *Les Idées et les lettres*, pp. 56–91.

all men, it is dispensed to each individual soul in the measure in which he is capable of receiving it, and only the wholly dedicated, the pure in heart can attain to that ecstatic union where they may contemplate in love what 'the heart of man cannot conceive nor tongue relate'. Hence there are only three knights who find their way to Sarras, the heavenly city, and there assist at the office of the Holy Grail, while Galahad alone, the perfect knight, is judged worthy to see the mysteries within the holy vessel and look on the ineffable.*

This making of the Grail into a symbol of divine grace involved the author in certain difficulties with his hero. It was plain that Lancelot, the subject as it were of the biography to date, must now be set aside. Several previous works treating of the Grail had Perceval as hero. However, different poets had furnished him with amatory exploits incompatible with the altered theme. Also his type-casting as the naïve, almost uncouth lad, whose simplicity wins him success where others more worldly-wise had come to grief, was too well established to be tampered with. While the author of the *Quest* saw fit to ignore a part of the tradition in making Perceval chaste, he obviously felt that the other aspects of his character were not consistent with his own conception of the Grail hero. The only solution that remained was the creation of a completely new personage, worthy in every way of the role he was destined from birth, one might almost say from all eternity, to fill. Being a man of daring vision he decided to make him a symbol and figure of Christ himself. Born to Lancelot and the daughter of the Fisher King as the result of a deception practised on the former, he was descended on his father's side by a mysterious filiation from King David, and on his mother's from the family of the

---

* Mme Myrrha Lot-Borodine, who has devoted several sensitive studies to the interpretation of the *Quest*, takes the theological discussion a stage further in an important article which at once deepens and to some extent corrects Gilson's thesis. She sees the work's immediate source less in the writings of St Bernard than in those of his contemporary and friend Guillaume de St Thierry. It is perhaps chiefly a question of emphasis, but she throws much valuable light on the Grail as a religious symbol. 'Les grands secrets du S. Graal dans la Queste du pseudo-Map' in Nelli: *Lumière du Graal*, Paris, 1951.

Grail-keepers. The object of messianic prophecies, awaited as the redeemer and deliverer of the kingdom of Logres, Christ-like in virtue, he is in a sense, or as the author would put it, 'in semblance' a second Christ. His name itself, found as Gilead in the Song of Songs, is one of the mystical designations of Christ. His arrival at King Arthur's court at Pentecost combines the themes of the descent of the Holy Ghost on the apostles and the appearance of the Resurrected Lord to the disciples in the upper room. He himself is not only perfect in virtue, he has an aura which draws men to him and makes it a matter of despair to his companions when, as he so often does, he vanishes without trace. It is their tragedy that they cannot keep abreast of this source of grace; he is always too far ahead, returning only of his goodness to rescue them in their moments of dire extremity. Eventually Bors and Perceval and, for a time, Lancelot, will have the joy of his company, but first they must be purified through trial and temptation. The companions of the Quest leave Camelot together, but only to separate, for each man makes his way alone through life with such grace as is sufficient to his needs; and of all who set out three, and only three, will ever be blessed with Galahad's continued presence, and Bors and Perceval alone will accompany him to his journey's end.

THE CHARACTERS

The *Quest* presents us with different types of humanity at varying degrees of spiritual development. Together with Lancelot, it is Bors, Perceval and Gawain who offer the most complete and interesting, the most subtly differentiated portraits. Of Galahad it has been alleged that he is a cardboard saint, that his austere virtue excludes humanity. A careful reading of the text will reveal on the contrary much tenderness in his relations with his father, with Melias his squire, with his companions Bors and Perceval, and with Perceval's sister, a feminine pendant to his own perfection.

If Galahad seems too rarefied a figure, Perceval is altogether human. He has a child-like simplicity and directness. This simplicity indeed is double-edged. On the one hand it engenders a total self-abandonment to God; on the other it leads him to gross imprudence and in the early part of his trials to excessive and childish despair when things go wrong. This holy simplicity verges at times on plain stupidity. Perceval never recognizes his demon temptresses and he fails to understand his holy visitor's message until it is spelled out, one might almost say in capitals. He has in fact an intuitive understanding of the divine, but, lacking common sense in a spectacular degree, he cannot relate this knowledge to what happens to him. In the end, however, the *sancta simplicitas* saves him from the consequences brought on him by the sillier sort and providence forestalls him in the nick of time. Despite his failings, or more probably because of them, he is a most endearing character and his charm is nowise lessened, at any rate for the modern reader, by an attendant lion and a visiting devil in feminine disguise.

Albert Pauphilet writes of Perceval: '*il est le type de ceux qui se justifient par la foi comme Bohort l'est de ceux qui se justifient par les œuvres,*' thereby drawing the essential distinction between the companions. He also describes Bors as a '*saint particulièrement laborieux*': a delineation as pleasing as exact. Bors is a plodder. He has neither Perceval's childlike grace nor his equally childlike failings. Where the one is rash the other is prudent, where the first is foolish the second is discerning. Bors is well instructed in the teachings of the Church and the temptations that beset him are not sensual but intellectual. He is the only character to be faced with a moral dilemma, a choice between conflicting duties: on the one hand the natural claims of his companion and brother, on the other the supernatural claims of his liege-lord, Christ. And Bors, unlike Perceval, and at whatever cost, is able to make a reasoned choice.

So much for the three heroes, the knights who finally win through to the vision of the Holy Grail. But what of the others, those whose success is partial, those who fall by the wayside? Lancelot presented perhaps the greatest difficulty, in that he had been until now the true hero of the romance, but from the outset of the *Quest* his former glory counts for nothing, and he finds himself condemned, because of the very wealth of his endowments, as the worst and most hardened of sinners, dashed at one blow from top to bottom of the ladder of excellence. His first encounter with the Grail finds him plunged in the spiritual torpor which disables those in whom repeated sin has blunted the soul's responses. And it is only after confessing, albeit with the greatest reluctance, his sin with the queen, that he can embark on the harsh path of penance which will lead him eventually to the Castle of the Grail and to a partial vision of his soul's desire. Bors and Perceval undergo temptation, but once they have overcome it salvation is assured. Lancelot needs continuous help and stumbles again and again on his way through the valley of humiliation. It is the dead weight of his past life that drags him down; this is no punishment but a weakness, a paralysis of soul and will. And when he finally attains his goal, he contemplates the mysteries not face to face, but suspended between life and death, deprived of the faculties he has misused, shorn of the liberty which marks the knights of God.

The Quest of the Holy Grail is not a comedy, unless it be in a Danteian sense, yet the figure of Gawain introduces a welcome lightness of touch which stands out all the better against the severity of the backcloth. Throughout Arthurian literature Gawain is seen as the paragon of knighthood. He epitomizes the courtly ideal: brave, magnanimous, unmatched in courtesy and *savoir-faire*, the staunchest and most discreet of friends. The *Quest* credits him with all these qualities and then sets out to show their bankruptcy in the spiritual order. Gawain is not without idealism: he has grace enough to wish for more; he is the first to leap to his feet and swear to ride in search of the Holy Grail. Indeed his intentions are always of the best. His fault lies in the fact that he never follows them up. He takes counsel of holy men and hermits only to make excuses when he finds their advice unpalatable. He fails to understand the nature of the Quest he is engaged in, and remains perpetually astonished by his failure to meet with any worth-while adventure. He is so rooted in the creed of his caste, so embedded in the secular that the sacred passes him by unrecognized. Inapt as he is for spiritual adventures, his virtues find no other outlet than in futile bloodshed, and he proceeds, unwilling and unwitting, to slaughter his companions one by one.

THE CISTERCIAN INFLUENCE

Having attempted somewhat briefly to outline the meaning of the Holy Grail and the roles of the main participants in the *Quest*, it remains to look more closely at the spiritual climate that infuses it. First however I must acknowledge my own incompetence in this field and my indebtedness for much of what follows to both Albert Pauphilet and Étienne Gilson who lit with such perceptive clarity the current of Cistercian doctrine that determines the whole structure of the work.

The Cistercian order came to birth in 1098 as part of that great movement of monastic reform that swept across France in the eleventh century. Those who embraced it did so with the purpose of returning to a stricter observance of the Benedictine rule; greatest among them was Bernard, abbot of Clairvaux, who exercised during his lifetime an extraordinary influence in matters spiritual and temporal, and whose authority and mystical writings gathered round him a group of like-minded men for whom the only way to God was through charity infused in the soul by grace. This was before men had a choice between Plato and Aristotle, between Augustine and Aquinas, for the Arabs had not yet let the lost writings of Aristotle loose on the Western world, and the twelfth century was nothing if not Augustinian. Reason has a very secondary part to play in a theology based on grace, which is why Gilson, referring to the terminology used by the author of the *Quest*, can say: '*Voir, connaître, autant de mots qui ne veulent dire autre chose qu'aimer*'.*

The Cistercian order had reached its highest point of expansion and influence by the beginning of the thirteenth century. The monks had houses all over Western Christendom and links with the military orders, such as the Knights Templar, which may not be without bearing on the conception of the *miles Christi*, so dear to the author of the *Quest*.† Certainly the

---

*The 'amor ipse intellectus est' of Guillaume de St Thierry suggests a veritable fusion on the spiritual plane of the affective and the intellectual.

† In St Bernard's own writings the athletes of God have already given way to the knights of Christ, a most natural change in a society where all supremacy affirmed itself on horseback.

latter's view of the Christian life is first and foremost a monastic one. It is monks and hermits who act as spiritual guides to the companions of the quest, and above all the white monks of the Cistercian observance, so called because of the colour of their habits. His hierarchy of virtues is also essentially monastic: chastity comes a clear first, lust, indeed, rather than pride is the root of evil, and an austere asceticism pervades the entire work. The practice that makes perfect is strictly orthodox: frequent confession, communion, fasting and abstinence, constant recourse to prayer. For specific examples of the Cistercian rule as followed by Lancelot after his conversion one cannot do better than consult Pauphilet.*

The continuous emphasis on asceticism may appear negative. This however is a rule of love. Again and again the author stresses God's infinite mercy towards sinners, and in this tale of jousting knights and hard-fought battles, death is a rare visitor. It is only those who reject God's grace, like Gawain and Lionel – the proud, the vainglorious and the empty-headed – who slay their adversaries, and they are specifically rebuked for doing so. But they themselves escape being killed – the author withholds judgement; and their victims, Owein and Calogrenant, die reconciled with God. As for those knights who are unhorsed or wounded, they are tenderly carried to the nearest abbey, there to be restored to health of body and, one hopes, of soul.

THE DEBT TO SCRIPTURE

So much then for the way that leads to perfection, but what of that perfection itself, how to describe the indescribable? Here the author had recourse to the Scriptures, to the wealth of symbolism contained in them, and particularly to the Song of Songs, the book of the Bible that above all others lends itself to mystical interpretation. He was able to draw upon a language hallowed by tradition, supple yet precise, carefully weighted, rich in overtones, a language whose full depths of meaning can only be plumbed by those as familiar as himself with both the biblical and apocryphal traditions. The fact that I have appended

* A. Pauphilet: *Études sur la Queste del Saint Graal*, 1921, pp. 75–83.

notes to those parts of the text which might require some elucidation implies on my part no such claim. I hope only that they may help the general reader and that those with greater knowledge will forgive my lack of it. The range of reference is wide, embracing certainly the first three books of the Pentateuch, Job, Psalms, the Song of Solomon and Ecclesiastes, one minor and two major prophets, three Gospels, Acts and two of the Pauline epistles as well as the Book of Revelation. The author seems to have been most deeply influenced by Chapter 6 of St John's Gospel in which Christ speaks of the foreshadowing of the Eucharistic bread in the manna dispensed to the Israelites in the desert, and by St Paul's description of the experience of mystical union with God, which he quotes again and again with reference to the Holy Grail. He also draws heavily, at the same time adapting it to his own ends, on the apocryphal tradition which has the Tree of Life providing the wood from which the Cross was made.

In rendering the quotations from Scripture I have used where possible the Authorized Version as being the most familiar to English readers. It must be remembered that the quotations in the Old French are themselves translated, since the author would have in mind the Vulgate text. He clearly worked from memory, often rendering the sense rather than the exact form of words, and in such cases I have followed his version where he deviates noticeably from the Bible.

FORM AND STYLE

The *Lancelot* cycle is a narrative of great complexity in which often concurrent adventures are interwoven, broken off, their threads to be picked up and knit together again after what sometimes seem to be interminable extrapolations. In fact the chronology and underlying pattern are far more rigorous than a superficial examination might allow. The author of the *Quest* retains the general form, adapting it to his own particular purpose. Here too heroes are left, at times in mid-adventure, with the words: 'But here the tale leaves Galahad (or Lancelot, or Bors) and returns to Sir Gawain', picking up a thread left hanging earlier and weaving another episode into the tapestry.

Within each section, though, the narrative is further broken up with passages of commentary or interpretation, placed in the mouths of holy men or hermits, in the manner of a gloss upon events.

The book is divided into fifteen chapters of unequal length, which usually correspond to a phase in the pilgrimage of one of the chief participants. It is worth noting that whereas 60 pages are consecrated to Lancelot's adventures, and more particularly to his spiritual regeneration, as against 45 to Perceval, and 25 and 20 respectively to Bors and to Gawain, Galahad rates no chapter exclusively devoted to his doings. He plays a prominent part of course in many episodes and is almost continually present in the last third of the book which relates the final adventures and the triumph of the heroes, but being in a state of grace from his first appearance at court there is no need to chart his spiritual progress.

The first chapter recounts Galahad's arrival at Camelot and the circumstances leading up to the quest for the Holy Grail. Thereafter two thirds of the book are devoted to the individual trials and adventures of the companions. This is the section where what Ferdinand Lot impatiently referred to as '*l'interminable kyrielle d'hermites*' make their frequent contribution to the heroes' understanding of the mysterious workings of providence in their lives. In the final section, with the exception of 15 pages telling of the end of Lancelot's quest, at once sublime and tragic, we see the three companions make their common way first to Corbenic and then, accompanied by the Grail, to Sarras and the apotheosis they have so long desired. The book falls therefore into two unequal halves, the first concerned with moral and spiritual shortcomings and their orthodox remedies, the second with the clarification of the mystical content.

The author is a master of narrative technique. In order to preserve the reader's interest he avoids giving too immediate and didactic an exposition of the meaning of the Grail Quest and adopts instead a method involving a series of flashbacks, enlightening his heroes at suitable moments in their journeyings with snippets of the history of the Holy Grail, constantly relating past to present, even to the extent of making King

Mordrain, the chosen companion of Joseph of Arimathea, survive for four hundred years in order at the last to die in Galahad's arms, another Simeon to his new Messiah. The element of repetition in the hermits' sermons may disconcert or irritate the modern reader, but this is a conscious and deliberate technique designed not merely to put across with maximum impact the moral and doctrinal content, but in Lancelot's case to underline the subtle gradations in his spiritual ascent.

The style itself is direct, at once dignified and unpretentious. There is little description and less poetry; one may regret the lack of it. It is a style, however, perfectly adapted to its purpose, clear, supple, analytical, reminding one by its magnificent use of rhythm and period of the Latin culture on which it substantially rested. I should like here to make some form of *apologia pro translatione mea*. Every translator is aware of traducing his original; the reader is usually aware of it as well, but unless he can compare the versions (in which case the translation is of little use) the exact virtues of the original are lost to him. Vocabulary and style are intimately bound to period, to social institutions, often to fad or fashion. Therefore when translating a work of another period, especially one as far removed not only in time but in social mores one can but attempt a timeless English, a language which, being of no period, is also lifeless and can never convey the freshness and immediacy of the work which enjoys unity of speech and spirit. A translation also suffers from dropsical tendencies. Each language has its own short-cuts and never do these correspond, so that in order to be faithful to the content one is forever expanding, slowing, deadening the form. Finally a point concerning medieval French. The vocabulary at the disposal of any thirteenth-century author was limited in extent. Because of this, each word carried an infinitely greater range of meaning which was largely determined by the context. This resulted in much repetition of words, expressions and phrases which does not seem to have shocked the medieval reader but which would produce a most tiresome effect today. To avoid this repetition and more particularly to render all the nuances implicit in the text I have considered myself justified in varying and widening very considerably the vocabulary of the original. This difference is deliberate: for all the others I apologize.

The penultimate sentence of the *Quest* states that its author was one Walter Map, who at King Henry's instigation translated into French the records of the adventures of Arthur's knights preserved in the library at Salisbury. This, the only information we are given about the author, is quite undoubtedly untrue. Walter Map, archdeacon of Oxford, author of *De Nugis Curialium* and protégé of Henry II, could not have written the *Quest* because he died in 1209, while modern scholarship is unanimous in dating the composition of the *Lancelot-Grail* cycle somewhere between 1215 and 1230. Since it seems likely that the writing of the work was spread over some 15 years it is reasonable to set an approximate date of 1225 for the *Quest*.

The identity of the author remains, and doubtless will remain, unknown. But over and above the question of who, there arises in the case of this huge cycle the more complex question of how many? The *Quest* is but a part of a much greater whole. Was one man responsible for this compilation, or did it grow up piecemeal, a sort of anthology of independent stories on one theme which were eventually slotted together to give an appearance of homogeneity? This last theory was widely held as late as this century; that it survived so long was due in part to the rambling nature of the work itself, to the existence within it of two apparently contradictory sets of moral values, and perhaps most of all to the longstanding lack of any comprehensive edition. The *Quest* and the *Mort Artu* were published separately in 1864 and 1910 respectively. The remaining and by far the greater part was accessible only in manuscript or in editions dating from the fifteenth and sixteenth centuries until Sommer brought out between 1909 and 1913 an edition of the whole based on manuscripts in the British Museum. The availability of the text in print inspired a renewal of interest in the work and in 1918 Ferdinand Lot published an important study of the cycle, stressing its fundamental unity of plan and structure, and presenting it as conceived and executed by one

man. Few scholars today would contest the overall unity which
Lot's careful spade-work and penetrating analysis brought to
light; many, however, do not subscribe to his theory of one sole
author. The vastness of the work, the discrepancies which
remain, the differences in tone, particularly between the
Lancelot on the one hand and the *Quest* on the other, have
led to the formulation of another thesis of which the most
notable exponent is Jean Frappier, whose position is best
summed up in his own words:

> In my opinion, a single man, whom I have called the 'architect',
> conceived the trilogy and outlined the plan of the whole. He was
> probably the author of the *Lancelot* proper, or at least the greater
> part of it. Two other authors then wrote the *Quest* and the *Mort
> Artu*, but in spite of their distinct personalities they conformed to
> the original plan. The *Estoire* was a later addition which supplied a
> portico for the edifice. Such a mode of collaborative creation may
> seem foreign and improbable, but the erection of the medieval
> cathedral presents an analogy. One may imagine the Prose *Lancelot*
> as the product of a sort of literary atelier. Several clues discovered
> by Lot – the mention of Meaux and of the feast of the Magdalen –
> would indicate a localization in Champagne. The Cistercian colour-
> ing of the *Quest* is not inconsistent with this view if we suppose that
> the author of that holy romance had attended the abbey school of
> Clairvaux, not far from Troyes ... Unless future editors turn up more
> significant facts, it is unlikely that we shall ever know more of
> the circumstances which surrounded the making of this literary
> monument. It stands, nevertheless, like a cathedral of which the
> *Quest* is the spire and bears mute witness to the genius of its
> architect.*

The theory is indeed both attractive and plausible and
respects the internal evidence. The unity of plan and conception must, I think, be admitted. The complex system of cross-
references, of early prophecies fulfilled in later sections, the
fact that Lancelot and Galahad are conceived from an early
moment as the twin pillars of the supporting arch, are proof
enough. For my part long and close study of the style, vocabulary and idiosyncrasies of the writer of the *Quest* have convinced me beyond doubt that the *Mort Artu* is from another

* In *Arthurian Literature in the Middle Ages*, ed. Loomis, pp. 316-17.

hand, and yet the *Quest* specifically looks forward to this sequel.

Whatever his relationship to the men who wrote the earlier and final parts of the cycle, one thing is certain: the author of the *Quest* was not a layman. Whether he was a monk remains open to doubt; it is not easy to see the abbots of Clairvaux giving their blessing to a literary exercise of this description. The *Quest* might pass muster, but the edifice into which it was to be incorporated would not have met with their approval. Most likely he was one of that great army of clerks who wandered anonymously in that no-man's land between the lay and ecclesiastical worlds. At all events his work speaks for itself and he would have wished for no other memorial.

MANUSCRIPTS AND EDITIONS

The *Quest* was first edited as a separate book by F. S. Furnivall in 1864. It is of course included in Sommer's complete edition of the cycle. There was, however, no critical edition until that of Albert Pauphilet, published in the *Classiques Français du Moyen Âge* in 1923 and reprinted in 1948. This is the most authoritative edition to date and it is this text that I have translated. A new edition of the first part of the Prose *Lancelot* is currently being prepared by Miss Elspeth Kennedy. There are some forty manuscripts of the *Quest* extant, ranging in date from the thirteenth to the fifteenth centuries. All these manuscripts would appear to stem from a lost original and though their variants are many they are mostly attributable to scribal quirks, errors or caprice; the version given in all but three of the manuscripts, where the story has been tampered with for particular reasons, is substantially the same. Therefore the problem is not one of determining the content of the original work but merely of establishing a text with the least number of errors and deviations from the author's copy.

POPULARITY AND INFLUENCE

The popularity of the Prose *Lancelot* in the Middle Ages is attested by the number of surviving manuscripts, about a hundred in all, though many are incomplete. It had a profound influence on other Arthurian romances, in particular on the later continuations of Chrétien's *Perceval*. The *Quest* itself was translated into Irish and Welsh and subsequently versified in Middle Dutch. But although the cycle retained its popularity in France until the sixteenth century, witness the seven printed editions which appeared between 1488 and 1533, it was England that assured it a new and glorious flowering which kept the legend alive throughout the centuries when the classical revival had killed all interest in it on the Continent. This home-coming produced a spate of literature on Arthurian themes in Middle English, but we have no rendering of the *Quest* itself or certain proof of its influence until Malory, who incorporated it under the title *The Tale of the Sangreal* in his great Arthurian canvas. Professor Vinaver has affirmed that Malory's version is based 'upon a text more closely related than any of the extant manuscripts to the lost original version of the French *Queste del Saint Graal*.'* Because of Malory's methods (he was concerned not primarily with translating but with recreating) it is doubtful whether his *Sangreal* can serve to bring us much closer to that lost original. Conversely the Old French *Quest* throws valuable light on Malory's use of his material and on his personality and stature as a creative writer. Firstly a comparison of the texts shows that he reduced the book to less than half its original length by curtailing or omitting the doctrinal glosses contained in the hermits' discourses. Whereas to the author of the *Quest* the tale was merely a vehicle for expressing spiritual truths in an idiom which would make them live in the minds of a sophisticated but secular public, for Malory the tale was paramount, the doctrines, in as far as he understood them, of very secondary importance. Furthermore the *Quest* with its overt condemnation of the pride and pomp of chivalry conflicted with Malory's conception of the knightly ideal. In his desire to soften or eliminate the antithesis between the Lancelot and the Grail stories he deprived the *Quest* of 'its spiritual foundation, of its doctrine and of its direct object'.† The qualities of Malory's genius have received their rightful measure of study

* E. Vinaver: *Malory*, 1929, pp. 141–7.
† Ibid., p. 84.

and of praise, sometimes to the detriment of the works that allowed that genius to come to its fruition. English readers who have hitherto had access to the *Quest of the Holy Grail* only in Malory's version, or through Tennyson's *Idylls of the King*, will now be able to read it as it was first conceived and penned, not as 'a beautiful parade of symbols and bright visions'* but as an authentic work of spiritual literature, starker perhaps, assuredly more powerful, and no less beautiful for its doctrinal underpinning.

Finally, instead of providing a list of books for further reading, which would either be too selective or too vast, I would like to suggest that readers anxious to extend their knowledge of the Grail legend and related themes consult the symposium by R. S. Loomis under the title *Arthurian Literature in the Middle Ages* (Oxford, 1959), which contains as well as articles by eminent scholars on every aspect of the 'matter of Britain' a useful bibliography appended to each chapter. And lest any think that the legend has lost its power to fire men's minds, I would mention, after T. S. Eliot's 'Waste Land', the 'Arthuriad' of Charles Williams and his posthumous essay 'Arthurian Torso', edited by C. S. Lewis with a critical commentary on Williams' poems.

* Ibid., p. 84.

[1]

Departure

ON the eve of Pentecost when the companions of the Round Table were all assembled at Camelot, at the hour of none[1] when the office was sung and the tables were being set up, a maiden of great beauty came riding into the hall. It was plain she had ridden hard for her horse was still lathered in sweat. She alighted and went straight to greet the king, who wished God's blessing on her.

'Sire,' she said, 'in God's name, tell me if Lancelot be here.'

'Yes, indeed, there he stands,' he answered, and pointed him out. And at once she went up to him and said:

'Lancelot, in the name of King Pellés, I bid you accompany me into the forest.'

Lancelot asked her whom she served.

'Him of whom I speak.'

'And what do you want with me?'

'You will know in good time.'

'As God is my aid,' he said, 'I will go with you gladly.'

Thereupon he called to a squire to saddle his horse and fetch his arms, and was obeyed directly. The king and those in the palace were grieved when they saw what was afoot, but, finding he would not be stayed, they did not press him. The queen, however, said to him:

'What is this, Lancelot, will you leave us on so high a feast-day?'

'Madam,' replied the maiden, 'be assured he will return to-morrow before the dinner-hour.'

'He may go then,' said the queen, 'but were tomorrow not to see him back, he should never have had my leave to ride today.'

With that Lancelot and the maiden mounted their horses, and with no further leave-taking they rode out of the castle, taking as sole companion the squire who had escorted her at her coming. Leaving Camelot behind, they rode on their way till they found themselves in the forest. There they took the wide, metalled road and held to it for a good half-league until they came to a valley and saw a nunnery lying ahead of them athwart their path. The young woman turned her horse as soon as they drew near, and when they stood before the gate the squire called out and it was opened to them, and they dismounted and entered. As soon as those within heard that Lancelot had come they all ran out to greet him and made much of him, and after they had led him to a chamber and unarmed him he spied his cousins, Bors and Lionel, lying asleep in two beds. Delightedly he woke them, and when they saw who it was they embraced and kissed him; and that was but a beginning of the joy which each showed unto each.

'Sweet Sir,' said Bors to Lancelot, 'what adventure brings you here? We thought we should find you at Camelot.'

Lancelot related to them then how a young woman had brought him there, but why he knew not.

As they stood in conversation, three nuns came into the room shepherding Galahad before them, a youth so fair and so well-made that it were hard indeed to find his peer. The noblest in rank had him by the hand and was weeping fondly. Approaching Lancelot she said:

'Sir, I bring you this boy whom we have raised, and who is all our joy, our comfort and our hope, that you may make a knight of him. For in our opinion he could receive the order of knighthood at no worthier hand.'

Lancelot looked at the youth, who appeared to him so wondrously adorned with every beauty that he thought that in all his days he had not seen so fair a human form. And the modesty of his bearing held promise of such virtue that Lancelot was gratified to knight him. He assured the ladies that he would not deny their suit, but would gladly knight the youth since they desired it.

'Sir,' said the nun who held him by the hand, 'we would have it take place tonight or tomorrow.'

'In God's name,' he answered, 'it shall be as you wish.'

Thus Lancelot lodged at the nunnery and saw to it that the youth kept night-long vigil in the church. In the morning he knighted him at the hour of prime, fastening on one spur himself while Bors attached the other. Lancelot then girded the sword about him and dubbed him, asking that God might make him as noble in spirit as he was fair of form. When he had done all those things that pertained to a new knight he said:

'Good Sir, will you ride with me to the court of my lord King Arthur?'

'No, Sir,' he replied, 'I will not go with you.'

At this Lancelot turned to the abbess:

'Madam, grant that our new knight accompany us to the court of my lord the king, for it will profit him more than staying here with you.'

'Sir,' she replied, 'he shall not go at present, but as soon as we deem it right and necessary we will send him.'

So Lancelot and his cousins took their leave, keeping company till they reached Camelot at the hour of terce, and found the king gone to hear mass in the minster with a great retinue of noble lords. As soon as the three cousins arrived they dismounted in the courtyard and made their way to the upper hall. There they began to talk of the youth that Lancelot had knighted. Bors thought he had never seen anyone so like in looks to Lancelot.

'Indeed,' he added, 'I will never hold anything true again if this is not Galahad, who was born of the Fisher King's beautiful daughter, for he bears an uncommon likeness both to that lineage and to ours.'

'Upon my faith,' said Lionel, 'I think it must be he, his resemblance to my lord Lancelot is truly striking.'

They continued awhile in this vein in the hope of eliciting some word from Lancelot, but to all their hints he vouchsafed at that time no reply.

When they had abandoned the subject they surveyed the seats of the Round Table and found that each bore the words: HERE SHALL SIT SUCH AN ONE. And thus until they came to the great seat known as the Seat of Danger. There they found letters which seemed to them freshly traced and which read: FOUR HUNDRED AND FIFTY YEARS HAVE PASSED SINCE THE PASSION OF OUR LORD JESUS CHRIST: AND ON THE DAY OF PENTECOST THIS SEAT SHALL FIND ITS MASTER. When they saw the inscription they exclaimed to one another:

'In truth, this is a singular adventure!'

'In God's name,' said Lancelot, 'it seems to me that he who reckoned aright the term set down here from the Resurrection of Our Lord to this present time, would find that the seat was to be filled this very day, for this is the first Pentecost to follow the span of four hundred and fifty-four years. Meanwhile I think it were best that no one else should see this prophecy until the coming of him who is destined to fulfil it.'

His cousins said they would soon prevent its being seen, and they had a silk cloth brought which they draped on the seat to hide the writing.

When the king came back from church and saw that Lancelot had returned bringing Bors and Lionel with him, he greeted them joyfully and wished them welcome. So it was that the revels in the palace were ushered in amid great rejoicing, for the arrival of the two brothers gladdened the hearts of all their companions. Sir Gawain asked them how they had fared since they left the court.

'Well, praise God,' they said, for they had kept in good health and spirits.

'I am happy to hear it,' he replied, and every knight at court joined him in fêting Bors and Lionel whom they had not seen for many months.

The king decided it was time to dine and ordered the cloths to be spread.

'Sire,' objected Kay the steward, 'in my opinion, if you sit down so soon to dinner you will infringe the custom of the court. On high feast-days we have never seen you seat yourself at table before some adventure has befallen the court in the presence of all the barons of your household.'

'Kay,' said the king, 'you speak the truth. I have always observed this custom and I will do so as long as I may, but in my great joy at seeing Lancelot and his cousins safe returned I had quite forgotten the practice.'

'You stand reminded,' retorted Kay.

Even as they talked a page came in and said to the king:

'Sire, I bring you news of a great wonder.'

'What is it? Tell me quickly.'

'Below your palace, Sire, I saw a great stone floating on the water. Come and look for yourself for I know it signifies some strange adventure.'

The king and his barons went down at once to see this marvel. When they came to the river bank, they found the great stone lying now by the water's edge. Held fast in its red marble was a sword, superb in its beauty, with a pommel carved from a precious stone cunningly inlaid with letters of gold. The barons examined the inscription which read: NONE SHALL TAKE ME HENCE BUT HE AT WHOSE SIDE I AM TO HANG. AND HE SHALL BE THE BEST KNIGHT IN THE WORLD. When the king saw the lettering he turned to Lancelot and said:

'Good Sir, this sword is yours by right, for I know you without a doubt for the best knight in the world.'

But Lancelot answered abruptly:

'Indeed, Sire, this sword is not meant for me, neither have I the courage nor the audacity to lay hand on it, for I am in no way worthy or fit to wear it. Wherefore I will refrain from putting my hand to it: such presumption would be folly.'

'Nonetheless,' said the king, 'try whether you can withdraw it.'

'Sire, I will not. For I know full well that none shall fail in the attempt but he receive some wound.'

'How came you by such knowledge?'

'Sire, suffice it that I know. And I will tell you more: I would have you know that this day shall see the beginning of the great adventures and the marvels of the Holy Grail.'

When the king saw that Lancelot would not be prevailed upon, he addressed himself to Sir Gawain:

'Good nephew, you try your hand.'

'No, Sire,' said he, 'saving your grace, since my lord Lancelot will not attempt it, neither will I. Nothing would be gained by my laying hand to it, for you are well aware that he is a far better knight than I.'

'You shall try all the same,' he insisted, 'not to win the sword, but because I ask it.'

Sir Gawain thrust out his hand and grasped the sword by the hilt, but tug as he would, he could not move it.

'Leave it be, good nephew,' interposed the king, 'you have done my bidding loyally.'

'My lord Gawain,' said Lancelot, 'know that you will see the day when you would not have touched this sword for a castle, for it will cut you to the quick.'

'Sir,' said Gawain, 'what is done, is done; were I to die of it here and now, I was only obeying my lord's command.'

When the king heard these words he repented his part in what Sir Gawain had done.[2]

King Arthur then bade Perceval try his fortune. Perceval agreed readily in order to keep Sir Gawain company. He took hold of the sword by the hilt and strained but could not shift it. The assembled knights were certain now that Lancelot spoke the truth and that the writing on the hilt was no fable, and there was none so bold that he dared touch the sword. Thereupon Sir Kay said to the king:

'Sire, Sire, upon my oath, you may surely sit down to dine at your pleasure, for I hardly think you have wanted for an adventure.'

'Then let us go in,' said the king, 'for the hour indeed is late.'

The knights returned to the palace leaving the stone on the river bank. The king had the trumpets sounded for water to be brought, and took his seat at his high table while the companions of the Round Table went each one to his place. That day saw four crowned kings serving at table, together with such a company of noblemen of rank that one might well have marvelled at the sight. When all were seated it was found that the fellowship of the Round Table was complete and every seat filled, excepting the one that was known as the Seat of Danger.

The first dish had just been served when a most extraordinary thing occurred: for all the doors and windows of the palace where the companions sat at meat closed of themselves without anyone setting hand to them; and yet the hall was not a whit the darker. This spectacle dumbfounded both the simple and the sage. King Arthur, who was the first to speak, exclaimed:

'In God's name, gracious lords, we have witnessed wonderful events this day, both here and at the river's bank, yet I think that before nightfall we shall see stranger still.'

As the king was speaking there appeared in the hall a man

robed in white, of venerable age and bearing, yet not a knight
there knew the manner of his entry. He came on foot leading
by the hand a knight in red armour who carried neither shield
nor sword, and as soon as he stood within the palace he said:

'Peace be with you.'[3]

Then turning towards the king, he addressed him, saying:

'King Arthur, I bring you the Desired Knight,* he who stems
from the noble house of King David and the lineage of Joseph of
Arimathea, and through whom the enchantments lying on this
and other lands are to be loosed. Behold him here.'

This news rejoiced the king exceedingly and he answered the
good man:

'Sir, if your words are true we wish you welcome here, and
welcome too to the knight! If he be indeed the one for whom
we have waited to bring to a close the adventures of the Holy
Grail, no man has ever met with greater joy than he shall have
of us. And whether he be the one whom you announce or
another I wish him well, since on your testimony he is of most
noble birth and ancestry.'

'Upon my faith,' said the old man, 'you shall see presently
your hopes take fair departure.'

With that he had the knight unarm till he stood in a tunic
of red sendal; then he handed him a red mantle to wear on his
shoulder, woven of samite and lined with whitest ermine.[4]

When the youth stood robed and ready the old man bade him
follow and led him straight to the Seat of Danger, alongside
Lancelot. He raised a corner of the silken cloth that Bors and
Lionel had placed there and uncovered an inscription reading:
THIS SEAT IS GALAHAD'S. The good man studied the letters,
finding them, as he thought, fresh-traced, and he was familiar
with the name they spelled. Then he said to the youth in a
voice so clear that the assembled company heard each word:

'Sir Knight, be seated, for this place is yours.'

The knight sat down with impunity and said in turn:

'Sir, you may return now for you have carried out your orders
faithfully. Greet all at the blessed castle on my behalf, especially
my uncle, King Pellés, and my grandsire, the Rich Fisher King.[5]

* Cf. Haggai 2, 8 (Vulgate): '... *et veniet desideratus* cunctibus
gentibus.'

and tell them from me that I will visit them as soon as I have the means and the occasion.'

Thereupon the good man turned to go, after commending King Arthur and his court to God. When they sought to ask him who he was he would have no talk with them, answering roundly that he would not tell them now, they would learn soon enough if they dared inquire. And going to the great door of the palace, which stood shut, he opened it and went down into the courtyard where an escort of knights and squires, numbering fifteen in all, had been waiting for him. There he mounted and rode away without the court discovering for the time being anything more about him.

When the barons saw the knight take his place in the seat which had struck fear into many bold hearts and where many an awesome event had been enacted, they were all astounded. Seeing him so tender in years, they could not conceive his meriting such a grace unless it were by the will of Our Lord. As the feast resumed with splendour the barons strove to honour the knight through whom, as they believed, the marvels attendant on the Holy Grail should find solution; for the trial of the Seat, where none but he had ever sat unscathed, was proof to them of his identity. So they did their best to honour and serve him, accounting him master and lord of all their fellowship. And Lancelot, driven in wonderment to watch him closely, recognized the youth he had knighted that very morning. In his delight he showed him the greatest honour and led him to converse on many topics, seeking especially to draw him out about himself. The other, who knew him a little and feared to offend him, gave him answers to a number of his questions. Bors, meanwhile, the happiest of men, well aware that this was Galahad, the son of Lancelot, who was to bring the adventures to their close, spoke to his brother Lionel, saying:

'Good brother, what do you know of the knight who sits in the Seat of Danger?'

'Only that he is the new-made knight, the same that was dubbed this morning by Sir Lancelot, whom you and I have talked of all day long and who was begotten by Lancelot of the Rich Fisher King's daughter.'

'Make no mistake,' said Bors, 'it is indeed he, and he is our near kinsman. This adventure gives us matter for rejoicing, for there is no doubt that he will achieve greater things than any knight I have known; here we already have a fair beginning.'

Thus ran the talk not only between Galahad's cousins but among all those assembled in the hall. And the rumour was bruited abroad so swiftly that it came to the ears of the queen, who was dining in her chambers when a page said to her:

'Madam, there have been marvellous happenings in the palace.'

'What do you mean?' she asked. 'Explain yourself.'

'Upon my faith, Madam, a knight has come to court who has triumphed in the adventure of the Seat of Danger, and yet he is so young that the whole world marvels how such a grace could be accorded him.'

'Indeed,' she replied, 'can this be true?'

'Yes, Madam, rest assured it is so.'

'In God's name,' said the queen, 'he has won great honour. No man has ever attempted this feat without death or injury forestalling him.'

'Ah God!' cried her ladies, 'this knight was born in an auspicious hour! No other man, however great his prowess, has achieved as much. This feat proves him the one who shall bring the adventures of Britain to their close and restore the Maimed King to health.'

'Friend,' said the queen, 'as God is your help, describe him to me.'

'Madam, as God is my help, in beauty there are few could match him, but he is amazingly young and looks so like Lancelot and the lineage of King Ban that they are all saying he must stem from that root.'

The queen's desire to see the knight quickened; what she heard of the resemblance convinced her that this must be Galahad, the son born to Lancelot by the daughter of the Rich Fisher King. She had heard many a time the tale of his begetting and of the deception practised on Lancelot, which softened the anger she would have borne towards him had the fault been his.[6]

When the king and barons had dined they rose from their seats and the king himself went to the Seat of Danger and lifted off the silk cloth to uncover the name of 'Galahad' which he had been impatient to learn. He showed it to Sir Gawain, saying:

'Now good nephew, we have Galahad among us, the good and perfect knight whom ourselves and the companions of the Round Table have waited so eagerly to see. Let us bestir ourselves to serve and honour him while he is with us; his stay will be but short, for the Quest of the Holy Grail will take him from us, and that soon, I fear. Lancelot made that clear to us this morning, and he would not have spoken unless he had some knowledge of the matter.'

'Sire,' said Sir Gawain, 'both you and we should serve him as one sent by God to free our country from the enchantments and the strange events that have troubled it so often and so long.'

After this exchange the king sought out Galahad and said to him:

'Welcome, Sir, we have greatly desired to see you. Now we have you among us, for which we thank God, and yourself for deigning to come.'

'Sire, I came because I must, for this is to be the starting point for all who would join fellowship in the Quest of the Holy Grail, which will be undertaken presently.'

'Sir,' said the king, 'many things have waited on your coming for their fulfilment, both the ridding of this land of its enchantments, and also an adventure that befell us this very day and which has defeated the best efforts of my barons. You, I know, will be equal to the challenge, for this is the purpose for which God sent you to us: to consummate what others have had to renounce, and to bring to conclusion all those things that no other was ever able to resolve.'

'Sire,' said Galahad, 'where is this adventure to be found? I would gladly see for myself.'

'And I will as gladly show you.'

With this the king took him by the hand and they went down out of the palace, and all the barons followed them to see what issue would be found to the adventure of the stone. They came hurrying from every side till there was not a single knight left within.

At this point the report reached the queen, and as soon as

she got word she had the tables removed and said to four of the noblest women attending her:

'Ladies, come with me to the river bank, for I am determined to see this adventure concluded if I can get there soon enough.'

And at that the queen left the palace accompanied by a great number of women and maidens. When they reached the water's edge and the knights saw them approaching, they cried:

'Make way, here comes the queen!'

And the most esteemed fell back to let her pass. The king said then to Galahad:

'Sir, here is the adventure I told you of. Some of the most valiant knights of my household have today failed to pluck this sword from the stone.'

'Sire,' said Galahad, 'that is not to be wondered at, for the adventure was not theirs but mine. I was so sure of this sword that I came to court without one, as you may have seen.'

Then he took hold of the sword and drew it as easily from the stone as if it had never been fast; and he sheathed it in the scabbard. Girding it on, he said to the king:

'Sire, now am I better equipped than before: I lack nothing but a shield.'

'Good Sir,' said the king, 'God will send you a shield from somewhere even as He did the sword.'

Then, as they stood looking along the river bank, they saw a maiden on a white palfrey approaching at full gallop. When she drew rein she greeted the king and all the company and asked if Lancelot were present. He was standing just in front of her and called out:

'Madam, here I am.'

She looked at him and, recognizing him, said weeping:

'Alas, Lancelot, this day has seen a sad change in your circumstance.'

'I pray you, tell me how.'

'In faith,' she said, 'you shall hear it in front of the whole court. Yesterday morning you were the best knight in the world; those who spoke of you as Lancelot, the paragon of chivalry, said but the truth, for so you were. But were anyone to call you that now, he would be a liar, for there is a better than you, as is clearly proved by this sword which you dared not set your hand to. This is the change in your name and title which I have brought to your mind lest you continue to think yourself the foremost of your peers.'

Lancelot replied that he would never think so again; the adventure had put any such claim far from his thoughts. Then the maiden turned to the king and said:

'King Arthur, I bring you word from Nascien the hermit that you will receive this day the greatest honour ever accorded to a knight of Britain, and that not for your own deserts but for another's. Do you know what this is? Today the Holy Grail will appear within your house and feed the companions of the Round Table.'

As soon as she had said this she turned her horse and departed the way she had come. There were many barons and knights there who would have stayed her, in order to know whom she was and where she came from, but she would not tarry for all their asking.

When she had gone, the king said to his barons:

'Gracious lords, we have now clear proof that you will embark very soon on the Quest of the Holy Grail. And because I know that I shall never again see you all assembled as you are today, I would have in the meadows of Camelot a tournament so splendid that after our death our heirs will talk of it still.'

Everyone fell in with this suggestion. They returned to the town and some fetched their harness to joust the more safely, while others took nothing but caparison and shield, for the majority were more than confident in their own prowess. Now the king had set this afoot in order to see something of Galahad's exploits, suspecting that once he left the court he would not soon return.

When people of every estate had gathered in the meadows of Camelot, Galahad, at the request of the king and queen, donned his coat of mail and put on his helm, but plead as they might, he would take no shield. This pleased Sir Gawain, who offered to break a lance with him, as did also Sir Owein and Bors of Gaunes. By then the queen and all her ladies had mounted the walls. And Galahad, who had ridden out into the meadow with the rest, began to shiver lances with a force and fury that astonished all the onlookers. He accomplished so much in so short a space that there was not a man or woman present but marvelled at his exploits and accounted him victor over all comers. And those who had never seen him before opined that he had made a worthy beginning in the way of chivalry, and that if his feats that day were proof, he would easily surpass all other knights in prowess. Indeed when the tournament was over it was found that of all the companions of the Round Table bearing arms that day there were only two that he had not unhorsed, and those were Lancelot and Perceval.

The tournament lasted without a break till past the hour of none, when the king, fearing lest passion prevail at the last, called for the combatants to part. Having made Galahad unlace his helm and given it to Bors to carry, he led him bare-headed from the meadows through the main street of Camelot, so that all might see his face. When the queen had looked at him well, she said that Lancelot must truly be his father, for there had never been two men so alike as these. It was thus no wonder that he was endowed with every knightly skill and virtue, anything less would be a betrayal of his heritage. One lady who had overhead a part of her remark was quick to ask:

'Madam, is this preeminence you speak of then his birthright?'

'Yes, indeed,' replied the queen, 'for he stems on both sides from the noblest knights the world has seen, and none has a prouder ancestry.'

The ladies then went down to hear vespers in honour of the day. And when the king returned from the minster and made his way to the upper hall of the palace he ordered that the tables should be set up. Every knight went to the place he had occupied that morning. When they were all seated and the noise was hushed, there came a clap of thunder so loud and terrible that they thought the palace must fall. Suddenly the hall was lit by a sunbeam which shed a radiance through the palace seven times brighter than had been before. In this moment they were all illumined as it might be by the grace of the Holy Ghost, and they began to look at one another, uncertain and perplexed. But not one of those present could utter a word, for all had been struck dumb, without respect of person.[7] When they had sat a long while thus, unable to speak and gazing at one another like dumb animals, the Holy Grail appeared, covered with a cloth of white samite; and yet no mortal hand was seen to bear it. It entered through the great door, and at once the palace was filled with fragrance as though all the spices of the earth had been spilled abroad.* It circled the hall along the great tables and each place was furnished in its wake with the food its occupants desired.[8] When all were served, the Holy Grail vanished, they knew not how nor whither. And those that had been mute regained the power of speech, and many gave thanks to Our Lord for the honour He had done them in filling them with the grace of the Holy Vessel. But greater than all was King Arthur's joy that Our Lord should have accorded him a favour never granted to any king before him.

This mark of Our Lord's goodwill was a source of joy to court and guests alike, who now felt sure that they were not forgotten. They talked of little else while the meal lasted. The king himself began to discuss it with those sitting closest to him, saying:

'In truth, my lords, our hearts should be lifted up for joy that Our Lord has shown us so great a sign of His love in deigning to feed us with His grace at this high feast of Pentecost.'

'Sire,' said Sir Gawain, 'you are not yet aware of the full extent of His favour: every man in this place was served with the food of his heart's desire. Such a thing was never seen at any court save that of the Maimed King. But we are so blinded and beguiled that we could not see it plain, rather was its true substance hidden from us. Wherefore I for my part make here and now this vow: in the morning I will set out on this Quest without more delay, and pursue it for a year and a day, or more if need be, nor will I return to court, come what may, until I have looked openly upon the mystery we have but glimpsed this day, provided that I am capable and worthy of such grace. And if it prove otherwise, I will return.'

When the companions of the Round Table heard these words, they rose one and all from their seats and took the same vow as Sir Gawain, swearing never to cease from wandering until they were seated at the high table where so sweet a food was served

* A recurring image. Cf. Song of Songs, 3, 6.

each day as they had just received. The king was sorely put out to hear them swear such an oath, for he realized that he would never turn them from their purpose. He said to his nephew:

'Ah, Gawain, this vow of yours is a mortal blow to me, for you have deprived me of the best and truest companions a man could find. I speak of the fellowship of the Round Table, for I am well aware that of those who leave my court when the hour comes, all will not return: on the contrary many shall fall in this Quest, and success will not come so swiftly as you think. This saddens me not a little. I have raised them up and advanced them to the utmost of my power, and have always loved them and indeed love them still like sons or brothers; how should I not grieve at their departure? I had grown accustomed to their presence and had learned to like their company; I cannot find in me the strength to bear this loss.'

The king fell silent and the tears that welled unchecked to his eyes for all to see bore witness to his distress of mind. When he spoke again it was in tones so loud that none could miss his words:

'Gawain, Gawain, you have filled my heart with anguish from which I shall have no relief until I know for certain how this Quest will end; for I have a great dread that those dearest to me will never return.'

'Sire,' said Lancelot, 'in God's name, what are you saying? A man such as you must not give way to fear, but should be resolute, sanguine and zealous for justice. Take comfort: for were every one of us to meet his death in this Quest, it would be a more honourable end than any other.'

'Lancelot,' said the king, 'it is the depth of my love for them that made me speak in that fashion, and it is no wonder that I am bitter at their departure. No Christian king ever had so many good knights or men of rank and wisdom at his table as I have had this day, nor will again when these are gone, nor shall I ever see them reunited round my table as before; it is this that hurts me most.'

Sir Gawain had no answer to this for he knew that the king spoke the truth. He would gladly have gone back on his word had he dared, but the occasion had been too public to permit it.

It was announced throughout the palace that the Quest of

the Holy Grail had begun and that all those who had sworn
fellowship would leave the court on the following day. There
were many present who were more vexed than joyful at the
news, for it was through the prowess of the knights of the
Round Table that King Arthur's court was feared and respected
above all others. Word came to the ladies as they sat at supper
with the queen in her rooms, and to many it was melancholy
news, not least to those who counted husbands and lovers
among the companions of the Round Table. Nor was this to be
wondered at, for they were honoured and cherished by the very
knights whom they feared to see perish in the Quest; and so
they fell to weeping and lamenting. The queen spoke to the
page standing before her:

'Tell me, boy, were you present when this vow was made?'

'Yes, Madam.'

'And Sir Gawain, and Lancelot of the Lake, are they to be
companions?'

'Yes, indeed, Madam; Sir Gawain was the first to take the
oath, and after him Lancelot and all the others; not one held
back of all that fellowship.'

When the queen heard this, her anguish for Lancelot was such
that she thought she should die of grief, and despite herself the
tears sprang to her eyes. There was no more wretched woman
than she when she spoke at last:

'It is a thousand pities! Since so many good knights have
embarked upon this Quest it cannot be achieved without the
loss of many noble lives. I wonder that my lord the king in his
great wisdom should allow it. For when the greatest and best of
his barons are leaving, the remainder can be of little worth.'

Thereupon she began to weep bitterly, as did all the ladies
attending her.

Thus the whole court was thrown into turmoil at the news of
this departure. And when the tables had been cleared from hall
and chambers and the ladies had come to join the knights, the
grief broke out afresh. For every lady, married or maid, offered
to accompany her knight in the Quest. And there were those
who would readily have agreed and indeed welcomed the
suggestion, had it not been for an old and venerable man wearing the religious habit, who entered the hall after supper.

Coming before King Arthur, he cried out in a loud voice:

'Hear my words, my lord knights of the Round Table, who have vowed to seek the Holy Grail! Nascien the hermit sends you word by me that none may take maid or lady with him on this Quest without falling into mortal sin; nor shall anyone set out unless he be shriven or seek confession, for no man may enter so high a service until he is cleansed of grievous sin and purged of every wickedness. For this is no search for earthly things but a seeking out of the mysteries and hidden sweets of Our Lord, and the divine secrets which the most high Master will disclose to that blessed knight whom He has chosen for His servant[9] from among the ranks of chivalry: he to whom He will show the marvels of the Holy Grail, and reveal that which the heart of man could not conceive nor tongue relate.'[10]

As a result of this warning none took with him wife or mistress. And the king, after seeing that the good man was lodged as befitted his rank, attempted to draw him into conversation about himself and his affairs, but he paid him little heed for his mind was on other matters.

The queen came and sat beside Galahad and began to ask him where he came from and to what country and what people he belonged. He answered her at some length, as one well informed – but made no mention of his kinship with Lancelot. What he did say, however, sufficed to convince the queen that he was the son of Lancelot and of King Pellés' daughter, whom she knew from frequent hearsay. Minded if possible to hear it from his own lips, she asked him to tell her the truth about his father. Galahad replied that he was not sure whose son he was.

'Sir,' she said, 'you are hiding it from me; why? As God is my help, you need never be ashamed to name your father. He is the finest knight on earth and is descended on both sides from kings and queens and from the noblest lineage known to man, and was reputed until now the best knight in the world; you, therefore, should by right surpass all men alive. Your resemblance, too, is so extraordinary that there is not a man here so simple he could overlook it if he gave it but a thought.'

Now Galahad reddened with shame and embarrassment.

'Madam,' he answered, 'since you are so certain of his identity you may tell me yourself. If it is he whom I believe to be my father, I will accept that you speak the truth, if another, nothing you could say would make me concur.'

'In God's name,' she said, 'if you will not name him, I will. He who begot you is known as Sir Lancelot of the Lake, the fairest and best and most gracious of knights, whose presence brings solace to rich and poor, and who is better loved than any man of his generation. It seems to me, therefore, that you should not hide this from me or from anyone else, for you could not be the son of a nobler man or better knight.'

'Madam,' he replied, 'since you are so well informed, what would have been the use of my telling you? Others will know soon enough.'

Dusk found the queen and Galahad still talking together. When the hour came to retire, the king led Galahad to his own room, where he made him, in honour of his high calling, lie down on the bed in which he himself usually slept. Thereupon the king went to rest, as did Lancelot and the other barons assembled at Camelot. That night the king was afflicted in mind for love of those whom his heart cleaved to, and who were to leave him next day for a place from which he feared they would not soon return. The thought of their absence, however long, did not dismay him unduly; his torment sprang from the fear that many would not come back at all. Thus racked in mind and spirit did the barons of the household and those of the kingdom of Logres* spend that night. And when it pleased Our Lord that the first signs of day should lighten the shadows of the night, those who had watched in heaviness of spirit rose at once to dress and prepare themselves. When the dawn was well advanced the king left his bed, and as soon as he was robed he went to the room where Sir Gawain and Lancelot had lain that night. He found them dressed and ready to hear mass. The king, who loved them as he might sons begotten of his own body, hastened to greet them, and they in turn rose to their feet and wished him good morning. He bade them be seated and sat down beside them. Then, looking at Sir Gawain he said:

'Gawain, Gawain, you have betrayed me! The lustre you conferred on my court was not so great as the loss it now suffers

*The Welsh name for Britain.

at your hand. Never again will my palace be graced by so brave and brilliant a company as you are stealing from it at your going. And yet their departure grieves me less than Lancelot's and yours. For no man can love another more than I have loved you, and that love is not new-born but dates from the hour when I first recognized the virtues lodged in you.'

With this the king lapsed into most sombre thoughts which brought tears coursing down his face. This sight wrung the hearts of the two who watched and dared not speak for the sorrow that they saw. He sat a long while plunged in his grief, and when he spoke it was with deep emotion:

'Ah, God, I never thought to see the day that would part me from this fellowship that fortune had gathered round me.' And then he said to Lancelot: 'Lancelot, by that faith and oath which bind us, I demand that you assist me with your counsel in this matter.'

'Sire, tell me how I may help you.'

'I would more than willingly call a halt to this Quest if it were possible.'

'Sire,' said Lancelot, 'I saw so many men of virtue and valour swear fellowship, that nothing, I think, will make them renounce the Quest. Any who did so would be forsworn, and he who would persuade them to such a course would be guilty of great disloyalty.'

'Upon my faith,' said the king, 'I know you speak the truth. But the great love I bear both you and them drove me to say it. And if it were a right and fitting request I would make it without hesitation, for their departure will be a grievous loss.'

They talked so long that the day was fair and bright, and the sun was drinking up the dew as the barons of the kingdom began to throng into the palace. The queen had risen and came to fetch the king, saying:

'Sire, your knights are waiting below for you to go to mass.'

The king stood up and wiped his eyes so that none might see he had wept. Sir Gawain had his arms brought to him and Lancelot also. When they were fully armed except for their shields they went into the great hall where they found their companions also ready and equipped. After going down to the minster, harnessed as they stood, and attending mass, they returned to the palace, and those who were to be companions in the Quest sat down together.

'Sire,' said King Baudemagus, 'since this matter is so far advanced that honour demands it be pursued to the end, I would recommend that the relics be brought and the companions swear such an oath as befits the occasion.'

'So be it, since it is your wish,' replied King Arthur, 'and since there is no other course.'

The clergy of the palace brought in the relics on which all oaths at court were sworn. When they had been borne before the high tables the king called Sir Gawain and said to him:

'You were the first to propose this undertaking; come forward now and be first to swear the oath proper to men entering on this Quest.'

'Sire,' said King Baudemagus, 'saving your grace, let not Sir Gawain swear first, but he whom we should hold as lord and master of the Round Table; let Sir Galahad precede us all. And we shall all swear without exception the selfsame oath as he, for that is the way it must be.'

So Galahad was summoned, and coming forward he knelt before the relics and swore on his faith as a knight to pursue the Quest for a year and a day, and more if need be, and never to return to court until he learned the truth about the Holy Grail, if it lay in his power to do so. Next came Lancelot who took the very same oath, and following him Sir Gawain and Perceval, Bors and Lionel, and then Helain the White; and after these the companions of the Round Table one by one. When all who were to take part in the Quest had taken the oath, those who were keeping the record found the tally to be one hundred and fifty, and not a coward among them. At the king's request they broke their fast, and when they had eaten they laced on their helms. Then at last it was certain that the moment of separation had come, and they commended the queen to God's keeping amid weeping and lamentation.

When she realized that her friends were set to go and could delay no longer, the queen fell to mourning as if she saw them dead before her eyes. In order to hide her suffering from the public gaze she went to her chamber and threw herself on her couch. There she gave rein to grief so pitiful that the most hardened man alive could not have looked on unmoved. Lancelot, whose heart was riven at the sight of his lady's hurt, turned back as he stood harnessed and ready to mount and followed her to the room he had seen her enter.

'Ah, Lancelot, you have betrayed me and delivered me up to death, you who would quit the service of my lord the king to go to foreign lands from which God alone can bring you safe returned.'

'Madam, I shall indeed return, if it please Our Lord, and that sooner than you think.'

'Ah, God! my heart tells me otherwise, that makes me sick with dread and teaches me all the anguish that ever lady suffered for her lover.'

'Madam, I will go with your leave, when it pleases you to give it.'

'You should never go,' she said, 'if I had my will. But since I cannot choose, I commend you to the safe-keeping of Him who suffered on the most Holy and True Cross to deliver mankind from everlasting death; may He protect and guide you in all your ways.'

'Madam,' he said, 'may God of His great mercy grant your prayer!'

Thereupon Lancelot took his leave of the queen and went down into the courtyard where he found his companions already horsed and awaiting only his coming to move off, so he went to his steed and mounted it. The king, noticing that Galahad was without a shield and would have set out defenceless with the rest, approached him and said:

'Sir, I fear you are ill equipped inasmuch as you carry no shield, as do your companions.'

'Sire, I should do myself an ill service if I took one from here. Nor will I ever take a shield till some adventure yield me one.'

'In that case,' said the king, 'may God protect you. I will say no more.'

Knights and barons spurred their horses and rode out one and all from the castle, wending their way down through the town until they left it behind them. Never had there been such weeping and wailing as was set up by the townspeople when they saw the companions setting out on the Quest of the Holy Grail; of those that remained behind there was not a man, were he baron or bondsman, rich or poor, who did not weep openly at their departure. Only the men who were leaving betrayed no outward sign of emotion; indeed to see them one would have thought them happy to be going, and so in truth they were.

When they had arrived in that part of the forest that lies around Castle Vagan they drew rein before a cross. There Sir Gawain said to the king:

'Sire, you have ridden far enough; you must turn back now, it is not for you to escort us farther.'

'The homeward path will seem longer by far than the outward, for it costs me dear to leave you; but, since it needs must be, I will return.'

Thereupon Sir Gawain bared his head and his companions did the same; and they went to embrace the king, he first and they after. When they had laced on their helms again they commended one another to God, weeping tenderly. And so their ways parted, the king returning to Camelot, while the companions took the forest track which led them to Castle Vagan.

This Vagan was a man of upright life, who in his youth had ranked among the foremost knights of his day. When he saw the companions passing through his castle he ordered all the gates to be shut, saying that since God had done him the honour of delivering them into his hands, they should not go free until he had served them with the best he had. He kept them there as it were by force and had them unarmed, and entertained them that night so lavishly that they were lost in wonder at such a display of wealth.

That evening they considered how best they might proceed, and agreed to separate the following day and go their several ways, for it would redound to their shame if they rode in a band together. The next morning at daybreak the companions rose, and taking their arms, went off to hear mass in a chapel within the walls. This done, they mounted their horses and commended the lord of the place to God's keeping, thanking him earnestly for the great honour he had shown them. Then they rode out from the castle and separated as they had decided amongst themselves, striking out into the forest one here, one there, wherever they saw it thickest and wherever path or track was absent. And even those men who fancied themselves hard and proud shed tears at this leave-taking. But here the tale leaves them and tells of Galahad, for he it was who had instigated this Quest.

[2]

The Shield

NOW the story relates that when Galahad had parted from his companions he journeyed three or four days without meeting with any adventure worth recording. On the fifth day, shortly after vespers, it so chanced that his path led him directly to an abbey of white monks. On arrival he knocked at the gate and the brethren came out, and recognizing him for a wandering knight, pulled him forcibly down from the saddle. One took charge of his horse and another led him to a ground floor room that he might be unarmed. When he had been divested of his armour he noticed two companions of the Round Table, of whom one was King Baudemagus and the other Owein the Bastard. These two, once they had scanned his features and recognized him, ran with arms spread wide to welcome him with joyful embraces in their delight at finding him there. When they had made themselves known in turn, Galahad matched his joy to theirs and showed them the honour due to men he must hold as companions and brothers.

That evening, when they had eaten, they went to take their ease in an adjoining orchard, a pretty, pleasant place, and as they sat down under a tree to talk, Galahad asked them what adventure had brought them there.

'Truth to tell, Sir,' they said, 'we came here to seek out a wonder which from all we have heard is passing strange. There is a shield in this abbey of such virtue, that the man who hangs it about his neck and bears it away prospers so ill that within one day, or two at the most, he lies dead or wounded or maimed. And we have come to test the truth of this report.'

'And in the morning,' added King Baudemagus, 'I will shoulder it myself, and then I shall know whether the adventure matches its repute.'

'In God's name,' said Galahad, 'if what you tell me of this shield is true it is indeed a marvel. And if you cannot win it, I will be the one to bear it forth, for I have no shield of my own.'

'Sir,' they said, 'in that case we will leave it for you, for we know, besides, that you will not fail the test.'

'I would like you to try your fortune first to ascertain the truth of your tale.'

The others agreed. That night the companions enjoyed the finest hospitality the monks could offer. The brethren showed Galahad great honour when they heard the testimony that the two knights bore him; they prepared the best room for him and all things fitting for such a guest, and King Baudemagus and his companion lay close by.

In the morning, when they had heard mass, King Baudemagus inquired of one of the brethren where he might find the shield of which there was so much talk in those parts.

'Sir,' said the good man, 'why do you ask?'

'Because I would take it away with me to see whether it has such powers as are commonly reported.'

'I do not advise you ever to carry it out of the abbey, for I fear you would only reap dishonour by so doing.'

'Nonetheless I should like to know where it hangs and how it is fashioned.'

So the monk led him round behind the altar where he found a shield bearing a red cross on a white ground.

'Sir,' said the good man, 'this is the shield you seek.'

When they had all surveyed it they declared they had never seen a shield more admirable in form or workmanship; and withal it was sweetly scented as though all the spices of the earth had been spilled on it. Seeing it Owein the Bastard said:

'So help me God, you are looking at such a shield as shall hang from no man's neck unless he be the very paragon of knighthood; and as for me, it shall not hang from mine, for I have neither valour nor virtue enough to wear it.'

'In God's name,' exclaimed King Baudemagus, 'come what may I will carry it off.'

Therewith he hung it round his neck and strode out of the church. Before mounting his courser he said to Galahad:

'Sir, if it please you, I should like you to wait for me here until such time as I can tell you the outcome of this adventure. Should it go ill with me I would gladly have you learn of it, for I know that you would accomplish the feat with ease.'

'I shall be happy to await your return,' said Galahad.

So King Baudemagus mounted and the brethren lent him a squire to attend him and bring the shield back should the need arise.

Thus Galahad stayed behind with Owein to keep him company until he should learn the truth of this matter. King Baudemagus, who had started out alone with the squire, rode for some two leagues or more until he came to a meadow sloping gently down towards a hermitage which lay in the bottom of a valley. Turning his glance in the direction of the hermitage he caught sight of a knight in white armour spurring towards him as fast as his steed could carry him. His lance was lowered as he rode at him full tilt. As soon as King Baudemagus descried him, he had at him in turn and shattered the haft of his own lance in the clash, projecting the splinters far and wide. And the white knight, who had caught him uncovered, dealt him such a blow that he sundered the steel rings of the hauberk and thrust the sharp steel into the king's left shoulder, pushing it home like one stout of heart and sinew, so that he unhorsed him. When King Baudemagus fell, the knight took the shield from him and spoke so loud that not only he, but the squire too, heard him plainly, saying:

'Sir Knight, it was overweening and foolish in you to hang this shield about your neck; for it is granted to no man to wear it unless he be the finest knight in Christendom. And for the sin you committed Our Lord sent me to exact vengeance in due measure.'

When he had spoken he went to the squire and said:

'Take this shield and carry it to the servant of Jesus Christ, the Good Knight they call Galahad, whom you left but now in the abbey, and say to him that the Master sends him word to wear it. For he will ever find it new and whole as it is today, and on this account he should cherish it. And greet him on my behalf as soon as you see him.'

'What is your name, Sir,' asked the lad, 'that I may be able to tell the knight when I find him?'

'My name is not for your knowing; it cannot be disclosed to you nor any mortal man;* and with this you must be content. Do only as I command.'

'Sir,' said the youth, 'since you will not tell me your name, I beg and constrain you by that which you hold most dear, to tell me the true story of the shield, how it was brought to this country and why so many marvels have attended it. For no man in living memory has hung it about his neck but it went ill with him.'

'You have pressed me so solemnly,' said the knight, 'that I will tell you. But it shall not be for your ears only. I want you to fetch the knight to whom you are to bear the shield.'

The lad promised to do so, adding:

'But where shall we find you on our return?'

'In this very place.'

Then the squire went to King Baudemagus and asked him whether he was badly wounded.

'Yes, indeed,' said the king, 'so grievously that I shall not escape with my life.'

'Could you ride?'

He said he would try, and injured as he was pulled himself to his feet and with the other's support he made his way to the horse from which he had fallen. The king mounted in front and the squire behind so that he might hold him fast round the waist, for he feared, and with reason, that he might otherwise fall.

In this manner they left the place where the king had received his wound and made their way back to the abbey they had so recently left. When the inmates saw them approaching they ran out to meet them, and having helped King Baudemagus down from his horse, they bore him to a chamber where they examined his wound, which was gaping and terrible. Galahad spoke to one of the brethren attending him, saying:

'Sir, do you think he can mend? It would be too great a pity in my opinion if he were to lose his life in this adventure.'

* Cf. Judges 13, 17–18.

'Sir,' replied the monk, 'he may recover, God willing, but believe me, he is sorely wounded. Still, one must not be too sorry for him, for we told him plainly that if he carried the shield away he would come to harm; yet he persisted despite our enjoinders, and must blame himself for his folly.'

When the brethren had done all that they could for the king, the squire said to Galahad in front of all those present:

'Sir, I bring you greetings from the good knight in white armour, he by whom King Baudemagus was wounded. He sends you this shield and bids you wear it from now on in the name of the Master. For there lives at this time, so he says, none but you that has the right to bear it. On this account has he sent it to you by me. And if you would know the cause of the adventures that time and again have attended it, we must go to him, you and I, and he will tell us, for so he promised me.'

When the monks heard these tidings they did Galahad reverence and cried blessings on the fortune that had bent his steps their way, for they held it certain that these perils and hazards would now cease troubling them. Then Owein the Bastard spoke and said:

'Sir Galahad, take up this shield that was made for none other than you, and you will be gratifying an earnest wish; for I have craved nothing more fervently than the acquaintance of the Good Knight who should prove himself its master.'

Galahad replied that since the shield had been sent to him he would wear it, but first he would have his arms; and these were brought at his asking. When he was armed and mounted he hung the shield about his neck and took his leave, commending the brethren to God. Owein the Bastard, accoutred too and horsed, offered to keep him company, but Galahad said that he could not accept; he would ride all alone except for the squire. So the two of them parted and went their separate ways.

Owein plunged into the thick of the forest, while Galahad and the squire rode on till they found the knight in white armour whom the lad had seen on the first occasion. At their approach the knight rode up and saluted Galahad, who returned the greeting as courteously as he knew how. After they had made one another's acquaintance and talked for a time, Galahad said to the knight:

'Sir, as I have heard it said, many strange adventures have come to pass in these parts by virtue of the shield I bear. I beg you in love and loyalty to disclose to me the meaning of these things and how and why they have come about, for I firmly believe you know the truth of it.'

'You are right, Sir,' said the knight, 'and as I know it I will tell you gladly. So listen, Galahad, if it please you, to my tale.

'Two and forty years after the Passion of Jesus Christ it happened that Joseph of Arimathea, the noble knight who took Our Lord's body down from the Holy Cross, left the city of Jerusalem accompanied by many of his people. It was Our Lord's command that set them on the road, and their wanderings brought them at last to Sarras, a city held by King Evalach, who was then an infidel. In the year that Joseph came to Sarras, Evalach was at war with one of his neighbours, a rich and powerful king called Tholomer whose lands marched with his own. When Evalach had gathered an army to ride against this Tholomer who had laid claim to his realm, Josephus, the son of Joseph, warned him that if he went into battle so destitute of true succour he would be worsted and put to shame by his enemy.

' "What counsel have you offered me?" asked Evalach.

' "Listen," replied Josephus, "and you shall hear."

'Thereupon he set about expounding the doctrine of the New Law and the story of the Gospel, and unfolded to him the truth concerning Our Lord's Crucifixion, and His Resurrection also. Then he had a shield brought, on the inner face of which he fashioned a cross of sendal, saying:

' "Now, King Evalach, I will show you how you may prove the power and the virtue of Him that was crucified. It is true that for the space of three days and three nights the worthless Tholomer will have the ascendancy over you, till he drive you to fear for your very life. But when death seems most certain, then unveil the shield and say: 'Most gracious Lord, the badge of whose death I bear, deliver me from this peril and lead me forth whole and unharmed to receive in faith Thy holy Law.' "

'Thus counselled the king rode out and led his army against Tholomer, and all came about as Josephus had prophesied. So when he saw himself in such danger that he thought he must surely die he uncovered his shield and beheld in the centre the bleeding figure of a man crucified. Then he spoke the words that Josephus had taught him and through them won victory and honour, for he was snatched from the hands of his enemies and overcame Tholomer and all his men. When he re-entered his city of Sarras he proclaimed to all the people the truth that Josephus had shown him and bore such witness to Christ Crucified that Nascien was baptized.[11] Now it happened that during his baptism a man passed by holding his severed hand which had been smitten off at the wrist. He approached when Josephus called him, and directly he touched the cross on the shield his hand was restored. Nor was that the end of the miracle. For the cross which had been on the shield imprinted itself on the arm of him that was healed and the shield itself remained blank ever after. Then Evalach was himself baptized and became a servant of Jesus Christ, whom he worshipped from that day on with ardent devotion, while the shield was ever the object of his greatest reverence.

'It came about later, when Josephus and his father had left Sarras, and were come to Britain, that they met with a cruel and wicked king who cast them into prison together with many other Christians. The news of Josephus' captivity was soon noised abroad, for no man was then held in such renown as he; indeed it travelled so fast and so far that it came to the ears of King Mordrain.[12] He and his brother-in-law Nascien summoned their vassals and fighting men and landing in Britain marched on Josephus' captor; they dispossessed him completely and routed all his barons, with the result that the Christian faith was established throughout the land. These two so loved Josephus that they never re-embarked but cleaved to him and followed him in all his journeyings. When Josephus lay at last on his death-bed and Evalach realized that he must leave this world, he came to his chamber and said to him, weeping tenderly:

' "Sir, when you leave me, I shall remain alone in this country, who left my kingdom for your sake and the solace of my homeland. Since you must depart this life, for the love of God leave me some relic of yourself which will be a remembrance of you when you are dead."

'Josephus fell in with his wish and began to consider what he might leave him. After much thought he said:

' "King Evalach, send for the shield I gave you when you went to do battle with Tholomer."

' "Most willingly," replied the king, for the shield was close by, as might indeed be an object which accompanied him wherever he went, and he had it brought before Josephus now. It so happened that at the moment when the shield was carried in, Josephus' nose was bleeding profusely and could not be staunched. He took hold of the shield at once and in his own blood traced the cross you see here (for I would have you know that this shield you carry is the selfsame one of which I tell). And when he had drawn this very cross, he said:

' "Behold this shield which I leave you as a token of remembrance. You will never look on it again without thinking of me, for you are witness that this cross is made in my blood, and it will ever be as fresh and bright as it is today, so long as the shield endures. And that will be no little space, for none, be he the best of knights, shall hang it about his neck without repenting the day, until the coming of Galahad, the Good Knight, the last of Nascien's line.[18] Let therefore none presume to take up this shield but he to whom God has destined it: for as this shield has outshone every other by the virtue vested in it, even so shall he outshine his peers in knightly deeds and holy living."

' "Since you are leaving me so precious a parting gift," said the king, "tell me, I pray you, where I must leave this shield when my hour comes. For I would wish to put it in some place where the Good Knight may be sure of finding it."

' "Listen," replied Josephus, "and I will tell you what you must do. There where Nascien shall leave orders for his body to be laid do you place the shield; for that is where the Good Knight will come on the fifth day after receiving the order of chivalry."

'And all has come to pass as he foretold, for you had been but five days a knight when you came to this abbey where Nascien lies buried. Now I have explained to you why a fearsome fate has befallen such foolhardy knights as ignored the proscription and would have carried off the shield to which you alone were entitled.'

When he had finished speaking he vanished in such a manner that Galahad never knew what had become of him nor where he had gone. The youth, who had heard the tale, jumped down from his cob and threw himself at Galahad's feet, begging him with tears, for the love of Him whose device he bore on his shield, to knight him and let him serve him as squire.

'If I wished for company,' said Galahad, 'be assured that I would not refuse you.'

'Sir,' implored the lad, 'make me a knight for God's sake and I swear that chivalry will find in me a worthy champion, so it please Him.'

As Galahad looked at the boy where he knelt weeping, he was moved to compassion and granted his request.

'Sir,' said the other then, 'return if you please to the abbey, for I shall get arms there and a horse. Indeed you must, not for my sake only, but on account of an adventure to be found there which you, I know, will bring to its conclusion, where all the world has failed.'

Galahad said that he would gladly go, and rode back to the monastery at once. There he received an enthusiastic welcome from the monks, who asked the youth the reason for their guest's return.

'To make me a knight,' he answered, and they rejoiced with him.

Then the Good Knight asked them where this adventure was to be sought.

'Sir,' they enquired, 'are you acquainted with its nature?'

He answered that he was not.

'Know then that there is a voice which proceeds from one of the tombs in our cemetery. Its power is such that those who hear it lie shorn of strength and wits for a long season.'

'Do you know the author of this voice?' asked Galahad.

'No, unless it be the enemy.'

'Lead me there,' he said, 'for I have a keen desire to learn.'

'Then you must come with us.'

Therewith they led him, armed as he stood except for his helm, to the farthermost end of the church, where one of the brethren said to him:

'Sir, do you see that great tree and the tomb beneath it?'

'Yes,' he answered.

'Then I will tell you what to do. Go to the tomb and raise the stone, and I give you my word that you will find a great marvel inside.'

Galahad waited no more but set out towards the tomb, and as he drew near he heard a rending shriek as of a being in torment, and a voice which cried:

'Stand back, Galahad, thou servant of Jesus Christ, and come not nigh me, for thou wouldst yet oust me from that place where I have lodged so long.'

But Galahad was undismayed and went up to the tomb, and as he bent forward to grasp the head he saw smoke and flame belch out, followed at once by a thing most foul and hideous, shaped like a man. At this sight he blessed himself, knowing it for the Evil One. And at the same moment he heard a voice which said to him:

'Ah! Galahad, most holy one, I see thee so girt about by angels that my power cannot endure against thee: I cede the place to thee.'

At this Galahad again made the sign of the cross and gave thanks to Our Lord. Then he raised the tombstone and discovered beneath the body of a man in armour, with a sword at his side and all that betokens a knight. When he had looked at it he called to the monks, crying:

'Come forward and see what I have found and tell me how I must proceed, for I am ready to do more if there is more to be done.'

When they drew near and saw the body lying in the grave, they said to him:

'Sir, it is not needful that you should do more than you have already accomplished, for in our opinion this body shall never be moved from its resting place.'

'Indeed it shall,' said the old man who had first described the adventure to Galahad. 'It must be taken from this graveyard and cast out, for since this ground has been blessed and hallowed, no body belonging to a wicked and recreant Christian ought to lie here.'

He ordered the servants of the abbey to raise it from the grave and bear it away, which they did. Then Galahad asked the venerable man whether he had done all that was required of him.

'Yes, indeed,' he replied, 'for the voice which engendered so many ills will never be heard here again.'

'Do you know the occasion of these mysteries?' asked Galahad.

'I do, and will be happy to tell you, and it is something that you should know, for the purport is most profound.

At this point they left the cemetery and returned to the abbey. Galahad told the youth that he must keep vigil all night in the church and that the following morning he would knight him as was his due. The lad replied that he asked no more, and they helped him array himself fittingly to receive the high order of chivalry which he had so ardently desired. Meanwhile Galahad was led to a room where he was relieved of arms and armour, and then sat down on a couch at the monk's request to listen to his tale.

'Sir, you asked me just now the meaning of the mysterious task you fulfilled, and I will gladly inform you. In this adventure there were three perils to be surmounted: the great weight of the tombstone which had to be raised, the body of the knight which must be cast out, and the voice which deprived the hearer of sense, movement and memory. I will now unfold to you the meaning of these three things.

'The tombstone covering the body signifies the obduracy of this world, which was so rife when Our Lord came down to earth that He met with nothing else. In those days sons loved not their fathers nor fathers their sons, and Satan bore them every one to hell on that account. When the heavenly Father saw that men's hearts were so hardened that they knew not their neighbour, nor trusted him, nor believed the words of the prophets, but daily raised up new gods, He sent His Son into the world to soften their hearts, that hardened sinners might become meek and tender as babes.* But when He was come to earth He found men so obdurate and steeped in sin, that one could as soon have melted the solid rock as their hard hearts. It was of this He spoke when He said through the mouth of David

---

* Cf. Ezekiel 36, 26.

the prophet: "I shall be alone until the hour of my death", which was to say: "Father, thou wilt have converted but a fragment of this nation ere I die."[14] Today the similitude is renewed whereby the Father sent His Son to earth for the deliverance of His people. For just as folly and error fled at His advent and truth stood revealed, even so has Our Lord chosen you from among all other knights to ride abroad through many lands to put an end to the hazards that afflict them and make their meaning and their causes plain. This is why your coming must be compared to the coming of Jesus Christ, in semblance only, not in sublimity. And even as the prophets who lived many years before the advent of Our Lord had announced that He should come to earth and deliver His people from the chains of hell, even so did the hermits and holy men foretell your coming fully twenty years ago. They predicted every one that the kingdom of Logres would never be loosed from its bondage until you came. We have waited so long for you that now, praise God, you are come.'

'Explain to me now,' said Galahad, 'what the body denotes, for you have made the meaning of the tomb quite plain.'

'I will tell you,' he replied. 'The dead body signifies mankind, for men had persisted so long in their obduracy, that they lay dead and blind beneath the weight of the sins they had committed down the years. This blindness was exposed by the advent of Jesus Christ. For when they had in their midst the King of kings and Saviour of the world, they held Him for a sinner, judging Him by themselves. They placed greater trust in Satan than in Him and delivered His body up to death at the behest of the devil, who was for ever whispering in their ears and had wormed his way into their hearts. It was this deed that led Vespasian, on learning the truth about the prophet they had betrayed, to seize their land and crush their nation under foot; thus was their downfall brought about by Satan's advocacy.

'Let us now consider how these interpretations concord with one another. The tomb signifies the hardheartedness of the Jews, while the body represents the death of them and their seed in that mortal sin whose shackles proved so hard to loose. The voice which proceeded from the tomb signifies the terrible words which they spoke to Pilate, the governor: "His blood be on us and our children!"* These were the words which led to their being put to shame and perishing with all that they possessed. Thus the adventure shows forth the meaning of the Passion of Jesus Christ, while at the same time it symbolizes His coming. It had too, formerly, another effect, for when wandering knights came here and approached the tomb, the enemy, knowing them for rank and wretched sinners, sunk in debauchery and all manner of wickedness, rendered them senseless with terror at the sound of his fell and gruesome voice. This peril would never have passed nor sinners ceased to be entrapped, had God not brought you here to draw its sting. As soon as you came, the devil, who knew you to be undefiled and as free from sin as is given to mortal man, dared not face your presence, but fled, and through your coming lost his sovereignty. So ended the adventure which many a knight of high renown had vainly essayed.'

And now, said the monk, he had told him the whole truth: to which Galahad answered that he had never thought the adventure held so high a meaning.

That night Galahad was served with the best the monks had to offer. And when morning broke he knighted the youth according to the custom of that time. When he had done all that was required of him he asked the youth his name, and he replied that he was called Melias and was the son of the King of Denmark.

'Good friend,' said Galahad, 'since you are now a knight and spring even from royal stock, take care so to acquit yourself in the service of chivalry that your lineage forfeit none of its lustre. For when a king's son receives the order of knighthood he must outshine all other knights in virtue even as the sun's light makes the stars seem pale.'

He replied that the honour of the order, so help him God, would be well safeguarded, for the prospect of pain or hardship would never make him shrink. Therewith Galahad asked for his arms, and as they were brought to him Melias said:

'Sir, you have made me a knight, for which I thank God and

*Cf. Matthew 27, 25.

T—C

yourself, and my joy is so great that I can scarce express it. You are not ignorant of the custom whereby he who dubs a man knight may not lawfully refuse his first request, so long as it is reasonable?'

'What you say is true,' said Galahad, 'but why do you ask?'

'Because I have a request to make; and I beg you to grant it for it can do you no possible harm.'

'I do so,' said Galahad, 'should it be to my hurt.'

'My grateful thanks,' he replied, and went on: 'My suit is that I may ride with you in this Quest until some adventure part us, and then if by chance we meet again, that you do not deprive me of your company in favour of another.'

Then he demanded a horse so that he might accompany Galahad, and when the animal was brought they left together, and rode all that day and a week beyond, until they came on a Tuesday morning to a cross where the road forked. They rode up to the cross and found an inscription carved in the wood, which read: GIVE HEED, THOU KNIGHT THAT GOEST ABOUT SEEKING ADVENTURE: BEHOLD TWO ROADS, ONE TO THY LEFT, THE OTHER TO THY RIGHT. THE LEFT-HAND ROAD THOU SHALT NOT TAKE, FOR HE THAT ENTERS THEREIN MUST BE SECOND TO NONE IF HE WOULD FOLLOW IT TO THE END: AND IF THOU TAKE THE RIGHT-HAND ROAD, HAPLY THOU MAYEST SOON PERISH. When Melias saw what was written, he said to Galahad:

'Ah, noble knight, in God's name let me take the left-hand path, for there I may prove my strength and find out whether there lie in me such seeds of prowess and valour as shall win me repute as a knight.'

'By your consent I would go that way myself, for I think I might win through easier than you.'

But Melias held stubbornly to his wish, so they went their different ways. And there the tale leaves Galahad to recount how Melias fared.

Presumption Punished. The Castle of the Maidens

Now the story relates that when Melias left Galahad he rode until he came to an ancient forest which he was two days traversing. The following morning at prime he came out into a meadow and saw a magnificent throne athwart his path. On the seat lay a crown of surpassing beauty, while a number of tables were arranged in front of it laden with delicacies. Melias halted in wonderment, but of all that met his gaze there was nothing he hungered after save that crown of rarest splendour, and he thought to himself that he would be a fortunate fellow indeed who could stand thus orbed before the people. Without more ado he took it, and swore he would carry it off, and ringing his right arm with it, he turned back into the forest. He had not gone far when he saw he was being followed by a knight who called to him from the height of his powerful charger:

'Sir Knight, lay down the crown: it is not yours to take and you will suffer for it.'

Melias turned his horse at this shout, and realizing that he must joust and no escape, he crossed himself with the prayer: 'Gracious Lord God, come to the aid of Thy new-made knight.' Thereupon the other rode at him and struck him so mighty a blow that he forced his lance through shield and hauberk into his side and bore him to the ground so fast impaled that the steel and part of the shaft remained embedded in his flank. Then the knight came up and took the crown from his arm, saying:

'Sir Knight, let go of the crown, for you have no right to it.'

And with that he rode off whence he had come. Meanwhile Melias lay there unable to rise, as one convinced he has a mortal wound. He reproached himself for not putting his trust in Galahad; the failure had already cost him dear.

As he lay in this agony of mind and body, it happened that Galahad, treading a random course, passed through that part of the forest. When he saw Melias lying wounded on the ground and seemingly close to death he was shocked and grieved, and going up to him, said:

'Ah! Melias, whose hand did this to you? Do you think you will live?'

Melias recognized Galahad by his voice and cried:

'Ah! Sir, for God's sake let me not die in this forest but carry me to some abbey where I may receive the rites of the Church and make a Christian end.'

'What? Melias, are you so badly hurt that you fear for your life?'

'Yes,' he replied.

At that Galahad was sick at heart and asked where they were who had done him such injury. Even as he spoke the knight who had wounded Melias emerged from the leafage and said to Galahad:

'Sir Knight, put up your guard, for I will do my worst!'

'Ah! Sir,' cried Melias, 'it is he that slew me. For God's sake defend yourself!'

Galahad made no reply but spurred to meet the knight who was charging towards him. In his headlong rush the attacker missed his mark and Galahad thrust at him so fiercely that the lance entered his shoulder and snapped, as man and horse crashed down together. His charger's impetus spent, Galahad wheeled to see a second armed knight who shouted as he came:

'Sir Knight, you will leave the horse for me!'

He couched his lance as he galloped forward and splintered it on Galahad's shield without shifting him a whit in the saddle, and as he thundered by Galahad struck off his hand with his sword. When he found himself crippled the victim turned tail and fled in fear of his life, and Galahad let him go, having no wish to do him greater mischief. Instead he returned to Melias' side without another glance at the knight he had felled.

He asked Melias how he might help him, for he was ready to do whatever he could.

'If I could bear the jolting, Sir, I should like you to mount me in front of you and take me to a nearby abbey where I know that the monks would do all in their power to heal me.'

Galahad agreed to this, but added:

'I think it were best if we first withdrew the spearhead from your wound.'

'Ah! Sir, I would on no account run such a risk before I am shriven, for I fear its removal will kill me. Do but bear me away from here.'

So Galahad lifted him up as gently as he could and propped him in front of him, and seeing how weak he was, clasped him tight against his falling. Thus they rode on their way till such time as they came to an abbey.

They called out as they stood before the gate, and the monks, who were good men, opened it wide and with a kindly welcome carried Melias away to a quiet room. There, when he had taken off his helm, he asked for his Saviour and they brought Him to him. And when he had confessed his sins and begged for mercy as a Christian should, he received the Lord's Body. Directly afterwards he said to Galahad:

'Sir, let death come when he will. I am well fortified against his assault. Now you may try to draw the steel out of my body.'

So taking hold of it, Galahad withdrew the spike with its splintered wood, while Melias fainted from the pain. Galahad next enquired whether there was any man present who was skilled to dress the knight's wounds. They replied that there was, and sent for an old monk who had once been a knight, and showed him the wound. He examined it and promised that he would restore Melias to health within a month. Galahad was much cheered by this news and had himself unarmed, announcing that he would stay at the abbey that day and the next until it was known whether Melias would indeed live.

When three days had passed he asked Melias how it went with him and learned that he felt himself on the road to recovery.

'In that case,' he said, 'I can be on my way tomorrow.'

'Ah, my lord Galahad,' replied Melias disconsolately, 'would you then leave me here? There is not a man on earth who desires your company more fervently than I, could I keep pace with you.'

'Sir', said Galahad, 'I am of no service to you here, and

instead of idling my time away, I should be better employed in seeking the Holy Grail and following up the Quest which I began.'

'What,' asked one of the brethren, 'is this Quest then begun?'

'Indeed it is, and we are both companions.'

'Then by my faith,' said the monk, 'I tell you, Sir Knight who lie sick, it was your sin that brought this evil upon you. And if you told me the tale of your wanderings since the Quest began I would show you which sin was to blame.'

'Sir,' said Melias, 'I will tell you all that has happened.'

So Melias told how Galahad had knighted him, and how together they had found the writing on the cross which warned against the left-hand road, and how he had taken it notwithstanding, and all that had befallen him since. At that the monk, who was a man both holy and learned, said to him:

'In truth, Sir Knight, these adventures pertain without a doubt to the Holy Grail, for everything you have told me has a meaning which I will interpret to you.

'When you were to be knighted you went to confession, and thus acceded to the order of chivalry cleansed from every stain and purged of the sins which sullied you; so it was that you entered upon the Quest of the Holy Grail in a fit state. Now when the devil saw this he was sorely put out and resolved to assail you at the very first juncture. This he did, and I will tell you how and when. After leaving the abbey where you were made a knight you first encountered on your road the sign of the true Cross: the sign in which a knight should place his greatest trust. Nor was this all. There was an inscription as well, which indicated the two roads open to you, one leading to the left, the other to the right. For the right-hand road you must read the way of Jesus Christ, the way of compassion, in which the knights of Our Lord travel by night and by day, in the darkness of the body and in the soul's light. In the left-hand road you perceive the way of sinners, which holds dire perils for those who choose it. Because it is far more hazardous than the first the inscription decreed that none should take it unless he were of uncommon valour, that is to say unless he stood so grounded in the love of Christ that no adventure could tempt him into sin. When you saw the writing you wondered what it could possibly signify; and at once the enemy pierced you with one of his darts. Shall I tell you which? It was the dart of pride, for you thought your prowess would see you through, but reason played you false, for the words referred to a spiritual order whilst you, seeing only the temporal, were filled with pride and fell headlong into mortal sin.

'When you had parted from Galahad, the enemy, who had probed your frailty, stayed at your side, counting his triumph paltry if he could not trip you again, and by luring you from sin to sin drag you down to hell. So he conjured up a golden crown before your eyes, causing you to stumble into covetousness as soon as you clapped eyes on it, so that in taking it you fell a prey to concupiscence, which made, with pride, two mortal sins. When he saw you implement your lust and bear away the crown he entered into the person of a reprobate knight, whose evil appetites he so excited, being already his master, that he itched to kill you. So he flew at you with brandished lance and would have killed you had the sign of the cross not been your safeguard. Nonetheless, as a punishment for straying from His service, Our Lord led you to the very brink of death, to teach you to trust another day in your Saviour's help sooner than in your own right arm. And to succour you in your extremity He sent you Galahad, the holy knight, to rout the two knights representing the two sins lodged in you; and because he was free from mortal sin they could not stand against him. Now I have expounded to you the meaning and cause of all your adventures.'

His listeners answered that they found the meaning admirable and much to be marvelled at.

Much talk passed that night between the two knights and their host about the adventures of the Holy Grail. And Galahad pleaded with Melias so earnestly that the latter gave him leave to go when he would, and having obtained his friend's consent, he said he would stay no longer. The following morning, therefore, as soon as he had heard mass, Galahad took up his arms and commended Melias to God. For many days he wandered without meeting with any adventure worthy of remark, until it fell one morning that he left the home of a vassal without hearing mass and journeyed till he came to a high mountain, where he chanced on an ancient chapel. He turned his horse towards it, for he always chafed if a day passed without his hearing the holy office. On arriving he found the place deserted and no one about; he knelt down however and prayed to Our Lord for counsel. When his prayer was done he heard a voice which said:

'Give ear, Knight Errant! Make thy way straight to the Castle of the Maidens and sweep away the evil customs which reign there.'

On hearing this he gave thanks to Our Lord for sending him guidance, and at once mounted and rode off. Some little way ahead he noticed a strong castle pleasingly sited in a valley which was watered by a broad, swift-flowing river called Severn. He headed towards it, and when he was not far off he met a man, very old and meanly clothed, who saluted him courteously. Galahad returned his greeting and asked him the name of the castle.

'Sir,' he said, 'it is called the Castle of the Maidens, and the castle and its inhabitants are accursed; for cruelty is enthroned there and all compassion banished.'

'How so?' asked Galahad.

'Because all who pass that road are brutally abased. Wherefore I advise you, Sir Knight, to return where you came from, for the way ahead holds nothing but dishonour.'

'Then God keep you, good Sir,' said Galahad, 'for turning back would go against the grain.'

With that he looked to his arms, and as soon as he was confident that all was in order he made off at a brisk pace towards the castle.

His way was soon barred by seven maidens mounted on richly caparisoned horses, who called out:

'Sir Knight, you have passed the bounds!'

He replied that no bounds would keep him from going to the castle. So he pressed on till he met a varlet who informed him that the rulers of the castle forbade him to proceed until they learned what he wanted.

'I ask only the custom of the castle.'

'Truly,' said the other, 'you are making a grave mistake in asking it, and what you will receive has proved beyond the strength of any knight. But wait for me here, and you shall have what you seek.'

'Bestir yourself then,' said Galahad, 'and speed my business for me.'

The varlet returned to the castle and within a short time there sallied out seven knights, all brothers, who shouted to Galahad:

'Sir Knight, put up your guard, for the only thing we warrant you is death.'

'What,' said he, 'would you all do battle with me in a body?'

'Yes,' they replied, 'for such is the adventure and the custom.'

Hearing this Galahad levelled his lance and sprang forward, felling the first with a blow that well-nigh broke his neck. Six lances clashed against his shield, yet he never moved in the saddle. However, the weight of their thrusts jerked his horse back on its haunches and almost brought it down. Every lance was shattered in this impact, and Galahad unhorsed three of his assailants. Now he drew his sword and he and his attackers clashed again in an affray so desperate and so long-drawn that those that had fallen first remounted, and the battle resumed more bloody than before. But he who was the paragon of knighthood strove so furiously that he drove his opponents back, doing them such damage with his keen sword-edge that no armour could prevent his spilling their bodies' blood. So strong and quick did they find him that he seemed to them more than mortal, for no man alive could have sustained the half of what he suffered. So when they saw that not only would he yield no inch but his strength never failed nor flagged, fear chilled their hearts. And indeed it is true, as the story of the Holy Grail testifies, that none ever saw him weary from the labours of his calling.

Thus did the battle rage until noon. Now the seven brothers were bold fighters and skilled in the art, but midday found them in such pitiable array that they were powerless to defend themselves, and he that never sued for mercy hewed them down as he would. When they saw they could not hold out any longer they turned and fled; Galahad, seeing this, did not pursue them, but went instead to the bridge that gave access to the castle. There he was met by a white-haired man wearing the habit, who handed him the keys of the castle, saying:

'Sir, receive these keys; you have won by your exploits this castle and all that is in it; they are yours to do as you will.'

Taking the keys he entered the stronghold, and as soon as he came within the walls he saw a great crowd of maidens thronging the streets, who cried out with one voice:

'Welcome! Sir, welcome! We have waited many a day for our deliverance! Blessed be God who has brought you here, for else we had never been freed from this castle of calamity.'

'God bless you all!' said he in return.

Thereupon they took his horse by the bridle and led him to the main keep where they stripped him of his arms, all unwilling, for he said it was far too soon to put up for the night.

'Ah! Sir,' cried one of the maidens, 'what are you saying? Most certainly, if you ride off again, those who fled before your sword will return this very night and re-establish the cruel custom which they enforced here for so long; and thus you will have striven to no purpose.'

'What would you have me do?' he asked. 'I am ready to execute your wishes, provided they seem to me right and lawful.'

'We would have you summon the knights and vassals of the locality, for they all hold their fiefs of this castle, and make them swear, both them and all that live here, that this custom shall never be instituted anew.'

This he agreed to do; and when they had escorted him to the principal dwelling he dismounted, and taking off his helm went up into the palace. At that moment a young woman appeared from a farther room carrying an ivory horn inlaid with bands of gold, which she handed to Galahad, saying:

'Sir, if you wish to summon those who will hold their lands of you henceforward, sound this horn that can be heard ten leagues away.'

This suggestion found favour with him. He passed the horn to a knight standing near, who took it in turn and blew it so loud and long that its note could be heard through all the surrounding countryside. When this had been done they all seated themselves round Galahad. First he asked the man who had given him the keys if he were a priest, and he said he was.

'Then tell me about the custom of this place and how these young women were made captive.'

'Gladly,' said the priest, and began his tale: 'It was fully ten years ago that the seven knights you vanquished came by chance to this castle and asked hospitality of Duke Lynor, who was lord of all the land and so fine a man that none could name a better. That night, after supper, a quarrel broke out between the seven brothers and the duke, touching one of his daughters whom they would have taken by force. It waxed so bitter that the duke was killed together with one of his sons, and she who had been the cause of the broil made prisoner. Having done this much, the brothers proceeded to seize the castle treasure, and, summoning knights and foot-soldiers, set about waging war on the neighbouring lords, till they forced them all to submit and become their vassals. The duke's daughter was grieved and angered by these events, and said to them, as though in prophecy:

' "In truth, my lords, we care not a straw that you are the masters of this castle now. For even as it was won on account of a woman it shall be lost through a maid; and one knight with his own arm shall discomfit seven."

'They took this in bad part, and swore that on account of her prediction they would let no maiden pass beneath the castle without holding her captive against the coming of the knight who was to prove their victor. And this they did until today, and the castle has been known since then as the Castle of the Maidens.'

'And the young woman over whom the quarrel arose,' asked Galahad, 'is she still here?'

'No, Sir, she is dead, but her younger sister is within.'

'And in what conditions were they held?'

'Sir, they suffered great wretchedness and discomfort.'

'They shall know it no more,' said Galahad.

Towards the hour of none the castle began to fill with those who had heard the news of its conquest. All showed Galahad every courteous attention, as to the one whom they held as lord. He invested the duke's daughter there and then with the castle and all its appurtenances and had the knights of that country swear fealty to her and vow to a man that they would never revive the custom. And the maidens dispersed to their respective homelands.

Galahad remained there, honoured and acclaimed, for the rest of that day, and in the morning came news that the seven brothers had perished.

'Who slew them?' he enquired.

'Sir,' said a squire, 'after leaving you yesterday, they encountered on that farther hill Sir Gawain and his brother Gaheriet, together with Sir Owein. Each party charged at the other, and the seven brothers went down in the affray.'

Galahad marvelled at the outcome of the adventure. He called for his arms, and when he was equipped he rode out from the castle. Its inmates escorted him a fair distance, until at the last he made them turn back and pursued his way alone. But here the tale leaves him and returns to Sir Gawain.

[4]

Sir Gawain Sets Out

Now the story relates that when Sir Gawain parted from his companions he journeyed many days without meeting with any adventure worth the telling, until he came to the abbey where Galahad had taken the white shield with the red cross, and learned of all the things he had accomplished. Having heard the tale of his exploits Sir Gawain asked the monks to show him the path which Galahad had taken, and struck out in pursuit. He rode on his way until he arrived by chance at the abbey where the injured Melias lay. The sick knight recognized Sir Gawain and gave him news of Galahad, who had left that very morning.

'God!' cried Sir Gawain, 'how unlucky I am! There is no more unfortunate fellow than I, who follow so hard on the heels of this knight and cannot come up with him! I swear that if God gave me to find him I should never leave his side, if he but loved my company as I should his.'

One of the monks caught Sir Gawain's words and answered:

'In truth, Sir, the two of you would be ill-yoked. For you are a bad and faithless servant and he a very model of knighthood.'

'Sir,' said Sir Gawain, 'from what you say I deduce you know me well.'

'I know you far better than you suspect.'

'In that case, Good Sir,' said Gawain, 'you may tell me, pray, how I fit your accusation.'

'That I will not,' said he, 'but when the time is ripe you will meet one who will tell you.'

During this exchange, a knight in full accoutrements rode into the abbey and dismounted in the courtyard. The brethren ran to help him and led him for unarming to the room where Gawain was waiting. As soon as Sir Gawain saw his face, he recognized his brother Gaheriet and ran to fold him in his arms with many expressions of delight, inquiring if he were in good health and spirits.

'Yes,' he replied, 'praise God.'

That night the monks attended to all their wants, and as soon as day dawned they heard mass in full armour, except for their helms. Then, arrayed and mounted, they left the abbey and went on their way till the hour of prime when they espied a little way ahead a solitary knight, whom they knew by his arms for Sir Owein. They shouted to him to halt. He looked round at the sound of his name and drew rein, recognizing their voices. They greeted him joyfully and asked what had befallen him since their parting.

'Nothing,' he replied, for he had met with no adventure that took his fancy.

'Then let us keep company,' said Gaheriet, 'till God send us some adventure.'

The two others assented and they pursued their common way till they found themselves in the neighbourhood of the Castle of the Maidens, on the very same day that it was conquered. When the seven brothers saw the three knights approaching, they said to one another:

'Let us at them and kill them, for they are of the same ilk as he that despoiled us: knights errant all.'

With that they spurred towards the three companions, shout-

ing to them to defend themselves, for their hour was come. At
this challenge the others wheeled their horses to face them, and
it happened that three of the seven brothers perished in the
first joust, for Sir Gawain slew one, and Sir Owein another, and
Gaheriet the third. Then they drew their swords and set upon
the survivors who defended themselves as best they could, but
that was but feebly, as men spent and shaken, for they had
already sustained a desperate combat against Galahad. And
the three, who were valiant knights, and skilled in warfare,
so set about them that they cut them down in no time at all.
And they left them dead on the field and went on their way
wheresoever fortune would lead them.

Now instead of heading towards the Castle of the Maidens
they turned away right-handed, and in so doing lost Galahad.[15]
Around the hour of vespers they separated from one another.
Sir Gawain proceeded alone till he came to a hermitage and
found the hermit in his chapel chanting the vespers of the
Blessed Virgin. He dismounted and stayed for the office, and
afterwards begged lodging in the name of holy charity; this the
hermit vouchsafed him cordially.

That evening the holy man asked Sir Gawain where he came
from, to which he gave a candid answer and told him also of the
Quest he had embarked on. On learning the identity of his
guest the hermit said:

'Indeed, Sir, did it please you, I should very much like to know
something of your life.'

Without more ado he began to speak to Sir Gawain of confession, calling to mind the most edifying texts of the Gospels
and urging the knight to confess his sins, and he would be at
pains to counsel him.

'Sir,' said Sir Gawain, 'if you would elucidate a remark that
was made to me two days ago I would unbosom myself to you,
for you seem to me a worthy man and you are, as I well know,
a priest.'

The good man assured him that he would do all he could to
assist him. Sir Gawain observed him and saw him so venerable
in age and demeanour that he was moved to confess himself to
him. So he told him of those offences against Our Lord which
lay heaviest on his conscience, nor did he omit the words which

the monk had spoken to him. The hermit, discovering that four years had elapsed since he had last been shriven, said to him then:

'In justice, Sir, were you called a bad and faithless servant. You were not admitted to the order of chivalry to soldier in the devil's cause thenceforward, but in order to serve our Maker, defend Holy Church and render at last to God that treasure which He entrusted to your safekeeping, namely your soul. To this end were you made a knight, and you, Gawain, have abused your knighthood. For you have been henchman to the enemy, forsaking your Maker and living the worst and most dissolute life that ever a knight lived. Now you can clearly see that he who called you a bad and faithless servant knew you well. And indeed, had you not been so hardened a sinner, the seven brothers would never have perished by your hand nor with your help, but would even now be doing penance for the wicked custom they established in the Castle of the Maidens and making their peace with God. He whom you seek, Galahad the Good Knight, did not act thus: he overcame without destroying them. And the fact that the seven brothers had brought this custom to the castle, whereby, without regard to justice, they held captive all the maidens who came to the country, is by no means devoid of meaning.'

'Ah! Sir,' exclaimed Sir Gawain, 'do tell me that meaning so that I can narrate it at court on my return.'

'Gladly,' said the other, and continued: 'By the Castle of the Maidens you are to understand hell, and by the maidens the souls of the just that were undeservedly imprisoned there before the Passion of Jesus Christ; and for the seven knights you should read the seven deadly sins, that in those days held such dominion over the world that justice was nowhere to be found. For when the soul left the body, were it of a just man or a sinner, that soul descended into hell and like the maidens was held captive there. But when the heavenly Father saw the corruption of all that He had made, He sent His son to earth to ransom the maidens, which is to say the souls of the just. And even as He sent His Son, who was with Him before the beginning of the world, even so did He send Galahad, His chosen knight and servant, to pluck from out of the castle the virtuous maidens, who are as pure and unsullied as the lily, which is never scorched by the heat of the day.'

This explanation left Sir Gawain at a loss for words; and the hermit said to him:

'Gawain, Gawain, if you would forsake this life of sin that you have led so long, you could yet be reconciled to Our Lord. For the Scriptures state that there is none so wicked but Our Lord will have mercy on him, provided he implore Him with a contrite heart. I therefore urge you most earnestly to accept a penance for your transgressions.'

But he said that the hardships of penance would be more than he could brook. So with that the good man let him be and held his peace, for he realized that all his admonishments would be so much wasted effort.

Come morning, Sir Gawain took his leave and continued his wanderings until he fell in by chance with Agloval and Girflet, son of Do. Four days they journeyed uneventfully, and on the fifth they parted each to his solitary course. And here the tale leaves them and tells of Galahad.

[5]

Lancelot's Conviction and Repentance

Now the story relates that after leaving the Castle of the Maidens, Galahad pressed on by stages till at last he found himself in the Waste Forest. There it fell one day that he met Lancelot and Perceval riding in company; and they took him for a stranger, being unfamiliar with the arms he bore. So Lancelot charged him at first, striking him full in the chest and snapping his lance, while Galahad met him with a blow that toppled horse and knight together, but did him no other injury.[16] Then, his lance being broken, he drew his sword and smote Perceval so hard that he cut through the helm and mail coif; and had the sword not twisted in his grasp he must have killed him. As it was, Perceval lost his grip on the saddle and hurtled to the ground so stunned and dazed from the blow he had received that he knew not whether it were day or night. This joust took place in front of a hermitage, the home of a recluse, and she, seeing Galahad riding off, cried out:

'Now, God go with you and guide you! Truly, if these had known you as well as I, they would never have ventured to attack you.'

When Galahad heard these words he was alarmed lest he be recognized, and pricking his horse, he galloped off at the roundest speed the animal could muster. The others, seeing him go, remounted with what haste they could, but when they found themselves outdistanced, they turned back so disconsolate and forlorn that they had welcomed death, for their lives were grown hateful to them; and in such despair they rode away into the Waste Forest.

So it was that Lancelot found himself back in the forest downcast and sore at heart for losing of the knight. He turned to Perceval for advice, but the other said that he had none to offer: the knight was riding at such a pace that they had no hope of catching him.

'And see,' he added, 'night has caught us in a spot so wild that we might never sally hence but by some happy chance. Therefore in my opinion we would do better to retrace our steps, for if we go astray at this point I fear it will be long before we find our road again. You may please yourself; for my part I see more to be gained from turning back than from pressing onward.'

However, Lancelot said he would never consent to return, but would rather follow the knight who carried the white shield, for he would have no peace of mind until he learned his name.

'You can wait at the least till morning breaks,' said Perceval, 'and then you and I will seek the knight together.'

But Lancelot said that he would not stay on any account.

'Then God keep you,' said Perceval, 'for I will ride no farther today; I shall go back instead to the anchoress who said she had cause to know him well.'

So the companions parted, and Perceval rode back to the recluse. Lancelot, however, took up his pursuit through the thick of the forest, keeping to neither track nor path, but following where fortune led. The darkness of the night served him ill, for he could make out nothing, either near or far, by which to steer his course. Notwithstanding, he came at last to a stone cross which stood on a lonely heath at the parting of two ways. Drawing near, he saw beside it a block of marble which bore, as it seemed to him, letters carved in the stone, but the night was so black that he was unable to decipher them. Not far from the cross he made out an ancient chapel and headed towards it, expecting to find some human presence. He rode up and dismounted, and having first tied his horse to an oak, he took his shield from his neck and hung it on the tree. But when he came to the chapel he found it abandoned and ruinous, and on passing the porch he came up against an iron grille whose close-set bars prevented farther access. Peering between them, he discerned within an altar richly hung with silken cloths and other trappings, and illumined by the radiance of six candles which burned before it in a massive silver candlestick. This fired him with a desire to enter and find out who abode there, for he was surprised to come upon such splendour in so strange a place. He examined the ironwork screen, but was so dismayed to find that he could not pass that he left the chapel, and going to his horse led it by the bridle as far as the cross. There he un-saddled it and turned it loose to graze. He unlaced his helm and placed it at his feet, then ungirding his sword he stretched out on his shield before the cross, where he slept but fitfully for, weary though he was, the Good Knight who carried the white shield was ever present to his mind.

When he had lain awake some while, he saw coming towards him in a litter slung between two palfreys, a sick knight who was moaning aloud in anguish. As he passed, he paused on his way and gazed at Lancelot, but gave him no greeting, for he thought he slept. And Lancelot, too, lay mute, as one who lies between sleeping and waking. Then the knight in the litter, who halted in front of the cross, set up a bitter lamentation, crying:

'Ah! God, shall my suffering never be abated? God, when shall I see the Holy Vessel which is to ease my smart? God, ah! God, did ever man endure such agony and for so venial an offence?'

Thus did the knight keep up his clamour, raving to God of his pain and torment. And all this while Lancelot lay without speech or movement, as though in a trance, yet he saw him clearly and heard his words.

When the knight had been long at his orisons, Lancelot looked about him and saw the silver candlestick issue from the chapel, the one he had observed there earlier with the tapers, and as he watched it moving towards the cross he marvelled to see that there was none to carry it. There followed on a silver table that Holy Vessel he had seen before in the castle of the Fisher King, the same men called the Holy Grail.* As soon as the sick knight saw it coming he let himself fall to the ground from where he lay, and with folded hands stretched out, cried:

'Gracious Lord God, who through this Holy Vessel that I now set eyes on hast performed so many miracles in this and other lands, Father, look on me in Thy mercy and grant that I may presently be healed of my infirmity so that I too may undertake the Quest wherein all worthy men are entered.'

Thereupon he dragged himself by the strength of his arms to the stone where the table stood that supported the Holy Vessel. He pulled himself up with his two hands until he could kiss the silver table and press his eyes to it. And immediately he knew relief from his suffering, and he groaned aloud and said:

'Ah! God, I am healed!'

And almost at once he fell asleep. When the vessel had remained some time in their presence, together with the chandelier it returned to the chapel as it had come, without Lancelot knowing who had borne them thither or thence. Yet it fell that, whether from exhaustion or from the weight of some sin that lay on him, he never stirred at the coming of the Grail, and gave no sign that he marked it; and for this he was to receive great blame and suffer many misadventures in the course of the Quest.

When the Holy Grail had regained the chapel, the knight of the litter stood up strong and hale and kissed the cross. At this moment a squire came up, carrying a magnificent suit of armour. He went up to the knight and asked him how it went with him.

*Cf. Hebrews 9, 2.

'Upon my faith, well, thanks be to God,' said he. 'I was healed but now through the visitation of the Holy Grail. But I marvel at that knight lying there asleep, who roused not once at its coming.'

'Of a truth,' said the squire, 'it is some knight who committed a grave sin, of which he was never shriven, and maybe so offended Our Lord thereby, that He would not have him witness this high adventure.'

'Whoever he be,' replied the knight, 'he is assuredly unfortunate, and I feel sure he is one of the companions of the Round Table who embarked on the Quest of the Holy Grail.'

'Sir,' said the squire, 'I have brought you your armour; you may take it when you please.'

The knight replied that he asked nothing better. And with that he armed himself, donning the mail leggings and the hauberk. And the squire fetched Lancelot's sword and handed it to him and also his helm. Then he caught Lancelot's horse and put on its saddle and bridle. When he had harnessed the animal he said to the knight:

'Mount, my lord, since you have not wanted for a good horse nor a good sword this night. I have certainly given you nothing that you will not put to better use than the worthless knight who lies there sleeping.'

The moon had risen and was shining bright in the sky, for it was past midnight. And the knight asked the squire how he had judged the worth of the sword.

'By its beauty,' he said. He had drawn it from the scabbard earlier and had seen it so fair that he had coveted it for himself. When the knight was accoutred and mounted on Lancelot's horse, he stretched out his hand towards the chapel and swore that, God and the saints aiding, he would never cease roving until he discovered how it came about that the Holy Grail was seen in many parts of the kingdom of Logres, and who first brought it to England and for what purpose, unless some other chanced to learn the truth before him.

'So help me God,' said the squire, 'you have said enough. God grant that in this Quest you save your honour and your soul, for the body will be exposed to mortal peril before you have gone far.'

'If I die,' said the knight, 'it will be accounted an honour and no shame. For no knight worthy of his calling may shrink from this Quest, whether the outcome be death or life.'

Thereupon, accompanied by the squire, he left the cross, bearing away Lancelot's arms and riding where adventure led.

He had travelled some half league or more when Lancelot sat up like a man first waking out of a deep sleep. He pondered awhile whether what he had seen were real or the fruit of fancy, not knowing if he had beheld the Holy Grail or had but dreamed it. Then he rose to his feet and saw the chandelier before the altar, but that which he most desired to look on was nowhere to be seen, namely the Holy Grail, whose true nature he longed to ascertain, if it were possible.

When he had waited and watched before the screen, hopeful of glimpsing something of his soul's desire, he heard a voice say to him:

'Lancelot, harder than stone, more bitter than wood, more barren and bare than the fig tree, how durst thou presume to venture there where the Holy Grail abides? Get thee hence, for the stench of thy presence fouls this place.'

These words so wrung his heart that he knew not what to do. He hastened out, his eyes blinded with tears, groaning and cursing the day that he was born,* for he knew he had come to that point where honour was forever forfeit, since he had failed to pierce the secret of the Holy Grail. But the words he had heard were graven in his memory and would not be forgotten as long as he lived, and he would have no ease till he knew why he had been thus styled. When he came to the cross he found neither helm, nor sword, nor horse: and then he knew that he had dreamed no dream. Thereupon he gave rein to the full tide of his grief, denouncing himself for a poor worthless wretch, and crying:

'Ah! God, my sin and the wickedness of my life now stand revealed. Now I see that above all else my weakness has been my undoing. For when I should have mended my ways, then did the enemy destroy me, blinding me so effectually that I could not discern the things of God. Nor should I marvel that

*Cf. Job 3, 1 ss.

I am purblind, for there has not passed an hour since I was first a knight but the murk of mortal sin has lapped me close, for more than any other I have given myself to lust and to the depravity of this world.'

Thus did Lancelot pass the night in lamentation and in bitter self-reproach. And when the day dawned fair and bright, and the birds broke into song throughout the forest, and the sun's rays filtered through the trees, and when he saw the beauty of the day and heard the birdsong that had often gladdened his heart, and saw himself stripped of arms and horse and all he had, and knew the sharpness of Our Lord's displeasure, then he thought the time would never come when anything on earth would yield him joy again. For there where he had thought to find all joy and honour and wordly acclaim, in the adventures of the Holy Grail, he had reaped only failure and its bitter gall.

After many hours spent in repining and heartburning and bewailing his misery, he left the cross and set out through the forest on foot, without helm or sword or shield. He did not go near the chapel where the heavenly voice had thrice rebuked him, but took another path which brought him at the hour of prime to a knoll crowned by a hermitage. The hermit was about to begin his mass and stood ready clad in the armour of Holy Church when Lancelot entered, the saddest and most dejected of men. He knelt down in the chancel and beat his breast, entreating Our Lord's forgiveness for the evil deeds he had wrought in the course of his life, and there he heard mass sung by the holy man and his clerk. When it was done and the hermit had put off the armour of Our Lord, Lancelot hailed him and drawing him to one side begged him for counsel in the name of God. The good man asked him where he came from, and he answered that he was of the household of King Arthur and a companion of the Round Table.

'What manner of counsel do you seek?' he asked. 'Is it confession that you want?'

'Yes, Sir,' he replied.

'Come, then, in the name of Our Lord.'

So saying, he led him towards the altar and the two sat down together. First he asked his name, and he replied that he was called Lancelot of the Lake and was the son of King Ban of

Benoic. When the hermit heard that he was Lancelot of the Lake, of all men the most lauded and admired, he was astonished to see him in such straits, and said to him:

'Sir, you owe God a great return for creating you so fair and valiant that the world cannot boast your peer. He has lent you understanding and memory, and you must so use them for good, that His love being kept perfect in you, the devil may derive no profit from the great gifts God has given you. Serve Him with your whole strength and keep His commandments, and do not use His gifts to serve His mortal enemy, the devil. For were you to squander His bounty which you have received in fuller measure than other men, you would be greatly to blame.

'Take care not to resemble the wicked servant of whom one of the evangelists speaks in the Gospel,* telling how a rich man gave a great part of his fortune in trust to three of his servants. For to one he gave one talent, to another two, and to the third five. He that had received the five talents multiplied them in such a way that when he came before his master to render account of what he had gained, he said: "Lord, thou gavest me five talents: behold them here, together with five other talents that I have earned beside." Hearing this the lord replied: "Come here, thou good and faithful servant, and be numbered among the members of my household." Then he that had received two talents came forward, too, and said to his lord that he had earned two more beside. The lord gave him the same answer that he had made to the first servant. But it happened that he that had received but one talent had buried his in the earth and had hidden himself from the face of his lord, and dared not come forward. This was the bad servant, the wicked simoniac, the dissembler in whose heart the fire of the Holy Ghost never burned,[17] and whose like are therefore unable to kindle or warm at the flame of Our Lord's love all those to whom they preach the holy word. For as Holy Scripture says: "He who is not aflame cannot burn", which is to say: If the fire of the Holy Ghost burn not in him who spreads the word of the Gospel, it will never ignite nor burn bright in the hearer.[18]

'I have told you this parable on account of the greatness of

*Cf. Matthew 25, 14–30.

Our Lord's gift to you. For I can see that He has created you
fairer of form than another, and endowed you more richly, if
I may judge from outward appearance. And should you turn
this gift against the giver, know that He will cast you down in
a short time if you do not speedily seek His mercy, confessing
your sins with true contrition, to the amendment of your life.
And yet I tell you truly that if you ask forgiveness in this
manner, He is so gracious to sinners, holding their repentance
dearer by far than their downfall, that He will raise you up
stronger and more vigorous than ever you were before.'

'Sir,' said Lancelot, 'this example that you have set before
me, of the three servants that had each received talents, dis-
heartens me more than anything you could say. For I am well
aware that Jesus Christ endowed me from infancy with all the
graces that a man could have, and since He lent so liberally
and I have made such sparing return, I know that I shall be
judged like the wicked servant who hid his talent in the ground.
All my life long I have served His enemy and have waged war
on Him with the arms of sin. And I have gone to my death down
that wide road which at the outset seems so smooth and honeyed
and is the portal and the path of sin. The devil showed me the
sweets and the honey, but he hid from my eyes the everlasting woe that lies in store for him who treads that road to its
end.'

At Lancelot's words the hermit fell to weeping and said to
him:

'Sir, I know full well that none may continue in the path you
speak of without dying an eternal death. But just as you may see
a man wander at times from his path when he falls asleep, and
retrace his steps at once on waking, so also is it with the sinner
who falls asleep in mortal sin and veers from the right way; he
too returns to his path, which is his Maker, and directs his steps
towards the Most High Lord who ever cries: "I am the way,
and the truth, and the life." '*

Then looking about him, the good man saw a cross on which
Our Lord was painted in effigy, and pointed it out to Lancelot,
saying:

*Cf. John 14, 6.

'Sir, do you see that cross?'

'Yes,' he answered.

'Then be assured,' said the other, 'that the arms of that figure are thus stretched wide to welcome all who come. In just the same way has Our Lord extended His arms to embrace every sinner that turns to Him, both you and others, calling evermore: "Come unto Me!" And since in His loving kindness He is always ready to receive each man and woman that comes back to Him, never doubt He will admit you if you offer yourself to Him in the manner I have described, which is that of oral confession, of true repentance and amendment. So bare your soul to Him now while I listen, and I will help and succour you to the utmost of my power, and will counsel you as best I can.'

Lancelot hesitated, for he had never avowed the matter concerning himself and the queen, nor would he while he lived, unless the moral pressure proved too great. His torment wrung a deep sigh from his breast, but not one word could he force from his lips. Yet he would gladly have spoken, but dared not, for fear was stronger in him than courage. And still the hermit urged him to confess his sin and renounce it utterly, for if he refused, confusion would overtake him; he promised him eternal life if he made a clean breast, and hell as the price of concealment. In short he plied him with so many wise words and meet examples that Lancelot's tongue was loosed at the last and he said:

'Sir, it is this way. I have sinned unto death with my lady, she whom I have loved all my life, Queen Guinevere, the wife of King Arthur. It is she who gave me abundance of gold and silver and such rich gifts as I have distributed from time to time among poor knights. It is she who exalted me and set me in the luxury I now enjoy. For her love alone I accomplished the exploits with which the whole world rings. She it is who raised me from poverty to riches and from hardship to the sum of earthly bliss. But I know full well that this bond is the sin that has earned me Our Lord's dire wrath which He showed me undisguised last night.'

Then Lancelot told him how he had seen the Holy Grail and how neither reverence for the vessel nor love for Our Lord had stirred him from his torpor.

And when he had laid open his life and soul to the gaze of the holy man, he besought him in God's name to counsel him.

'In truth, Sir,' said the other, 'there is no counsel will avail you in your plight, unless you first vow in the sight of God never to fall into this sin again. Yet, if you would wholly forsake it, seeking His pardon with tears of true repentance, I believe that Our Lord would number you again among his servants and open to you the gates of heaven, where eternal life awaits all those who enter. But to give you advice would profit you nothing in your present state, for it would be like the man who builds a tall, strong tower on shifting ground; and it happens that when the work is well advanced, the whole edifice comes crashing down.* Even so would our striving come to nothing, if you failed to receive our words in a spirit of sincerity and put them to good account. It would be like the seed that is cast upon the rocks, which the birds carry off and scatter, so that it bears no fruit.'†

'Sir,' replied Lancelot, 'there is nothing you can say that I will not do, if God gives me life.'

'Then I demand of you,' said the good man, 'that you promise me never again to trespass against your Maker by committing mortal sin with the queen, nor with another woman, nor in any other way that might offend Him.'

Lancelot plighted his troth as a true knight.

'Now tell me once more,' said the hermit, 'what befell you when you saw the Holy Grail.'

And Lancelot told him, repeating the three solemn words that the voice had spoken to him in the chapel, where he was compared to stone and wood and fig tree.

'For the love of God,' he added, 'tell me the meaning of these three words. For I never heard any thing said, which I so thirsted to understand. Wherefore, I pray you, set my mind at rest, for I am certain that you know the truth.'

The hermit pondered a long while in silence, and when he spoke again it was to say:

'Truly, Lancelot, I am in no way amazed that these three words were spoken to you. For you have ever been the most

*Cf. Luke 6, 49.
†Cf. Matthew 13, 4–6.

wondrous of men, therefore it is no marvel if more wondrous things are said to you than to another. And since you would know the truth I will gladly tell it you: so heed my words.

'You say that a voice said to you: "Lancelot, harder than stone, more bitter than wood, more barren and bare than the fig tree, get thee hence." Now it is indeed significant that you were termed harder than stone. All stones are of their nature hard, and some more so than others. And by the temper of the stone one should understand the sinner whose heart is so numbed and hardened by sin that it cannot be softened either by fire or by water. Not by fire, for the fire of the Holy Ghost cannot enter or find lodging there for the filth of the vessel, where day on day aberrant sins have gathered and accumulated. Nor by water, for the word of the Holy Ghost, which is the sweet water and the gentle rain,* cannot penetrate such a heart. For Our Lord will never lodge under one roof with His enemy, but would have His abode swept and cleansed of all impurity and vice. Thus the sinner is likened to the stone on the grounds of the hardness which Our Lord finds in him. But now must we rightly examine how it comes that you are harder yet than the stone, which is to say more culpable than any other sinner.'

When he had said this he fell to thinking, and presently spoke again:

'I will tell you in what way you are more culpable than any other sinner. You heard the parable of the three servants to whom the rich man delivered his talents to multiply and increase. The two that had received the most were good and faithful servants, wise furthermore and prudent. But the other, he that received the least amount, showed himself faithless and improvident. Consider now whether you could be among those of His servants to whom Our Lord entrusted the multiplication of the five talents. As I see it He gave you far more. For I believe that were a man to search the ranks of chivalry, he would not find a single knight to whom Our Lord had imparted such graces as He lent to you. He gave you beauty in full measure; He gave you understanding, and wit enough to distinguish good from evil; courage He gave you and skill in battle; and over and above He gave you such good fortune that success has crowned

* Cf. Deuteronomy, 32, 2.

your every undertaking. All these things did Our Lord vest in you that you might be His knight and servant. Not that His gifts might lapse in you did He furnish you thus, but to their increasing and betterment. And you were so careless of your trust that you basely forsook Him to serve His enemy, waging incessant war on your Creator. You were no better than the mercenary who, his wages taken, deserts his lord and goes to aid his foe. You behaved thus towards Our Lord, for as soon as He had paid you lavishly and in full, you left Him to serve the one who harries Him night and day. No man, to my knowledge, has ever acted thus after taking such generous payment as yours; and by this token you can see that you are indeed harder than stone and the most sinful of sinners. Now the stone, for such as can understand, bears yet another meaning. For was not a certain sweetness seen to well from stone, in the desert beyond the Red Sea, where the children of Israel dwelled so long? There, when the people thirsted and murmured among themselves, Moses was plainly seen to go up to a hard and ancient rock, and say, as though he did not hold it possible: "Can we fetch water even from this rock?" And at once water gushed out of the rock in such quantity that all the people drank of it, and so their chiding was stilled and their thirst quenched.[19] Hence one can say that sweetness sometime came from stone; but since none has ever flowed from you it is obvious that you are harder yet than stone.'

'Sir,' said Lancelot, 'tell me now why I was called more bitter than wood.'

'I will tell you,' said the holy man, 'if you but listen. I have shown you that your hardness is inordinate, and where there is such hardness, sweetness can find no room, nor should we think that anything remains save bitterness; thus you are bitter where you should be sweet and in equal measure. You resemble in that the dead and rotten wood whose sweetness has given place to gall. Now have I shown you how it is that you are harder than stone and more bitter than wood.

'It remains to show thirdly how you come to be more barren and bare than the fig tree. This is that very fig tree which the Gospel mentions there where it speaks about Palm Sunday: the day that Our Lord entered the city of Jerusalem riding upon an ass; the day on which the children of the Hebrews hailed His coming with those sweet chants that Holy Church rehearses every year; the day that is called the day of Palms. On that day the Lord of Majesty, the Most High Master, the Glorious Prophet, taught in the city of Jerusalem, among those whose hardness of heart was absolute. When He had striven with them all day, He left the place of His discourse, and finding in all the city none that would give Him lodging, He went out of Jerusalem, and passed on His road a fig tree which, for all it was well grown and amply furnished with leaves and branches, carried no fruit. Our Lord went up to the tree, and when He saw it was bare of fruit He spoke as it might be in anger and cursed the barren tree. Such was the lot of the fig tree that stood outside Jerusalem.* Now consider whether you could be like that tree, save only more barren and bare. The Lord Most High found leaves on the tree when He approached, that He might have taken had He wished. But when the Holy Grail came there where you were lying, it found you barren even to the want of every right thought and all good intent; foul and besmirched and polluted with lust did it find you, and denuded of leaves and flowers, which is to say of all good works; it was on this account that you were upbraided later in the terms you told me: "Lancelot, harder than stone, more bitter than wood, more barren and bare than the fig tree, get thee hence!" '

'In truth, Sir,' said Lancelot, 'you have said enough to prove to me that I was properly called stone and wood and fig tree: for in all respects I am as you portrayed me. But since you told me that I have not gone so far but I may yet turn back, if by vigilance I keep from mortal sin, I swear to God and secondly to you that I will never return to the life I led so long, but will observe chastity and keep my body as pure as I am able. But while I am fit and hale as I am now I could not forswear chivalry and the life of arms.'

The hermit was overjoyed to hear such sentiments, and said to Lancelot:

'Assuredly, if you would abjure your sinful commerce with the queen, I warrant you that Our Lord would love you yet

* Cf. Matthew 21, 19.

and send you succour. He would look on you with compassion
and empower you to accomplish many things from which your
sin debars you.'

'Sir,' said Lancelot, 'I renounce it, and that so wholly that I
will nevermore sin with her or another.'

When he heard this promise the good man imposed on
Lancelot such penance as he felt he could perform, and gave
him absolution and blessing, requesting him further to bide with
him that day. Lancelot answered that he had no choice, since
he had neither horse to ride, nor shield, nor lance, nor sword.

'I can be of service to you there, and that before nightfall
tomorrow. Not far from here lives a knight, my brother, who
will send me a horse and arms and all things needful as soon as
I send him word.'

Lancelot answered that such being the case he would be
happy to stay, and the hermit rejoiced exceedingly.

So the hermit kept Lancelot by him, urging him always to
live aright, and admonishing him with words of wisdom till
Lancelot bitterly rued his former conduct. For it was plain to
him that if he died in that sin he would lose his soul; while he
ran a great chance of bodily hurt if the offence could be proved
against him. So he came to deplore his sinful love for the queen,
in which he had squandered his years, and with self-reproach
and execration he vowed in his heart never to revert to it again.
But here the tale leaves him and returns to Perceval.

[6]

The Peregrinations of Perceval

NOW the story relates that when Perceval had parted from
Lancelot he went back to the recluse, hopeful of gleaning some
news of the knight who had eluded them. But it so happened
that on retracing his steps he could find no path to take him
there direct. However, he steered the best course he could towards the point where he judged the house to lie. When he
arrived at the chapel he tapped on the little casement of her
cell, and she opened it with the promptitude of one who keeps

vigil, and, putting out her head as far as she could, she asked him who he was. He replied that he was of King Arthur's house and was called Perceval of Wales. At the sound of this name she was filled with joy, for she loved the bearer dearly, as indeed she should, since he was her nephew. She called up her people and ordered them to open the door to the knight who stood without, and to give him to eat if he were hungry and show him every attention, for she loved him more than any man in the world. They did as she told them and unbarred the door, and, having bidden the knight welcome, they unarmed him and served him with food. He asked if he might speak with the recluse that same evening.

'Oh no, Sir,' they answered, 'but in the morning after mass we think that you will surely be able to see her.'

So he contented himself with that and lay down on the bed which the servants made up for him, and there he slept the night through like a man tired and spent.

Next morning when it was light Perceval rose and heard mass, which was sung by the priest of that place. Then, when he had armed, he presented himself before the recluse, saying:

'Madam, for the love of God give me some tidings of the knight who passed here yesterday, and with whom, as you told him, you are well acquainted: for I cannot wait to find out who he is.'

When the lady heard of Perceval's impatience she asked him why he sought the knight.

'Because I shall know no ease until I find him and join battle with him. For he has done me such violence that it would be to my shame to let the matter rest.'

'Ah! Perceval,' she exclaimed, 'what are you saying? Would you measure yourself with him? Are you anxious to die like your brothers, who perished victims of their own arrogance? Assuredly, if you meet a similar death it will be a great misfortune and a stain upon your lineage. Are you even aware of what you would lose by joining battle with this knight? Let me tell you then. It is true that the great Quest of the Holy Grail is begun, among whose companions you, I believe, are numbered, and it will shortly be brought to its close, so it please God. And at its term a far higher honour than you thought to find awaits you, if you will but refrain from breaking lances with that knight. For here, as in many other parts, it is well known that when the goal is reached, there will be three knights beyond compare to whom above all others the glory and the guerdon of this Quest shall fall: and two shall be virgins and the other chaste. And of the two that are virgins one will be the knight whom you seek and the other yourself, while the third will be Bors of Gaunes. These are the three that shall complete the Quest. And since God has prepared this honour for you, it would be a dire misfortune if meantime you sought to bring about your death. And to engage in battle with him whom you seek would be to hasten it most surely, for without a doubt he is a much better knight than you, or any man now known.'[20]

'Madam,' said Perceval, 'from what you say of my brothers I hold it you know who I am.'

'I know very well,' said she, 'and have good reason to do so, for I am your aunt and you my nephew. Mistrust me not because you see me in so mean a dwelling, but know in truth that I am she who once was called the Queen of the Waste Land. Then you might have seen me in circumstances far removed from these, for I was one of the richest ladies in the world. And yet those riches never pleased nor became me as well as does my present poverty.'

Perceval's heart was so moved at these words that he fell to weeping, and as he cast his mind back he knew her for his aunt. Then he sat down before her and asked her for news of his mother and kindred.

'What, good nephew,' she asked, 'have you no tidings of your mother?'

'No, Madam, none. Indeed I know not whether she be alive or dead. But she has often appeared to me in my sleep, saying she had greater cause to chide me than commend me, for I had used her ill.'

As she listened the lady grew pensive and answered him sadly:

'You have lost all chance of seeing your mother again, except it be in dream, for she died as soon as you left for King Arthur's court.'

'Madam, how did this come about?'

'In truth, your mother was so broken-hearted at your going that she died that very day, as soon as she had sought confession.'

'May God have mercy on her soul,' said he, 'it grieves me deeply; but since this thing has come to pass I must bear with it, for that is our common end. It is true that I never had word of her since. But that knight whom I seek, in God's name, do you know who he is or where he comes from, and whether he be the same who came to court armed all in red?'

'Yes,' said she, 'upon my oath, he came by virtue of his right; and I will tell you whence he holds it.

'You are well aware that since the advent of Jesus Christ the world has seen three great fellowships. The first was the table of Jesus Christ, where the apostles broke bread on many occasions. That was the table where the bread of heaven sustained both souls and bodies, while they that sat around it were one in heart and soul, as King David prophesied when he wrote in his book the wonderful words: "Behold, how good and how pleasant it is for brethren to dwell together in unity."* Peace and long-suffering and concord reigned among the brethren seated at that table, and all good works could be seen in them; and that table was established by the Lamb without spot who was sacrificed for our redemption.

'Thereafter there was instituted another table in memory and in likeness of the first. This was the table of the Holy Grail which, in the days of Joseph of Arimathea when the Christian faith was first brought to this land, saw the enacting of miracles so great that godly men and unbelievers both should ever hold them in remembrance. It happened at the time when Joseph of Arimathea landed here with a host of followers, at least four thousand strong, and poor men all. When they came to this country they were worried by fears of a shortage of food, for their numbers were great. One day as they traversed a forest and found it as bare of provender as of inhabitants, they grew dismayed, being unaccustomed to privation. They fasted all that day, and on the next they foraged by hill and by dale till they met an old woman bringing twelve loaves home from the oven, and bought them of her. But when they went to portion them

*Cf. Psalm 133, 1.

out, anger and resentment flared up, for some refused to agree to what the rest proposed. This circumstance was reported to Joseph and made him exceedingly angry. He ordered the loaves to be brought before him, and the men who had purchased them came to him too, and themselves related to him the facts of their dispute. So he ordered all the people to be seated, as it might be at the Last Supper. And he broke the bread and placed pieces here and there, and at the head of the table he put the Holy Grail; and as he set it in place the twelve loaves were multiplied in such miraculous profusion that those present, who numbered four thousand and more, had every man his fill. And all who were witness to the event gave praise and thanks to Our Lord for this manifest sign of His succour.[21]

'At that table there stood a seat where Josephus, the son of Joseph of Arimathea, should sit. Now this seat was set apart for the use of their master and shepherd, and none but he might sit there, for it had been blessed by the hand of Our Lord Himself, as the story relates, and consecrated to the ministry that Josephus was to exercise over the Christian people; and Our Lord having set him in that seat, there was none so bold as dared usurp his place. The seat itself had been fashioned after the one in which Our Lord had sat at the Last Supper, when He had presided as master and shepherd among His apostles. And even as He was the master and lord of the apostles, so was Josephus to lead the company who sat at the table of the Holy Grail: he was in turn to be their master and their lord. But it happened, after their landing here and wandering for some time in alien lands, that two brothers of Josephus' lineage were eaten up with envy that Our Lord had exalted their kinsman over them and had chosen him for chief among them all. They discussed it privily and vowed they would not stomach his authority: they were as nobly born as he, and so would no longer account themselves his disciples, nor call him master. So next day when the people, having climbed a high knoll and set up the tables on its summit, would have placed Josephus in the highest seat, the two brothers disputed his right and one of them sat there himself in view of the whole assembly. At once, by a miracle, the earth swallowed up the usurper.* Word of

* Cf. Numbers 16, 3, 13 and 31-3.

this happening spread like wildfire through the land; the seat was known thereafter as the Seat of Dread, and nobody was bold enough to sit there since, save only the appointed of Our Lord.

'This table was succeeded by the Round Table, devised by Merlin to embody a very subtle meaning. For in its name it mirrors the roundness of the earth, the concentric spheres of the planets and of the elements in the firmament; and in these heavenly spheres we see the stars and many things besides; whence it follows that the Round Table is a true epitome of the universe.[22] For from every land, be it Christian or heathen, where chivalry resides, knights are seen flocking to the Round Table. And when by God's grace they are made companions, they count themselves richer than if they had gained the whole world, and to this end forsake father, mother, wife and children too.[23] You have seen this happen in your own particular case. From the day you left your mother and were made a companion of the Round Table, you had no wish to go back, but fell at once captive to the sweet intimacy and brotherly love that binds its members.

'When Merlin had established the Round Table, he announced that the secrets of the Holy Grail, which in his time was covert and withdrawn, would be revealed by knights of that same fellowship. He was asked by what sign the foremost might be known, and he replied:

' "There will be three shall triumph in this undertaking: two will be virgins, and the other chaste. And one of the three shall surpass his father as the lion surpasses the leopard in strength and hardihood. He shall be held as master and shepherd over all his fellows; and the companions of the Round Table will consume their days in bootless pursuit of the Holy Grail until such time as Our Lord shall send him among them so suddenly as to confound them all."

'When they had heard this prediction, they said:

' "Well, Merlin, since he shall be so peerless as you say, you should contrive a special seat where none but he shall sit, and so much bigger than the rest that no one could mistake it."

' "That will I do," said Merlin.

'So he made a seat that passed in size and splendour every

other. And when it was finished he fell to kissing it, for love, he said, of the Good Knight who was to rest his limbs there. Then they asked him again:

' "Merlin, what virtue will be vested in this seat?"

' "It will give rise to many a marvel," he answered, "for none shall ever sit here, but shall suffer death or injury, until the True Knight take his rightful place."

' "In God's name," they exclaimed, "then he who sat there would be in danger of his life?"

' "He would indeed," said Merlin, "and on account of the dangers that shall follow on it, it shall be known as the Seat of Danger."

'Good nephew,' continued the lady, 'I have explained to you how the Round Table came to be established, and the Seat of Danger too, where many a knight has perished who was unfit to sit there. Now I will tell you why.it it was that the knight arrived at court in red accoutrements. You are not ignorant that Jesus Christ presided as shepherd and master among His apostles at the table of the Last Supper. Later the Table of the Holy Grail acquired this meaning through Josephus, and the Round Table through this knight. Our Lord, before His Passion, promised the apostles that He would come to them and visit them, and as they awaited the fulfilment of that promise in anxiety and sorrow, it came to pass that on the day of Pentecost, when they were met together in a house with fast-closed doors, the Holy Ghost came down upon them as a flame of fire, comforting them and banishing their misgivings. Then He dispersed them, and sent them abroad through every land to convert the people and preach the Holy Gospel. So it was that on the day of Pentecost Our Lord visited and comforted His apostles. And it seems to me that in like guise there came to comfort you the Knight whom you should hold as master and shepherd. For just as Our Lord appeared in the likeness of fire, so did the Knight come armed in red, which is the colour of fire. And just as the doors of the house where the apostles sat were closed at Our Lord's coming, just so did the palace gates stand shut before the Knight appeared among you. He came in consequence so suddenly as to confound the wisest. And that same day was vowed the Quest of the Holy Grail, which will never cease until the truth is known concerning the Grail, and the Lance, and the hazards that have beset this land so long. Now I have told you the truth about the Knight in order that you may never match yourself against him; indeed, you must at all costs refrain from such a course forasmuch as you are brothers one of another in the fellowship of the Round Table, and again because you could never withstand him, for he is a far better knight than you.'

'Madam,' said Perceval, 'after all that you have said I shall never itch to fight with him again. Yet teach me, in God's name, what I must do, and how and where I can find him. For if I had him as companion, I would never leave his side again, while I could keep abreast.'

'I will help you in this as best I can,' she said. 'I could not tell you where he is at present, but I will give you certain pointers which will lead you to him shortly; then, once you have found him, stay with him as long as you can. From here you must go to the Castle of Gort, where he probably slept this night, for he has a very dear cousin who lives there. If she can tell you where he is bent, follow as fast as you can; if she cannot help you, go straight to the Castle of Corbenic where the Maimed King lies, and if by chance you do not find him there, you will at least have some positive report.'

Perceval and the recluse talked of the Knight all morning, and when noon came she said to him:

'Sweet nephew, you shall stay with me this night; I shall be the happier for it. It is so long since I set eyes on you that my heart will ache at your departure.'

'Madam,' he said, 'so much awaits my doing that I can hardly linger here today. I beg you in God's name to let me go.'

'If you ride this day it will be without my leave. Tomorrow, though, as soon as mass is said, I will grant you leave most gladly.'

So Perceval agreed to bide with her and had himself unarmed at once; and when her people had set up the table, they ate of the meal that she had had prepared.

Perceval lodged that night with his aunt. They had spent many hours conversing together of the Knight and of other matters when she said to him:

'Sweet nephew, it so happens that you have kept so close a watch upon yourself till now that your virginity was never once abused nor smirched, nor have you ever known in verity the nature of the flesh or carnal union. And this was most essential for your good; for had your body been violated by the corruption of sin, you would have forfeited your primacy among the companions of the Quest, even as Lancelot of the Lake, who through the lusts and fevers of the flesh let slip long since the prospect of attaining what all the rest now strive after. Therefore I implore you to keep your body as undefiled as the day Our Lord made you a knight, so that you may come pure and unsullied before the Holy Grail, and without stain of lechery. Where is the knight can boast so fair an exploit? There is not a man of all your fellowship that has not sinned in this respect, save only you and Galahad, the Good Knight I have told you of.'

To this he answered that with God's help he would ever keep himself as it behoved him.

During the remainder of that day Perceval's aunt applied herself to his instruction, exhorting him to virtue and begging him above all else to observe the chastity required of him, to which he pledged his faith. And when they had talked at length of the Knight and of King Arthur's court, Perceval asked what cause had prompted her to leave her lands and settle in so wild a haunt.

'As God is my witness,' she said, 'it was mortal fear that spurred me to take refuge here. At the time when you went to court my lord the king, as you know, was at war with King Libran, so that on my husband's death it followed that I, being but a fearful woman, was afraid his foe might kill me if I fell into his hands. So hastily snatching up a large part of my fortune, I fled to this lonely place to escape discovery. Here I had this hermitage built and the house as it stands today, and established myself with my chaplain and household in this retreat, never to leave it more, so it please Our Lord, but serving Him while I live and dying in that service.'

'Upon my faith,' said Perceval, 'this is a remarkable story. But do tell me now what happened to your son, Dyabial, I am most curious to know how is he doing.'

'He went to serve your kinsman King Pellés in order to win his arms; and I have heard since that he made him a knight. But more than two years have passed since I saw him, for he travels the length and breadth of Britain in the wake of the tournaments. If you go to Corbenic I expect you will find him there.'

'Truly,' said he, 'I would go there for his sake alone, if I went for nothing else, for it is my very real wish to keep him company.'

'And I,' she said, 'wish too that you had met, for it would make me very happy to know you were together.'

So Perceval stayed that day with his aunt and left the hermitage promptly in the morning, his mass heard and himself harnessed. The long day through he traversed the vast sweep of the forest without encountering a living soul. Soon after vespers he heard to the right of him the tolling of a bell and headed towards it, certain of coming on a hermitage or some religious house. He had gone but a short distance when he saw an abbey encircled by high walls and moats as deep, and riding up he shouted and hailed till the inmates opened the gate. The sight of his arms told them at once that this was a wandering knight, and helping him divest himself they gave him a cordial welcome. They took his horse and led it to the stables where they foddered it well with oats and hay, and one of the monks conducted him to a room where he might rest. Perceval enjoyed that night the best lodging the monks could offer, and never awoke, as it turned out, until the hour of prime, when he rose at once to hear mass in the abbey church.

As he entered he saw on his right an iron grille and beyond it a monk, ready vested in the armour of Our Lord, who was about to intone mass. Intent on following the service, Perceval made his way across to the screen, fully expecting to enter, but realized when he found no gate that it was not to be. He resigned himself accordingly and knelt down without; and looking past the priest he saw a bed richly spread, as it might be with silken sheets and such like stuff: for nothing that decked it was other than white. As he gazed intently at the bed he made out a recumbent form, whether man or woman he knew not, for the face was covered with a fine white cloth which masked the features. When Perceval saw that he was musing to no purpose, he ceased his staring and attended to the office which the priest had already begun. At that point where the celebrant went to elevate the Body of Our Lord, he that lay in the bed sat up and uncovered his face. And Perceval saw a white-haired ancient, very full of years; his shoulders and trunk were bare to the navel and he wore a gold crown on his head. As Perceval gazed, he saw that his body was striped with gashes and wounds, and also his face and arms and the palms of his hands. When the priest held the Body of Christ aloft for all to see, he stretched out his hands towards the host and cried:

'Most gracious and loving Father, be not unmindful of my dues!'

Nor would he lie down afterwards, but passed his time in prayers and orisons with his hands extended towards his Maker and his head still orbed with the golden crown. Perceval closely observed the man who sat in the bed, for he seemed in acute discomfort from his wounds, and he judged him, so stricken in years did he appear, to have passed three hundred winters. So he stared at him constantly, marvelling at all he saw. When mass was over he watched the priest take the Lord's Body in his hands and carry it to him who lay in the bed, that he might partake of it. And as soon as he had received the host, he took the crown from his head and had it placed on the altar; then he lay back on his couch, to be covered up as before so that none of his person was visible. Meanwhile the priest, having sung mass, unrobed without more delay.

When Perceval had witnessed these things he left the church, and returning to the chamber where he had slept, he called one of the brethren and said to him:

'Sir, in God's name, give me an answer to my question: for I am sure that you must know the truth.'

'Sir Knight, first ask it of me, and if I know the answer I will be pleased to tell you, if so be I may.'

'Very well,' he said, 'I will tell you what perplexes me. I was in the church just now attending mass; and there I saw beyond an iron grille an old, old man who lay in a bed before the altar, wearing a gold crown on his head. And when he sat up I saw that his body was covered in wounds. When mass was sung, the priest gave him to partake of the Lord's Body, and as soon as he had received it he lay back and put off his crown. Good Sir, such things cannot be void of meaning, and since I crave, if possible, to understand, I beg you to explain what I have seen.'

'Gladly,' replied the worthy man, and began his tale:

'It is true, and you have heard it said by many, that Joseph of Arimathea, that noble man and veritable knight, was first sent by the Master to this land in order, with his Maker's help, to implant and establish here our holy Christian faith. After he landed he had to endure much persecution and obstruction at the hands of the enemies of the Law, for in those days they were all infidels in this country. The land hereabouts was ruled by a king named Crudel who was the most savage and cruel of lords, as proud as he was pitiless. When he heard that the Christians had landed in his realm, bringing with them a precious vessel, so miraculous in its effects that the greater number lived by its grace alone, he held this report for a fable. His informers insisted again and again and swore it was the truth, to which he retorted that he would soon find out. So he seized Josephus, Joseph's son, together with two of his nephews, and some hundred of those whom he had chosen as leaders and shepherds of the Christian people. Now when they were taken and thrown into prison, they had the Holy Vessel with them, whose presence left them carefree for their bodies' food. The king held them forty days in his gaol without sending them food or water, and on the strict injunction that none should make so bold as to give them assistance within the term prescribed.

'The news that King Crudel held Josephus in prison with many of his followers spread quickly through all the countries where he had been, till it came to the ears of King Mordrain in his city of Sarras, which lies towards Jerusalem: the same Mordrain who had been converted by Josephus' wisdom and preaching. He was deeply grieved, for it was thanks to Josephus that he had won back his land that Tholomer would have snatched, and with success, had it not been for Josephus' counsel and the help of his brother-in-law, named Seraph.[*] When King Mordrain heard that Josephus lay in prison, he swore that he would do all in his power to deliver him. He

---

[*] Later Nascien, see note 11.

summoned as many troops as he could raise at short notice and put to sea with a full complement of arms and horses, and by dint of much sailing came at last to these shores. When he had disembarked with all his men, he sent word to Crudel that he would seize his country and dispossess him unless he released Josephus. But Crudel, who had no great opinion of him, chose to ride against him under arms. The parties clashed in battle, and the outcome, by the will of Our Lord, was a victory for the Christians, King Crudel being slain on the field with all his men. As for King Mordrain, who bore the name Evalach before he was baptized, he acquitted himself so stoutly in the combat that all his people marvelled. And when they had unarmed him they found that his body bore more wounds than would have killed another man. They asked him then how he was, and he said that he felt no pain from any of his injuries. He had Josephus freed from prison and met him with all the joy such love as his could prompt. When Josephus asked him what had brought him to those parts, King Mordrain answered that his friend's deliverance had been the only object of his journey.

'On the following day the Christians gathered before the table of the Holy Grail to offer up their prayers. When Josephus, their master, had robed in preparation and was about the service of the Holy Grail, King Mordrain, who had always longed, if it were possible, to contemplate the mystery openly, drew nearer than he should; and a voice was heard in their midst, saying: "King, go no closer, it is forbidden thee!" He had already advanced so far that the tongue of man could not relate nor human heart conceive what he now saw, and his yearning was so strong that he kept inching farther forward. Then suddenly a cloud came down before him which robbed him of his sight and strength, so that he stood there blinded and scarcely able to move. When he saw that Our Lord had exacted such terrible vengeance for his disobedience, he said in the hearing of all those gathered there: "Gracious Lord Jesus Christ, who hast shown me here the folly of breaking Thy commandment, even as I truly welcome this affliction Thou hast sent me and endure it joyfully, even so grant me by Thy pleasure and as a guerdon of my service not to die until such hour as the Good Knight, the ninth descendant of my line, he who is to see unveiled the marvels of the Holy Grail, shall come to visit me, that I may clasp him to my breast."

'When the king had made his plea to God, he heard the voice answer: "King, be not dismayed: Our Lord has heard thy prayer and thou shalt have thy wish, for thou shalt not die until the hour when the knight thou askst for shall come to thee, and on that day when he shall stand before thee, thy sight shall be restored and thou shalt see him plain; and then shall thy wounds be healed that will not close before." Such were the words that the voice spoke to the king, promising him that he should see the coming of the knight, in accordance with his fervent wish. And surely they have proved true in every respect. For four hundred years have now elapsed since this adventure befell him, and all this time he has lain blind and helpless, and his wounds have never healed. And now they say that the knight is in these parts who is to bring all these things to their conclusion. What is more, we firmly believe, from the signs already vouchsafed to us, that he will see again and regain the strength of his limbs; but from then he will not have long to live.

'I have told you the story of King Mordrain according as it happened, and you can accept in truth that it is he you saw today. For four hundred years he has lived a life so holy and devout that he never tasted any earthly food but that which the priest holds up to our view at the sacrament of the mass, which is the body of Jesus Christ. You saw this much yourself today; for as soon as the priest had finished singing mass he took the Lord's Body to the king and gave him to partake of it. From the time of Josephus to this present hour the king has lain waiting thus for the coming of that knight whom he has yearned to see: waiting as did the aged Simeon who watched so long for the advent of Our Lord that the babe was brought to the temple, and there the old man met him and took him in his arms in his joy and glee that what had been promised him was now fulfilled. For the Holy Ghost had made it known to him that he would not die until he had looked on Jesus Christ. And when he saw him he broke into that sweet song which is foreshadowed by the prophet David.* And even as Simeon thirsted

---

* Cf. Luke 2, 29–32, and Psalm 97 (Vulgate), A.V. 98.

after Jesus Christ, the Son of God, the most high Prophet and the one true Shepherd, even so this king now waits for the coming of Galahad, the good and perfect Knight.

'Now I have told you the truth you asked of me just as it came about; and in turn I request you to tell me who you are.'

Perceval replied that he was of the household of King Arthur and a companion of the Round Table, and was called Perceval of Wales. The good monk, when he heard this name, responded joyfully, for he had often heard its bearer spoken of. He begged him to spend that day at the abbey: the brethren would entertain him and do him honour, as was only right. But Perceval answered that so much remained for him to do that he would not tarry on any account, but must be off at once. With that he sent to fetch his arms, and when he was equipped, he mounted and bade them farewell, and leaving the abbey he rode on his way through the forest till noon.

Around mid-day his path brought him out into a valley where he encountered some twenty armed men escorting a horse-drawn bier on which lay the body of a man but newly slain. When they saw him they asked him where he hailed from.

'From the house of King Arthur,' he replied, and at that they shouted in chorus:

'Have at him!'

Seeing their temper Perceval prepared to defend himself dearly and spurred to meet the foremost, felling him with a blow that brought his horse crashing down on top of him. But his charge was checked before he could complete it, for more than seven struck him on the shield, while the others killed his horse and he himself fell to the ground. Being strong and brave, he tried to rise and drew his sword in readiness. But his enemies pressed him so sorely that all defence was useless; they struck him on shield and helm and rained so many blows on him that he could not stand and was knocked off his balance, falling heavily on one knee. They went on battering and hammering at him so savagely that they would have killed him there and then, for they had already torn off his helm and wounded him, had it not been for the knight in red armour who was passing by chance that way. When he saw the lone knight on foot surrounded by so many foes all striving to kill him, he galloped up as fast as his horse would carry him and shouted to them:.

'Leave the knight be!'

He hurled himself into the group with lowered lance and unhorsed the nearest with a mighty blow. Having broken his lance he grasped his sword and galloped up and down striking to right and left so powerfully that none received the full brunt of his blows but hurtled to the ground. In a short space of time he had done them such damage by the strength and speed with which he laid about him that there was none so bold as would barter blows with him. Instead they all turned tail and fled, some here, some there, scattering through the great deeps of the forest till only three were left, of whom Perceval had felled and wounded one and he the others. When he saw that they had all departed and Perceval had no more to fear from them, he made off into the forest at the point where the trees stood thickest, like a man who seeks at all costs to evade pursuit.

When Perceval saw him leaving in such haste he shouted after him at the top of his voice:

'Sir Knight, for God's sake stay awhile till you have talked with me!'

The Good Knight gave no sign that he had heard Perceval, but pressed on at full speed in the manner of one loth to return. And Perceval who had no horse, for his own had been killed by the knights, went after him on foot as best he could. As he ran he met a squire who was riding a strong cob, fleet and built to gallop, and leading a tall black war-horse. When Perceval saw him he did not know what to do. For he badly wanted the horse in order to follow the knight, and he would have gone to any lengths to acquire it, provided the squire would cede it of his own free will, for he would not take it by force unless he were driven to it by crucial need, not wishing to be held a knave. He greeted the youth as soon as he drew close and the other returned his salutation.

'Good friend,' said Perceval, 'I beg you in return for any service or guerdon you may name, and on my undertaking to be your man on the first occasion that you call on me, to lend me that horse for the time I will need to overtake a knight who has just left this spot.'

'Sir,' said the squire, 'I will do no such thing, for it belongs to such a man as would do me some bodily injury if I failed to return it to him.'

'Good friend,' said Perceval again, 'pray do as I ask. For if I lose this knight for want of a horse I shall suffer such grief as I have never known.'

'By my faith,' he answered, 'I can do no different. You will never have it by my consent while it is in my charge, you will have to take it from me by force.'

Perceval was so anguished at this reply that he thought he would go out of his mind. For he would not basely molest the youth, yet if he lost the speeding knight his joy would be fled for ever. This dilemma so tore at his heartstrings that he was unable to stand and collapsed half-fainting under a tree, while the colour drained from his face and the strength from his limbs. In his extreme distress he wanted to die forthwith, and thereupon took off his helm and held out his sword to the squire, saying:

'Good friend, since you will not remedy the grief from which death alone can offer me escape, I beg you to take my sword and kill me now: and then my suffering will have an end. And if the Good Knight, whom I was seeking, hears that I have died for sorrow at his loss, he will not be so churlish but he will pray Our Lord to have mercy on my soul.'

'In Heaven's name!' cried the other, 'I will never kill you, please God, for you have done nothing to deserve it.'

With that he went on his way at a round pace, leaving Perceval so prostrated that he thought he should die of grief. When the squire had gone from view, leaving him quite alone, he gave full vent to his misery, calling himself a sorry creature and exclaiming:

'Alas, unhappy wretch, now has your quest miscarried since he has eluded your pursuit. You will never be so well poised to find him as you were but now!'

As Perceval was bewailing his tribulations in this fashion, the clatter of a horse's hooves broke on his ears. He opened his eyes and saw an armed knight riding along the high road through the forest mounted on the charger that the squire had lately been leading. Perceval recognized it at once but it never occurred to him that the rider had possessed the beast by force. When they had passed out of sight he returned to his sorrow, but had not long to wait before he saw the lad appear on his cob, railing and weeping. On seeing Perceval he cried:

'Ah! Sir, did you see an armed knight pass this way on the war-horse that you asked me for just now?'

'Yes, truly,' answered Perceval, 'but why do you ask?'

'Because he stole it from me by force, and so contrived my death and destruction; for my lord will kill me for this wherever he happens to find me.'

'And what would you have me do about it? I cannot retrieve it for you, since I am on foot. Now had I a horse I would hope to recover it soon enough.'

'Sir,' said the young man, 'take my cob, and if you can win the other it is yours.'

'And how will you recover the cob if I manage to secure the horse?'

'Sir, I will follow you on foot and if you can conquer the knight I will take my cob and you may keep the horse.'

To this Perceval answered that he asked nothing better.

So he laced on his helm again and taking up his shield he mounted the cob and urged it on in hot pursuit of the knight. When he had gone some way he came to a small clearing of which there were many such in the forest. And there in front of him he spied the knight fleeing apace on the charger. As soon as he glimpsed him he shouted from afar:

'Sir Knight, turn back, and give the varlet back his horse to which you have no right!'

When the other heard himself hailed he lowered his lance and charged across the glade, and Perceval drew his sword, as one who sees the combat is upon him. But the knight, who wished to be rid of him quickly, galloped flat out towards him and struck the cob so hard in the chest that he speared it clean through the body, and it dropped in its tracks and fell dead, pitching Perceval over its head. When the knight had marked the result of his blow he resumed his flight down the glade and plunged into the densest part of the forest. Perceval was so disconsolate at the outcome of this encounter, that he knew not what to do or say. He shouted after the fleeing knight:

'You craven, lily-livered coward, turn back and fight, all mounted as you are, with one who is on foot!'

But the knight never answered his challenge, for he held him of small account, and the forest engulfed him directly he reached its edge. When he was lost to view Perceval threw down his shield and sword in despair and tearing off his helm abandoned himself more violently than ever to his grief. He wept and cried aloud, swearing he was the most wretched, unhappy and luckless of knights, and exclaiming:

'Now I have failed in all my heart's desires!'

In such distress and torment did Perceval repine the whole day through, for no one came along to comfort him. And when dusk fell he found himself so weak and faint that it seemed to him his limbs were sapped of strength. A longing for sleep came over him and he yielded to it and slept until the middle of the night. He looked up on awaking and saw a woman standing before him who asked him very timidly:

'Perceval, what are you doing here?'

'Nor good nor ill,' he answered, adding that if he had a horse he would soon be gone.

'If you but promised to do my bidding when I called on you, I would give you at once a fine and hardy animal that would carry you wherever you wished to go.'

These words saw Perceval the happiest of men, all careless in his joy of whom he was addressing. He believed it was a woman that he spoke to, yet he erred, for it was none other than the enemy, agog to trick him and bring him to that pass where he should lose his soul eternally. When he heard her promise him the thing he most desired, he replied that he was ready to give her every assurance she needed, and that if she furnished him with a good horse he would perform as best he could whatever she demanded of him.

'Do you pledge your faith thereto as a true knight?'

'Yes, yes, indeed!' he answered.

'Wait for me then, for I will presently return.'

With that she disappeared into the forest and came back almost at once leading a huge and wondrous horse, so black as to be quite remarkable.

When Perceval saw the horse he looked it up and down and

felt a shudder of fear; none the less he had mettle enough to climb into the saddle, as one unwary of the enemy's snare. Once mounted he took up his shield and his lance and she that stood before him then enquired:

'Perceval, are you going now? Be mindful of the quittance that you owe me.'

Perceval said that he would not forget, and galloped off into the forest under the bright moonlight. But once there his steed swept him along so fast that in no time at all it had carried him through the forest and out again and borne him thence a three days' journey and more. He continued his headlong flight till he saw in his path a wide river rushing along a valley bottom. The horse headed straight towards it and made as though to plunge into the flood. The prospect of crossing so great a river filled Perceval with alarm, for he could see neither bridge nor planks in the darkness. So he raised his hand to his forehead and made the sign of the cross. When the enemy felt himself weighted down with the burden of the cross, which was exceedingly heavy and hateful to him, he gave a great shake, and freeing himself of Perceval, rushed into the water howling and shrieking and making a yammer such as was never heard. And it came about then that bright sheaves of fire and flame shot up from the river in several places, so that the water itself appeared to burn.

Observing this phenomenon, Perceval understood in a trice that it was the enemy that had carried him thither in order to trap him and place him in jeopardy of body and soul. So making the sign of the cross he commended himself to God, and prayed to Our Lord that he might not fall into temptation and so forfeit the company of His knights above. He stretched out his hands towards heaven and gave Our Lord heartfelt thanks for helping him in his hour of need. For had the enemy carried him into the river he would undoubtedly have thrown him off and exposed him to death through drowning and the loss of both soul and body. He drew back then from the water's edge, for he still mistrusted the enemy's assaults, and kneeling down with his face to the east he recited his prayers and orisons as he had learned them. He was impatient for daybreak to show him where he was, for he was sure that the enemy had borne him a far cry from the abbey where he had yesterday seen King Mordrain.

Perceval passed the hours until dawn at his devotions, wait-ing till the sun had circled the firmament to rise again on earth's horizon. When it had risen bright and beaming and had dried the dew a little, he looked about him and found that he was on a soaring peak, eerie and utterly desolate, and girt on all sides by so wide a sweep of sea that he could see no land but in the farthest distance. He realized then that he had been con-veyed to an island, but which he could not tell; he would have liked to know, and yet it seemed he never would, for there was neither castle, fortress, refuge, nor house in sight where men might dwell. His solitude, however, was not entire, for round him roamed wild beasts, bears and lions and leopards and winged serpents. When Perceval saw what mannner of place it was he was ill at ease, for he feared the wild beasts, which would not leave him be, but would kill him as well he knew, if he could not defend himself. None the less if He that rescued Jonah from the belly of the whale and watched over Daniel in the lions' den would be his shield and guard in this predicament, nothing he saw had power to dismay him. He trusted more in His help and succour than in his sword, for he saw most plainly that no prowess achieved with this world's arms would suffice to save him unless Our Lord came to his aid. Looking about him he saw in the centre of the island a strange and beetling crag, and thought that if he could scale it he need not fear the attacks of any wild beast. So with that in mind and armed as he was he set out towards it. As he was making his way there he spied a serpent carrying a lion cub; it held it in its teeth by the scruff of its neck and settled on the summit of the mountain. Swiftly behind the serpent followed a lion, rending the air with its roars and making such a hideous clamour that Perceval felt it must be mourning the little cub which the serpent was carrying off.

At the sight of this adventure Perceval ran as hard as he could up the mountainside. But the lion, being fleeter, had already outstripped him and fallen on the serpent before he could get there. As soon as he had scrambled up the crag, however, and looked at the two beasts, he decided to go to the aid of the lion, as being the more natural animal and of a nobler order than the serpent. So he drew his sword and covered his face with his shield against the searing fire, and went to beard the serpent, dealing it a fearsome blow between the ears. The monster spewed out a sheet of fire and flame that burned his shield and all the front of his hauberk, and would have wreaked worse havoc yet; but Perceval was quick-footed and jumped aside so that instead of catching the full brunt of the flame, he received but, as it were, the ember glow, and suffered less harm in consequence. He was frightened none the less for he feared that the fire might be mingled with venom. But for all that he ran at the serpent again, hacking at whatever part he could reach, and as he strove with it he happened to catch it on the very spot where he had struck it first. Since the hide was already split and the bones were soft, the light, sharp sword cut easily down through the monster's head and dropped it dead at his feet.

When the lion saw that the knight's assistance had rid it of the serpent, it gave no sign that it wanted to attack him, but padded up to him with downbent head and fawned on him as best it knew, so that Perceval realized that it had no wish to harm him.[24] He slid his sword back in the sheath and threw down his shield which was burned and charred, and then took off his helm to let the wind play on his head, for the serpent had well-nigh roasted him. And always the lion stayed close on his heels, wagging its tail in pleasure and affection. Seeing this, Perceval began to stroke its head and neck and shoulders, saying that Our Lord had sent this beast to keep him company; and he set great store by the incident. The lion meanwhile paid him such joyous court as a dumb beast can to a man and stayed with him a great part of the day. But as soon as the hour of none was passed it bounded down the rock-face and bore its whelp off by the scruff to its lair. When Perceval saw himself alone and friendless on the desolate peak his apprehension needs no asking, and he would have been more anguished still but for the trust he placed in his Maker, for he stood out among all the knights of his time for his perfect faith in Our Lord. Yet such was not the custom of his land, for in those days the people of Wales were so insensate and fanatical that if a son found his father lying in bed by reason of some sickness, he dragged him out by the head or the arms and made a summary end of him, for he would have been held dishonoured had the father died in his bed. But when it came about that son killed father or father killed son and the whole clan died a violent death, then the neighbours proclaimed them nobly born and bred.

Perceval whiled away the day on the rock gazing out to sea in the hope of sighting a passing ship. But however he scanned the horizon not a single vessel hove in sight. In the face of this, he summoned up his courage and sought comfort in Our Lord, asking Him so to keep him that he might not fall into temptation either through the deceits of the devil or his own sinful thoughts, but to protect and nurture him rather, as a father would his son. And he held out his hands to heaven, saying:

'Gracious Lord God, who didst suffer me to aspire even to the dignity of the high order of knighthood, and didst choose me for Thy servant for all I was unworthy, grant of Thy mercy, Lord, that I may never leave that service, but may ever resemble the good and trusty champion who defends his lord's quarrel stoutly against him that arraigns him without warrant. Most sweet and gracious Lord, grant that I may thus defend my soul, which is Thy quarrel and Thy just heritage, against him who would wrongfully possess it. Sweet Saviour, who didst say of Thyself in the Gospels: "I am the Good Shepherd: the good shepherd lays down his life for the sheep, but not so the hireling, for he leaves the sheep unguarded, and directly the wolf comes it seizes them by the throat and devours them;"* Lord, be Thou my shepherd, my defender and my guide, that I may be counted among Thy sheep. And should it happen, gracious Lord, that I were the hundredth sheep, the silly one and weak, that strayed away in its folly into the wilderness, do Thou have pity on me, Lord, and do not leave me in the wilderness, but bring me back to Thy fold, that fold which is Holy Church and holy faith, there where all good sheep are, and upright men and faithful Christians all, so that the enemy, who wants nothing of me but the substance, which is the soul, may not find me unguarded.'

When Perceval's prayer was done he saw the lion, on whose behalf he had grappled with the serpent, heading once more in

*Cf. John 10, 11–14.

his direction; but again it showed him no ill-will but approached with every sign of friendliness. So Perceval called to it, and going straight up to the animal he fondled it on head and neck, and the lion lay down at his feet as it might be the tamest of household beasts. And Perceval propped himself against it and rested his head on its shoulders, waiting quietly at its side till night fell dark and deep, and sleep surprised him of a sudden where he lay. In all this time, he felt no wish to eat, his mind being taken up with other things.

Now a strange adventure befell him while he slept; for it seemed to his sleeping mind that two ladies appeared before him, of whom one was as old as the hills and the other much younger, and beautiful to boot. They did not go on foot but were mounted on two most singular beasts, for the younger rode a lion and the other was seated on a serpent. Perceval stared at them in amazement that they could master two such animals. The younger lady led the way and addressed him, saying:

'Perceval, my lord sends you greetings and bids you prepare yourself as best you can: for tomorrow you will have to fight the most dreaded champion in all the world. And if you are vanquished you will not escape with the loss of a limb, but will receive such punishment as shall be to your everlasting shame.'

To these words Perceval replied:

'Madam, who is your lord?'

'Truly,' she said, 'there is none mightier than he. Look to it therefore that by your valour and your constancy you reap some honour in this combat.'

And with that she vanished so suddenly that Perceval knew not what had become of her.

Then the lady who was seated on the serpent came up and said to Perceval:

'Perceval, I have a quarrel with you: for you have done an injury to me and mine which I had not deserved.'

When he heard himself reproached Perceval replied in great bewilderment.

'Assuredly, Madam, I am not aware of having wronged you or any lady living. So tell me, I pray you, what disservice I have done you; and if it lie in my power to make amends I will do so gladly, as and how you will.'

'I will tell you straight,' she said, 'how you have wronged me. I had long nurtured in my castle a beast of mine, such as is called a serpent, which was more useful to my purposes than you imagined. This beast flew yesterday by chance to this high mountain and found a lion cub which it carried to this rock. And you came running after with your sword and slew it unprovoked. Now tell me why you killed it. Had I done you some wrong whereby you felt constrained to shed its blood? Was the lion yours or was it subject to you that you must fight its battle? Are the beasts of the air so disinherited that you should slay them without cause?'

When Perceval heard the lady's words he said:

'Madam, you had not wronged me that I knew of, nor was the lion mine, nor are the beasts of the air in my disposal. But because the lion is a nobler creature by nature and condition than the serpent, and because I saw it was less baleful than its adversary, I fell upon the serpent and killed it. And it seems to me the wrong is far less grievous than you claim.'

To this defence the lady made rejoinder:

'Perceval, have you no more to offer me?'

'Madam, what would you have me do?'

'I want you to do me homage in reparation for my serpent.' But he answered that he would not.

'No?' she said. 'You were my liegeman once: before you swore fealty to your lord you first belonged to me. And because I had first claim on your allegiance the debt is not expunged; instead I warrant you that on the first occasion that I find you undefended I will snatch back the chattel that was mine.'

Having issued this warning the lady left, and Perceval slept on, much wearied by his vision. Indeed he slept so soundly that he never stirred the whole night through. Next morning when the sky was bright and the sun had risen so high that its fiery rays shone warm upon his head, Perceval opened his eyes and saw that all was light. He sat up then and making the sign of the cross he begged Our Lord to send him some counsel which might profit his soul, for he gave less thought to his body than he used, having given up all expectation of leaving the rock where he found himself. He looked about him, but saw neither the lion that had kept him company nor the serpent he had slain, and he wondered greatly at their disappearance.

While he was turning this matter over in his mind his gaze strayed out to sea; and there he saw a ship with sail spread taut skimming the waves and making straight for the spot where he waited to learn whether God would send him some good fortune. The ship sped on apace, for she had the wind abaft to chase her on and she flew like an arrow towards him, coming right to the foot of the peak.[25] As he observed this from his lofty perch Perceval knew his fill of joy; convinced that there would be many men on board he jumped to his feet and took up his arms. As soon as he was accoutred he made his way down the crag with all the eagerness of a man impatient to know who the occupants might be. On drawing near he saw that the ship was shrouded within and without with white silk, so that nothing met the eye but perfect white. And when he reached the ship's side he found a man robed like a priest in surplice and alb and crowned with a band of white silk two fingers deep; and this circlet bore a text which glorified Our Lord's most holy names.* Perceval was filled with wonder at this sight and drawing closer he greeted the man and said:

'Welcome, Sir, and God be with you!'

'Good friend,' said the venerable man, 'who are you?'

'One of King Arthur's household.'

'And what adventure brought you to this place?'

'Sir, I do not know the mode nor manner of my coming.'

'And what is your wish?'

'Sir,' he said, 'so it please Our Lord I would leave this island and rejoin my brethren of the Round Table in the Quest of the Holy Grail, for I left the court of my lord the king for that sole purpose.'

'You will get away in God's good time,' said the worthy man. 'He will not be slow to deliver you when it pleases Him to do so. If He deemed you His servant and saw that you would further His purpose better in some other place He would convey you away from here without delay. But this is now your testing

* Cf. Revelation 19, 12.

ground where He would try you to determine whether you are indeed His faithful servant and true knight, even as the order of chivalry demands. For since you are come to such a high estate, no earthly fear of peril should cause your heart to quail. For the heart of a knight must be so hard and unrelenting towards his suzerain's foe that nothing in the world can soften it. And if he gives way to fear, he is not of the company of true knights and veritable champions, who would sooner meet death in battle than fail to uphold the quarrel of their lord.'

Then Perceval asked him whence he came and from what land he hailed; and he said that he came from a far country.

'And what adventure,' Perceval enquired, 'brought you to so remote and wild a spot as this appears to be?'

'Upon my faith,' he answered, 'I came thus far to visit and sustain you and to hear from you how you fared. For if you have need of counsel and will confide in me, there is no matter in which I am not supremely fitted to advise you.'

'You amaze me greatly,' said Perceval, 'when you say that you came here for the purpose of counselling me. I do not understand how this can be, for none knew I was on this rock save only God and I. And even had you known of my presence here, I am sure that you cannot know my name, for you never yet beheld me to my knowledge. And so I can but marvel at your words.'

'Ah, Perceval,' said the other, 'I know you very much better than you think. There is nothing you have done in many a year but I have more inward knowledge of it than yourself.'

When he heard himself named, Perceval was lost in astonishment and found himself repenting his remarks. He asked the good man's pardon, crying:

'Ah! Sir, in God's name, forgive me what I said. I thought you did not know me and now I see that you are better acquainted with me than I with you: I stand a fool and you a wise man proved.'

Then Perceval rested his elbows on the ship's side and he and his visitor talked of many things. The latter displayed such wisdom on every topic that Perceval wondered greatly who he could be. Meanwhile he took such a delight in his company that had their converse been prolonged for ever, he would have had no wish for meat or drink, so sweet and so refreshing were the words he heard. When they had talked a good long while together, Perceval said to him:

'Sir, help me to the understanding of a vision which I had this night as I lay sleeping, and which seems to me so singular that I shall never rest content until I know the meaning of it.'

'Speak,' said the other, 'and I will give you clear and certain proof of what it signifies.'

'Very well,' said Perceval. 'I will acquaint you with it. Last night as I slept two ladies came before me, the one mounted on a lion and the other on a serpent. The one that sat on the lion was young, while she of the serpent was old, and the younger spoke to me first.'

Then he related in order all that he had heard in his sleep, just as the words had been spoken to him, for nothing had as yet slipped his memory. When he had told his dream he asked the good man to explain it to him, and he said he would do so gladly and began at once:

'Perceval, the meaning of the two ladies, whom you saw riding on such unwonted beasts as are a lion and a serpent, is truly marvellous, as you shall learn. The one who sat upon the lion signifies the New Law, that is set upon the lion which is Christ; it had its footing and its ground in Him, and by Him was established and raised up in the sight and view of Christendom to serve as a mirror and true light to all that fix their hearts upon the Trinity. This lady sits upon the lion, Christ, and she is faith and hope, belief and baptism. This lady is the firm and solid rock on which Our Lord announced that He would set fast Holy Church, there where He said: "Upon this rock I will build my church."* Thus the lady seated on the lion denotes the New Law which Our Lord maintains in strength and vigour, even as a father does his son. Nor is it surprising that she seemed younger to you than the other, for she is not so old in age or aspect, since she had her birth in the Passion and Resurrection of Jesus Christ, while the other had already reigned on earth through untold generations. The former came to talk to you as to her son, for all good Christians are her sons, and she

*Cf. Matthew 16, 18.

proved herself your mother by the great solicitude which drove her to forewarn you of what the future held. She came on behalf of her lord, who is Jesus Christ, to tell you you were doomed to fight a battle. By that faith I owe you, if she loved you not, she had not come to caution you, for your defeat had touched her not a whit. But she made haste to tell you so that you might be better equipped for the encounter. With whom? With the most dreaded champion in the world. This champion is he on whose account those stalwart men of God, Enoch and Elijah, were caught up from earth to heaven and there await the Judgment Day, when they shall come again to battle with the one whom all men fear.[26] This champion is the enemy, who with ceaseless toil and striving lures men into mortal sin and leads them thence to hell. This is the champion whom you needs must fight, and, should you be worsted, you will not be quit for the losing of a limb, but dishonour without end shall be your lot, as the lady warned. You can see the truth of that for yourself; for if the enemy succeeds in getting the better of you, he will place you in jeopardy of soul and body and haul you thence to the abode of darkness, even hell, where you will suffer shame and pain and torment as long as the dominion of Jesus Christ shall last.

'I have now explained to you the meaning of the lady in your dream who rode upon the lion; as for the other, from what I have told you you can easily tell who she must be.'

'Sir,' answered Perceval, 'you have said quite enough about the first to make the interpretation clear to me; tell me now, though, about the one that rode on the serpent, for I could never figure out the meaning by myself.'

'Very well, I will tell you,' said his visitor, 'so listen carefully. The lady whom you saw astride the serpent, she is the Synagogue, the first Law, that was put aside as soon as Jesus Christ had introduced the New. The serpent that carries her denotes the Scriptures wrongly understood and misconstrued; it is hypocrisy and heresy, iniquity and mortal sin, it is the enemy himself: the serpent who through pride was hurled from paradise, the same which said to Adam and his wife: "If you eat of this fruit you shall be like God,"* and by this saying im-

* Cf. Genesis 3, 5.

planted the seed of concupiscence in their hearts. For they itched at once to be greater than they were, and heeding the enemy's prompting, committed the sin for which they were cast forth from paradise and into exile: the sin which all their heirs had part in, and for which they daily pay the price. Now when the lady came before you, she complained that you had killed her serpent. Do you know which serpent she referred to? It was not the one that you slew yesterday, but the serpent that she rides on, which is the enemy. And do you know when you did her this hurt? It happened as the enemy was bearing you towards this rock, at the instant when you crossed yourself. For the cross you traced on your brow, whose weight was altogether unendurable, inspired him with a mortal terror, and he fled headlong like one unable to abide your company. You dealt him thus a lethal blow and robbed him of his power and his hegemony just when he thought to have you in his grasp: this is the grievance that his mistress holds against you. Now when you had countered her questions as well as you knew how, she asked you, in reparation for the wrong you did her, to become her man. And you refused. To which she answered that once long ago you had been hers before you swore allegiance to your lord. You have puzzled your head about this thing today, yet you should have understood her meaning. For without a doubt before you were baptized into the Christian faith you were in the enemy's thrall. But in the moment you received the seal of Jesus Christ, which is the holy oil with which you were anointed, you renounced the enemy and escaped his jurisdiction, having done homage to the Lord who made you. Now I have told you the meaning which attaches to both ladies, and now I must leave you, for I have much to do. You will stay here awhile, and make sure you bear in mind the fight that lies in store, for if you lose you will fare no better than was promised you.' [27]

'Good Sir,' said Perceval, 'why would you go so soon? I take such pleasure in your commerce that, as for me, I should never seek to part myself from you. For the love of God, bide here a little longer if you can, for what you have already said to me will make me, I am sure, a better man for all my life to come.'

'I must go,' said the good man, 'for there are many waiting

for me, and you will stay behind. And look to it that you be not unfurnished against the coming of your adversary; for if he finds you undefended it will go ill with you, and that right fast.'

With these words he cast off and the wind filled the sail and bore the ship away so swiftly that the eye could scarcely follow, and in a short time it had disappeared from Perceval's view. When he had quite lost sight of it he clambered back up the rock with his harness on his back, and there he found the lion that had kept him company the previous day. The beast fawned on him so delightedly that he began to fondle it again. He stayed atop the rock till past mid-day, and then as he gazed far out to sea he saw a boat heading towards him, cleaving the waves as though all four winds were driving it along; it was preceded by a whirlwind that created a huge swell and whipped up waves on every side. At first sight Perceval wondered what he was looking at, for the whirlwind hid the craft from view. However, it drew near enough for him to see it really was a ship, and curtained all from stem to stern with draperies of black linen or maybe of silk. When it had come close inshore he went down to find out who there was on board, wishing it might be the visitor with whom he had spoken earlier. And it happened, moreover, whether by the power of God or for some other reason, that no beast, however savage, on that mountain dared venture to molest or pounce on him. So he came safely down the crag and hurried to the ship's side. There he saw, seated in the tented entrance, a maiden of dazzling beauty, decked out as splendidly as any woman could be.

As soon as she set eyes on Perceval she rose to her feet and said without other greeting:

'Perceval, what are you doing here? Who brought you to this mountain, so lonely that your rescue hangs on a quirk of chance, and so utterly desolate that you will die of hunger and distress before anyone notices your presence?'

'Damsel,' he answered, 'if I should die of hunger it would be proof that I was not a faithful servant. For none is servant to so great a lord as mine, provided he serve him loyally and well, without receiving everything he asks. Himself says that His door is shut to none that come, but he that knocks, enters and he that asks, receives.* And if any seek Him, he does not hide Himself away but is easily accessible to all.'

When she heard him quoting from the Gospels she made no rejoinder, but changed the subject, saying:

'Perceval, do you know where I come from?'

And he, surprised, asked her from whom she had learned his name.

'I know it well,' she said, 'and am better acquainted with you than you suspected.'

'And where have you come from in this wise?'

'In truth,' she said, 'I came from the Waste Forest where I witnessed the strangest adventure imaginable that overtook the Good Knight.'

'Ah, damsel,' cried Perceval, 'tell me about the Good Knight, by the faith you owe to that which you love most in all the world!'

'On no account will I tell you what I know of him unless you pledge me on your honour as a knight that you will do my bidding whensoever I call upon you.'

Perceval answered that he would if it lay in his power to do so.

'You have said enough,' she said. 'Now I will tell you what happened. It is true that I was but recently in the very heart of the Waste Forest, where the great Median River flows. Thither I saw the Good Knight galloping in hot pursuit of two knights whom he sought to kill. They plunged into the water in fear of their lives, and as luck would have it reached the further bank. But their pursuer fared less well: for his horse was drowned in the river and he would have drowned as well had he not scrambled out in all haste, only saving himself by turning back. Now you have heard what befell the knight you were asking for. And now I want you to tell me how you have managed since you were stranded on this island, where all will soon be up with you unless you are rescued. For you can see for yourself that none lands here from whom you can get help, and you must either get away or die. Therefore, unless you want to perish, you needs must make a pact with someone for your rescue. And since I am the only one who can get you off, you are

* Cf. Matthew 7, 7, and Luke 11, 9.

obliged to come to terms with me – if you have any sense, that is, for there is nothing worse in my opinion than people who refuse to help themselves.'[28]

'Damsel,' said Perceval, 'if I could leave this place and if I thought it was God's will that I should do so, then would I go, but only then. For there is nothing in the whole wide world that I would wish to have done if I thought that it displeased Him: I should indeed have been knighted in an evil hour were I to use my arms against my Maker.'

'Leave all these matters be,' she said, 'and tell me whether you ate today or no.'

'In truth, I had no earthly meat today, but a holy man came here earlier to comfort me, who fed me with words of wisdom in such plenty that I should never want to eat or drink again for as long as his memory endured in me.'[29]

'Do you know who he is?' she asked. 'He is a sorcerer, a spawner of phrases who makes words breed a hundredfold and never tells the truth if he can help it. If you heed him you will be lost, for you will never get off this rock, but will die of hunger and be eaten by wild beasts. The prospect should be plain enough by now; you have been here for two days and two whole nights and as much of this day as is already sped, and he whom you speak of never once brought you food, but left you stranded then and will so leave you, for he will never come to your aid. It will be a pity and a great misfortune if you die; for you are yet young and skilled enough in arms to do great service both to me and others if you escaped from here. And I tell you straight that I will take you off if you wish.'

When Perceval heard her offer, he replied:

'Damsel, who are you who show yourself so eager to deliver me if I choose?'

'A maiden,' she replied, 'who has been disinherited, one who had been the greatest lady in the land if she had not been driven from her heritage.'

'Damsel in exile, tell me who despoiled you: I feel more compassion for you now than at any time today.'[30]

'I will tell you how it was,' she answered. 'It is true that a mighty lord once placed me in his household to wait upon him, and this great lord was the mightiest king of all. I was then so

fair and radiant that none could fail to wonder at my beauty:
for I was beautiful beyond compare. And no doubt, being so
lovely, I grew a little vainer than I ought, and passed some com-
ment that he took amiss. Hardly was it said, than his anger
waxed so fierce against me that he would not tolerate me in his
presence any longer, but drove me out unportioned and despoiled; nor did he ever relent toward me, or toward anyone
who took my part. And so the great lord banished me and my
retainers and sent me into desolate exile. He thought I was well
punished, and so I should have been, had not my resource-
fulness enabled me to take the field against him right away. Since
then my cause has met with such success that I have made much
headway; for I have won over many of his men, who deserted
him to side with me when they saw how generously I dealt
with them. For I give them everything they ask and more
besides. So it is that I wage war night and day on him who dispossessed me; and I have gathered together knights and soldiers
and all conditions of men; and I assure you there is no
knight or man of worth and standing that I know of, to whom
I do not make the offer of a fee if they will join with me. And
because I knew you for a valiant knight and honourable man I
came here to enlist your help. Indeed, you cannot refuse my
support, being, as you are, a companion of the Round Table, for
no knight of that fellowship may turn a deaf ear to the plea of a
maid who has been wrongly used. You know very well that this
is true, for when you took your seat there at King Arthur's
bidding, you swore by your very first oath that you would never
fail to succour any maiden who asked for your aid.'

Perceval agreed that he had indeed sworn such an oath, and
promised her the assistance she demanded, whereat she thanked
him warmly.

They talked so long that mid-day came and went, and the
hour of none drew near. The sun was blazing down so torridly
that the maiden said to him:

'Perceval, I have on board the most magnificent silk tent you
ever saw. If you wish, I will have it brought ashore and set up
here in case the heat of the sun prove harmful to you.'

Directly he agreed to her suggestion she went into the ship
and got two servants to erect the tent on the strand. When they

had done the job to the best of their ability the maiden said to Perceval:

'Come and rest yourself, and sit here out of the sun till nightfall, for I fear you are getting overheated.'

He stepped inside the awning and fell asleep almost at once; but first she divested him of helm and hauberk and sword, and when he was stripped to his tunic she let him sleep.[31]

When he had slept long and deep he awoke and asked to eat; and she ordered her servants to prepare the table, which they did. Perceval watched them load the board with a choice of dishes which seemed to him prodigious, and he and the maiden took their meal together. When he asked for drink it was brought to him, and he found that it was wine, the best and most potent he had ever drunk, and he wondered greatly where it could have come from. For in those days there was no wine in Britain save in princely households, and they commonly drank ale and other local brews. He drank so much of the stuff that it went to his head somewhat. Then he looked at the young woman and found her so lovely that he thought he had never seen her match for beauty. Indeed he found her so much to his taste and liking, both for the gorgeousness of her attire and all the gracious things she said to him, that his feelings for her grew unduly warm. He chatted with her about this and that, till finally he wooed her openly, begging her to be his and to let him be hers. She held him off as long as she could on purpose to increase his ardour, while he continued pleading. When she saw that he was all aflame, she said to him:

'Perceval, you must understand that I will on no account give way to your desire unless you pledge me that you will be mine henceforward and help me against all opponents, and will do nothing but what I command you.'

He agreed eagerly.

'Do you give me your oath as a true knight?'

'Yes,' he replied.

'Then I will be content with that and do whatever you desire. And believe me, you have not hungered to possess me one half so much as I have wanted you, for you are one of the knights I was most passionately set on having.'

Then she ordered her servants to prepare within the tent

the most beautiful and luxurious bed they could, and complying
at once they made ready a couch, and taking off the maiden's
slippers they put her to bed, and Perceval beside her. When he
was already lying in bed with her and would have pulled up
the coverlet, it happened by chance that he caught sight of his
sword which the servants had laid on the ground when they
unbuckled it. As he went to place it against the bed his glance
fell on a red cross which was inlaid in the hilt. Directly he saw
it he came to his senses.[32] He made the sign of the cross on his
forehead and immediately the tent collapsed about him and he
was shrouded in a cloud of blinding smoke, while so foul a
stench pervaded everything that he thought he must be in hell.
Then he cried out in a loud voice:

'Gracious Lord Jesus Christ, let me not perish here but succour me by Thy grace or I am lost!'

When he had said this he opened his eyes, but the tent in
which he had been lying had vanished. Looking seawards he
saw the ship as he had seen it earlier, and in it the maiden who
called out to him:

'Perceval, you have betrayed me!'

Immediately she pushed out to sea and Perceval saw such a
violent storm following in her wake that it seemed that the ship
must be driven off its course, and the whole sea suddenly burst
into flame till it looked as though all the fires on earth were
burning there, and meanwhile the ship sped on its way faster
than any wind could blow.

When Perceval understood what had happened to him he
thought he should die of grief. He stood gazing after the ship for
as long as it stayed in view, wishing the direst of dooms might
overtake it; and when he could see it no longer he exclaimed:

'Alas, I am undone!' and yearned for death in the extremity
of his distress. Then drawing his sword from its scabbard he
stabbed himself so savagely that he drove the point through his
left thigh and the blood spurted out in a rain. When he saw
what he had done he said:

'Gracious Lord God, this is to atone for the offence I did Thee.'

Then he took stock of himself, and saw that he was naked save
his breeches, while his clothes lay scattered here and his arms
there, and he cried aloud:

T—E

'Alas! miserable wretch that I am, I have been vile and wicked beyond measure, to let myself be brought so swiftly to the brink of losing what is irredeemable, namely virginity, which cannot be recovered since it is lost but once!'

He withdrew his sword from the wound and sheathed it. The thought that God was angered with him pained him more acutely than his injury. He put on his shirt and frock, and having made himself as presentable as he could, he lay down on the rock and besought Our Lord to send him some counsel whereby he might find mercy and forgiveness, for he felt that his sin had rendered him so guilty in God's sight that His mercy could alone restore peace to his soul. So Perceval waited all that day on the rock and lost much blood from his wound. But when night drew on and cloaked the world in shadow he dragged himself to his hauberk, and, resting his head on it, he begged Our Lord of His sweet pity so to watch over him that the enemy of mankind, the devil, might gain no hold on him whereby he could lead him into temptation. When his prayer was finished he stood up and cut off the end of his shirt, and plugged his wound lest it should bleed too freely. Then he spent the hours until dawn reciting the many prayers he knew. And when it was Our Lord's good pleasure to pour out the light of His day on every land, and the sun shone its beams on the place where Perceval lay, he looked about him at the sea on the one hand and the rock on the other. And when he remembered the enemy, for such he thought it must have been, who in the guise of a maiden had clasped him close the day before, he fell to weeping and wailing and swore he was dead in very truth if he were not comforted by the grace of the Holy Ghost.

As he uttered these words he glanced eastwards across the sea and espied the ship he had seen before, that was dressed overall in white silk and had borne the visitor in priestly robes. When he recognized it he was reassured by the memory of the salutary words the good man had spoken to him on the first occasion, and of the great wisdom he had found in him. When the ship touched land and he saw his visitor at the rail, he sat up with an effort and wished him welcome. Stepping ashore, the good man approached and seated himself on the rocks, where he said to Perceval:

'And how have you acquitted yourself?'

'Poorly, Sir, for a maiden well-nigh lured me into mortal sin.' And Perceval recounted all that had happened to him. The good man asked him whether he knew who the maiden was.

'No, Sir,' he answered, 'but I know that the enemy sent her to confound and trick me. And she would have gained her ends but for the sign of the Holy Cross which needs brought me to my right mind and senses. As soon as I had made the sign of the cross she hurried away and I never saw her since. I beg you, in God's name, to tell me what I must do, for I never stood in such desperate need of advice as I do now.'

'Ah, Perceval,' sighed the other, 'you will ever be simple. So you have no idea who the young woman was that brought you to the verge of mortal sin, when the sign of the cross preserved you?'

'I am certainly in doubt. And I pray you for the love of God to tell me who she is and from what land she hails, and who the great lord is that dispossessed her, against whom she was asking for my help.'

'I will make all plain to you. Do you but listen.

'The maiden whom you spoke with is the enemy, the master of hell, he who lords it over all the rest. It is true that he was once an angel of the heavenly host, and so resplendent that he swelled with pride at his own beauty and would have set himself beside the Trinity, saying, "I will climb the heavens and will be even as the Lord of Glory." But as soon as the words were spoken, Our Lord, who would not have His house fouled with the poison of pride, flung him down from the high throne where He had placed him and condemned him to the abode of darkness we call hell.* When he saw himself cast down from his high seat and the great position he had occupied, and found himself in everlasting night, he resolved to wage war on Him who had abased him with every means at his disposal. He did not see his way clearly at first, but eventually he won the ear of Adam's wife, the first woman of the human race; he laid a snare for her until by guile he lured her into that same mortal sin, concupiscence, for which he had himself been hurled from

* Cf. Isaiah 14, 12–15.

heaven's glory. He played on her criminal desire until she culled the deadly fruit of the tree her Maker had forbidden her to touch. And having plucked it, she ate of it and gave it also to her lord, Adam, to eat, with such results that all their seed endures the mortal pangs. The enemy that urged her to that course was the same serpent that you saw the ancient crone bestride; he was the maiden, too, that visited you yesterday. And in telling you she battled night and day she spoke the truth, as you yourself well know; for the hour will never come that does not see her lying in wait for the knights of Jesus Christ, and for the good men, free and bond, in whom the Holy Ghost abides.

'When she had won your confidence by dint of lying words and artful ruses, she had her tent spread to receive you, saying: "Perceval, come and rest yourself and sit here until nightfall out of the sun, for I fear it is too hot for you." These words of hers were far from trivial, inasmuch as she construed them differently from you. The tent, round in shape like the earth's environment, quite plainly signifies the world, which will never be free from sin; and sin being ever present in the world, she did not want you to stay outside the tent: that was the reason for its setting up. And when she called to you she said: "Perceval, come and rest yourself and sit down until nightfall." By sitting and resting she meant that you should be idle and give your body its fill of earthly cheer and gluttony. She did not exhort you to work in this life and sow your seed against the day when good men reap their harvest, the day of eternal judgement. She entreated you to rest until night came, which is to say till you were snatched by death, which is termed night most aptly whenever it catches unawares a man in mortal sin.[33] She called you in lest the heat of the sun should be too much for you, and it was no wonder that she feared its strength. For when the sun, for which we must read Jesus Christ, the one true light, warms the sinner with the fire of the Holy Ghost, the chill and ice of the enemy can do him little hurt if he has fixed his heart on the heavenly sun. Now I have told you enough about this lady for you to realize who she is, and that her visit boded you more harm than good.'

'Indeed, Sir,' answered Perceval, 'you have told me enough

about the lady for me to recognize in her the champion I was to fight against.'

'In faith,' said the good man, 'you are right. Consider now how you did.'

'Badly, Sir, I fear. For I would have been vanquished but for the grace of the Holy Ghost, who saved me from destruction, all thanks to Him!'

'However you fared this once,' said the other, 'be on your guard henceforward. For if you fall a second time you will not find any to help you to your feet as promptly as today.'

The good man lingered long to talk with Perceval; he admonished him earnestly to live aright, and assured him that God would not forget him but would come to his rescue shortly. Then he enquired after his wound.

'Upon my faith,' said Perceval, 'from the moment of your arrival it has been as though I had never been wounded, for since I set eyes on you I have felt no pain or discomfort, nor do I now while I listen to you; instead, your words and looks impart such balm to soul and body, that I must believe you are no mortal man but a spiritual being. I know beyond question that if you stayed with me for ever I should know neither hunger nor thirst. Indeed, if I dared speak the words, I would say you are the Living Bread that comes down from heaven, which is a pledge of everlasting life to all who partake worthily thereof.'[84]

He had hardly finished speaking when his visitor vanished without Perceval knowing what had become of him. Then he heard a voice which said:

'Perceval, thou hast conquered and art healed. Enter this ship and go wheresoever adventure leads thee. And be not dismayed by anything thou seest, for wherever thou goest God will be thy guide. Thou hast borne thyself so well that thou shalt meet one day with Bors and Galahad, the two whose company thou most desirest.'

These words filled him with the greatest joy a man can know, and he stretched his hands heavenwards, giving thanks to Our Lord that he had weathered the storm. He took up his arms, and when he was harnessed he stepped aboard the ship and pushed out to sea where the wind caught the sail and carried him swiftly away from the island. But here the tale leaves him and takes up the story of Lancelot, who was lodging still with the hermit from whom he had received so clear an explanation of the words the voice had spoken to him in the chapel.

[7]

Lancelot: The Slow Ascent

Now the story relates that the holy man persuaded Lancelot to stay with him three days, and took advantage of his presence to exhort him ceaselessly with homily and discourse, saying:

'Lancelot, you will most certainly pursue this Quest in vain, unless you seek wholeheartedly to keep from mortal sin and to withdraw your affections from worldly thoughts and pleasures. Be assured that your prowess as a knight will avail you nothing in this Quest unless the Holy Ghost first pave your way in all the adventures that you meet with. You are aware that this Quest was undertaken to glean some knowledge of the mysteries of the Holy Grail, which Our Lord has promised to reveal to the true knight who shall transcend in chivalry and virtue his fellows past and future. You saw that knight on the feast of Pentecost seated at the Round Table in the Seat of Danger where none but he had sat and lived, as you yourself were witness more than once. This knight is the paragon who in his lifetime shall exemplify the sum of earthly chivalry. And when by dint of his achievements he shall live wholly in the spirit, he will slough off the garment of the flesh and join the company of the knights of heaven. Such was Merlin's prophecy concerning this knight whom you have seen, and he had great knowledge of things to come. None the less, for all it is true that this knight has now a greater share of valour and hardihood than any other, you may be sure that if he gave himself to mortal sin – from which Our Lord preserve him in His pity – he would get no further in this Quest than any other ordinary knight. For this service in which you are entered does not pertain in any way to the things of earth, but of heaven, whence you can see that he who would embrace it and attain his goal must firstly purge and cleanse himself of the corruption of this world, so that the enemy may have no part in him. In this way, having utterly renounced the devil, and being washed clean of every mortal sin, he will be able to enter safely on this high Quest and most exalted service. And if he is a man so weak and wanting in faith that he thinks he can achieve more by his prowess than by the grace of Our Lord, know that dishonour lies in wait for him, and that at the last his hopes will come to naught.'

So ran the hermit's discourse during the three days he kept Lancelot by him. And Lancelot held himself thrice-blest in that God had led him to this venerable priest who had instructed him so wisely that he must ever be the better for it.

On the fourth day the hermit sent word to his brother, asking him to send arms and a horse to a knight who had been lodging with him, and the other met his wish most graciously. On the fifth morning after mass, when Lancelot had armed and mounted, he bade his host a sorrowful farewell and asked him urgently and before God to pray that Our Lord should never so forget him that he relapse into his former misery. This the hermit promised to do and Lancelot went on his way.

Having taken his leave he rode through the forest till the hour of prime when he met a squire who greeted him with the question:

'Sir Knight, where do you hail from?'

'The household of King Arthur,' he replied.

'Tell me, what is your name?'

He answered that he was called Lancelot of the Lake.

'Lancelot,' said the other, 'in God's name, you are the last man I was bent on meeting: for there is no sorrier knight than you.'

'Good friend, what do you know of it?'

'I am well informed,' replied the squire. 'Are you not he who saw the Holy Grail appear and work an undoubted miracle before his eyes, and lay as wooden at its coming as might an unbeliever?'

'It is true,' said Lancelot. 'I saw it and stirred not; it is no cause for glory but for grief.'

'It is no wonder that it grieves you, for you proved beyond a doubt that you had no loyalty or virtue in you, showing yourself faithless both as a Christian and a knight. And since you would not honour the vessel of your own accord, be not surprised if, in the course of this Quest you have embarked on with your peers, dishonour follow fast on your demur. In truth, you miserable defaulter, you have good cause to grieve, you who once were held to be the best knight in the world and now are shown the worst and most disloyal!'

Lancelot knew not what reply to make, for he felt himself guilty of the offence the squire taxed him with. However, he said:

'Good friend, you may say what you like to me and I will hear you out. For no knight may show anger at the words of a squire, unless they pass the bounds of calumny.'

'There is nothing left you but to listen,' said the other, 'for no other good will ever come of you. And yet you were the very flower of knighthood! Wretch! You have been properly bewitched by her who loves you little and esteems you less. She has brought you to such a fix that you have lost the joys of heaven and the company of the angels and every honour that the world can give, and are condemned to drain the cup of shame to the very dregs.'[35]

Lancelot was so mortified that he did not trust himself to answer and wished that he were dead. And the varlet continued to revile and taunt him and heap the grossest insults on his head. Lancelot listened notwithstanding, as one so abashed that he cannot bear to look at his accuser. When the varlet tired of speaking his mind and saw that he would not answer, he went on his way. And Lancelot, without a glance at him, rode off weeping and sorrowing and begging Our Lord to lead him back into a path which would profit his soul; for he realized he had sinned so grievously in this life and so offended his Maker, that Our Lord's mercy must be truly boundless for him to find forgiveness. So he came at the last to this: that however much his former life had pleased him, his present practice pleased him ten times more.

When he had ridden until noon he saw a low dwelling ahead of him, standing back from the road, and turned towards it, knowing it must be a hermitage. On coming close he found a small chapel and a modest house. An old man wearing a monk's white habit was sitting in front of the entrance, distraught with grief and crying:

'Gracious Lord God, why hast Thou suffered this to be? He had already served Thee for so long and striven in that service heart and soul!'

The sight of the old man's tears moved Lancelot to pity and he greeted him, saying:

'God keep you, Sir.'

'I pray He may, Sir Knight,' replied the hermit. 'For unless He keep me close I have no doubt that the enemy will easily contrive to catch me out. And may God deliver you from your sin: for you are certainly in direr straits than any knight I know.'

When Lancelot heard the hermit's words he dismounted, thinking he would ride no more that day, but would take counsel of this holy man who seemed, judging by what he said, to know him well. So he tied his horse to a tree and was going forward when he caught sight of a white-haired man lying in the chapel porch, seemingly dead, and clothed in a soft white shirt, while another of rough and bristling haircloth lay beside him. Filled with amazement at so strange a death, Lancelot sat down and asked the hermit how his friend had died, to which he answered:

'Sir Knight, I know not; but it is plain to me he did not die a godly death, nor one consistent with his vows. For no such man as he can die in the garb you see him in without having broken his rule; which proves to me it was the enemy who launched the assault that brought about his death. The pity of it breaks my heart: for he had served Our Lord most faithfully for over thirty years.'

'Before God,' said Lancelot, 'it is indeed a grievous pity that he should lose his years of service, and also that at such an age the enemy should have caught him off his guard.'

The good man went into his chapel then to fetch a book and a stole which he put round his neck, and on his return he set about conjuring the enemy. He had been reading the invocation for some while, when he looked up and saw the enemy before him in such hideous guise that the stoutest of hearts would have quailed at the sight of him.

'Thou dost plague me cruelly,' said the enemy. 'Here am I now. What is thy business?'

'I want thee to tell me how my companion met his death, and whether he is lost or saved.'

Then, in a gruesome and repulsive voice, the enemy spoke out the words: 'He is not lost but saved.'

'How can this be?' asked the hermit. 'I think thou liest. For our rule does not command, nay stringently forbids that any man should wear a linen shirt; and he who does so contravenes the rule. And it is a grave matter, as I see it, to die in such transgressing of the rule.'

'I will tell thee,' said the enemy, 'how it came about. Thou knowest that he is a man of noble birth and lineage, and still has nephews and nieces in these parts. Now it fell the day before yesterday that the count of the Vale went to war with one of these nephews, Agaran by name. When the fighting had begun and Agaran saw he was getting the worst of it, not knowing what to do, he came to seek counsel of his uncle, whom thou seest here, and implored him so persuasively that he left his anchorage and went to help him prosecute his war against the count. Thus he reverted to his former calling and carried arms once more. When he had joined his kinsmen he performed such prodigies of valour that the count was taken during the third day's fighting, and he and Agaran made peace, the count giving firm pledges that he would never march on him again.

'When the war was at an end and the strife stilled, the good man went back to his hermitage and resumed the service in which he had laboured many a year. But when the count learned that his discomfiture lay at the old man's door, he asked two of his nephews to avenge him, and they agreed to do so. They hurried over at once and dismounted in front of this chapel where they found the hermit engaged in saying mass. Not daring to assail him at such a juncture, they decided to wait until he came outside, and set up a tent close by. When he had recited the office and left the chapel, they shouted to him that he was a dead man, and grabbing hold of him, drew their swords. But just as they thought to make short work of beheading him, He whose servant he had ever been wrought in him now so clear a miracle as to preserve him unhurt beneath the sword-strokes, for all he was wearing nothing but his habit. His aggressors' blades splintered and rebounded as if they had been hacking at an anvil, and they flailed away till their swords were shattered and they were weary and sore from their efforts, and still they had not wounded him to the extent of drawing blood.

'This threw them into such a mindless rage that, fetching flint and kindling, they lit a fire out here and said that they would burn him, for fire would make an end of him soon enough. They stripped him naked, even to the hair-shirt you see beside his body. And when he saw his nakedness he was mortified and ashamed, and begged them for some garment which would save him having to look on his disgrace. But these two harsh and cruel men swore he should never more wear flax or fleece, but should most surely die. Hearing this, he began to smile and answered: "What? Did you think that this fire you have prepared for me can kill me?" "It spells your death, and nothing else," they said. "In truth, Sirs," he replied, "if it pleases Our Lord that I should die, it pleases me as well. But if I die it will rather be by the will of God than by the fire: for this fire will have no power to burn a single hair of me; nor is there in the world a shirt so fine that the flames could mark or mar it, were I to put it on and wear it in the blaze." When they heard what he said they held it all for moonshine; however, one of the two asserted that his words could be put to the test, and that right soon. So he took off his shirt, and they made the old man put it on and threw him into the fire which they had built so high that it lasted from yesterday morning till late at night. When it had burnt itself out they found the old man indeed dead; but his flesh was as perfect and intact as you can see, and the shirt he had donned bore no other mark than it does now. The sight of this frightened them out of their wits; they took his body from the ashes and laid it where you see it now, and placing his hair shirt beside him they took to their heels. And by this miracle which He whom he had served so long performed for thy companion, thou canst plainly see he is not lost but saved. Now with that I will be off, for I have explained everything thou wast in doubt about.'

Having said this he departed suddenly, razing the trees in his path and whipping up such a violent storm that it seemed as though all the fiends of hell were tearing through the forest.

The good man was much cheered by what he had heard. He put away the book and the stole, and returning to the dead man he began to kiss him, saying to Lancelot:

'In faith, Sir, Our Lord has worked a wonderful miracle for this man, who I thought had died in some mortal sin. But thanks be to God it was not so, instead he is saved, as you yourself were able to hear.'

'Sir,' asked Lancelot, 'who was it that spoke to you at such length? I could not see him, but I heard his voice, which is grisly and dreadful enough to strike fear into any heart.'

'And it is right that men should fear it,' said the other, 'for nothing merits to be dreaded like its author, for he it is who lures men to damnation.'

Now Lancelot knew for certain whom he spoke of. The hermit asked him next to keep him company while he watched by the body of the holy man, and to help him on the morrow with the burial. He said he would do so gladly, and that he was happy that God had put him in the way of serving so holy a man as this had been.

He took off his armour, which he put in the chapel, and went to remove his horse's saddle and bridle before returning to keep the hermit company. When they had sat down together the good man questioned him, saying:

'Sir Knight, are you not Lancelot of the Lake?'

'I am,' he answered.

'And what do you go about seeking, thus accoutred?'

'Along with the rest of my companions, Sir, I am seeking the adventures of the Holy Grail.'

'Seek them you may,' replied the priest, 'but find them you will not. For were the Holy Grail to appear before you, I do not think you would be able to see it any more than a blind man would a sword before his eyes. And yet many people have dwelt long in darkness and in the murk of sin, whom Our Lord has recalled to the true light, as soon as He saw they willed it in their hearts. Our Lord is not slow to succour the sinner: the moment He sees him turn towards Him in heart or mind or some good work, He visits him without delay. And if he has swept and garnished his lodging as a sinner should, Our Lord comes down and makes His abode there,[36] and the sinner need not fear His leaving unless he turn Him out of doors. But if he opens the door to His adversary, Our Lord takes His departure, unable to tarry longer when he who ever wages war on Him is welcomed in.

'Lancelot, I have shown you this example on account of the life you have led so long since you gave yourself to sin, which is to say since you received the order of knighthood. For before you were made a knight, all the virtues inhered in you so naturally, that I know of no young man to rival you.[37] First of all was virginity so innate to your being that you had never violated it in thought or act. Even in thought you had kept it undefiled; for many a time, as you meditated on the abomination of the sin of the flesh by which virginity is lost, you spat with disgust and swore you would never fall into such wretchedness. In those days you affirmed that there was no prowess to compare with being a virgin, shunning lust and keeping one's body pure.

'Besides this virtue, of itself sublime, you had humility. Humility is meek and gentle, and goes about with downbent head. It does not imitate the Pharisee who said as he prayed in the temple: "Gracious Lord God, I give thee thanks that I am not as sinful and wicked as my neighbours." This was not your way; you resembled rather the publican who dared not raise his eyes to the image, lest God should be angered with him for the greatness of his sins; instead he stood far from the altar and smote his breast, saying: "Blessed Lord Jesus Christ, be merciful to me, a sinner."* He who would practise humility should pattern himself on the publican. And so you did as a youth, for you loved and feared your Maker above all else, and said one should dread no power on earth, but him alone who is able to destroy body and soul and clap the sinner into hell.†

'As well as these two virtues which I have told you of, longsuffering was yours. Long-suffering is like the emerald whose colour never varies. For no temptation, of whatever magnitude, can overpower long-suffering, which always gleams with a green and constant light; and who so strives against it, it wins each

* Cf. Luke 18, 10–13.
† Cf. Matthew 10, 28.

time the honour and the palm. For none can better overcome his enemy than by long-suffering. Whatever other sins you have committed, you know at heart that this virtue was inherent to your nature.

'There was another virtue that flowered in you so naturally that it seemed it was inborn, and this was rectitude. Rectitude is so robust and sovereign a virtue that it maintains all things in true perspective; it is undeviating, and renders unto each his true deserts and what is rightly his. Rectitude neither favours friend nor wrongs a foe, and never spares its own, but holds to its unwavering course so steadfastly that no eventuality can shift it from that path.

'Over and above all these, there was charity present in you in marvellous measure. For had you held all the riches of the world at your disposal you would have given them away without a qualm, for the love of your Maker. The fire of the Holy Ghost burned warm and bright in you then, and you were heart and soul intent on holding fast to the yield these virtues made you.

'Thus endowed with every good quality a mortal man could have, you entered the high ranks of chivalry. But when the enemy, who first brought man to sin and led him to damnation, saw you so armed and girt on every side, he feared that he would never catch you out. He realized that he stood to gain a great advantage if he could force you out of any of your positions. He saw, too, that you had been enrolled in Our Lord's service and brought to such a high degree that you ought never to abase yourself to serve His enemy. And he was apprehensive of attacking you, for he feared his labours would be wasted. He gave much thought to the best way of ensnaring you and making you commit a mortal sin, and concluded at the last that the shortest cut to success lay through a woman. He told himself that the father of mankind had been deceived by woman, and Solomon, the wisest of the human race, and Strong-arm Samson the invincible, and Absalom, son of David, the fairest man the world has seen. "And since," he inferred, "all those were brought low by a woman's wiles, I hardly think this youth could hold out long."

'With that he entered into Queen Guinevere, who had not

made a good confession since she was first married, and roused
her to cast frequent looks at you as you tarried in her apart-
ments on the day you were knighted. Growing conscious
of her glances, you turned your thoughts to her; and at once
the enemy let fly a dart which caught you undefended and
knocked you off your balance with such force that you stumbled
from the path of righteousness and set your feet in one unknown to you till then, the path of lust, the path which
degrades both body and soul to a degree that none can really
know who has not tried it. From that time on the enemy robbed
you of your sight. For as soon as your eyes were glazed by the
fever of lust you sent humility packing and opened the door to
pride, wishing to hold up your head with the best and stalk
about like a very lion; at the same time you swore in your heart
that you neither should nor would set store by anything unless
you had your will of her who was so lovely in your sight. When
the enemy, who hears each word as soon as the tongue has
formed it, knew that you had sinned in thought and intent, he
entered wholly into you and drove out Him whom you had
lodged so long.

'Thus were you lost to Our Lord, who had nurtured and
enhanced you and equipped you with every virtue, and had
called you even to the honour of His service. Thus, when He
thought that you would be His servant and use the riches He had
loaned you in His employ, you quitted Him there and then;
thus, when you should have been the servant of Jesus Christ
you joined the devil's train and took to yourself as many of the
enemy's attributes as Our Lord had given you His. For in the
place of virginity and chastity you installed lust, which is the
ruin of both; and in lieu of humility you embraced pride, as
one who holds no man his equal. And then you drove out all the
virtues I have named and welcomed in their opposites. However,
Our Lord had furnished you so lavishly, that out of such profusion there needs must be some leavings. With the residue God
left you, you performed the wondrous feats in far-flung lands
which won you such renown the whole world over.[38] Think then
what more you might have done had you kept intact in you all
those virtues which Our Lord had planted there. You would not
have failed in the adventures of the Holy Grail, which all the

rest are now at such pains to achieve, but would have triumphed in a greater number than any other man save the True Knight; you had not lain blinded in the presence of your Lord, but would have seen Him face to face. I have told you all these things because of my sorrow at seeing you so abased and shamed that instead of honour attending you wherever you go, you will meet with nothing but slights and derision from all who know the true account of your fortunes in the Quest.

'None the less you have not so offended, but you may find forgiveness, if you implore it unreservedly of Him who had furnished you so nobly and called you to His service. But should your heart not be entire, I do not recommend you to pursue this Quest. For know that not one of those who have embarked on it will come away without dishonour unless he be truly shriven. For this is no Quest for earthly things, but those of heaven; and who would enter heaven foul and sinful is cast out with such force that he bears the mark his whole life long. So is it with those who have entered on this Quest defiled and soiled with this world's vices, for they will find themselves unable to hold to track or trail, but will wander footloose in outlandish parts. For now is brought to pass in simile the parable we read of in the Gospel:

' "There was once a great lord who had prepared a marriage feast and who summoned his friends and kinsmen and neighbours. When the tables had been set up, he sent out his messengers to those he had invited and bade them come, for all was ready. But they tarried and delayed so long that the lord took umbrage and said to his servants: 'Go out into the highways and byways and summon friend and stranger, poor and rich to come and eat, for the tables are set up and all is ready.' They did as their lord commanded and brought along so many that the house was filled. When all were seated the lord looked round and saw a man who had no wedding garment. Going up to him, he said: 'Good friend, what sought you here?' 'Sir, I came along like all the rest.' 'In faith,' said the lord, 'you did not so: for they came joyous and jubilant and dressed in a manner fitting to a wedding. But you have brought nothing proper to a feast.' And he had him thrown out of his house, forthwith, and said in the hearing of all who sat at the tables that he had summoned ten times more than had come to his wedding; whence one can truly say that many are called but few are chosen."*

'What we read here in the Gospel we can see again in semblance in this Quest. For by the wedding feast the lord proclaimed, we must understand the table of the Holy Grail, where the worthy men, the true knights, shall be fed, those whom Our Lord shall find arrayed in wedding garments, which are the graces and the virtues he bestows on them that serve him. But those whom He shall find there unprovided and lacking their raiment of confession and good deeds He will not welcome in, but will have them cast out from the society of the rest, so that shame and humiliation shall be theirs in just such measure as the others shall have honour.'

With that he fell silent and looked at Lancelot who was weeping as bitterly as if he had seen the object of his dearest love lying dead before him, and with the desperation of a man at his wit's end for grief. When the hermit had observed him for a space, he asked him if he had been shriven since entering on the Quest. Lancelot answered with an effort that he had, and then disclosed the details of his plight and of the three words that the first hermit had explained to him, together with their meaning. Having heard all this, the good man said to him:

'Lancelot, I adjure you by your Christian faith and by the order of knighthood you received long since, that you tell me which life you prefer, the one you led before or that which you have recently embraced.'

'Sir, I swear by my Maker that I like my present way of life a hundred times better than ever I did the old, nor while I live will I ever break with it, betide what may.'

'Be not dismayed, then,' said the hermit. 'For if Our Lord sees that you are wholehearted in asking His forgiveness, He will send you grace unstinted, and you shall be His temple and His lodging, and He will take up His abode in you.'†

The whole day passed in such-like conversation, and when the night drew in they made a meal of some bread and ale which they found in the hermitage. Then they stretched out on

* Cf. Matthew 22, 2–14, and Luke 14, 10–24.
† Cf. 1 Corinthians 3, 16, and 2 Corinthians 6, 16

the ground beside the corpse, where they slept but little, for their minds were less intent on the things of earth than of heaven. Next morning, when the worthy man had buried the body of his friend before the altar, he entered into the hermitage saying he would never leave it again in this life, but would spend his days in the service of his heavenly Lord. When he saw that Lancelot would have taken his arms, he said to him:

'Lancelot, I command you in the name of holy penance to wear this holy man's hair-shirt from this day on. Be assured you will derive such benefit that you will not commit a mortal sin while it is next your skin. And furthermore I charge you that you eat no meat and drink no wine while you pursue this Quest, and that you go to church each day to hear the service of Our Lord, if circumstance permits.'

Lancelot accepted this command in penance's name, and stripping in the good man's sight, he received the discipline with a willing spirit. Then he took the hair-shirt with its rasping bristles and donned it first beneath his tunic. When he was fitted out he took up his arms and mounted, asking the hermit's leave to go. He gave it him gladly, but pressed him still to live aright and on no account to neglect to seek confession every week, so that the enemy might have no power to harm him, and Lancelot assured him he would do so. So he went on his way, and rode all day through the forest until the hour of vespers without meeting with any adventure worth recounting.

Shortly before vespers he met a young woman riding apace on a white palfrey, who greeted him on approaching with the words:

'Sir Knight, where are you going?'

'In truth, young lady,' he replied, 'I do not rightly know, save there where fortune takes me. For I have no notion of the whereabouts of what I seek.'

'I know very well,' she said, 'what you are seeking. You once were closer to it than you are today, and yet are closer now than ever you were before, if you hold fast to what you have embarked on.'

'Damsel,' answered Lancelot, 'your two remarks appear to contradict each other.'

'Do not concern yourself,' she said, 'there will come a time when you will see it plainer than you see it now, and I have told you nothing you can fully comprehend as yet.'

When she had said this much and would have ridden off, Lancelot asked her where he could put up that day.

'There will be no roof for you tonight; but tomorrow you will find a lodging to meet your need, and there your fears and doubts will be allayed.'

They commended one another to God and went their ways, Lancelot following the forest track, till nightfall found him at a fork where a wooden cross was planted at a parting of the roads. He was happy to have found the cross and said that this should be his lodging for the night. He bowed in reverence and then dismounted, unsaddling his horse to let it graze; next he took his shield from his neck and unlaced his helmet and eased it from his head; then he knelt down before the cross to recite his prayers, entreating Him who on one Cross had hung and in whose honour and remembrance this other was erected, so to watch over him as to prevent his lapsing into mortal sin. For there was nothing he feared so much as his own backsliding.

When he had finished his devotions and spent a long time praying to Our Lord, he pillowed his head and arms on a stone which lay at the foot of the cross. Watching and fasting had tired him out and made him so drowsy that he fell asleep directly he settled himself on the stone. It seemed to him as he slept that there came a man before him set all about with stars; two knights and seven kings attended him, and he wore on his head a golden crown. When they had come before Lancelot they halted and fell on their knees before the cross in worship and adoration. Eventually, after kneeling for a term, they all sat down and stretched out their hands to heaven, crying:

'Heavenly Father, come to visit us, render unto each his due,* and take us into Thy mansion, the abode of our hearts' desire!'

Having made this plea, they fell silent. And Lancelot looking heavenwards saw the clouds riven asunder, and a man come forth amid a throng of angels; he came down among them and blessed them severally, calling them good and faithful servants and saying:

* Cf. Matthew 16, 27, and Revelations 22, 12.

'My mansion is made ready for you all: enter into the joy that has no end.'*

When he had done this, he went up to the elder of the two knights and said:

'Get thee hence! Thou hast been my son in name but not in nature; thou hast shown thyself my foe and not my friend. I tell thee thou shalt perish if thou render not my treasure up again.'

The knight, when he heard these words, fled from their midst, pleading for mercy and distraught with grief. And the man said to him again:

'It is for thee to choose whether I love or hate thee.'

At once the other left the company. And he who had come down from heaven went up to the youngest knight of all and changed him into the likeness of a lion, and gave him wings, and said:

'Beloved son, now canst thou range over all the world and soar above the ranks of chivalry.'

And straightway he took wing, and his pinions waxed so huge and wondrous that they shadowed all the earth. And having left everyone breathless with his powers of flight, he soared up to the clouds; and at once the heavens opened to receive him and he entered in without further stay.

Thus it was that Lancelot had this vision while he slept. Next morning, when he saw that it was light, he raised his hand to his forehead and made the sign of the cross, commending himself to Our Lord with the prayer:

'Blessed Lord Jesus Christ, who art the true Saviour and the certain comfort of all who earnestly invoke Thee, I adore Thee, Lord, and render thanks to Thee that Thou hast shielded and delivered me from the dire shame and tribulation that I must have suffered but for Thy loving-kindness. Lord, I am Thy creature, to whom Thou hast shown such infinite love, that when my soul was set to go to hell and everlasting death, Thou in Thy pity didst snatch it from the brink and call it back to the knowledge and fear of Thee. Lord, of Thy mercy, let me not stray anew from the path of righteousness, but hold me so close

---

* Cf. Matthew 25, 21, and 25, 31 ss.

that the enemy, who is bent but on deceiving me, may ever find me in Thy hands.'

Having said this, he got to his feet and went to saddle and bridle his horse. Then he laced on his helm and took up his shield and lance and mounted, striking out down the path he had followed the previous day and pondering on what he had seen in his sleep, for he could not fathom it at all, and would have come at its meaning if he could. Mid-day found him riding through a valley, sweltering with heat, when he met the knight who two days earlier had carried off his arms. When the latter saw him coming, he gave no greeting, but shouted out:

'Defend yourself against me, Lancelot! For you are dead unless you hold your own.'

He levelled his lance as he galloped up, and struck Lancelot so hard that the point pierced shield and hauberk, but did not graze his flesh. And Lancelot, putting all his strength behind the thrust, felled horse and knight with a violence that well-nigh broke the rider's neck. He galloped past and came back on his tracks to see the horse already struggling to its feet. He caught it by the bridle and tied it to a tree so that the knight might find it to hand when he revived. This done, he set off again and rode on until evening. By then he was tired and weak, having eaten nothing all that day nor the one before, while two long days in the saddle had fagged and wearied him.

His journeying brought him as far as a hermitage, set on a mountainside. Looking across at it, he saw an aged hermit sitting before the door. Happily he called a greeting, which the venerable man returned with gracious courtesy.

'Sir,' enquired Lancelot, 'could you give lodging to a wandering knight?'

'Good Sir,' replied the hermit, 'if it please you, I will put you up this night as best I can, and give you to eat of that which God has lent me.'

Lancelot answered that he asked for nothing better; and the good man took his horse and led it to a lean-to which stood against his dwelling. There he unsaddled it himself and fed it some grass from a plentiful supply nearby. Then taking Lancelot's shield and lance he carried them into the house.

Lancelot had already unlaced his helm and pushed down his
aventail; now he took off his hauberk and carried it in-
doors. When he had finished unarming, the hermit asked him if
he had heard vespers, and he said he had seen neither man, nor
woman, nor house, nor hovel, save one man only he had encountered at noon. At that the good man entered his chapel
and calling to his clerk, began to say vespers, appending to the
office of the day that of the Blessed Virgin. Having recited
what was proper to the day he left the chapel and started to
question Lancelot about his homeland and identity. And he told
him who he was, concealing nothing of what had befallen him
in the Quest of the Holy Grail. The hermit was moved to pity
by his tale, for he saw that Lancelot started to weep when
recounting the incident of the Holy Grail. He adjured him, in
the name of the Virgin Mary and by his holy faith, to make a
full confession and lay bare his life. Lancelot said he would do
so gladly since he asked him. So the hermit led him back to the
chapel, where Lancelot told him the burden of his story as he
had told it twice before, and after begged him in God's name
to counsel him.

When the worthy man had heard his confession and the
story of his life, he eased his penitent's mind and reassured him
with such words of comfort, that Lancelot was much relieved
in spirit and said to him:

'Sir, there is a matter on which, if you can help me, I would
be glad of your direction.'

'Speak,' said the other, 'for there is no subject on which I will
not give you what advice I can.'

'It happened, sir, last night as I was sleeping, that a man
appeared before me, all set about by stars, and in his company
there came two knights and seven kings.'

And he related everything as he had seen it, word by word.
The hermit heard him out and then exclaimed:

'Ah! Lancelot, you witnessed there the glory of your lineage
and what manner of men you stem from. Know, too, that the
significance of what you saw is more profound than many
people think. So listen, if you will, and I will tell you whence
you take your origin. But it is requisite I start a long while
back.

'True it is, that two and forty years after the Passion of Jesus Christ, Joseph of Arimathea, that worthy man and perfect knight, left Jerusalem at Our Lord's behest to proclaim and preach the truth of the New Law and the commandments of the Gospel. When he came to the city of Sarras he found a pagan king – one Evalach by name – who was at war with a rich and powerful neighbour. Once he had gained the king's ear, he gave him such good counsel that the latter overcame his enemy and, with the help God sent him, defeated him in battle. Immediately on his return to the city he was baptized by Josephus, Joseph's son. Now Evalach had a brother-in-law whose pagan name was Seraph, but who took the name of Nascien on abandoning his cult. This knight, when he became a Christian and forswore the heathen law, came to believe so steadfastly in God, and loved his Maker with such fervour, that he was a very pillar and mainstay of the faith. That he was an upright man and true was made apparent when Our Lord vouchsafed to him the vision of the high secrets and the mysteries of the Holy Grail, which no knight of his time had seen, except for Joseph, unless it were fleetingly, nor have they been contemplated since by any knight, save as it were in dream.

'It appeared to Evalach at that time that from his nephew, Nascien's son, there issued a great lake which welled from out his loins. And from that lake there flowed nine rivers, eight of which were of the selfsame breadth and depth. But the last was broader and deeper than all the rest and so swift and rushing that nothing could withstand it. This river was cloudy at its source and thick as mud,[39] and in its middle stretches clear and sparkling, while the farther reach was different again, being fairer and more limpid by a hundred times than was its source, and so sweet to the taste that none could drink his fill. Such was the last of the nine rivers. King Evalach was still gazing when he saw a man come down from heaven, in outward sign and feature like Our Lord. When he had come to the lake he washed his hands and feet in it and in the rivers one by one, and when he came to the ninth river he washed his hands and feet and all his body.[40]

King Mordrain saw this vision in his sleep; and I will now show you the meaning of it and what it signified. King Mor-

drain's nephew, he from whom the lake gushed out, was Celydoine, the son of Nascien, whom Our Lord sent to this land to
confound and crush the unbelievers. This man was verily a
servant of Jesus Christ and God's true knight. He knew as much
as the philosophers, or more, about the course of the stars and
planets and the laws that govern the firmament. And because
he was supremely learned in every field of knowledge and of
science, he came before you set about with stars. He was the
first Christian king to hold sway over Scotland. He was a very
lake of learning and of science in which the fisher after truth
might find the principles and moving force of the divine ordin-
ance. And from this lake nine rivers flowed, betokening the nine
men descended from him; not indeed that they were all his
sons, but each begat the other in unbroken line. King Narpus was
the first of Celydoine's descendance, and he was a worthy
man and noted for his love of Holy Church. Nascien was the
next, so called after his grandsire; in him was the indwelling
of Our Lord so perfect that in his day no nobler man was
known. The third king was called Elian the Fat; he would sooner
have died than offend against his Maker. The fourth, Isaiah, was
a true and upright man who feared Our Lord above all else,
a man who never wittingly displeased his heavenly Lord. The
fifth was named Jonaan, a good knight and a loyal one, and
brave beyond compare; he never to his knowledge did any
deed that might offend Our Lord. He left this land and went to
Gaul, where he took to wife the daughter of Maronex, who
ceded him his kingdom. This king begot your grandsire,
Lancelot, who returned from Gaul to make his home in Britain
and wedded the daughter of the king of Ireland. You heard
about his gifts of heart and spirit the day you found his
body at the fountain, watched over by two lions.[41] King Ban,
your father, was his heir, a man of greater worth and holier life
than many men surmised who thought that sorrow at his
country's loss had killed him, but this was not the case: he had
daily begged Our Lord to let him leave this life at the hour of his
own choosing. And Our Lord showed clearly He had heard his
prayer; for no sooner did he sue for bodily death than it was
granted, and he lived in spirit.

'The seven men I have named to you are the founders of your

line; these are the seven kings who appeared to you in dream, and they were seven of the rivers that flowed out of the lake which King Mordrain saw sleeping; and in all seven did Our Lord wash both his hands and feet. It remains for me to tell you who the two knights were that kept them company. The elder of the two who followed after, which is to say, who was descended from them, is you yourself: for you are the offspring of King Ban, the last of these seven kings. When all were assembled in front of you they made this prayer: "Heavenly Father, come to visit us, render unto each his due, and take us into Thy mansion!" By saying: "Father, come to visit us," they included you in their company and begged Our Lord to come and fetch both them and you, since they were the root from which you sprang. And by their saying: "Render unto each his due", you are to understand that rectitude was so innate in them, that despite the love they bore you they would not ask Our Lord for anything save what they ought, which was to render unto each his due. When they had made their suit, it seemed to you that a man appeared from heaven amid a throng of angels, and coming down among them blessed each one. And everything has come to pass exactly as you saw it in your vision: for there is not one but is gathered in to the company of the angels.

'When the man had addressed the elder of the two knights and spoken the words which you remember well, and should take to heart as he of whom and for whom they were spoken, for the elder knight is but the image of yourself, he turned to the younger who is descended from you, for you begot him on the daughter of the Fisher King; and he changed him into the likeness of a lion, which is to say that he set him so far beyond all manner and class of men that none resembled him in valour or in strength. And he gave him wings that none might be as swift or fleet as he, nor rise as high in prowess or any other sphere, and said to him: "Beloved son, now canst thou range over all the world and soar above the ranks of chivalry." And straightway he took wing and his pinions waxed so huge and wondrous that they shadowed all the earth. All that you saw has already fulfilled itself in Galahad, this knight that is your son: for he has attained to such holiness of life that all must marvel; nor can he be matched for chivalry, by you or any other. And because he has risen there where none can follow, we must say that Our Lord has given him wings to fly above mankind; and we are to see in him the ninth of the rivers in King Mordrain's dream, the one that was broader and deeper than all the rest together. Now I have told you the names of the seven kings whom you saw in your dream, and that of the knight who was cast out of their company, and who the last one was on whom Our Lord had bestowed such grace that He enabled him to outsoar all mankind.'

'Sir,' said Lancelot, 'I am greatly amazed by what you say about the Good Knight's being my son.'

'You must not be amazed nor marvel at it. For you are well aware that you had carnal knowledge of King Pellé's daughter, and have heard many a time how Galahad was there begotten. And that same Galahad, whom you fathered on that maiden, is the knight who sat at Pentecost in the Seat of Danger; he is the knight you seek. I have told you this and made it plain to you, that you may never join in battle with him; for by doing you some bodily hurt he would commit a mortal sin. And you can depend upon it that it would soon be up with you, were you to fight him, since no prowess can match itself with his.'

'Sir,' said Lancelot, 'I am greatly comforted by what you say. For it seems to me that since Our Lord has suffered me to get such fruit, he that is so peerless would not allow his father, whatever his faults, to perish everlastingly; rather ought he pray to Our Lord by day and night that He of His sweet pity should pluck me from the evil ways in which I have dwelt so long.'

'I will tell you,' said the hermit, 'the right of the matter. The father bears his load of mortal sin, and the son his; neither shall the son have any part in his father's guilt, nor the father answer for the son's transgressions; but each will be paid according to his deserts.* Your hope, therefore, should not be in your son, but in God alone, for if you ask His help, He will sustain and succour you in all your needs.'[42]

'Since it is so ordained,' said Lancelot, 'that none but Jesus

---

*Cf. Jeremiah 31, 29–30, and Galatians 6, 4–5.

Christ can avail or help me, I pray that He may be my staff and shield and may not let me fall into the enemy's clutches, enabling me to render unto Him the treasure He demands of me, which is my soul, at that dire day when He shall say to the wicked: "Depart from me, ye accursed, into everlasting fire!"* while the just shall hear the sweet command: "Come, ye blessed heirs and children of my father, and enter into the joy that has no end!" '†

Lancelot and the worthy man talked long together; and when it was time to eat they left the chapel and sat down in the hermit's cell to a meal of bread and ale. When they had eaten, the hermit, as one who had no better bed to offer, made Lancelot lie down on a couch of grass, where he slept well enough, being tired and spent and less intent on worldly comforts than before. Had he craved them he would never have slept a wink for the hardness of the ground and the hair-shirt's pricking and scratching next his flesh. But he had been driven to the point where he found greater pleasure and beauty in the chafing garment and unyielding earth than in anything he had experienced theretofore. In consequence nothing that he did was irksome to him.

Lancelot slept that night and took his rest in the hermit's house, rising at daybreak to hear the service of Our Lord. When the hermit had sung the office, Lancelot armed and mounted, commending his host to God. The holy man implored him to hold to his new-found path, and he assured him that he would, so be God gave him health. Then he rode away, forging steadily through the forest without following track or path, for his thoughts were wholly on his life and his soul's weal, and he bitterly rued the grievous sins he had committed, which were the cause of his exclusion from the glorious company he had beheld in vision. Such was his anguish at this exile that he feared despair might seize him, but having fastened all his trust on Jesus Christ he was hopeful still of coming to that place from which he had been banished, and keeping company with those from whom he sprang.

Having pressed on until midday, he debouched in a vast clearing in the forest and saw ahead of him a strong and well-

* Cf. Matthew 25, 41.
† Cf. Matthew 25, 34.

positioned castle, beset with walls and ditches. A meadow stretched beneath the castle, decked with some hundred tents, whose silken awnings winked with many hues. Before these tents five hundred knights at least, mounted on great war-horses, had commenced a tournament, most strange and splendid. Some of the combatants wore white accoutrements, the others black; no other variants could be seen among them. The knights arrayed in white had taken up their stand towards the forest, while their adversaries had the castle side. The tournament was in full progress and already a prodigious count of knights had been unhorsed. Lancelot watched the jousting for some time until it seemed to him that the knights in black were having the harder time and losing ground, although they were more numerous by far. He therefore spurred towards them, bent on lending them what help he could. He lowered his lance and gave his horse its head and rammed his first opponent with such force that horse and rider fell. Thundering on he broke his lance against the next man's shield, but managed to unhorse him all the same. He drew his sword then and began to mete out swinging blows along the ranks like the champion he was, wreaking such damage in so short a space that all who saw him there accorded him the palm and guerdon of the tournament. But for all his pains he could not get the whip hand of his adversaries, whose powers of endurance left him quite aghast. He slashed and struck at them as he might upon a log; but they gave no sign they felt his blows, and yielded not an inch, but pressed inexorably forward. They wore him down till presently he could not hold his sword for weariness, and suffered such exhaustion that he thought he should never have the strength to carry arms again. Then they seized him by main force and led him off to the forest where they turned him loose. His companions were defeated to a man the moment his support was lost to them; and those who were leading Lancelot away said to him:

'Lancelot, thanks to our efforts you are on our side now, and in our custody; and if you would regain your freedom you must agree to do whatever we may stipulate.'

He pledged his willingness, and left them there in the forest, riding off down a different path to the one he had come by.

When he had put a good distance between himself and his captors, he reflected that this day had brought him to a pass to which nothing had yet succeeded in reducing him, for in every joust to date he had emerged the victor, and had never been taken prisoner in a tournament. These thoughts brought bitter chagrin in their train, and made him recognize that he was deeper sunk in sin than any other, for his crimes and his ill-fortune had robbed him of both sight and strength. His loss of sight had been made clear in his failure to discern the Holy Grail, when in its presence. And now the loss of physical strength was well and truly proved, for until this tournament, however great the crush that pressed about him, he had never been fatigued or jaded, but had driven his rivals willy nilly from the field. Thus sorrowing and disconsolate he rode on his way, till nightfall caught him in a valley flanked by great escarpments. When he saw he could not make the heights he dismounted under a tall poplar and relieved his horse of saddle and bridle and himself of his helm, at the same time pushing down his aventail. This done, he stretched out on the grass and was soon asleep, being wearier from the day's exertions than he had been for many a month.

As he lay sleeping it seemed to him that a man of noble aspect came down to him out of heaven, and spoke to him seemingly in anger, saying:

'Ah! man of little faith and most infirm belief, why is thy will so easily bent towards thy mortal foe? If thou dost not take heed he will plummet thee down into the bottomless pit whence none return.'

With these words he vanished, Lancelot knew not whither. This remonstrance disturbed his mind but not his sleep, for it so happened that he slept on solidly through the night till daylight flooded back, when he got to his feet and, tracing the sign of the cross on his brow, commended himself to Our Lord. Then he looked about for his horse which was nowhere to be seen; however, he found it after a search, and saddled it and mounted as soon as he was equipped.

As he went to move off he glanced to his right and spied a chapel only a bow's shot from the track, the retreat of an anchoress who passed for one of the holiest ladies in the land.

This caused him to exclaim that he was ill-starred indeed, and that without a doubt his sin deflected him from every good. For he had come this far the previous evening, early enough to have gone to the chapel by daylight and asked for counsel touching his life and person. He turned in and dismounted at the entrance, tying his horse to a tree and laying down shield and helm and sword before the threshold. When he entered he saw the vestments of Holy Church lying ready on the altar and a chaplain praying on his knees in front; it was not long before he took up the armour of Our Lord, and donning it commenced the mass of the glorious Mother of God. When he had sung the office and unrobed, the recluse, who had a small embrasure through which she could see the altar, called Lancelot over, judging him on appearance to be a wandering knight and in need of counsel. On his approach she asked him who he was and whence he came and what he sought. He answered all her questions one by one, and then proceeded to relate the adventure of the tournament in which he had taken part the day before, and how the knights in white had captured him, and what they had said to him on that occasion. He then recounted the vision that had come to him in his sleep, and having unbosomed himself on every matter, he begged her to give him what advice she could. And at once she began:

'Lancelot, Lancelot, while you strove for worldly prizes you were the finest knight on earth and the richest in adventures. Therefore you should not wonder now if, at your first endeavours in the heavenly lists, adventures yet more wonderful befall you. Nevertheless I will unfold to you the meaning of the tournament you saw; for, depend upon it, whatever you saw was but as it were a figuration of Jesus Christ. The jousting, however, without any question or deception, took place between mortal knights, who themselves were far from realizing its full significance. But first I will tell you why the tournament was arranged and who took part in it. It was arranged in order to find out who should have the biggest following of knights, Elyezer, the son of King Pellés or Arguste, the son of King Herlen. So that the parties might be told apart, Elyezer had his knights put on white coverings. And when they met in joust the black were beaten, despite your help and despite their greater numbers.

'Now let me explain to you the meaning of it. The other day, on the feast of Pentecost, the earthly knights engaged in tournament with the knights of heaven, which is to say that both embarked upon the Quest. The earthly knights, being those in mortal sin, and the knights of heaven, the true knights, the righteous men unsoiled by sin's defilement, together began the Quest of the Holy Grail: this was the tournament that they engaged in. The earthly knights, whose eyes and hearts were choked with earth, put on black wraps, as those enwrapped in black and hideous sin. The others, whose allegiance was to heaven took to themselves the white garb of virginity and chastity, unsmirched by speck of black. When the tournament, which is the Quest, had started, watching the sinners and the righteous men you fancied that it went ill with the former. And because you were on the sinners' side, being in other words in mortal sin, you joined with them and turned your lance against the just, never more notably than when you sought to joust with Galahad, your son, the day he felled your horse and Perceval's as well. When your long struggle in the tournament had drained you of resistance, the just men took you captive and led you to the forest. The other day when you set out on the Quest and the Holy Grail appeared to you, you found you were so foul and soiled with sin that you thought you never would be fit to carry arms again: so foul and soiled that is to say, that you never thought Our Lord would make of you His knight and servant. Then it was that the just men took you by the rein, the hermits and religious who set your feet upon the path of Jesus Christ, which quickens with life and greenness like the forest. They counselled you what would benefit your soul; and when you had left them, you shunned the path you had followed earlier, the mortal sins which were your former habit. As soon, however, as you bethought yourself of the empty glories of the world and the prideful life you used to lead, you began to regret you had not carried all before you, and so attracted the just displeasure of Our Lord, of which He gave you proof when He came to reproach you in your sleep with your lack of faith and trust, warning you that the enemy would plummet you into the bottomless pit, which is hell, if you were not on your guard. I have explained to you now the meaning of the tournament and of your dream, that neither vain ambition nor any other motive should tempt you from the path of truth. For you should know that having so transgressed against your Maker, if now you aggrieve Him further, He will leave you to lurch from sin to sin till you come to the everlasting pains of hell.'

With that the recluse fell silent and Lancelot replied:

'Madam, both you and those holy men with whom I have talked have filled my ears with so much wisdom that if I fall into mortal sin I shall be worthier of blame than any sinner living.'

'May God of His pity grant that never happen,' she said, and added:

'Lancelot, this forest is vast and labyrinthine in its depths; a knight can ride a whole day long and never find a house or refuge; I want you therefore to tell me if you ate today, for if you have not eaten I will give you of the alms that God has lent us.'

Lancelot said he had had no food either that day or the one before; so she had bread and water brought him, and he went into the chaplain's house and accepted the charity that God sent him. When he had eaten he took his leave, commending the lady to God, and rode on his way until evening.

He spent that night on a wild and towering crag, with no other company save that of God, dividing the hours of darkness between prayer and sleep. When he saw dawn break on the morrow he made the sign of the cross on his forehead and, facing east, prostrated himself on knees and elbows and prayed as was now his wont. Then he went to his horse, which he saddled and mounted, and set out anew on his journeyings. He rode till he came to a valley most beautiful in aspect and deeply sunk between prodigious bluffs. When he set foot in this valley he began to give serious thought to his position. Looking ahead he saw the stream known as the Median River which cut the forest in two.[43] The sight of it placed him in a quandary, for it was obvious to him that he must ford the river, which was deep and dangerous, and the realization filled him with dismay. However, his trust and confidence in God were so entire that he shrugged his fears aside, and said that with God's help he would make the passage.

While his mind was thus intent a strange adventure befell him; he saw a knight come out of the river wearing armour blacker than sloe and bestriding a huge black charger. Without a word he headed for Lancelot with his lance levelled at him and struck his horse so violently that he killed it, but never touched the rider, galloping off so fast that he was lost to view in a matter of seconds. When Lancelot found his horse slain under him he scrambled to his feet, not fretting overmuch since such was Our Lord's pleasure. He strode off, shouldering his arms and without a backward glance. When he reached the river and saw no means of crossing, he halted, and laying down helm and shield and sword and lance, stretched his length under a rock, intending to wait there until Our Lord should send him succour.

Thus was Lancelot hemmed in on all sides: in front flowed the river, to either side rose the cliffs, and at his back lay the forest. With whatever attention he considered these obstacles, he could see no salvation here below. For if he clambered up the cliffs and needed to eat he would find nothing to satisfy his hunger, unless Our Lord saw to it. And if he entered the forest, which was more treacherous than any he had known, he could lose his way and wander many days without finding a soul to help him. And as for the river, he did not see how he could make the crossing safely, for the water was so dark and deep that he would have no footing. These three considerations kept him in prayer and supplication on the bank, beseeching Our Lord to come in His mercy to comfort and visit him with His counsel, lest through the devil's wiles he fall into temptation or be dragged down into despair. But here the tale leaves him and returns to Sir Gawain.

T—G

Sir Gawain and Hector Warned in Vision

Now the story relates that when Sir Gawain took leave of his companions he rode for many a day both near and far without meeting with any adventure worth setting down in story.[44] His companions fared no better, for they met with ten times fewer adventures than was usual; this was indeed the aspect of the Quest which irked them most. Sir Gawain pursued his wanderings from Whitsun to St Magdalene's day* without coming across an adventure that merited recounting; he found it most surprising, having expected the Quest of the Holy Grail to furnish a prompter crop of strange and arduous adventures than any other emprise. One day he happened to come upon Hector of the Marsh riding alone; the two knights recognized each other at once and expressed their delight at the meeting. Sir Gawain asked Hector how it went with him.

'Well as to health and spirits,' he replied, but added that for a long spell now his travels had brought him no adventure.

'Upon my faith!' exclaimed Sir Gawain, 'that is just what I wanted to complain about to you. As God is my witness, not a single adventure has come my way since leaving Camelot. Nor do I know the reason for it: it is not for want of journeying through foreign parts and far-flung lands and riding day and night. For I swear to you, as you are my companion, that in the course of merely going my way, and no other measures taken, I have slain more than ten knights already, the worst of whom was more than adequate, and still have met with no adventure.'

Hector crossed himself in amazement.

'Now tell me,' Sir Gawain went on, 'whether you fell in with any of our companions since you left.'

'Yes, indeed,' said Hector, 'in the past two weeks I have met more than twenty, all alone, and all complaining of the lack of any adventure.'

* 22 July.

'Upon my oath,' replied Sir Gawain, 'this is most extra-ordinary. Have you any recent report of Sir Lancelot?'

'No, none; I found no one who could give me news of him, no more than if a chasm had engulfed him. It makes me very uneasy on his behalf, for I fear he may lie captive somewhere.'

'And Galahad, and Perceval, and Bors, did you hear tell of them?'

'No, never a word,' said Hector. 'These four have vanished so completely that one gets neither wind nor wake of them.'

'God guide them wherever they be,' said Sir Gawain, 'for if these should strive in vain in the adventures of the Holy Grail, the rest will stand no chance at all. I expect they will attain their goal, for they are the foremost of their peers in the Quest.'[45]

When they had been some time in conversation Hector said:

'Sir, you have ridden long alone, and so have I, and to no purpose. Let us now keep company to see if we have more luck in meeting with adventures than each man by himself.'

'Well spoken, by my faith! I agree to that. Let us go on to-gether, and may God lead us to a place where we shall find some part of what we seek.'

'Sir,' rejoined Hector, 'we shall find nothing in the direction that I come from, nor in the quarter you have traversed.'

Sir Gawain admitted it was unlikely.

'Then I suggest we take another road, untried as yet.'

Sir Gawain agreed, and Hector set out down a path which led across the plain where they had met, and so they left the high road.

They pursued their course for a week without meeting with any adventure, which disheartened them a lot. Then one day they happened to ride through a huge expanse of unfamiliar forest where no one, man or woman, crossed their path. To-wards evening they chanced upon an ancient chapel set on an upland in between two crags, and seemingly abandoned and deserted. They dismounted on arriving and stood their shields and lances against the outer wall before unsaddling their horses and turning them loose to graze on the hillside. Then they un-buckled their swords and laid them down and knelt before the altar to recite their prayers and orisons as good Christians should. Their devotions completed, the companions sat down on a bench in the chancel and chatted together of this and that, but avoided the subject of food, well aware that to repine would be pointless under the circumstances. It was very dark inside, for there was no lamp or candle burning there, and having watched a while they slept where best they could.

When they had fallen asleep, each knight had a vision, strange and wonderful; both merit setting down in story lest they be forgotten, for both were rich in meaning. It seemed to Sir Gawain as he slept that he stood in a meadow of greenest grass all studded with flowers. There was a hayrack in this field where a hundred and fifty bulls were feeding. The bulls were proud, and all but three were dappled. Of these three, one was neither truly dappled nor truly white, but bore traces of spots; and the other two were as white and resplendent as they could be. These three bulls were coupled together at the neck by strong, unyielding yokes. The bulls exclaimed in a body:

'Let us go farther afield to seek out better pasture!'

And with that they all moved off and wandered, not in the meadow, but out across the moor, and were a long time gone. When they returned there were many that were missing, and those that came back were so thin and weak they could hardly stand. Of the three without spot, one returned and the other two stayed behind. When they were all assembled round the hayrack they fell to fighting among themselves till their fodder was destroyed and they were forced to go their several ways.[46]

Such was the vision of Sir Gawain. But Hector had a different and quite dissimilar vision. It seemed to him that Lancelot and himself stepped down off a throne and mounted two powerful horses, saying:

'Let us set out to seek what we shall never find.'

They set off at once and wandered for many days till Lancelot fell from his horse, struck down by a man who stripped him of all he wore. And when he stood naked the man arrayed him in a robe all spiked with holly, and set him on an ass. Thus mounted, he went on his way till he came at last to a spring, the clearest he had ever set eyes on. But when he stooped to drink the spring hid itself from his sight, and Lancelot, seeing he might not drink of it, went back the way he had come.

Hector meanwhile, his mode of life unaltered, wandered aimlessly hither and yon till he came to a great man's house where a splendid wedding feast was in progress. He stood outside the gate shouting: 'Open up!' And the lord came out and said to him:

'Sir Knight, this is not the house you are looking for: for no one enters here so proudly mounted as yourself.'

Hector turned away at once, as crestfallen as might be, and made his way back to the throne that he had left.

This dream left Hector so disturbed in mind that the worry of it woke him up, and he began to toss and turn in the manner of one who cannot get to sleep. Sir Gawain, who had also been roused by his dream, and hearing Hector stirring, asked him:

'Sir, are you asleep?'

'No, Sir, far from it; I was woken up just now by a vision, passing strange, that came to me in my sleep.'

'Upon my faith,' said Sir Gawain, 'I too can say the same. I had a most extraordinary vision, and I assure you I shall never rest content until I know the truth concerning it.'

'And I likewise promise you that I shall never rest content until I know the truth concerning Sir Lancelot, my brother.'

As they were speaking thus, they saw a hand and forearm draped in bright red samite entering through the door of the chapel. A bridle, plainly fashioned, hung down from it, while clasped in the fist was a big candle, burning brightly; this apparition passed in front of them and up the chancel where it vanished without their knowing what became of it. Thereupon they heard a voice say to them:

'Knights, weak in faith and erring in belief, these three things you have just looked on are wanting in you; and this is the reason why you cannot attain to the adventures of the Holy Grail.'

They listened awestruck to these words, and when they had sat in silence for a space Sir Gawain spoke first and said to Hector:

'Did you understand that saying?'

'Indeed, sir, I did not, and yet I heard it clearly.'

'In God's name,' went on Sir Gawain, 'we have seen such things this night, both sleeping and waking, that the best course open to us in my view, is to seek out some hermit or some man of God, who can tell us the meaning of our dreams and interpret what we have heard. And we will do whatever he advises; for else we shall but waste our time and energies, as we have done till now.'

Hector said he could find nothing but good in this suggestion. Thus the two companions spent the night in the chapel, and slept not another wink after their first waking, but each man brooded urgently on what he had seen in his sleep.

When morning broke they went to look for their horses, searching until they found them. Having saddled and bridled them they took up their arms and mounted, and made their way down from the hilltop. When they arrived in the valley they met a squire riding alone on a cob. They greeted him and he returned their courtesy.

'Good friend,' said Sir Gawain, 'do you know of a hermitage or some religious house nearby to which you could direct us?'

'Yes, indeed, Sir,' said the youth and he pointed out a narrow path to their right and said to them:

'This path will take you straight to the upper hermitage which is perched upon a hill; but the approach is far too steep for the horses, so you will have to dismount and go on foot. There is no worthier or more saintly man in all this land than the hermit you will find at the end of your climb.'

'May God keep you, good friend,' said Gawain, 'for what you have said has been of the greatest help to us.'

Then he and they went their separate ways; and when the companions had ridden a while up the valley they saw in the distance a knight in full accoutrements who shouted out: 'Joust!' as soon as he clapped eyes on them.

'In God's name,' said Sir Gawain, 'I never met a knight since leaving Camelot who challenged me to a joust, and since this fellow wants one, he shall have it.'

'Let me be the one to go, Sir,' said Hector, 'if it please you.'

'That I will not,' replied the other, 'but should he fell me, I would not object to your going after me.'

Then he placed his lance in its rest and charged at the knight who thundered up as fast as his horse would gallop. They clashed with a force that pierced their shields and ruptured both their hauberks, and each sustained a wound, but not of equal gravity. Sir Gawain was speared in the left side, but the wound was superficial. His assailant, however, received such a fearful thrust that the lance went right through his body. Both flew out of their saddles, and the shaft was snapped in the fall so that the knight remained transfixed and lay where he fell, too grievously wounded to rise.

When Sir Gawain found himself on the ground he jumped to his feet at once, and grasping his sword and holding his shield before his face, he put on the greatest show of valour that a man already well endowed with it could do. But when he saw that the knight lay prone, he had no doubt he was mortally wounded. Thereupon he said to him:

'Sir Knight, you must fight on, or I will slay you.'

'Ah, Sir Knight, believe me, I am slain already. And I beseech you on that account to grant the request I have to make of you.'

Gawain replied that he would gladly do so if he could.

'Then, Sir, I beg you to carry me to an abbey close at hand and have me watched and buried with the ceremonies proper to my station.'

'Sir,' replied Sir Gawain, 'I know of no religious house near here.'

'Ah, Sir,' rejoined the other, 'mount me on your horse and I will lead you to an abbey that I know which lies at no great distance.'

So Sir Gawain lifted him into the saddle in front of him, and handed his shield to Hector to carry, and clasped him round the waist to keep him from falling. And the knight guided the horse straight to the abbey which stood in a neighbouring valley.

When they came to the entrance they set up a clamour which reached the ears of those within, who came out to unbar the gate and gave them a friendly welcome; they helped the wounded knight down and bedded him as softly as they could. As soon as he was settled he asked to receive his Saviour, and they brought him the host. At his Lord's coming he began to weep most bitterly and stretched out anxious hands; then he made public confession of all the sins against his Maker which troubled his conscience and with most contrite tears besought forgiveness. When he had set forth all that he could call to mind, the priest gave him his Saviour, whom he received with great devotion. After receiving the Lord's Body the knight asked Sir Gawain to pull out the spearhead from his breast. The latter first asked him who he was and from what land he came.

'Sir,' he answered, 'I am of the household of King Arthur and a knight of the Round Table; Owein the Bastard is my name and I am the son of King Urien. I set out on the Quest of the Holy Grail with the rest of my companions. But now it has come about, by the will of God or through my sin, that you have killed me; the which I forgive you cordially, and may Our Lord do likewise!'

At this Sir Gawain exclaimed in an extremity of grief and wretchedness:

'Oh God! how terrible a misadventure! Ah! Owein, I am sick at heart for you!'

'Sir,' asked the knight, 'who are you?'

'I am Gawain, King Arthur's nephew.'

'Then I set my death at naught,' said he, 'if it comes at the hand of so fine a knight as you. For the love of God, when you come to court, take greetings from me to all of our companions whom you find alive, for I know that many will die in this Quest, and tell them, for the sake of the fellowship that bound us, to remember me in their prayers and orisons, and to pray to Our Lord to have mercy on my soul.'

Hector and Sir Gawain both fell to weeping. And then Sir Gawain took hold of the spearhead which was embedded in Owein's chest; and as he pulled it forth Owein stretched out in anguish and his soul at that instant left his body, so that he died in Hector's arms. Sir Gawain was heartbroken and so was Hector: for they had seen him perform many a brilliant exploit. They had the body richly wound in a cloth of finest silk which the brethren brought them when they heard that he was a king's son, and had the funeral rites said for him, and buried him in front of the high altar in the abbey church, where they covered him with a fine tombstone, inscribed at their bidding with his name, and the name, too, of the man who killed him.

Then Sir Gawain and Hector left that place, saddened and depressed by the misadventure that had befallen them and which in their eyes was plainly rank ill-luck; and they rode on

their way till they came to the foot of the hermitage on the hill.
There they tied their horses to two oak trees and set out to
climb a narrow path which led up to the tor, soon finding it
so steep and toilsome that they were tired and weary before
they reached the top. When they had made the ascent, they
spied the hermitage where the good man dwelled, one Nascien
by name. It comprised a little chapel and a modest hut. Walking across, they saw in a plot adjoining the chapel an aged man
gathering nettles for his dinner, as one who had not tasted
other fare for a long time past. Directly he saw their arms he
concluded they were wandering knights engaged in the Quest
of the Holy Grail, of which he had heard previous report. He
left what he was at and went to greet them, and they returned
his greeting with a reverent bow.

'Good Sirs,' he asked, 'what adventure has brought you here?'

'Sir,' replied Sir Gawain, 'our great desire and longing to talk
with you, to be enlightened where we were in darkness and to
receive assurance where we are in error.'

When the hermit heard Sir Gawain speak thus he judged him
well endued with worldly wisdom, and said to him:

'Sir, all that lies within my power and ken I hold at your disposal.'

With that he led them both into his chapel and asked them
who they were, and they gave him their names and told him as
much about themselves as made him well acquainted with each
one. Then he asked them to tell him in what respect they were
in darkness, that he might enlighten them to the best of his
ability. Sir Gawain began at once:

'Sir, it happened yesterday that I and my companion here
rode all day long through a forest without encountering a living
soul, till we found a chapel on an upland. There we dismounted,
preferring the shelter of a roof to the open air. And after reliev-
ing ourselves of our armour we went inside and slept where
best we could, and while I slept I had a strange and wondrous
vision.'

He went on to describe it and Hector followed suit. Later
they told him about the hand they had seen when they awoke
and the words the voice had spoken to them. When they had
recounted it all they asked him in the name of God to tell

them what it meant: for no such vision would have come to
them in their sleep unless it had some signal meaning.

When he had heard them out and learned why they had come
to him, the holy man replied to Sir Gawain:

'Now, good Sir, in the meadow you saw there was a hayrack,
by which we should understand the Round Table: for even as
the spaces at a hayrack are marked off by wooden bars, so
are there pillars at the Round Table which separate the seats
from one another. The meadow signifies humility and patience
which spring ever vigorous and quick.[47] And since neither
humility nor patience can be conquered, it was on them that
that same fellowship was founded, where chivalry has since
derived such vigour from the fraternal love that binds its
members that it has shown itself unconquerable. And this is
the reason it is said that it was founded on humility and
patience. There were one hundred and fifty bulls feeding at the
hayrack. It was there that they found their fodder, and not in
the meadow, else they had stayed patient and humble of heart.
The bulls were proud and all but three were dappled. For the
bulls you must read the companions of the Round Table, who
through their lechery and pride fell so deeply into mortal sin
that their guilt could not stay hidden in the inner man but
must affect the outer, with the result that all are dappled and
spotted and foul and unsightly as were the bulls. Among the
bulls were three that were unspotted, or in other words were
without sin. Two were white and fair, and the third bore traces
of spots. The two that were white and fair signify Galahad and
Perceval, who are whiter and fairer than any other knight. They
are truly fair, being perfect in every virtue, and their whiteness
is so immaculate and pure that one could scarcely find today
the smallest spot upon them. The third, that bore traces of spots,
is Bors, who once abused his virginity, but has since atoned so
fully by his purity of life that the offence is wholly pardoned.*
The three bulls were yoked together at the neck, which is to
say that virginity is so engrafted in these knights that they are
powerless to lift their heads: meaning they are secure against
the assaults of pride. The bulls said: "Let us go farther afield to

* See p. 179.

seek out better pasture." On the feast of Pentecost the knights of
the Round Table declared: "Let us set out on the Quest of the
Holy Grail, and we shall have our fill of worldly honours and of
the heavenly food the Holy Ghost dispenses to such as sit at
the Table of the Holy Grail. There is the good pasture. Let us
leave this and go thither!" They left the court and wandered
not in the meadow but out across the moor. When they left
court they did not go to confession, as men ought who enter the
service of Our Lord. They did not walk in humility and patience,
signified by the meadow, but wandered over the moor, the
wasteland, taking the way which is barren of flowers and fruit,
even the path of hell, the way in which all things are laid to
waste and nothing salutary can survive. When they returned
there were many that were missing, which is to say that all will
not come back, but many instead shall die. And those that did
come back were so thin and weak that they could scarcely
stand, meaning that those who return will be so blinded with
sin that some will have killed their fellows; they will have no
limb sound enough to sustain them, no virtue, that is, such as
keeps a man upright and prevents his falling into hell, but will
be lapped in every possible filth and mortal sin. Of the three
without spot, one will return and the others will stay behind;
which is to say that of the three good knights one will return
to court, not a whit for the fodder in the hayrack, but to
announce the good pasture that those in mortal sin have forfeited. The other two will stay behind, for the food of the Holy
Grail will be so sweet to them that having once savoured it,
nothing on earth could part them from it more. The last part of
your dream,' he said, 'I will not interpret to you, for no good
would come of my doing so, and you might be improperly prevented from fulfilling it.'*

'Since it is your pleasure, Sir,' said Sir Gawain, 'I rest content with that. And it is right I should; for you have given me
such certitude in place of my confusion that the true meaning
of my dream is quite apparent to me.'

Then the good man spoke to Hector, saying:

'Hector, it seemed to you that you and Lancelot both stepped

* See note 46.

down off a throne. The throne is the sign of power or sovereignty, and the throne that you vacated is the honour and prestige which you enjoyed at the Round Table, and which you abdicated the day you left King Arthur's court. Both of you mounted next the high horses of pride and arrogance, which are the enemy's steeds, saying: "Let us set out to seek what we shall never find," which is the Holy Grail, the mysteries of Our Lord, which will never be revealed to you, for you are not fit to look on them. When you two had parted, Lancelot went on his way till he fell from his horse, which is to say that he turned his back on pride and espoused humility. Do you know who weaned him from his pride? He who cast pride out of heaven: even Jesus Christ, who humbled Lancelot to the point where He stripped him bare. He stripped him of his sins, and Lancelot found he was naked of all the virtues that should clothe a Christian, and pleaded for forgiveness. And Our Lord made haste to array him, but in what? In patience and humility: this was the gown He gave him, spiked with holly, this is the hairshirt, barbed like the holly leaf. Then He set him on an ass, humility's own beast, as Our Lord Himself made plain by riding on an ass when He entered His city of Jerusalem, He that was King of kings and held all power and wealth in His dominion, and yet chose not a charger nor a palfrey but came on the lowliest and most abject beast, the ass, that poor and rich might take example from it. It was on such a beast that you saw Lancelot riding in your sleep. And when he had ridden some way he came to a spring, the clearest he had ever seen, and got off his ass to drink: but when he stooped towards it the spring hid itself from his sight; and Lancelot, seeing he might not drink of it, returned to the throne that he had left. The waters of this spring will never fail, however deep the draughts one draws from it: it is the Holy Grail, the grace of the Holy Ghost. This spring is the gentle rain, the Gospel's dulcet words, from which the heart of the penitent derives such sweet refreshment that the more he savours it the greater is his craving: it is the grace of the Holy Grail.* For the more amply and abundantly it flows, the more remains, which is why it must properly be

* Cf. John 4, 14; also the 'fountain of the water of life', Revelation; 21, 6, and 22, 1.

likened to a spring. When Lancelot came to the spring he lowered himself from his ass, which is to say that when he comes before the Holy Grail he will abase himself and hold himself less than a man, by reason of the sins he once committed. And when he shall stoop down, which will be when he kneels to drink his fill of its abounding grace, then will the spring, the Holy Grail, secrete itself. For in the presence of the sacred vessel his eyes will lose their sight because he sullied them by gazing on the midden of this world, and his body will be sapped of strength for the years in which he used it in the enemy's service. This retribution will last four and twenty days, and will be so absolute that he will neither eat, nor drink, nor speak, nor move hand, foot or limb, yet it will seem to him that he will always know such bliss as in the moment when his sight was ravished. After, he will divulge a part of what he saw, and then he will leave that country straight away and make his way back to Camelot.

'As for you, who will spend your life astride the powerful war-horse, meaning that you will always live in mortal sin, a prey to pride and envy and many other vices, you will wander at random hither and yon, till you come to the house of the Great Fisher, there where the faithful and deserving knights will hold their feast to celebrate the finding of the treasure without price. And when you get there, confident of entry, the king will tell you that he has no use for a man as proudly mounted as yourself, to wit one steeped in mortal sin and pride. On hearing this you will return to Camelot, having won yourself scant profit in this Quest. Now I have told you and explained a part of what the future holds.

'It is required besides that you should understand the meaning of the hand which passed before your eyes, holding a candle and a bridle, and of the voice which told you that these three things were wanting in you. The hand spells charity, the vermilion samite represents the grace of the Holy Ghost, which burns in charity with a constant flame. And he that harbours charity is ardent and aglow with love of Our Lord in heaven, Jesus Christ. The bridle stands for abstinence; for even as by the bridle a man governs his horse and guides it where he would, so is it too with abstinence. It is so firmly fixed in the

Christian's heart that he cannot stumble into mortal sin, nor follow his own volition unless it lie towards good works. The candle held in the hand denotes the truth of the Gospel: it is Jesus Christ, who restores the light of sight and sense to all who turn from sin and seek His path again. When therefore it so fell that charity and abstinence and truth appeared before you in the chapel, when Our Lord, that is to say, sought out His own abode within those walls, which He had not built to shelter arrant sinners polluted with every filth, but for the preaching of the truth, and when on entering He saw you there, He left the place your presence had defiled, and leaving, said to you: "Knights weak in faith and erring in belief, these three things you have just looked on are wanting in you; and this is the reason why you cannot attain to the adventures of the Holy Grail." I have now unfolded to you the meaning of your dreams and of the hand as well.'

'Indeed,' said Sir Gawain, 'you have explained the last so well that it is as clear as the day to me. Pray tell us now why it is we no longer meet with as many adventures as we used to do.'

'I will tell you why,' replied the holy man. 'The adventures that you are now to seek concern the nature and manifestations of the Holy Grail; these signs will never appear to sinners or men sunk deep in guilt, and never therefore to you, for you are most heinous sinners. Do not imagine moreover that the adventures now afoot consist in the murder of men or the slaying of knights; they are of a spiritual order, higher in every way and much more worth.'

'Sir,' said Sir Gawain, 'by reason of what you say it seems to me that since we should be in mortal sin, it would be pointless for us to pursue this Quest any further; for I should accomplish nothing.'

'Indeed, you speak the truth; there are many engaged in it who will never reap anything but shame.'

'Then, Sir,' asked Hector, 'if we took your word for it, we would return to Camelot?'

'That is my advice,' said the other. 'And I assure you further that while you are in mortal sin nothing you do there, either, will bring you honour.'

When he had spoken these words they turned to leave. They

had not gone far, however, when the good man called Sir Gawain back. He retraced his steps, and the hermit said to him:

'Gawain, it is a long time since you were knighted, and in all these years you have done little enough for your Maker. You are an old tree, bare now of leaves and fruit. Bear this in mind, if nothing else, that Our Lord should have the pith and bark, since the enemy has had the flower and the fruit.'

'Sir,' replied Sir Gawain, 'had I the leisure to talk to you I would do so gladly. But you see my companion making off down the hill, and I must needs go too. But believe me, I shall return as soon as opportunity allows, for I am most anxious to speak with you in private.'

With that they separated; and the two knights hurried down the hill till they found and mounted their horses, and rode on until evening. They spent that night with a forester who received them with open arms and gave them of his best. They left the following day and set out on their travels again, pursuing their way a long time without finding any adventure worthy of note. But here the tale leaves them and returns to Sir Bors of Gaunes.

[9]

Trials and Temptations of Bors

NOW the story relates that when Bors and Lancelot had parted, as was recounted earlier, the former went on his way till the hour of none, when he overtook a very aged man wearing a monk's habit and riding along on an ass, quite alone, without squire or servant. Bors hailed him with the greeting:

'God be with you, Sir!'

The other looked up at him, and recognizing him for a wandering knight, wished God might be his guide. Bors asked him then where he came from thus alone.

'I have been to visit a servant of mine who is ill, and who used to do my errands. And you, who are you and where are you bound?'

'I am a wandering knight,' replied Bors, 'engaged upon a quest, and very wishful that Our Lord should help me to my goal. For this quest is the most sublime that was ever instituted, the Quest of the Holy Grail, which holds in store for him who shall see it through such honour as passes man's imagining.'

'Indeed,' said the good man, 'what you say is true, great honour will be his, and it will be no marvel, for he shall be a truer and more faithful servant than any of his fellows. He will not be vile and sullied and defiled at his setting out, like the shameless sinners who have embarked on the Quest without first setting their lives to rights: for this is the service of Our Lord Himself. Consider then their folly. They are well aware, having heard it again and again, that none can come to his Maker save by the gateway of cleanness, which is by confession; for none can be made clean and pure unless the spirit of true confession visit him: confession it is that rids him of the enemy. For when a knight, or any man at all, commits a mortal sin, he takes the enemy into himself and cannot stop his dwelling cheek by jowl with him thereafter. And when the fiend has dwelt in him for ten or twenty years, or whatever the term may be, and that man seeks confession, he spews him out and ejects him from his body, receiving in his place another and more salutary guest, even Jesus Christ. Our Lord has furnished for a long time past His earthly warriors with their bodies' food. Now He has shown His bounty and benevolence more plainly than before. For He has given them the food of the Holy Grail which fills the soul to overflowing and sustains the body too. This is the sweet food He has filled them with, even as He sustained the Israelites for so long in the desert. Thus He has shown Himself more bounteous now towards them, for He promises them gold in lieu of the lead they used to have. But just as the earthly food has been changed for that of heaven, even so must those whose affections have been earthbound until now (meaning that they were sinners), transmute them to the heavenly plane, and must leave their sins and wickedness and come to confession and repentance, becoming the knights of Jesus Christ and carrying His shield, the shield of patience and humility. For He bore none other against the enemy when He vanquished him on the Cross, Himself suffering death to save

His knights from the death of hell and the bondage they were in. It is through this gateway, called confession, the only door that leads to Jesus Christ, that every man must enter on this Quest, and each must change his inner state to fit it to receive a different food. As for those who would enter by another door, content to labour lustily without first being shriven, their search will be quite bootless, and they will return without having touched or tasted of this food that has been promised them. And worse will yet befall them. For by their false pretensions to be the knights of Christ (for they will hold themselves erroneously companions of the Quest, but will instead be deeper-dyed in wickedness than I could apprehend), some will fall into adultery, some into fornication, and others into murder. Thus their sins and the devil's wiles will make them the butt of mockery and insult and they will come empty-handed back to court, save for the wages that the enemy gives his servants, shame and dishonour to wit, of which they will have their fill before returning home. Sir Knight, I have told you all this because you are engaged in the Quest of the Holy Grail. For I should by no means recommend you to labour longer in this Quest if you are not all you should be.'

'Sir,' said Bors, 'by reason of what you have said I cannot but think that each and all will be companions if it lies with them, for it is my certain opinion that none ought ever to enter so high a service as this, which is the service of Jesus Christ Himself, but through confession. Nor can I believe that he that neglects this course could prosper in his search for so sublime a treasure.'

'You are quite right,' replied the worthy man.

Thereupon Bors asked him if he were a priest.

'Yes,' he answered.

'Then I adjure you in the name of holy charity to counsel me as a father should his son, he being the penitent who seeks confession; for the priest stands in the stead of Jesus Christ, who is a father to all true believers. Counsel me then, I pray you, to the profit of my soul and to the increase of my honour as a knight.'

'In God's name,' said the good man, 'it is no small thing you ask. Were I to fail you in this, and you fell later into mortal sin or error, you could summon me at the day of doom before the face of Jesus Christ. I will give you therefore all the help I can.'

He proceeded to ask him his name, and he replied that he was Bors of Gaunes, the son of King Bors and cousin to Sir Lancelot of the Lake.

Hearing this, the good man answered:

'Truly, Bors, if the words of the Gospel were fulfilled in you, you would be a good knight and a true one. For, as Our Lord once said: "The good tree brings forth good fruit"; so you should by rights be good, since you are the fruit of a tree that was good indeed. Your father, King Bors, was among the most virtuous men I ever saw; and I have not seen the like of your mother, Queen Evaine, in many a year. The marriage tie made of these two but one tree and one flesh. And you, their fruit, should be as good as the tree that bore you.'

'Sir,' said Bors, 'for all that a man stems from an evil stock, namely from wicked parents, this gall is changed to sweetness the moment he is anointed with the holy chrism; therefore it seems to me that it is not fathers and mothers that determine whether a man be bad or good, but his own inclinations. A man's heart is the helm of his ship and steers it where he lists, to harbour or to hazard.'

'At the helm,' rejoined the priest, 'there stands a master who holds and governs it and turns it where he would; so it is too with the human heart. For a man's good works proceed from the grace and guidance of the Holy Ghost, the evil from the enemy's seduction.'[48]

The two pursued their theme until they saw a hermitage ahead. The good man made towards it, bidding Bors to follow, for he would lodge him overnight, and next morning discuss with him in private the matter on which he sought advice. Bors agreed readily to this suggestion. They dismounted on arriving, and were met by a clerk who unsaddled Bors' horse and saw to its needs, and helped the knight unarm. This done, the hermit told his guest to go and attend vespers.

'Willingly,' he replied.

They went into the chapel and the priest intoned the office. When it was sung he had the table set up and gave Bors bread and water with the words:

'Sir, it is with such food as this that the knights of heaven should sustain their bodies, not with strong meats that rouse a man to lust and mortal sin. And as God is my help,' he went on, 'if I thought you would wish to do me a favour, I would ask one of you now.'

Bors inquired what it was.

'It is something which will benefit your soul while providing adequately for the body's needs.'

Thereto Bors gave his promise.

'Many thanks,' said the other, adding: 'Do you know what you have undertaken? Not to regale yourself with any different food until you are seated at the table of the Holy Grail.'

'And how do you know that I shall ever sit there?'

'I have sure knowledge that you will be there, the third of three companions of the Round Table.'

'Then I pledge you on my faith as a knight that I will eat nothing but bread and water, till the hour that finds me at this table that you speak of.'

The holy man thanked him for consenting to this abstinence for the love of Him who was crucified.

Bors slept that night on a couch of fresh green grass, cut by the clerk outside the chapel. He rose promptly at daybreak on the morrow, and received the visit of the priest, who said to him:

'Sir, here is a white frock for you to wear in lieu of a shirt. It will be a mark of penance, and serve to chasten the flesh.'[49]

So Bors took off his gown and shirt and put on the garment in the spirit in which it had been given him, pulling on over the top a gown of fine red cloth. Then he crossed himself and accompanied the priest into the chapel, where he made a full confession of the sins against God his conscience taxed him with. The hermit was lost in wonder at discovering how good and holy a life he led, and he learned besides that Bors had never sinned in the flesh, save the once when he had begotten Elyan the White;* and for this he owed Our Lord a debt of gratitude. When the priest had absolved him and imposed such penance as he judged suitable, Bors asked to receive his Saviour: he

* Cf. Sommer, Vol. IV, pp. 268–70.

would be the better protected wherever he might go, for he did not know if he was to die in the Quest or whether he might survive. His host asked him to wait until he had heard mass, and this he agreed to do.

So the good man began mattins; and having sung that office he robed and commenced the mass. After the blessing he took the Lord's Body and beckoned to Bors to come forward. He obeyed, and knelt before the priest, who said to him:

'Bors, do you see what I am holding?'

'Yes indeed, Sir. I see that you are holding my Saviour and Redeemer under the guise of bread. I should not be looking on Him in this wise were it not that my eyes, being mortal clay, and thus unapt to discern the things of the spirit, do not permit my seeing Him any other way, but rather cloak His true appearance. For I have no doubt that what I look on now is truly flesh and truly man and wholly God.'

At these words he was overmastered by weeping, and the good man said to him:

'You would surely be insensate if you received so holy a thing as you describe, without manifesting your love and loyalty all the rest of your living days.'

'Sir,' affirmed Bors, 'while I live He shall have my whole allegiance, and I will ever do as He commands.'

Then the hermit gave him the host, and he received it with great devotion, and knew such joy and bliss that he thought no circumstance would have the power to gall him ever again.

After receiving the host and remaining on his knees for the time he chose, he sought out the priest and told him he wanted to leave, having tarried there long enough. The other replied that he could please himself when he left, for he was armed as a knight of Christ should be, and could not be better furnished against the enemy. So Bors went and fetched his equipment and armed himself, and when he was ready harnessed he bade his host farewell, commending him to God. The worthy man requested his prayers when he should come before the Holy Grail, and Bors in turn asked him to pray to Our Lord that he might be kept from falling into mortal sin through the enemy's blandishments; and the good man promised he would remember him in every way he could.

With that Bors left and rode through the day till the after-noon. A little past the hour of none he looked upwards and saw a great bird circling above an ancient, blasted tree, with neither leaves nor fruit on its rotten limbs. After flying re-peatedly round and round, it alighted on the tree where it had its young, how many Bors could not tell, but they all lay dead in the nest. When it settled on them and found them lifeless, it stabbed at its breast with its beak until it made the blood spurt out. As soon as the warm blood touched them, the young revived, while the big bird sank among them dying, so that the offspring were reborn in the blood of the parent bird.[50] As Bors stood watching this phenomenon, he wondered, awe-struck, what it signified, not knowing what reality might underlie the form. He knew enough, however, to recognize it for a sign of great significance. He stayed there gazing for some time in case the big bird should rise again, but since it was already dead, this could not be. Once he was certain of this he resumed his course, pressing on until after vespers.

Evening brought him, as chance would have it, to a tall, strong tower, where his request for a night's lodging was granted without demur. When he had been unarmed in a chamber, he was taken to a hall above, where he found the lady of the place, who was young and beautiful, but poorly dressed. Seeing Bors enter she hurried over to him and bade him wel-come. He greeted her with the respect due to her station; she, for her part, received him most joyfully, seating him next to her and showing him every honour and attention. When it was time to dine she again made Bors sit beside her, and her people brought in great joints of meat and set them on the table. When Bors saw what was offered he bethought himself that it was not for him, so he called to a squire, bidding him fetch some water. The lad brought water in a silver goblet; and Bors put it down in front of him and made three sops. The lady noticed what he did and asked him:

'Sir, do you not like the meat that has been set before you?'

'Yes, indeed, Madam,' he answered, 'yet today I shall take nothing but what you see.'

She did not insist, as though fearing to displease him. When they had finished their meal and the cloths had been removed, they rose and walked over to the windows of the hall, where Bors sat down beside the lady. They were conversing together, when a squire came into the room and said to his mistress:

'Madam, it goes ill with us. Your sister has taken two of your castles, along with the men who held them for you, and sends you word that she will not leave you one square foot of land if tomorrow, by the hour of prime, you have not found a knight to fight for you against Priadan the Black, who is her lord.'

The lady, hearing this, began to weep and wring her hands, crying:

'Ah! God, why didst Thou ever suffer me to govern a domain if I was to be stripped of it, and that unjustly?'

Bors, who overheard these words, asked the lady what she meant.

'Sir,' she answered, 'it is the most extraordinary story in the world.'

'I pray you, tell it me.'

She assented graciously, and began at once:

'It is a fact that King Love, who held in his jurisdiction all the country round and as much and more again, once loved a lady, my sister and my elder by some years, to whom he abandoned his dominion over lands and men. While she was close to him she brought in harsh and prejudicial customs which, far from having any jot of equity, were patently unjust, and by means of which she had large numbers of his people put to death. When the king saw the evil of her ways, he drove her from his realm and made me suzerain of all he had. Directly he died, however, my sister began the war which has since led to her winning the greater part of my lands, along with the allegiance of many of my vassals. Yet, not content with her success to date, she threatens to disinherit me completely, and has made so good a start that I am left with nothing but this tower; and that will not be mine much longer, unless by tomorrow I can find a knight to fight for me against Priadan the Black, who intends to take the field to vindicate her quarrel.'

'Tell me,' said Bors, 'who is this Priadan?'

'The most dreaded champion in these parts, and the most skilled in warfare.'

'And your battle is to take place tomorrow?' he enquired.

'That is so,' she answered.

'Then you can send word to your sister and this Priadan that you have found a knight to fight for you; that you are to hold the land since it was you that King Love gave it to, and that no portion can revert to her since she was driven from it by her lord.'

These were not words to cause the lady sorrow, on the contrary it was the height of happiness that made her exclaim:

'How fortunate, Sir, your coming here today! For by your promise you have given me great joy. God give you now the strength and power to defend my cause, as verily as I am in the right: I would not ask it else.'

Bors took pains to reassure her, telling her she need have no fear of losing her due right while health and strength were his. So she sent word to her sister that her champion would hold himself ready on the morrow to perform whatever the knights of the land should stipulate, and after some parleying on either side, the battle was fixed for the morning following.

That evening Bors was fêted and feasted, and a magnificent bed prepared for him at the lady's orders. When it was time to retire and he had been unshod, he was led to a fine and spacious room. As soon as he entered and saw the bed that had been made up for him he asked his entourage to leave, which, since it was his wish, they did. Then hastily snuffing the candles, he lay down on the hard floor, with a box under his head, and bent his mind to prayer, beseeching God of His mercy to help him in his battle with the knight, as truly as he fought to further justice and good faith and thwart brutality.

When his prayer was ended he fell asleep, and directly it seemed to him that two birds appeared before him, one of which was as white as a swan and about as big, and indeed resembled a swan very closely. The other bird was as black as black and of no great size at all. It seemed to Bors, as he marked it, to be very like a rook, but the jet-black plumage gave it a rare beauty. Then the white bird approached and said to him:

'If you would serve me, I would give you all the riches in the world, and you should be as fair and white as I.'

Bors asked it who it was.

'Can you not see for yourself? I am so white, so very beautiful, and yet I am lovelier still than you imagine.'

Bors made no reply to this, and the bird flew off, its place being taken at once by the black, which spoke in turn:

'You ought and must serve me tomorrow. Do not despise me for my blackness, but know that my black hues are better worth than others' whiteness.'*

Then it, too, went away, and both were gone from sight.

This vision was followed by another, no less extraordinary. Bors thought he was entering a large and handsome building, which might have been a chapel. Once inside, he found a man seated on a throne. To the left of him, and at a distance, there was a rotten and worm-eaten tree trunk, so tottery that it could barely stand; and to his right hand were two lilies. One of the flowers bent towards the other and would have robbed it of its whiteness. But the venerable man parted them, so that neither touched the other, and in a short space of time there grew out of each flower a tree, laden with fruit. When this had occurred, the man said to Bors:

'Bors, would it not be folly to let these flowers perish in order to save that rotten trunk from falling to the ground?'

'Yes, sir, it would indeed. For in my opinion the tree-trunk must be worthless, whereas these lilies are much more wonderful than I had thought.'

'Then take heed,' said the other, 'if you meet with a similar adventure, that you do not leave these flowers to die in order to save the rotten trunk. For if too hot a flame should sear them, they could die of a sudden.'

Bors assured him that, should the occasion arise, he would bear his words in mind.

So it came about that night that Bors had these two visions which left him amazed and perplexed, for he could not at all conceive what they might mean. So troubled was he by them that he woke from his sleep, and making the sign of the cross on his forehead, commended himself most devoutly to Our Lord and settled down to wait for the dawn. When the sun had

* Cf. Song of Songs, 1, 6.

risen bright, he got into the bed and rumpled the bedclothes so that nobody could tell he had not slept in it. Next came the lady of the tower and greeted him.

'Madam, God give you joy,' he answered, and followed her to a chapel where he heard mattins and the office proper to the day.

A little before prime he left the chapel and joined a great gathering of knights and soldiers in the hall, whom the lady had summoned as witnesses to the combat. On Bors' entering the palace the lady enjoined him to eat before he armed: he would be the stronger for it. He said, however, that he would eat nothing until he had seen his battle through.

'In that case,' declared the others, 'it only remains to take your weapons and arm yourself, for doubtless Priadan is already armed and on the field where the battle is to be.'

So Bors asked for his arms, which were brought him at once, and when he was fitted out to the last detail he got on to his horse, requesting the lady that she and her retinue should mount and lead him to the field appointed for the contest. She mounted accordingly, along with her followers, and he and they set off on a route which brought them to a meadow at the head of a valley, from where they espied in the dale a great concourse of people, all awaiting the coming of Bors and the lady whose battle he was to fight. They spurred down the hillside and when they reached the venue and the ladies caught sight of one another they both closed in, and the younger, she for whom Bors was fighting, said at once:

'Madam, I call you to account, and with just cause. For you have robbed me of that heritage and right with which King Love invested me, and of which no portion can revert to you, whose title was revoked in person by the king.'

The other replied that she had never been dispossessed and was ready to prove as much if her sister dared dispute it. Seeing there was no other way out, the younger said to Bors:

'What think you, Sir, of this lady's suit?'

'I think she is attacking you in bad faith and unjustly, and that all who help her are as false as she. I have heard enough from you and from others to convince me that she is in the wrong and you are in the right. And if there is a knight prepared to say that she has the right of the matter, I am ready this very day to make him rue the saying.'

His antagonist sprang forward to say that he gave not a fig for such threats, and was all ready to defend his lady.

'And I, too, am ready,' said Bors, 'on behalf of the lady who has brought me here, to prove in combat with you that she should have the land since it was she to whom the king assigned it, and that the other lady should lose it as of right.'

At that the onlookers dispersed and vacated the area chosen for the joust. The two knights pulled back, and having retreated some distance, they charged at each other, and the speed of their gallop put such power behind the blows that shields were pierced and hauberks ruptured in the clash. And if the lances had not shattered they must have both been killed. As it was, shields and bodies collided with a force that propelled both knights to the ground over their horses' croups. They were soon on their feet, as became men of such mettle, and raising their shields above their heads and drawing their swords, they dealt one another great blows where they thought to do most damage. The shields were hacked to pieces and great shards sent flying earthwards, and the mail shirts burst asunder on arms and haunches where the sharp, flashing blades carved deep and gaping wounds and made the red blood run. The knight defended himself more stubbornly than Bors had looked for; however, he drew much comfort from the knowledge that his was a just and honourable cause. So he let his opponent hammer away, albeit not too forcefully, while he put up his guard and waited till the other should wear himself out. When he had borne the brunt some time and saw that the knight was badly winded, he went into the attack, as fresh and quick on his feet as if he had never struck a blow. He began to belabour the knight with his sword, and soon reduced him to such a pass that he could no longer defend himself for the blows he had suffered and the blood he had lost. When Bors saw his adversary thus exhausted he pressed him even harder, and the other stumbled this way and that till he measured his length backwards on the ground. Then Bors grabbed hold of his helm and tugged so hard that he wrenched it off and threw it aside, and struck him on the head with his sword-hilt, making the blood spurt out and driving the links of the mail into the wound; then, swearing that he would kill him unless he admitted defeat, he made as if to behead him. When the other saw the sword raised high above his head, he was mortally afraid and cried for quarter, saying:

'Ah! noble knight, for God's sake have mercy on me and spare my life! And I give you my oath that I will never attack the younger lady while I live, and will play no further part.'

So Bors at once let him be. When the elder of the two saw that her knight was beaten she fled the field as quickly as she could, deeming herself dishonoured. Bors now approached all present who held land of her, and swore he would destroy them unless they left her faction. Many of the vassals there did homage to his lady, and those that refused were slain and dispossessed and driven from their fiefs. So it was that by Bors' valour the lady regained that dignity to which the king had raised her. Notwithstanding, the other harried her always and in every way she could, as one who nursed an undying envy all her life.

When the country had been pacified to the extent that the enemies of the younger sister dared not raise their heads, Bors set off again, pondering as he rode through the forest on the things he had seen in his sleep, and desiring most earnestly that God might lead him to some place where he could hear his dream interpreted. He lodged the first night with a widowed lady who saw to all his wants, and whose pleasure at his coming quickened to joy at learning who he was.

The following morning at dawn he left her dwelling and struck out down the wide road through the forest. He had ridden until noon when he met with a most singular adventure. For he encountered at a crossroads two knights who were leading away his brother Lionel mounted, stripped to his breeches, on a big strong cob, with his hands pinioned across his chest; each one had hold of a switch of spiny thorn branches with which they were beating Lionel so mercilessly that his back was bleeding in more than a hundred places and his whole body was streaked and spattered with blood. But he, great-hearted as he was, said never a word, but endured all their brutalities as though he never felt them. As he prepared to hasten to the rescue, Bors glanced the other way and caught sight of an armed knight who was forcibly carrying off a beautiful young girl, and would have taken her into the thickest part of the forest, the better to hide her from her rescuers, should any follow him with that intent. But she, aware of her danger, called over and over again:

'Holy Mary, save your maid!'

When she saw Bors riding all alone she concluded he must be one of the wandering knights engaged in the Quest. So she turned towards him and shouted as loudly as she could:

'Ah! Knight, I adjure you by the faith you owe to Him you serve and whose liegeman you are, to come to my aid and prevent my being dishonoured by this knight who carries me off under duress!'

When Bors heard himself thus conjured in the name of his liege-lord, he was plunged in an agony of indecision: for were he to allow his brother to be dragged off by his captors, he did not expect to see him whole again; yet if he failed to go to the assistance of this maiden, she would be ravished shortly and dishonoured, and he would be to blame for her disgrace. So he raised his eyes to heaven and, weeping, said:

'Gracious Lord Jesus Christ, whose liegeman I am, protect my brother for me so that he die not at the hands of these two knights. And I, for the love of Thee and mercy's sake, will succour this maiden lest she be dishonoured, for I fear the knight is bent on her defilement.'

With that he galloped off in pursuit of the maiden's ravisher, spurring his horse so furiously that he drew blood from either flank. As he closed on him he shouted:

'Sir Knight, let the maid alone or you are a dead man!'

At the sound of this challenge the knight set the maiden down; he was armed and wanted nothing but a lance; he slipped his arm through the straps on the shield and drawing his sword he charged at Bors. But Bors struck him so hard that he pushed the spearhead home through shield and hauberk and the other fainted with the pain that racked him. Then Bors went up to the girl and said:

'Damsel, to all appearances you are delivered of this knight. What more would you have me do?'

'Sir,' she replied, 'since you have saved me from trucking honour for disgrace, I beg you to return me to the place whence I was taken.'

Bors said that he would do so with pleasure. So he fetched the wounded man's horse, and mounting the maiden on it he led her away as she directed. When she had gone some distance from the scene, she said:

'Sir Knight, you achieved more than you thought in coming to my rescue. For had I been deflowered five hundred more would have perished, who are now reprieved.'

Bors asked her who her ravisher was.

'In fact,' she said, 'he is a close cousin to me, and I know not by what devilish trick the enemy managed so to inflame him that he abducted me secretly from my father's house and carried me off into this forest to abuse me. For had he gained his ends he would have forfeited his soul and suffered bodily hurt, and I should have been disgraced for evermore.'

Their talk was interrupted by the approach of twelve armed knights who were scouring the forest searching for the maiden. Their joy on catching sight of her was wonderful to see. She asked them to show her companion every honour and offer him hospitality, for she would have been dishonoured but for God's help and this man's strength. The newcomers took Bors by the bridle, saying:

'It is but proper, Sir, that you should come with us. And we add our prayers thereto, for you have rendered us such service that we should be hard put to make a due return.'

'Good Sirs,' he answered, 'it is out of the question that I go with you. I have that to do elsewhere which makes it impossible for me to stay. I beg you not to take offence; for believe me, I would accompany you gladly, but the need of my presence is so desperate, and the loss, should I delay, would be so grievous, that none but God could make it good.'

When they heard that it was a matter of such urgency they dared not press him further, but commended him to God; and the maiden begged him very sweetly in God's name to come and see her as soon as he had the time, and explained to him where he would find her. He answered that if fortune bent his steps that way, he would be mindful of her invitation. With that he left them and they escorted the maiden safely home.

Bors, meanwhile, rode back to where he had last seen his brother Lionel. When he came to the selfsame spot where he had seen Lionel turn off, he looked each way as far as the forest allowed, and strained his ears in hope of catching some sound. Hearing nothing which might afford him hope of finding his brother, he struck out down the path which he had seen the three men take. When he had ridden some way he caught up with a man in monk's attire riding a horse blacker than any sloe. When the latter heard Bors coming up behind he called him on and said to him:

'Knight, what do you seek?'

'Sir,' replied Bors, 'I seek my brother whom I saw lately being led away and scourged by two armed knights.'

'Ah! Bors,' said the other, 'if I did not think it would harrow you too sorely and plunge you into despair, I would tell you what I know and show you your brother plain.'

These words immediately gave Bors to think that the knights had murdered Lionel, and he began to weep most piteously. When he was able to speak again, he said:

'Ah! Sir, if he be dead, show me his body, and I will have him buried with the honours befitting a king's son: for he sprang truly from a noble stock.'

'Look, then,' said his companion, 'and you will see him.'

Bors looked, and saw a body sprawled upon the ground, grimed in its still-fresh blood. He scanned it well and recognized, or so it seemed, his brother. Then his anguish caused him to reel, and falling in a faint, he lay some time unconscious. When he got to his feet again he cried out:

'Ah! sweet Sir, who is it used you so? Now of certainty my joy is fled for ever, unless He who visits sinners in their sorrows and tribulations comfort me in mine. And since, sweet brother, it so happens that our companionship has been dissevered, may He whom I have taken to companion and to master be my guide and guardian in every peril. For from now on I have but my soul to think of, since you have left this life.'

Then he took the body and lifted it onto the saddle, finding it almost weightless in his arms, and turned to the man at his side, saying:

'Sir, for God's sake tell me whether there be a church or chapel nearby where I can bury this knight.'

'Yes,' he replied, 'there is a chapel that stands before a tower quite close at hand where he can well be buried.'

'Then in God's name, Sir, lead me there.'

'Most willingly,' he answered. 'Follow me.'

Bors sprang onto his horse's croup, bearing in front of him, as he thought, the body of his brother. They had not gone far when they saw ahead a tall and well-defended tower, with an old tumbledown building built on the plan of a chapel in the foreground. They dismounted before the door and, going in, they laid the body on a big marble tomb which stood in the centre of the building. Bors searched high and low but could find no holy water, nor cross, nor veritable symbol of Jesus Christ.

'Let us leave him here,' said the man, 'and spend the night in the tower, and I will come back tomorrow to conduct a service for him.'

'What, Sir,' asked Bors, 'are you then a priest?'

'Yes, I am.'

'Then I beg you to give me the true explanation of a dream I had last night as I slept, and of another incident besides which leaves me much perplexed.'

'Speak on,' said the man.

So Bors recounted there and then the episode of the bird he had seen in the forest, and went on to tell him about the two birds, one white and the other black, and also about the rotten trunk and the white flowers.

'I will explain a part of it now,' said the man, 'and the rest tomorrow.

'The bird that appeared to you in the guise of a swan signifies a maiden who is aflame with desire for you, one who has loved you long and who will come soon to invite you to be her lover and her paramour. The pledge you would not give means that you will reject her suit, whereupon she will hasten away and die of grief if you do not relent. The black bird signifies the grievous sin which will be the cause of your rejecting her. For it is not the fear of God, nor any innate virtue that will cause you to repulse her: you will do it so that men may hold you chaste, to win the world's applause and its transient renown.

This chastity will itself breed such ills, that Lancelot, your cousin, will die its victim, slain by the maiden's kindred, and she herself will die of grief at being thus repulsed. It might therefore well be said that you are the murderer of them both, as also of your brother, you who could easily have saved him had you wished, when you abandoned him to go instead to the rescue of the maiden who had no claim upon you. Consider now where the greater evil lies: that she should be deflowered, or that your brother, one of the finest knights on earth, should perish? It were better for sure that every maiden in the world lost her virginity than he his life.'

When he heard the man whom he took for a model of holy living condemn what he had done on the girl's behalf, Bors was lost for a reply, and the other asked him:

'Well, have you heard the meaning of your dream?'

'Yes, Sir,' said Bors.

'Then the fate of your cousin Lancelot rests with you. For if you wish you can prevent his death, and if you so wish you can bring it about. It is in your hands now: whatever you want will come to be.'

'One thing is certain,' said Bors, 'there is nothing I would not sooner do than kill Sir Lancelot.'

'We shall see that soon enough,' rejoined the other.

Then he led Bors into the tower. On entering he was met by knights and ladies and maidens who bade him welcome one and all. They took him into the hall and there unarmed him; and when he stood stripped to his body-linen they brought him a splendid mantle lined with ermine and put it round his shoulders, and sat him down on a white couch, where they set about comforting him and reviving his spirits till they managed to make him forget some part of his grief. While they were all intent on cheering him a young woman came into the hall, so lovely and so gracious that it seemed all earthly beauty was embodied in her; and she was as gorgeously attired as if she had had the pick of the most magnificent dresses in the world.

'Sir,' said a knight, 'behold the lady whom we serve, the richest and most beautiful the world can boast, and the one who has loved you best. She has been waiting long for you, wanting no other knight but you for lover.'

This news left Bors aghast. He greeted the lady on her approach, and she returned his salutation and sat down next to him. Their conversation touched on many things till finally she asked him to become her lover, for she loved him more than any man under the sun; and if he would plight his love to her she would give him greater power and wealth than any man of his lineage before him.

When Bors heard this profession he was very embarrassed, being determined on no account to infringe his rule of chastity: he sat nonplussed and silent, till the lady said to him:

'What is it, Bors? Will you not grant my prayer?'

'Madam,' he said, 'there is not a lady in the world, however exalted her rank, whose pleasure I would do in this. Nor is it a fit request to make of me in my present situation: for my brother lies dead without, who was slain this day I know not how.'

'Ah! Bors,' she said, 'give that no further thought! It is imperative you do what I am asking. And be assured that, were it not that I love you more than ever woman loved a man, I should not ask it of you: for it is neither customary nor becoming for a woman to solicit a man's favours, for all she loves him well. But the passionate desire that I have always felt for you constrains my heart and forces me to say what I have ever hidden. I beg you therefore, dear, sweet friend, to do as I entreat and lie this night with me.'

Bors answered that he would nowise grant her suit, at which reply she made such a show of grief that she appeared to him to weep and be beside herself with woe. All this, however, gained her no advantage.

When she saw that nothing she did would win him over, she said to him:

'Bors, you have driven me to such an extremity by your refusal, that I will kill myself before your very eyes.'

So saying, she took him by the hand and leading him to the door of the palace, she added:

'Wait here, and you shall see how I will die for love of you.'

'Upon my faith,' he retorted, 'I shall see no such thing.'

She ordered her people to retain him there, and they promised that they would. Then, taking twelve maidens with her she climbed up onto the battlements. When they had made the ascent, one of her maidens cried out:

'Ah! Bors, have pity on us all, and grant my lady her desire! If you refuse, we shall most certainly precede her in throwing ourselves from this tower, for on no account would we be witness to our lady's death. There was never a knight displayed such perfidy as will be yours, if you allow us to die for such a trivial matter.'

He looked at them, believing them to be, in fact, ladies of high descent and rank; and he felt great pity for them. Nevertheless, his dispositions were not such, but that he preferred them all to lose their souls rather than he his: so he shouted that, whether they lived or died, he would do nothing of the kind.[51] Thereupon they let themselves fall to the ground from the summit of the tower; and Bors raised his hand and crossed himself at the sight. Immediately he was enveloped in such a tumult and shrieking that it seemed to him that all the fiends of hell were round about him: and no doubt there were a number present. He looked round, but saw neither the tower nor the lady who had been soliciting his love, nor anything he had seen earlier, save only the arms he had brought with him and the building where he thought to have left his brother's body.

He knew then straight away that it was the enemy who had laid this ambush for him, being bent on bringing him to death and to damnation; but by the power of Our Lord he had escaped the net. Therewith he lifted up his hands to heaven, saying:

'Gracious Lord Jesus Christ, blessed be Thou who hast given me strength and power to wrestle with the enemy and hast granted me the victory in this combat.'

Then he went over to where he had left, as he thought, his dead brother, but found no trace of him. This made him easier in his mind, for now he firmly believed that Lionel was not dead and that it was but a phantom he had seen. Next he went to pick up his arms, and, donning them and mounting, quitted that spot, determined to linger there no longer, it being, as he affirmed, the devil's haunt.

When he had ridden some little way, his ear caught the sound of a bell tolling to right of him. It made him happy to

hear it, and he turned towards it and had not long to wait before he saw an abbey girt with good, strong walls, with white
monks for its inmates. He rode up to the gate and knocked until
it was opened to him. When the monks saw him armed they
promptly concluded that he was one of the companions of the
Quest. They helped him down and led him to a chamber to
unarm him, and ministered to him in every way they could.
Bors said meanwhile to one of the monks whom he presumed
to be a priest:

'Sir, in God's name, take me to that member of your community whom you esteem mostly highly. For I met today with a
most singular adventure, and would be counselled both of God
and him.'

'Sir Knight,' replied the other, 'if you want my advice you
will go to the lord abbot: for he is first among us in learning
and in holiness.'

'For the love of God, Sir, lead me to him.'

The monk complied gladly and took him to a chapel where
the abbot then was, and having pointed him out he went back
whence he had come. Bors stepped forward and greeted the
holy man, who bowed towards him and asked him who he was.
Bors answered that he was a wandering knight, and told him
what had happened to him that day. When all was told, the
abbot said:

'Sir Knight, I know not who you are, but upon my oath, I
had not thought that a knight of your age could be so established in the grace of Our Lord as you are. You have told me
something of your affair, upon which I could not advise you
today as I would wish, for it is too late. But you shall go and
rest yourself today, and in the morning I will counsel you as
best I can.'

Bors left him, with the wish that God might keep him; he,
for his part, stayed in the chapel, meditating on what the knight
had told him, and gave instructions to the brother that Bors
should get princely hospitality, for he was a man of nobler
stamp than anyone suspected. That evening Bors enjoyed
greater ease and finer fare than he had wished, and meat and
fish were both prepared for him. However, he ate of neither,
helping himself instead to bread and water, of which he took

as much as he needed and tasted nothing else, in the manner of one who would not for the world infringe the penance put upon him, whether touching bed or board or any other matter. Next morning, as soon as he had heard mattins and mass, the abbot, who had not forgotten his guest, came to him saying:

'Sir, God give you good day!'

Bors gave him a like greeting. With that the abbot drew him to one side in front of an altar where they were alone and bade him recount what had befallen him in the Quest of the Holy Grail. So Bors repeated word for word what he had heard and seen both sleeping and waking, and asked the abbot to tell him the meaning of all these things. The latter considered a while and then, replying that he would gladly do so, he began:

'Bors, when you had received the most high Master, the true Companion, which is to say when you had received the Lord's Body, you set out to discover whether Our Lord would grant your finding the glorious treasure which awaits the knights of Jesus Christ, the true champions of this Quest. You had not gone far when Our Lord appeared to you in the shape of a bird and revealed to you the pain and anguish that He suffered for our sakes. When the bird came to the leafless, barren tree it began to look over its young and saw that there was not one of them alive. Forthwith it settled down among them and began to strike its breast with its beak till the blood gushed out; and there it died, while from this blood the young took life, as you observed. Now I will tell you the meaning there enacted.

'The bird signifies our Maker, who created man in His own image. When Adam was expelled from paradise for his transgression, he found himself on earth, and there he met with death, in life's default. The tree without leaves or fruit plainly signifies the world, where in those days was nothing but adversity and poverty and want. The young birds signify the human race whose members, unredeemed as yet, went every one to hell, the good men with the sinners, being equal in deserts. When the Son of God saw this, He climbed onto the tree, which is the Cross, and there was struck in the right side with the lance's beak, namely the point, until the blood gushed out. And from this blood the young received new life, those that had done His works: for He delivered them from hell, where all was death, and is so still, without a spark of life. This boon that God conferred upon the world, on me and you and every other sinner, He came in the semblance of a bird to show it you, that you should no more fear to die for Him than He for you.

'Next he led you to the house of the lady to whom King Love had entrusted the defence of his domain. King Love is Jesus Christ Himself, who loved in greater measure than any other king; there is no mortal man in whom lie depths of mansuetude and pity such as one finds in Him. The other sister, she who had been banished from the realm, was waging war on her with every means in her power. You took the combat on yourself and vanquished her: now I will tell you what and why you fought.

'No sooner had Our Lord shown you that He had shed His blood for you than you engaged in battle on His behalf. For in fighting the lady's battle it was His you fought – since in her we see Holy Church portrayed, who holds all Christendom in true, unerring faith and strict belief, who is the domain and rightful heritage of Jesus Christ. By the other lady who had been dispossessed and was waging war on her, we understand the Old Law, the enemy who ever wages war on Holy Church and her defenders. When the younger had disclosed to you the reason of this harassment, you undertook the combat, as was proper; for being the knight of Jesus Christ it was your bounden duty to defend His Church. You were visited that night by Holy Church in the guise of a woman sorrowing and stricken, one who has been unjustly dispossessed. She did not visit you in a festal gown, but in the gown of sorrow, which is black. She appeared to you in the weeds of grief on account of that sorrow which her own sons cause her, the sinning Christians who should be sons to her, and yet betray their kinship; they should protect her as their mother, but do no such thing; instead they harry her day and night. And this was why she came to you in the guise of a woman sorrowing and stricken, that you should be moved to greater pity for her plight.

'In the black bird that came to visit you we should see Holy Church who said: "I am black, but I am beautiful:* know that

* Cf. Song of Songs 1, 5.

my black hues are better worth than others' whiteness." The white bird shaped like a swan denotes the enemy, and I will tell you how this is. The swan is white without and black within, it is the hypocrite, who is fair-hued and pale and who gives every outward sign of being among the servants of Jesus Christ: but inwardly he is so black and hideous with the sludge of sin that he deceives the world most grossly. This bird appeared to you in your sleep, but you saw it also when you were awake. This was when the enemy appeared to you in the guise of a religious who told you you had sent your brother to his death. In that he lied to you, for your brother is not slain, but is even now alive. He said it so that you, embracing a delusion, might thence be led into despair and lust.[52] Thus he would have caught you fast in mortal sin, which would have spelled your failure in the adventures of the Holy Grail. Now I have told you who the black and the white birds were, and who the lady was for whom you undertook the battle, and whom it was you fought against.

'It remains for me to explain to you the meaning of the rotten trunk and of the flowers. The shaky and decrepit tree trunk signifies your brother Lionel, who lacks the sustaining power of Jesus Christ. The rotten pith denotes that store of mortal sins which he has amassed and added to from day to day, earning himself the just description of rotten and worm-eaten trunk. The two flowers on the right represent two virgins: one the knight you wounded yesterday, the other the maiden whom you rescued. One of these flowers bent towards the other: this was the knight who wanted to take the maid by force and would have ravished her and robbed her of her whiteness. The venerable man, however, parted them, which is to say that Our Lord, not wanting her to lose her whiteness thus, led you to the spot, enabling you to part them and keep the purity of each intact. He spoke to you, saying: "Bors, he would indeed be foolish who let these flowers perish in order to shore up that rotten trunk. Take heed if you meet with a similar adventure that you do not leave these flowers to die, so as to save the rotten tree." That was His command to you which you obeyed, earning yourself His boundless gratitude. For you saw your brother being taken away by his captors, and saw the maiden whom the knight was carrying off. She entreated you so poignantly that you were vanquished by compassion, and for the love of Jesus Christ set natural love aside and hastened to her rescue, leaving your brother to be dragged away in peril of his life. But He whom you had gone to serve went with him in your stead, repaying the love you showed the King of heaven by a great miracle that struck your brother's captors dead in their tracks, while he, their victim, loosed his bonds and taking the arms of one of them, mounted and set out anew on the Quest in the wake of his companions; it will not be long before you have living proof of what I say.

'The fact that you saw leaves and fruit growing out of the flowers signifies that the knight shall yet beget a rich inheritance, which shall include true knights and men of honour who can most justly be accounted fruit; and the same will be true of the young woman. And if it had come about that so foul a sin had robbed her of her maidenhead, the wrath of God would have condemned them both to sudden death and the loss of body and soul. This you averted, and must therefore be deemed a good and faithful servant of Jesus Christ. And, as God is my help, if your allegiance had been to the world, so high an adventure would never have been yours, one that empowered you to deliver Our Lord's own children, the body from mortal suffering and the soul from the pains of hell. Now I have told you the meaning of the adventures that have fallen to your lot in the Quest of the Holy Grail.'

'That, Sir,' said Bors, 'is very true. You have explained them so admirably that I shall be a better man for the telling all my days.'

'Now I beg you,' said the other, 'to pray for me, for so help me God, I think He would listen more readily to you than He would to me.'

Bors kept silent at this, as one ashamed that the abbot should have so high an opinion of him.

When the two men had conversed at length Bors took his leave, commending the abbot to God. Having armed, he set out on his travels and rode until evening, when he put up with a widow who gave him of the best she had. Next morning saw him back in the saddle and pressing onward till he came to a fortress known as Castle Tubele, sited in a valley. He was quite close to the castle when he met a youth cantering off in the direction of a wood. Bors rode up to him and asked him if he knew anything worth telling.

'Yes, indeed,' replied the youth, 'there is to be a most splendid tournament tomorrow in front of this castle.'

'Between whom?' asked Bors.

'The Count of the Plain's men and those of the widow of the castle.'

This piece of news determined Bors to stay, for it was impossible he should not see one or more of the companions of the Quest there: such might come as would bring him word of his brother, perhaps his brother himself might be there, if he was in the vicinity and was strong and fit. So thinking, he turned towards a hermitage which stood at the forest's edge. When he got there he found his brother Lionel sitting all un-armed on the chapel steps; he had put up there so as to be present at the tournament which was to be fought next day in that very meadow. Bors' joy at the sight of his brother defied description. Jumping down from his horse, he cried:

'Sweet brother, when did you come here?'

Lionel knew Bors at these words, but he budged not an inch as he said to him:

'Bors, Bors, it was no thanks to you that I was not killed the other day, when the two knights were beating me and dragging me away, and you let me go without lifting a finger to help me, dashing off instead to the rescue of the maiden whom the knight was carrying off, and leaving me in peril of my life. There was never a brother guilty of such gross betrayal, and in requital of your crime I pledge you nothing but the death you have so well deserved. So be on your guard against me, for you had better know that death is all you can expect from me, wherever I first fall in with you when I am armed.'

His brother's anger cut Bors to the quick. He knelt down on the ground in front of Lionel with both hands joined in suppli-cation, and begged him in God's name to pardon him. It was out of the question, said the other, and swore that he would kill him, if God lent him strength and he could get the better of him. And loth to listen to him further, he went into the hermit's house where he had left his arms, and taking them he donned them hurriedly. This done, he fetched his horse, mounted and said to Bors:

'Defend yourself against me! For if God grants me aid and I can worst you, you shall have such justice as is rightly meted out to traitors and to knaves. For you are the most false-hearted scoundrel ever to spring from such a noble stock as was King Bors, who begot both me and you. So get on your horse, it will be more becoming, and if you don't I shall kill you where you stand; the shame will be mine and the hurt yours, but I care nothing for the shame, for I would sooner taste a little such and be reproached by many, than see you escape the punishment you deserve.'

When Bors saw there was nothing left him but to fight, he knew not what to do: for to fight one's brother was not a course in any circumstance to be commended However, for prudence' sake he resolved to mount his horse: but first he would approach him once again to see if he could win forgiveness. So he knelt down on the ground immediately in front of Lionel's horse and weeping piteously, he said to him:

'For the love of God, sweet brother, have pity on me! Forgive me this offence and kill me not; think rather of that great love which should be between you and me!'[53]

But Lionel was deaf to Bors' entreaties, being passionately set, under the enemy's goading, on shedding his brother's blood. And still Bors knelt before him, asking his forgiveness with humbly folded hands. When Lionel saw he would make no headway and that there was no getting Bors to rise, he sent his horse plunging forward, so that its chest struck the kneeling man so brutally that he was bowled over backwards and injured himself severely in his fall; and Lionel rode straight over his body, breaking it under his horse's hooves. The agony he felt caused Bors to faint, and he thought he must die unshriven. Lionel meanwhile, having rendered him incapable of getting to his feet, dismounted, bent upon beheading him.

When he had got off his horse and was about to wrench Bors' helm from his head, the hermit came running up: he was a very aged man and had overheard everything that had passed between them. When he saw Lionel preparing to cut off his brother's head, he threw himself down on the injured man and cried:

'Ah, noble knight, for God's sake take pity on yourself and on your brother! For in killing him you will kill your soul as well, and his death will be a most unspeakable loss, for he ranks among the noblest men and finest knights in the world.'

'As God is my help, Sir,' said Lionel, 'unless you get out of the way directly I will kill you, too, and his account will still be left to settle.'

'Truly,' said the good man, 'I had sooner you killed me than him, for my death will be by far the slighter loss: better, therefore, that I should die than he.'

So saying, he stretched his length on top of Bors, clasping him round the shoulders; and Lionel, at the sight, unsheathed his sword and struck the hermit such a vicious blow that he split the back of his skull and his body stiffened in the throes of death. This deed put no curb on his malevolence, instead he grabbed his brother by the helm and unlaced it prior to beheading him. He was making short work of the business when, by the will of Our Lord, Calogrenant, a knight of King Arthur's household and a companion of the Round Table, came riding by. The sight of the hermit lying dead both startled and amazed him. Then looking beyond, he saw where Lionel, having already loosed his brother's helm, was making ready to kill him, and he recognized Bors at once, a man he loved with all his heart. He jumped to the ground, seized Lionel by the shoulders and tugged so hard that he dragged him back, the while exclaiming:

'What is this Lionel? Are you out of your senses that you would kill your brother, who is one of the finest knights there are? By God, no man of any mettle would let you do this thing!'

'What?' demanded Lionel, 'have you a mind to help him? If you meddle in this any further I shall leave him and attend to you.'

The other stared at him in blank astonishment, and then said:

'What, Lionel? Do you really mean to kill him?'

'Kill him I will and shall, nor will I stay my hand for you or any other for he has done me such injury that he has more than earned his end.'

At that he rushed at him again and would have struck him on the head, but Calogrenant stepped in between and said that if he ventured to do Bors any further violence that day, he would have a battle on his hands.

At the sound of this challenge Lionel took up his shield and asked Calogrenant who he was. He named himself, and Lionel, on learning his identity, defied him and ran at him, brandishing his sword, and brought it down with all the force at his command. When the other saw that he was come to the fray, he ran to fetch his shield and he too drew his sword. He was a knight both skilled and strong, and defended himself most strenuously. The struggle was so long-drawn that Bors had raised himself to a sitting position, albeit so painfully that he did not think he would regain his strength in months without Our Lord's assistance. The sight of Calogrenant doing battle with his brother filled him with dismay; for if Calogrenant slew his brother before his eyes he would never know joy again, while if Lionel gave the death-blow, himself would bear the shame; for he was well aware that it was only for his sake that Calogrenant had started the fight at all. This dilemma caused him great distress; had he been able, he would readily have gone to part them, but he was in such pain as rendered defence and attack alike beyond his powers. Having watched for a while he saw that Calogrenant was getting the worst of the contest. For Lionel was a mighty warrior, fierce and resolute, and had breached his shield and helm and reduced him to a plight where death seemed certain: indeed he had lost such quantities of blood that it was a wonder he should still be standing. When he saw that he was overmatched the fear of death seized hold of him; he looked about him and seeing Bors sitting up, he cried out:

'Ah! Bors, come to my help and save me from this mortal peril in which I placed myself to rescue you, who were closer still to death than he whom you see before you. Truly, if I die now, it is you must bear the general reproach.'

'One thing is certain,' broke in Lionel, 'all this avails you nothing. You will pay for this intrusion with your life, there is none could prevent my killing both of you with this sword edge!'

Such talk was far from reassuring Bors, who knew full well that if Calogrenant were slain, his own life would be little worth; he struggled to his feet, went to his helm and settled it on his head. He was much grieved to see the hermit lying dead and implored Our Lord to have mercy on him, for never had one so good and brave died for so trifling an offence. Meanwhile Calogrenant was shouting to him:

'Ah! Bors, are you going to let me die? If it be your wish that I should die in this affair death will be sweet to me, for I could not die to save a better man.'

At that Lionel, with a blow of his sword, struck off his helm; and when he felt his head unshielded and saw there was no escape, Calogrenant cried out:

'Ah! gracious Lord Jesus Christ, who didst suffer me to serve Thee in spite of the shortcomings of my service, have mercy on my soul in such a wise that this anguish which my body shall endure in lieu of the good deeds and the almsgiving that I intended, may be accounted to me as a penance and be an easement to this soul of mine.'

As he was speaking these words, Lionel struck him with such force that he dashed him to the ground and his body stiffened in its last agony.

When he had slain Calogrenant, he would not stop at that, but rushed at his brother and dealt him a blow that sent him staggering. And Bors, in whom humility was rooted as of nature, begged him for the love of God to spare him this encounter:

'For should it happen, sweet brother, that one of us should kill the other, we both should be dead in sin.'

'May God never come to my aid,' swore Lionel, 'if I ever give you quarter, staying my hand, if I can get the better of you: for it is no thanks to you that I am alive today.'

Bors drew his sword then, weeping as he said:

'Gracious Lord Jesus Christ, may it not be set against me as a sin if I defend my life against my brother!'

So saying he raised his sword above his head, and as he was about to strike he heard a voice say to him:

'Bors, stay thy arm, for thou wouldst smite him dead!'

Immediately a ball of fire akin to a thunderbolt plummeted

down from heaven between the two, and from it there shot so prodigious and searing a flame that both their shields were burned and they themselves so terrified that each fell to the ground and lay there stunned and senseless. When at length they recovered consciousness they stared at one another; and they saw that the ground between was red from the fire that had scorched it. But when Bors saw that his brother was quite unharmed he held up his hands towards heaven and thanked God with all his heart.

Then he heard a voice which said to him:

'Bors, arise and leave this place. Do not keep company with thy brother any longer, but make thy way towards the sea, and tarry nowhere along thy road, for Perceval awaits thee there.'

When he heard these words Bors got to his knees, and stretching his hands aloft he said:

'Father of heaven, blessed be Thou when Thou dost deign to call me to Thy service!'

Then he went up to Lionel, who was still dazed, and said to him:

'Dear brother, you have done evil by this knight whom you have killed, and by this hermit. For God's sake do not leave this place until the bodies have been placed in the ground and every honour rendered them that is their due.'

'And you, what will you do? Will you wait here until they are interred?'

'No,' said Bors, 'I shall go to the sea where Perceval awaits me, as the heavenly voice gave me to understand.'

Then he left the spot and set out down the track that led towards the sea. He rode day in, day out, until he came to an abbey situated on the coast. He put up there that night; and when he had fallen asleep, there came a voice which said to him:

'Arise, Bors, and go straight down to the sea, where Perceval is waiting for thee by the shore!'

He jumped up at these words, making the sign of the cross on his brow and asking Our Lord to be his guide. He went to where he had left his arms and took them up and armed in haste. Then he sought out his horse and put on saddle and bridle. When he was equipped, not wanting to let the brethren know that he was leaving at such an hour, he wandered around looking for some place which would afford him passage, till he lit on a breach in the rear wall which left him room enough. So he went back to his horse and mounted, and then returning to the gap in the wall, he passed through.

So he slipped away from the abbey without a soul noticing his going; he rode on till he came to the sea and found a ship by the shore dressed overall in white samite. He dismounted and went on board, commending himself to Jesus Christ. He had no sooner entered the ship than he saw it drawing away from the shore, and the wind filled the sail and drove it along so swiftly that it seemed to fly over the waves. When he saw that he had missed embarking his horse he resigned himself to the loss. He looked around the ship, but could make nothing out, for the night was too dark and thick to permit of seeing much. So he went and leaned on the ship's side, and asked Our Lord to guide him where his soul's salvation was. His prayer done, he went to sleep until morning.

When he awoke he looked about the ship and saw a knight, fully armed with the exception of his helm, which lay in front of him, and whom Bors knew at second glance for Perceval of Wales. Without waiting, he ran to clasp him in his arms, hugging him for joy. The other was dumbfounded at being confronted with this knight, having no notion how he could have come aboard. He asked him who he was.

'What' said Bors, 'do you not know me?'

'No, I certainly do not. I marvel moreover how you got here, unless it were Our Lord Himself who brought you.'

Bors smiled at this and took off his helm. Perceval recognized him then; and it would be no easy matter to describe the joy that each showed to the other. Bors began to tell how he came to the ship, and by what guidance. Perceval recounted in turn the adventures that had befallen him on the rock he had been marooned on, there where the enemy appeared to him in the likeness of a woman and led him to the brink of mortal sin. Thus it was that the two friends found themselves together even as Our Lord had fore-ordained, and there they awaited whatever adventures He would choose to send them: meanwhile they tacked back and forth across the sea at the wind's pleasure, talking of many things and each encouraging the other. Perceval said that it wanted only Galahad now for his promise to be fulfilled, and he told Bors of the promise made to him. But now the tale leaves them and returns to the Good Knight.

[10]

The Miraculous Ship

Now the story relates that when the Good Knight left Perceval, after rescuing him from the twenty knights who had set upon him, he took the wide road that runs through the Waste Forest, and spent many days roving now this way, now that at the beck of chance. He met there with many adventures, which he brought to an end, and which the story passes over, forasmuch as it would be too great a task to relate them one by one. When the Good Knight had visited every corner of the kingdom of Logres from which report of some adventure reached his ears, he finally left the country and headed towards the sea, such being his inclination. His road as it happened led him past a castle where a great tournament was under way. But those without had already striven with such effect that the defenders of the castle were in full flight, for the others far outnumbered and outmatched them.

When Galahad saw that those within were in such straits and were being hewn down before the castle gate, he turned their way and thought he would go to their aid. He lowered his lance and spurred his horse, and struck the first knight he met so hard that he sent him hurtling to the ground, and his own lance flew to pieces. He drew his sword then, like a man practised in its use, and plunging in where he saw the battle thickest, he started felling knights and horses and performed such stupendous feats of arms that all who saw him held him for a champion. Sir Gawain had come to the tournament together with Hector, and they were helping those without; but as soon as they caught sight of the white shield with its red cross, the one said to the other:

'Look, there goes the Good Knight! None but a fool will wait for him, for there is no armour proof against his sword.'

As they were speaking Galahad, as chance would have it, came spurring towards Sir Gawain, and dealt him a blow so fierce it split his helm and the steel coif beneath. Sir Gawain pitched out of the saddle, convinced the blow was mortal, and Galahad, unable to arrest his stroke, caught the horse in front of the saddle bow and severed neck from shoulders, dropping it dead on top of its rider.[54]

When Hector saw Sir Gawain on the ground he beat a retreat, both because he saw that it would not be sensible to wait for a man who could deliver such blows, and because he was bound to love and cherish him as his nephew. Galahad meanwhile galloped up and down and worked such wonders in no time at all that those within, but now discomfited, took heart again, and hacked and hewed without a pause till the others were overwhelmed by force of arms and fled to save their lives. Galahad pursued them for some distance, and when he saw that they were gone for good, he slipped away so discreetly that none could tell which way he had gone;[55] at the same time he was held by both sides to have won the palm and honour of the tournament. Sir Gawain, who was in such pain from the blow dealt him by Galahad that he despaired of coming through alive, said to Hector, whom he saw standing over him:

'Upon my oath, now are the words proved true that were spoken to me the other day, on the feast of Pentecost, about the stone and the sword to which I had set my hand: that it should cut me so sorely before the year was out, that not for a castle would I have tasted its bite. And upon my soul, the knight used that same sword to strike me down. Thus I can truly say that the thing has come to pass just as I was forewarned.'

'Sir,' asked Hector, 'has the knight wounded you so gravely then?'

'He has indeed, so gravely that my life will be endangered, unless God intervene.'

'Then what can we do?' asked Hector. 'As I see it now our quest is at an end, since you have suffered such an injury.'

'Sir,' replied Sir Gawain, 'yours is by no means at an end, but only mine, till it please God that I should follow you.'

While they exchanged these words the knights of the castle were mustering close by, and many of them were distressed at recognizing Sir Gawain and learning how badly he was wounded: for beyond a doubt he enjoyed a more widespread popularity than any man alive. So they lifted him up and carried him into the castle and laid him in a quiet room, away from noise and bustle. Then they sent for a physician, and after getting him to examine the wound they asked him if Sir Gawain would live. This leech assured them he would have Sir Gawain within a month so hale and hearty that he would be fit to ride and carry arms. The others promised him that if he did as much they would give him silver enough to keep him a rich man for the rest of his days. He told them they might depend on it, for he would be as good as his word. So it was that Sir Gawain stayed at the castle, and with him Hector, who stead-fastly refused to leave until his companion should be healed.

On quitting the tournament the Good Knight, riding as fortune shaped his course, covered so much ground that dusk found him some two leagues from Corbenic. It happened that he was passing a hermitage as it grew dark, and seeing that night was falling he dismounted and stood calling at the door until the hermit came and opened to him. This good man, when he saw his guest was a wandering knight, wished him most welcome, and saw to the stabling of the horse and the unarming of its rider. When the latter had been divested, the hermit had him served with whatever alms he had himself re-ceived of God, and Galahad accepted with the gratitude of one who had not eaten all that day. Then, having finished his meal, he stretched out on a pile of grass and fell asleep.

When the two men had gone to rest, a young woman came and knocked on the door, calling persistently for Galahad, till the good man went to the door and asked who it was that sought admittance at such an hour.

'Sir Ulfin,' she answered, 'it is a maiden who wishes to speak with the knight who is here, for I have urgent business with him.'

The hermit woke Galahad and said to him:

'Sir Knight, there is a young woman outside who is anxious to speak with you, and her affair would seem to be most pressing.'

Galahad rose at once, and going to her, he asked her what she wanted.

'Galahad,' she replied, 'I want you to arm and mount your horse and follow me. And I declare to you that I will show you the highest adventure that ever knight was witness to.'

Galahad, at these tidings, went and armed himself, and saddling his horse, he mounted and commended the hermit to God. Then he said to the maiden:

'Now you may go where you wish: for I will follow you wheresoever you lead.'

At that she set off at the fastest gallop she could urge from her palfrey and he kept close on her heels. They were still riding when dawn began to break, and the sky was fully light when they entered a forest known as the forest of Celibe, which stretched as far as the sea. All day they pressed on down the high road, without even a pause to eat or drink.

It was just past the hour of vespers when they came to a castle sited in a valley and superbly furnished against attack, girt with running water and well-built walls, high and massive, and deep, steep-sided ditches. The maiden was still riding in front when she entered the castle, and Galahad followed after. When the inmates saw her come, they cried out:

'Welcome, Madam!'

And they received her with all the marks of joy due to their mistress, as in fact she was. She bade them give the knight a royal welcome, for no better man had ever carried arms. They ran to help him down, unarming him at once; and he turned to the young woman and said:

'Madam, are we to stay here for the remainder of this day?'

'No,' she answered, 'directly we have eaten and slept a little we shall be off again.'

They sat down then to dine, and after went to rest. As soon as the first sleep was upon her, the maiden called to Galahad, saying:

'Up, Sir, arise!'

Galahad rose and her people brought candles and torches to light him as he armed. He mounted his horse, and the maiden took a casket of the most exquisite workmanship, which she set in front of her when she too was mounted. Then they rode out of the castle and set off at a great pace, riding that night both fast and far until they arrived at the sea. When they came to the shore they found the ship which carried Bors and Perceval; the two companions were standing, wide awake, at the ship's side and shouted to Galahad when he was still afar off, crying:

'Welcome, Sir! We have waited for you so long that at last you are come to us, thanks be to God! Come up here, for nothing remains but to seek the high adventure which God has prepared for us.'

When Galahad heard their shout, he asked them who they were and why they said they had waited for him so long; and he asked the maiden whether she would dismount.

'Yes, Sir, I shall. And turn your horse loose here, as I am leaving mine.'

So he dismounted promptly and unsaddled his horse and the maiden's palfrey too. Then he made the sign of the cross on his forehead and commending himself to Our Lord he stepped aboard the ship, while the maiden followed behind him. The two companions could not have given them a more jubilant welcome. A strong wind got up almost at once, and drove the ship swiftly out to sea, till soon they had made such headway as to have lost all sight of land, whether near or far. By this time it was light, and they knew one another; and all three wept for the joy they felt at their coming together again.

Bors took off his helm then, and Galahad laid aside both helm and sword, but kept on his shirt of mail. And when he beheld the beauty of the ship, as well without as within, he asked the two companions if they knew where so fair a craft had come from. Bors said that he had no idea, while Perceval related what he knew, telling Galahad just what had happened to him on the rock, and how the holy man with the air of a priest had bidden him embark.

'And indeed he told me it would not be long before I had you as companions; but of this maid he spoke no word at all.'

'In faith,' said Galahad, 'to the best of my knowledge I should never have come to this place if she had not brought me here.

So it can be said that my coming was more her doing than my own. For I never passed this road before, and never did I think to hear of you, my friends, in so strange a place as this.'

At this they all began to laugh.

Then each began to relate his adventures to the other, till at length Bors said to Galahad:

'Sir, if only my lord Lancelot, your father, were with us now, it seems to me that we should want for nothing.'

Galahad answered that it could not be, since it was not God's will it should be so.

The hour of none came round and found them talking still; by then they must have been some way from the kingdom of Logres, for the ship had sped all night and all day long with sail spread wide Then, slipping between two rocks, they came to a lonely islet, so tucked away as to fill the mind with wonder, and found themselves in what was undoubtedly a hidden creek. When they hove to they saw ahead, beyond a rocky outcrop, another ship which could only be reached on foot.

'Good Sirs,' said the maiden, 'in that ship yonder is the adventure to be found for which Our Lord has gathered you together; you must therefore leave this vessel and board the other.'

They expressed their readiness, and jumping ashore, they helped the maiden over the side; then they moored their boat lest the tide should carry it out to sea. Once they were all on the rocks they made their way in single file to where they saw the ship. On their approach they found it more magnificent by far than the one that they had left; but they were most amazed at seeing no soul on board. They drew nearer in the hope of making some discovery, and looking at the ship's side they saw an inscription written in Chaldean which bore a dire and alarming message to all intending to embark; and it ran thus:

GIVE EAR, O MAN WHO WOULDST SET FOOT IN ME: WHO-
SOEVER THOU ART, TAKE HEED THAT THOU BE FULL OF
FAITH, FOR I AM FAITH ITSELF. THEREFORE LOOK TO IT,
ERE THOU ENTEREST HERE, THAT THOU BE WITHOUT
SPOT, FOR I AM NAUGHT BUT FAITH AND TRUE BELIEF, AND

AS SOON AS THOU DOST LAPSE FROM FAITH, MYSELF
SHALL CAST THEE DOWN IN SUCH A WAY THAT THOU
SHALT FIND IN ME NOR HELP NOR FOOTING, BUT I SHALL
FAIL THEE WHOLLY, WHERESOEVER THOU ART CON-
VICTED OF UNBELIEF, AND HOWEVER SLIGHT THE
MEASURE OF THY DEFAULT.[56]

When they had taken stock of the inscription they looked at
one another. And then the maiden said to Perceval:

'Do you know who I am?'

'Indeed I do not; I never saw you to my knowledge.'

'Let me then tell you that I am your sister, the daughter of
King Pellehen. Do you know why I am making myself known
to you? In order that you should give greater credence to what
I am about to say. Firstly, I warn you, as the person I hold most
dear, on no account to step aboard this ship if you have not
perfect faith in Jesus Christ, for in so doing you would bring
about your death forthwith. For the ship is so sublime a thing
that none who bears the taint of vice can sojourn there secure.'

Hearing this Perceval looked at her anew and having observed
her closely he knew her for his sister. Then he embraced her
joyfully and said to her:

'In truth, fair sister, I will go aboard; and shall I tell you
why? so that, were I to prove no true believer, then might I
die a traitor's death, and if I am strong in faith and such as a
knight should be, I may be saved.'

'Then enter in safety,' she replied, 'and may Our Lord be
your defence and safeguard.'

While she was speaking, Galahad, who was standing in
front, raised his hand to bless himself and stepped aboard.
Standing in the ship he began to look around, and the maiden
followed him in, making the sign of the cross as she entered.
Seeing this the other two hesitated no longer, but went on
board as well. When they had looked the ship carefully up
and down they opined that nowhere on land or sea could there
be a vessel to compare in beauty or splendour with what now
met their gaze. After exploring fore and aft they turned their
attention amidships, where they saw a most costly fabric spread
to form a canopy, and curtaining a wide and sumptuous bed.

Galahad went to the baldachin and lifted it to look beneath, and there his eyes lit on the most magnificent bed he had ever seen, both in its size and its adornment. At its head was a glorious golden crown, while a sword of burnished beauty lay across its foot, with more than a handsbreadth of blade drawn clear of the scabbard.

This sword was very curiously fashioned: for the pommel was formed of a stone combining all the colours found on earth; and, for another and greater singularity, each colour had its own specific virtue. The tale states furthermore that two ribs composed the hilt, and each of these was taken from a most unusual beast. The first belonged to a species of serpent more often found in Caledonia than elsewhere; this snake is called the papalust, and it has this special property, that if a man has hold of one of its ribs or any other bone of it, it renders him insensible to heat. The second came from a fish, which is not unduly big and which lives in the river Euphrates and no other. This fish is known as the ortenax, and its ribs have this peculiarity, that if any man takes one, for as long as he holds it in his hand he has no recollection of any joy or sorrow he has known, but only of the purpose for which he took it up. Directly he puts it down again he starts to think once more as he was wont, after the fashion of a normal man.[57] Such were the attributes of the two ribs which were set in the sword hilt, and covered with the richest of red cloths, which in turn was embroidered all over with letters spelling this message:

I AM A MARVEL TO BEHOLD AND APPREHEND. FOR NONE WAS EVER ABLE TO GRIP ME, HOWEVER BIG HIS HAND, NOR EVER SHALL, SAVE ONE ALONE; AND HE SHALL PASS IN EXCELLENCE ALL WHO PRECEDED AND SHALL FOLLOW HIM.

So said the inscription on the hilt, and the knights, directly they had read it (for they were well-lettered men), gazed at each other and said:

'Of a truth, there are wonders to be witnessed here.'

'In God's name,' said Perceval. 'I will see if I can grip the sword.'

He stretched out his hand, but could not encircle the hilt.

'Upon my faith,' he exclaimed, 'this has convinced me that the letters spoke the truth.'

Then Bors set hand to it, but his efforts too were unavailing. Seeing this, the other two addressed themselves to Galahad:

'Sir, you try your luck with the sword. For our failure is the gage of your success in this adventure.'

But Galahad said he would make no such attempt, for he was standing in presence of a marvel that far transcended any he had witnessed. Next he looked at the blade of which a section, as you have heard, emerged from the scabbard, and he noticed other letters, red as blood, which said:

LET NONE PRESUME TO DRAW ME FROM THE SCABBARD, UNLESS HE CAN OUTDO AND OUTDARE EVERY OTHER. HE WHO IN ANY OTHER CIRCUMSTANCE UNSHEATHES ME SHOULD KNOW HE IS FOREDOOMED TO INJURY OR DEATH. THE TRUTH OF THIS REQUIRES NO FURTHER PROVING.

When Galahad had read these words, he said:

'Upon my faith, I wished to draw this sword, but since the caution is so ominous I shall not touch it.'

Perceval and Bors were of a like opinion.

'Know, good Sirs,' said the maiden then, 'that all are forbidden to draw it, save only one; and I will tell you something touching it that happened not long since.

'It is the truth,' she went on, 'that this ship arrived in the kingdom of Logres at a time when a bloody war was raging between King Lambar, the father of that king who is known as the Maimed King, and King Varlan, who had been a pagan all his life, but had lately been baptized, and so was considered one of the finest men alive. It happened one day that the armies of the two kings met upon the shore where the ship was lying, and the tide of battle went against King Varlan. When he saw himself defeated and his soldiers slain he trembled for his life, and running to this ship, which was lying close inshore, he jumped aboard. Finding this sword, he drew it from the scabbard and went ashore again. There he met King Lambar, in all of Christendom the man who had the staunchest faith and trust in Jesus Christ and in whose soul Our Lord abode most inwardly. At the sight of his foe, King Varlan raised the sword and brought it crashing down on the other's helm, splitting man and horse clean through. This was the first blow struck with this sword in the kingdom of Logres. It unleashed such wrack and ruin on both the countries that never again did the land requite the ploughman's toil, for no corn sprouted there, nor any other crop, nor did the trees bear fruit, and there was a dearth of fish in pond and stream. This is why the land of these two kingdoms was called the Waste Land, seeing that it had been laid to waste by this terrible blow.

'When King Varlan found the sword so keen, he thought he would go back to fetch the scabbard. So, returning to the ship, he stepped inside and slid the blade back into the sheath; no sooner had he done so than he fell down dead beside the bed. Thus was it proved that none might draw this sword without being maimed or killed. What is more, the king's body lay in front of the bed until a maid removed it, for of all the bold men round about, not one dared step aboard this ship on account of the warning painted on the hull.'[58]

'Upon my honour,' said Galahad, 'that was a most remarkable adventure; and I can well believe it happened thus, for I have no doubt this sword has properties more strange and wonderful than any other.'

So saying, he advanced to draw it.

'Stay, Galahad!' exclaimed the maiden. 'Forbear yet a little longer, till we have scrutinized the marvels to be found upon it.'

He drew back his hand at once, and they turned their attention to the scabbard, but were unable to think what it could be made of, unless it were snakeskin. They noticed, however, that it was red as a bright red rose, and was inscribed with letters, gold and blue. But when they came to look at the belt their astonishment redoubled, for what they saw was most ill-suited to the splendour of the weapon: it was made, of all cheap and common stuffs, of hempen tow, and so flimsy was its appearance that it looked to the knights as if it could not support the sword an hour without breaking. The letters on the scabbard read:

HE WHO WEARS ME SHALL DO GREATER DEEDS THAN ANY

OTHER AND NEED FEAR NO PERIL IF HE KEEP HIMSELF
THE WHILE AS SPOTLESS AS HE OUGHT. FOR I MUST NOT
ENTER ANY PLACE WHERE SIN OR VICE ARE FOUND. SHOULD
I BE TAKEN INTO ANY SUCH THE WEARER SHALL BE THE FIRST
TO RUE HIS ACT. BUT IF HE KEEP ME CLEANLY HE SHALL BE
SAFE WHEREVER HE SHALL GO FOR NO BODILY HURT CAN
COME TO HIM AT WHOSE SIDE I SHALL HANG, WHILE HE IS
GIRDED WITH THE BELT THAT SHALL SUPPORT ME. LET
NONE BE SO BOLD AS TO REMOVE THIS PRESENT BELT ON
ANY GROUNDS: THIS IS NOT GRANTED ANY MAN NOW LIVING
OR TO COME. IT MUST NOT BE UNFASTENED SAVE BY A
WOMAN'S HAND, AND SHE THE DAUGHTER OF A KING AND
QUEEN. SHE SHALL EXCHANGE IT FOR ANOTHER, FASHIONED
FROM THAT THING ABOUT HER PERSON THAT IS MOST
PRECIOUS TO HER, WHICH SHE SHALL PUT IN THIS ONE'S
STEAD. IT IS ESSENTIAL THAT THIS MAIDEN BE THROUGH-
OUT HER LIFE A VIRGIN BOTH IN DEED AND IN DESIRE. AND
IF IT HAPPEN THAT SHE LOSE HER MAIDENHOOD, SHE MAY
BE SURE THAT SHE WILL DIE THE BASEST DEATH THAT CAN
BE A WOMAN'S LOT. THIS MAID SHALL CALL THE SWORD BY
ITS TRUE NAME, AND ME BY MINE, AND NEVER TILL THAT
DAY SHALL THERE BE FOUND A MAN TO NAME US BY OUR
PROPER NAMES.

When the knights finished reading the inscription they broke
into laughter, exclaiming that what they saw and heard was
marvellous indeed.

'Sir,' said Perceval, 'turn the sword over, and see what there is
on the other side.'

Galahad promptly did so, and when he had turned it over,
they saw that the underside was red as blood and bore the
following message:

HE THAT SHALL PRIZE ME MOST SHALL FIND ME WORTHIER
OF REPROACH IN TIME OF NEED THAN HE COULD DREAM.
AND TO HIM TO WHOM I SHOULD BE KINDEST I SHALL SHOW
MYSELF MOST CRUEL. THIS WILL OCCUR BUT ONCE, FOR SO
IT IS ORDAINED.

Such were the words inscribed on the reverse, and the reading of them left the knights more baffled than before.

'In God's name,' said Perceval to Galahad, 'I intended urging you to take this sword. But since the letters state that it will fail the wearer in his greatest need and show itself cruel where it should be kind, I would not advise your taking it: it might at one stroke expose you to disaster, which would be a thousand pities.'

The maiden, overhearing this, turned to Perceval, saying:

'Sweet brother, these two predictions have already been fulfilled, and I will tell you when it was and who the persons were; for which reason none should be afraid to take this sword, provided he be worthy of it.

'Long ago, a good forty years after the Passion of Jesus Christ, it came to pass that Nascien, the brother-in-law of King Mordrain, was at Our Lord's command rapt in a cloud and carried some two weeks' journey from his country to an island known as the Turning Isle, far out towards the Kingdom of the West. On coming there, he found this ship we are standing in hoveto in a little creek. When he had gone on board and come upon this bed, with the sword lying on it, just as it is today, he stood gazing at it and was filled with a desperate longing to have it for his own. He had not, however, the temerity to draw it, so the ambition and desire to own it burned within him. He spent eight days in the ship and took scant meat or drink the while. Then it fell on the ninth day that a strange and mighty wind swooped down on him and drove him away from the Turning Isle and thence to a western island, far removed. He sailed straight up to a landing point and stepped ashore to be met by a huge giant, the most monstrous in the world, who shouted out to him that he was a dead man. Nascien feared for his life when he saw this ogre bearing down on him. He looked around him, but seeing nothing with which he might defend himself he ran to the sword, like a man distrained by terror and the fear of death, and drew it from the scabbard. When he looked on the naked steel, he prized the sword beyond all that earth could offer. He started then to brandish it aloft, but it came to pass at its first circling that the blade snapped in half, and Nascien cried then that the thing he had most prized in all the world was made the object of his bitterest reproach, and rightly so, since it had failed him in his time of need.

'Then he replaced the pieces of the sword upon the bed, and, leaping out of the ship, he ran to fight the giant, whom he slew, and after went back to the ship again. When a chance wind had swelled the sail he drifted at random over the sea, till he met another ship carrying King Mordrain, who had been fiercely attacked and harried by the enemy upon the rocks of Port Perilous. When the two men caught sight of one another they met with all the joy that marks such love as theirs. Each asked the other how he fared and what adventures had befallen him, till Nascien said at last:

' "Sir, I know not what you have to relate to me about the world's adventures. But since you saw me last I assure you that I have met with one of the strangest adventures earth can boast or, to my knowledge, any man encountered."

'He proceeded to tell King Mordrain of his fortunes with the magnificent sword, and how it had broken at the critical time, when he had thought to kill the giant with it.

' "Upon my faith," replied the other, "it is a wondrous tale you are telling me. What did you do with this sword?"

' "Sir," said Nascien, "I put it back where I had found it. You can see it if you like, it lies in here."

'At that King Mordrain left his ship and clambered aboard the other. When he stood in front of the bed and saw the broken pieces of the sword he prized it above anything that he had ever set eyes on. He said, too, that the fracture had not occurred through any flaw or defect in the sword, but because of some hidden meaning or some sin of Nascien's. Thereupon he took the two sections of the sword and fitted them back together; and as soon as the edges of the metal touched, the sword knitted again as easily as it had broken. At this sight King Mordrain gave a sudden smile and said:

' "Before God, how wonderful are the powers of Jesus Christ who joins and parts with greater ease than one would think it possible!"

'Then he sheathed the sword and laid it where you see it now. And straightway they heard a voice which said to them:

' "Go out of this ship and board the other, for if you fall into sin and are found here in that state, you will not escape un-scathed."

'They did as they were bid without delay, and as Nascien was passing from one ship to the next a flying sword entered his shoulder with an impetus that flung him backwards into the ship, and he cried out as he fell:

' "Ah, God, I am sorely wounded!"

'At that moment he heard a voice say to him:

' "This is for the wrong thou didst in drawing the sword: thou shouldst not have touched it, for thou wert unworthy. Another time take greater care not to offend thy Maker."

'So it was that the prophecy comprised in the words: HE THAT SHALL PRIZE ME MOST SHALL FIND ME WORTHIEST OF REPROACH IN TIME OF NEED, fulfilled itself in the manner I have described. For Nascien was the man who prized this sword most highly, and it failed him as I have told you in the hour of his greatest need.'

'In God's name,' said Galahad, 'you have given us a full account of this matter. Tell us now how the other prediction came to be realized.'

'Gladly,' replied the maiden, and continued:

'For as long as he was able to ride, King Parlan, who is known as the Maimed King, was a man who greatly furthered the Christian cause; there was none paid greater honour to the poor nor was there his equal in all Christendom for virtuous and upright living. One day, however, as he was hunting in one of his forests that stretched as far as the sea, he strayed so far that he lost hounds and huntsmen and all his knights save one, who was close kinsman to him. When he realized that he had cut adrift from all his retinue, he did not know what course to take; for he saw that he had pushed too deep into the forest to find his own way out, being unfamiliar with its paths. So, accompanied by his knight, he set off down a track, pressing ever onward till he came out on the coast that faces Ireland. There he found this ship that we are in today, and riding up to it he noticed on the side the same inscription that you saw your-selves. He felt no apprehension as he read it, for with every virtue that could grace an earthly knight, he was not sensible of having sinned against Our Lord. He boarded the ship alone, for the knight who was with him had not the audacity to enter. When he had found this sword he unsheathed it by as much as you can see (for nothing of the blade was visible before), and would have lost no time in baring the remainder, had he not been transfixed at that instant by a flying lance which pierced him through the thighs, inflicting a wound that never healed but left him maimed, as to this day he is and shall remain until you come to him. Thus was he crippled by his presumptuous gesture; and it is because of the vengeance then exacted that it was said the sword proved cruel to him it should have shown itself most kind to: for there was no better man or knight than was King Parlan in his day.' [59]

'In God's name, damsel,' said the three companions, 'you have said enough to convince us that the lettering ought not to discourage anyone from laying hand on this sword.'

Next they examined the bed and saw that it was made of timber hewn from the living tree. In the centre of the side that faced them there was a post let into the wooden beam that extended the length of the bed, in such a way that it was perpendicular to the frame. And on the far side in the other truss there was another post, exactly opposite the first. These posts were separated by the width of the bed, and on them lay a slender cross-piece, squared and bolted to the two uprights. The post on the nearer side was whiter than fallen snow; while the further one was as red as drops of bright red blood; and the one which joined them overhead was emerald green. Of these three hues were the three posts over the bed; and it is the undoubted truth that these were natural colours, not painted on, for they owed naught to any human hand. And forasmuch as many might hear of it who would take it for a lie if they were not informed how such a thing could be, the tale now turns aside a while from the mainstream of its subject to explain the origin of the three posts which were of those three different hues.

The Legend of the Tree of Life

HERE the tale of the Holy Grail relates that when it came to pass that sinful Eve, the first woman, had taken counsel of the mortal enemy, the devil (who from that day on set about ensnaring the human race by guile), and when he had goaded her into committing mortal sin, even the sin of concupiscence, through which he himself had been cast out of Paradise and hurled down from heaven's great glory, he worked upon her criminal desire until he made her pluck the deadly fruit from the tree, breaking off as she did so a twig of the tree itself, as it often happens that the twig adheres to the gathered fruit. As soon as she had taken it to her husband, Adam, to whom she recommended and urged its eating, he took hold of it in such a way as to tear the fruit from the branch, and ate it to our hurt and his, and to his dire perdition and our own. When he had torn it from the stem as you have heard, this branch by chance stayed in the woman's hand, as one may sometimes hold an object in one's hand without remarking it. Directly they had eaten of the deadly fruit, which must rightly be termed deadly since death first came thereby to these two and to others afterwards, their former attributes were changed and they saw that they were flesh and naked, where before they had been spiritual beings, for all they had had bodies. Notwithstanding this, the story does not affirm that they were wholly spiritual; for a thing that is formed of such base stuff as clay cannot be clean in essence. But they resembled spiritual beings in that they were created to live for ever, if it so happened that they kept from sin. When, then, their eyes were opened, they knew that they were naked and knew, too, the shameful members and felt ashamed in one another's sight: thus far did they already feel the consequences of their fault. Then each one covered the basest parts of his person with his hands. Eve however, was still clutching the branch in her hand, nor did she ever let it drop, either then or later.

When He who knows all thoughts and plumbs the human heart* knew that they had committed this sin He called to Adam first. And it was right that he should be held more culpable than his wife, for she was of a frailer nature, having been fashioned from the rib of man; and it was right that she should obey him, but not he her; and for this reason God called Adam first. And when He had spoken those harsh words to him: 'In the sweat of thy brow shalt thou eat bread,' He did not wish the woman to get off scot free, nor escape her share of the punishment where she had been a partner in the fault, so He said to her: 'In pain and sorrow shalt thou bring forth children. Thereupon He drove them both from Paradise, which the Scriptures call the garden of delight. When they stood without, Eve still had hold of the little branch, but never marked its presence in her hand. But when, on taking stock of herself, she saw the twig, it caught her eye because it was still as fresh and green as if it had just been picked. She knew that the tree from which it had been broken was the cause of her exile and her misery. So she said then that, in remembrance of the cruel loss she had suffered through that tree, she would keep the branch for as long as she could, where it would often be before her eyes to remind her of her great misfortune.

Then Eve bethought herself that she had neither casket nor any other box in which to house it, for no such things as yet existed. So she thrust it into the ground, so that it stood erect, saying that in this way it would often catch her eye. And the branch that had been stuck in the earth, by the will of Him whom all created things obey, quickened and took root in the soil and grew.

This branch which the first sinner brought with her out of Paradise was charged with meaning. In that she held it in her hand it betokened a great happiness, as though she were speaking to her heirs that were to follow her (for she was still a maid), and saying to them through the medium of this twig:

'Be not dismayed if we are banished from our inheritance: it is not lost to us eternally; see here a sign of our return hereafter.'

* Cf. Psalm 7, 9, and Revelations 2, 23.

As for him who might ask of the book why it was not the man rather than the woman who carried the branch out of Paradise, since he is her superior, the book makes answer that the bearing of the branch pertained not to the man but to the woman. For in that the woman bore it, it signified that through a woman life was lost, and through a woman life would be regained, meaning that through the Virgin Mary the inheritance that had just then been lost should one day be recovered.

With that the tale returns to the twig that was stuck in the earth and tells how it grew and shot up apace, till within a little lapse of time it had become a tree. When it had grown into a tall, shade-giving tree, its trunk and boughs and leaves were all as white as snow. This was the mark of virginity; for virginity is a virtue whereby the body is kept clean and the soul white. And the tree being white in all its parts signified that she who had planted it was still a virgin at the hour of its planting: for at the time when Adam and Eve were cast forth from Paradise they were still virgins, unspotted by the shame of lust. It must furthermore be understood that virginity and maidenhood are nowise identical, indeed there is a deep distinction to be drawn between them. Maidenhood is not to be equated with virginity for reasons I will show. The former is a virtue common to those of either sex who have not known the contact born of carnal commerce. But virginity is something infinitely higher and more worth: for none, whether man or woman, can possess it who has inclined in will to carnal intercourse. Such virginity did Eve still have when she was driven out of Paradise and the delights it held; nor had she lost this virtue at the time of the branch's planting. But after, God commanded Adam that he know his wife, which is to say that he lie with her carnally, as nature requires that a man lie with his wife and a woman with her lord. So Eve lost her virginity, and from then on the two lived as one flesh.

A long time had elapsed since Adam, as you have heard, first knew his wife, when it happened that the two of them were sitting beneath this tree. Adam looked up at it, and started to bewail his sorrows and his exile. At that they both began to weep most bitterly, each for the other. Then Eve said that it was no wonder if the spot reminded them of grief and suffering, for such was the very substance of the tree, and none, however happy he might be, could sit beneath it but went sad away; and it was only right they were unhappy, since this was the Tree of Death. She had no sooner said this than a voice was heard, saying to them:

'Ah! poor wretches, why do you thus pronounce its nature to be death, persuading one another? Be not governed in your thinking by despair, but comfort one another, for the tree has more of life in it than death.'

Thus spoke the voice to the unhappy pair; and they were greatly cheered, and called it ever after the Tree of Life; and because of the great joy it had brought them, they planted many slips, each struck from the first. For as soon as they broke off a branch and stuck it in the ground, it took at once and rooted freely, always retaining the colour of the parent tree.

Meanwhile the original tree continued to grow in size and beauty. Adam and Eve were readier than before to sit beneath it and often did so, till it happened one day – a Friday as the true story states – when they had been sitting there some time, that they heard a voice speak to them and command them to unite as man and wife. The shame that filled them both was so intense, that the thought of seeing one another openly in the performing of so base an act was unbearable, to the man no less than the woman. And yet they did not know how they should dare to disobey Our Lord's command, still smarting as they were under the punishment that followed the first fault. They had begun to look at one another in extreme embarrassment, when Our Lord, seeing their shame, took pity on them. But since His order could not brook transgression, it being His will that through this couple the human race should be established to the end of restoring the tenth legion of angels cast down from heaven for their pride, He intervened to mitigate their shame and put between them so thick a pall of darkness as to hide each from each. They for their part wondered, all amazed, how they came to be plunged so suddenly in darkness. They called to one another and stretched out groping hands. And because all things must come to pass according to Our Lord's command, it had to be that these two came together, even as the Father of mankind had bidden them. And when they had lain together, a new seed had been sown, by which their sin was somewhat remedied; for Adam had begotten, and his wife conceived, Abel the just, the first to give satisfaction to his Maker by rendering up to Him his rightful portion.

Thus was Abel the just begotten under the Tree of Life upon a Friday, just as you have heard. Afterwards the darkness lifted and the couple saw each other as before, and were filled with joy at the realization that Our Lord had acted thus to hide their shame. Another miracle stemmed from this event, for the tree which had been white till then in all its parts, became forthwith as green as the grass of the field; and all the saplings which were struck from it after this union grew green in wood and leaf and bark.

So it was that the tree passed from white to green; but those that had sprung from it retained their original hue, and the green was never seen in any other. The Tree of Life, however, flaunted its emerald tints from bole to crown, and from that time on it began to carry flowers and fruit, which it had never done before. The loss of its whiteness and its dressing itself in green signified that virginity had gone from her who planted it, and the green that it put on, and the flowers and fruit it bore, were symbols of the seed that had been sown beneath it, the life that was to be ever green in Jesus Christ, quickened, that is to say, by pious thoughts and love for Him who made it. Now the flower signified that the creature there begotten was to be chaste and clean and pure in body; and lastly the fruit betokened that he should be active in good works and hold a mirror up to goodness and religion in all he was and did.

The Tree stayed green for many years, and just as green were all those struck from it from the day of Abel's begetting until he was a grown man, and the love and good-will that he bore his Maker led him to offer up to Him the tithes and first-fruits of the finest things he had. But Cain, his brother, far from doing likewise, took the scurviest and worst part of his harvest to offer to his Maker. In result Our Lord bestowed such graces on the one who paid his tithes, that when Abel had climbed the hill where he was in the habit of burning his offerings, as Our Lord had commanded him, the smoke rose up in a column to heaven. Not so the smoke from the offerings of his brother Cain: it spread out over the fields, black and foul and rank, while the smoke from Abel's sacrifice was white and sweet to the nostrils. When Cain saw that his brother was more blessed in his sacrifice than he, and that it was more acceptable in God's sight than was his own, he grew embittered and conceived a virulent hatred of Abel which increased till it passed all measure.* He began then to ponder how he could be revenged on him, and resolved at last to kill him; for there was no other way he could see of gaining satisfaction.

Cain harboured this hatred in his heart over a long period, never betraying in look or manner any sign which might bring it to the notice of his brother, who had no inkling of evil. He kept his enmity concealed until a day when Abel had gone to a pasture somewhat remote from his father's manor, which was at some little distance from the Tree where, in fact, Abel was keeping watch over his sheep. The day was warm and Abel, finding the blazing sun too hot for comfort, went and sat down beneath the Tree. Soon feeling sleepy, he stretched out in its shade and began to doze. His brother, who had long been hatching his treachery, had observed and trailed him till such time as he saw him settle to rest under the Tree. He followed on his heels meaning to kill him suddenly before the other could realize what was happening. But Abel heard him coming; he looked around, and seeing it was his brother whom he sincerely loved, he rose to greet him, saying:

'Welcome, sweet brother.'

Cain saluted him in turn and made him sit down again; then flashing out a curved knife he was holding, he stabbed him in the heart.

Thus it was that Abel met his death at the hand of his false brother in the very spot where he had been conceived. And just as he was conceived on a Friday, as the true witness positively states, the same authority affirms it was on a Friday that he met his death. And the death that Abel met through treachery, at the time when there were but three men on earth, was a symbol of Christ's death upon the Cross, for Abel signified Our Lord, and Cain prefigured Judas, who brought about His death.

---

* Cf. Genesis 4, 3–6.

And just as Cain greeted his brother Abel and slew him after, even so did Judas greet his Lord, although he had been compassing His death. There are then many points where these deaths correspond, not in degree, but in their outward signs. For even as Cain killed Abel on a Friday, so it was that Judas slew his Master on a Friday, not with his hand but by his tongue. Indeed, the points where Cain foreshadows Judas are many and remarkable: for the latter could find in Jesus Christ no cause for hurting Him; one cause he had, and that unwarrantable: he hated Him for no evil he had seen in Him, but just because he could find nought in Him but good. For it is always the way of wicked men to envy and molest the good; if so false a blackguard as was Judas had seen as much bad faith and infamy in Jesus Christ as was in him, instead of hating, he would have loved Him for that very reason, seeing Him as the mirror of himself. Our Lord refers in the Psalter to this treachery of Cain's towards his brother, where He puts harsh words into King David's mouth (who spoke them all unwitting), making him say as it were to Cain: 'Thou hast devised slanders and spoken them of thy brother, thou hast laid gins and snares for thine own mother's son. These things hast thou done and I kept silence, wherefore thou thoughtest that I was like to thee because I held my peace, but I am not, nay rather will I reprove thee and chastise thee harshly.'* Long before David spoke of it Cain had paid the penalty of his crime, the day Our Lord appeared to him and asked him:

'Cain, where is thy brother?'

His reply was that of a man who knew himself guilty of his brother's murder, having already covered the body with leaves of that same Tree, that it might not be found. So he said, when Our Lord had asked him where his brother was:

'Lord, I know not; am I my brother's keeper?'

Our Lord said to him then:

'What hast thou done? The voice of thy brother's blood cries unto me from the ground where thou didst spill it. And because thou hast done this thing, thou shalt be accursed upon earth; and the earth shall be cursed in all thy labours, because

* Psalm 50, 20–21.

it drank thy brother's blood, which thou perfidiously didst spill upon it.'*

Thus did Our Lord curse the earth, but not the Tree beneath which Abel had been slain, nor the others of its stock, nor those which by His will sprang up on earth thereafter. Now at the hour of Abel's death a marvellous transformation overtook this Tree, for its green tints veered to scarlet in remembrance of the blood poured out beneath it. And there was an end, too, of its issue, for all the slips that were taken afterwards shrivelled and died. But the parent tree increased so wondrously in size and beauty that none could since compare with it in splendour, nor any so delight the beholder's eye.

Over the years the Tree lost nothing of the loveliness of form and hue that I have just described to you, nor did it age or wither, nor suffer any falling-off at all, save only inasmuch as it never carried flower or fruit from the hour that Abel's blood was shed; but the others that had sprung from it flowered and bore fruit as the nature of a tree demands it should. And it remained that way till men had greatly increased and multiplied upon the earth. The descendants of Adam and Eve held the Tree in the utmost reverence, and honoured it one and all, and each generation told the next how the mother of mankind had planted it. And young and old found solace there and came to refresh themselves beside it when in distress of mind or body, because it was called the Tree of Life and held for them memories of joy. If this Tree grew and added to its beauty, so also did its offshoots, both the white ones and the green; and there was none on earth so bold as to break off a branch or leaf of them.

Time saw another miracle befall this Tree. For when Our Lord had sent the flood to cover the earth, by which the world with all its wickedness was swallowed up, and the fruits of the earth, the forests and the ploughlands suffered such ravages that their first sweet savour was for ever lost, then all things everywhere acquired a bitter taste; those trees, however, that were descended from the Tree of Life betrayed no sign of degradation either in flavour or in fruit or in the sameness of their pristine hues.[60]

*Cf. Genesis 4, 9–12.

Indeed they were still unchanged in the reign of Solomon, King David's son, who ruled the land after his father's death. This Solomon was wise with all the knowledge that could be grasped by human understanding; he knew the powers of every precious stone, the virtues of all herbs, and had a more perfect knowledge of the course of the firmament and of the stars than any saving God Himself. Nonetheless, all his sagacity could not combat the cunning of his wife, nor prevent her from deceiving him as frequently as she took pains to do so. Nor is this anything to wonder at; for without a doubt, when woman gives her mind and heart to guile, no mere man's wit can prove a match for her; and this is nothing new, but dates back to the mother of us all.

When Solomon saw he was powerless against his spouse's wiles he was mystified as to the reason why, and much put out as well; however, he did not dare do anything about it. He alludes to this in his book entitled 'Parables': 'I have,' he says, 'gone round about the world and searched it high and low with all the powers of human understanding, but in all my wanderings I found not one good woman.'* These words expressed Solomon's anger that he could not get the better of his wife. He strove by different means to wean her from her ways, but all in vain. Seeing this, he began to ask himself why women took such pleasure in annoying men. As he reflected, a voice replied in answer to his questions:

'Solomon, Solomon, if sorrow came to man through woman's wiles, and comes so still, let it not trouble thee. For there shall come a woman through whom man shall know joy greater an hundred times than is this sorrow; and she shall be born of thine inheritance.'

These words caused Solomon to hold himself a fool for finding fault with his wife, and led him to study every sign accorded him, whether waking or in dream, in the hope of coming at the truth about the ending of his line. He sought so diligently that the Holy Ghost revealed to him the coming of the glorious Virgin, and a voice told him in part what was to be. When Solomon learned of this, he asked whether this maid was to mark the end of his lineage.

* In fact a free rendering of Ecclesiastes 7, 27–8.

'No,' said the voice, 'a man, himself a virgin, shall be the last: one who shall pass in valour Josiah, thy step-brother, by as much as that Virgin shall surpass thy wife. Now I have set the seal of certitude upon thy glimmerings.'

Hearing these words, Solomon declared himself most happy that the last scion of his lineage should be rooted in such virtue and high valour. He bethought himself how he could make known to the last of his line how Solomon, who had lived so long before him, had had foreknowledge of his coming. He pondered long and deep upon this matter, not seeing how he could inform a man to live so many generations after him, how he had known of him. His wife perceived he was wrestling with a problem that he could not solve. She loved him well, if not so well that many love their lords still better, and she was a most designing woman. She did not want to ask him straight out, but waited until she saw her opportunity one evening when she observed him in blithe spirits and well disposed towards her. She requested him then to answer whatever question she would put to him, and he agreed readily enough, little suspecting where her aspirations lay. At once she said to him:

'Sir, this week, and last, and for a long time now you have been racking your brains without respite, which tells me plainly that you have a problem you cannot solve. This very reason makes me want to know it, for there is no problem in the world I am not confident of solving, what with your wisdom and my ingenuity.'

When Solomon heard what she said, it struck him that if this business could be forwarded by human wit, she would be the one to do it, for he had found in her such a wealth of ruse that he did not think the world could boast her match for subtlety. The desire grew on him to open his mind to her, and he told her the whole mattter, keeping nothing back. When he had finished, she thought a while, and then said promptly:

'Is it that you are at a loss to know how to inform this knight that you knew all about him in advance?'

'Yes indeed,' he answered, 'I cannot see how it can be arranged. The thought of the years that sunder us leaves me aghast.'

'Upon my faith,' said she, 'since you are so benighted, I will show you the way. First tell me, though, how great you estimate the gap.'

Solomon answered that he thought it must be two thousand years and more.

'I will tell you then what must be done. Have a ship built of the best and most durable wood that can be found, such wood as neither water nor anything else can rot.'

And Solomon agreed.

The following day he sent for all the carpenters of his kingdom and ordered them to build the finest ship that was ever seen, and all of rot-proof wood, and they said they would build it according to his instructions. When they had assembled wood and timbers and made a start, Solomon's wife said to her lord:

'Sir, since this knight you speak of is to surpass all those who ever lived or are to follow, it would be a great honour if you were to furnish him with some weapon, itself as peerless among arms as he shall be unrivalled among men.'

Solomon answered that he knew not where to find a weapon such as she described.

'I will tell you,' said his wife. 'In the temple you built in honour of your Lord lies the sword of your father King David, the keenest and noblest blade that ever a knight wielded. Take it and strip it of its hilt and pommel, so that we are left with the naked steel. And you who know the powers of stones, and the virtues of herbs, and the nature of all other things on earth, you must fashion a pommel out of precious stones so cunningly joined that after your time no human eye shall be able to discern the seams, but all who look on it shall think it is entire. Next you must make a hilt of such extraordinary virtue that it shall have no equal in the world. And after, do you make a sheath worthy in all respects of such a sword. When you have done all this I shall provide a belt after my own liking.'

Solomon followed his wife's suggestions in every detail, save the pommel, for which he used only one stone, but one which contained every colour; and he fitted it with the strange and wonderful hilt described elsewhere.

When the ship was built and launched the lady had a magnificent great bed set in it, which she overlaid with coverlets to embellish and adorn it. At its head the king placed his own crown and covered it with a white silk cloth. He had given his wife the sword for her to fix on the belt, and he said to her:

'Bring the sword here; and I will lay it across the foot of the bed.'

She fetched it, and he looked at it: and then he saw that she had put on a belt of hemp; he was about to show his annoyance when she said to him:

'Know, Sir, that I have nothing, however rich or rare, that is worthy to support so glorious a sword.'

'Then what is to be done?' he asked.

'You must leave it as it is, for it is not for us to equip it with a belt; a maiden will provide one, but I know neither the time nor circumstance.'

So the king left the sword just as it was; and later they had the ship dressed with white silk sheeting which was proof against the elements. When this was done the lady looked at the bed and declared that something was still lacking.

Whereupon, taking two carpenters with her, she left the ship and set off to the Tree beneath which Abel had been slain. When she came to it she said to the carpenters:

'Cut me as much of this wood as I need to make a post.'

'Ah! Madam,' they exclaimed, 'we would not dare do such a thing. Do you not know that this is the Tree which was planted by our mother Eve?'

'You needs must do it,' she retorted, 'for else I shall have you put to death.'

They gave way, pushed to this extreme, preferring the guilt of the offence to certain death. They set at once about cutting into the Tree, but at the first strokes they were appalled to see, quite plainly, drops of blood as bright as the reddest rose exuding from the wood. They would have ceased their work, but she made them carry on whether they would or no, and they chopped off enough timber to provide them with a post. When they had done this, Solomon's wife forced them to cut some wood from one of the green-hued trees that were descended from the Tree of Life, and finally from one of those that were white in every part.

Once they were provided with these three woods, each of a

different hue, they returned to the ship. The lady went aboard and bidding them follow her, she said to them:

'Out of this timber I want you to hew me three posts, the one to be fixed to the side of this bed, the other opposite to it on the farther side, and the third to form a cross-piece overhead bolted to each of the others.'

The carpenters carried out her orders and set the posts in position, not one of which suffered any change in colour for as long as the ship was in being. When the job was done, Solomon looked at the ship and said to his wife:

'You have done a marvellous work. For if all earth's inhabitants were here, they would not be able to spell out the meaning of this ship unless Our Lord revealed it to them, nor do you understand it yourself, for all that you have built it. Nor will anything you have done serve to inform the knight that I had heard of him unless Our Lord give him some other help.'

But she said: 'Leave the ship as it is, for you will have news of it yet that you did not look for.'[61]

Solomon spent that night in a tent in front of the ship with but a few companions. When he had fallen asleep it seemed to him that a man came down towards him out of heaven amid a throng of angels and alighted in the ship. Having set foot in it, this man took water from a silver pail which one of the angels brought him and sprinkled it over all the ship; next he went to the sword and inscribed both pommel and hilt; and then he went to the side of the ship and wrote upon it too. Having done these things he laid himself down on the bed, and from that moment Solomon knew not what became of him, for he vanished, he and all his company.

At daybreak on the morrow, as soon as Solomon awoke, he went over to the ship and found letters painted on the side, which read:

GIVE EAR, O MAN WHO WOULDST SET FOOT IN ME, TAKE HEED THOU ENTER NOT SAVE THOU BE FULL OF FAITH, FOR I AM NAUGHT BUT FAITH AND TRUE BELIEF. AND AS SOON AS THOU DOST LAPSE FROM FAITH, MYSELF SHALL CAST THEE DOWN IN SUCH A WAY THAT THOU SHALT FIND IN ME NOR HELP NOR FOOTING, BUT I SHALL LET THEE FALL

IN THE SAME HOUR THAT THOU ART BRANDED WITH THE
MARK OF UNBELIEF.

Solomon was so taken aback at the sight of this inscription
that he dared not step aboard, but retreated a little, and as he
did so, the ship slid down into the sea and sped away so swiftly
that he soon lost sight of it. He sat down on the shore and began
to reflect on what he had seen. Then he heard a voice from
above say to him:

   'Solomon, the last knight of thy lineage will lie on this bed
that thou hast made and will have tidings of thee.'

   This made Solomon more than happy; he woke his wife and
companions and recounted what had happened, and he told
friends and strangers how his wife had solved the problem
which had baffled him. And so the tale relates to you, for the
reasons set out earlier, for what end the ship was built, and
why and how the posts were naturally tinted white and green
and red, without recourse to paint. And now the tale speaks no
more of this matter but tells of other things.

[12]

Adventures of the Three Companions

NOW the story relates that the three companions gave the bed
and the posts most careful scrutiny, till they recognized that
the colours of the wood were natural, not painted on, and they
marvelled at it, for it passed their comprehension. Having gazed
their fill, they lifted the cloth and uncovered the gold crown,
which in turn overlay a purse of rich confection. Perceval took
and opened this, and found a letter inside which the others
hoped, God willing, would furnish them with some sure testimony concerning the ship, the place it came from and the man
who built it. Then Perceval began to read out what was written
there, describing to them bit by bit the origin of the posts and
of the ship exactly as the story has narrated it. As they stood
listening, there was not one who did not shed abundant tears,

for they were put in mind of solemn deeds and men of high descent.

When Perceval had given them the explanation of the ship and posts, Galahad said:

'Good Sirs, we must seek out the maiden now who is to change this belt and put another in its place: for none must move the sword from here without this being done.'

The others protested that they did not know where they should find her. 'None the less,' they added, 'we will willingly set about searching, since needs must.'

When Perceval's sister overheard these cheerless words, she said to them:

'Sirs, do not lose heart: so it please God, the belt will be attached before we leave, as rich and beautiful a belt as circumstance demands.'

With that she opened a casket she was holding and drew out a belt woven of threads of richest gold, and silk, and strands of hair. And the hair was so bright and burnished that one could scarce distinguish between it and the gold. The belt was encrusted, too, with priceless gems and fastened with two gold buckles, hard to match for cost and beauty.

'Good Sirs,' she said, 'here is the belt that belongs to the sword, and be assured that I made it of the most precious thing I had, which was my hair. Nor was it any wonder that my hair was dear to me, for on the feast of Pentecost when you, Sir,' here she spoke to Galahad, 'were knighted, I had the finest head of hair of any woman in the world. But as soon as I learned that this adventure awaited me, and that this was what I must do, I had my hair shorn in haste and made it up into the braids you are looking on.'

'In God's name, damsel,' answered Bors, 'welcome again for this! You have saved us from the trials we must have faced but for this news.'

The maiden went swiftly over to the sword and removing the hempen belt she affixed the other as skilfully as if it were her daily task. This done, she said to the companions:

'Do you know the name of this sword?'

'Damsel, we do not. It is for you to tell it us, for so the inscription says.'

'Know then,' she said, 'that this sword is called the Sword of the Strange Belt, and the name of the scabbard is Memory of Blood. For no man of understanding will be able to look at that part of the scabbard which was made from the Tree of Life without recalling to mind the blood of Abel.'[62]

When Bors and Perceval heard what she said they turned to Galahad:

'Sir, we beg you now in the name of Our Lord Jesus Christ, and so that all chivalry may gain a greater lustre, to gird on the Sword of the Strange Belt, which has been more impatiently desired in the kingdom of Logres than was Our Lord Himself by His apostles.'

For they were convinced this sword would be the means whereby the awesome happenings attendant on the Holy Grail would cease to be, and the perilous adventures, too, which they encountered daily.

'Let me first,' said Galahad, 'make good my right to it. For none may have the sword who cannot grip the pommel. So if I fail you will have proof that it is not meant for me.'

The other two agreed; so Galahad put his hand to the hilt, and as he took hold of it and gripped it tight he found that his thumb and finger easily overlapped each other. His watching companions said to him then:

'Sir, we are sure now that the sword is yours: henceforth there will be no disputing your right to gird it on.'

Galahad unsheathed it, and when he saw the blade, whose brilliance was a mirror to the face, he prized it more than anything on earth was ever prized. He slid it back into the scabbard, and the maiden unbuckled the sword he was wearing and girded the other about him by the belt. When she had hung it at his side she said to him:

'Truly, Sir, it matters no more to me when death shall take me; for now I hold myself blessed above all maidens, having made a knight of the noblest man in the world. For I assure you, you were not by rights a knight until you were girded with the sword which was brought to this land for you alone.'

'Damsel,' answered Galahad, 'your part in this makes me your knight for ever. And my heartfelt thanks for all that you have told us.'[63]

'Now we can leave this ship,' she said, 'and go about our other business.'

They disembarked at once and as they stepped onto the rocks, Perceval said to Galahad:

'Truly, Sir, no day shall pass without I thank Our Lord that it pleased Him I should see the consummation of so high an adventure as the one we have just witnessed: for I have never seen any marvel to compare with it.'

Directly they got to their own ship they went on board; and the wind, catching and filling the sail, carried them swiftly away from the islet. When night was come upon them they began to wonder aloud if they were close to land, but each in turn confessed his ignorance. They spent that night at sea without either meat or drink, having no stores aboard. It happened the following morning that they made landfall at a fortress known as Castle Carcelois, on the Scottish marches. When they had accosted and given thanks to Our Lord for having guided them to the adventure of the sword and brought them back in safety, they entered the castle. Once they were past the gate the maiden said to them:

'Sirs, this is no safe haven we are come to: for if it is known we are of King Arthur's household we shall be attacked on sight: there is none so hated here as he.'

'Damsel,' said Bors, 'be not dismayed, for He who brought us off the rock will deliver us from here at His good pleasure.'

As they were speaking a youth came out to meet them and hailed them with the words:

'My lords, who are you?'

'Knights of King Arthur's household,' they replied.

'Well,' he declared, 'upon my honour, your arrival is most untoward.'

And he turned on his heel and went back to the keep. Scarcely a few moments later they heard a trumpet sound and reverberate throughout the castle. Then a maiden came up to them and asked them whence they came. On their telling her, she exclaimed:

'Ah! Sirs, for God's sake, if you can, return! For as God is my help, you are come to your deaths, for which reason I would urge you in all sincerity to retreat before our people catch you within the walls.'

The companions said they had no intention of turning back.

'Are you then determined to die?'

'Have no fear,' they said, 'for He whom we serve will be our guide and ward.'

As they said this they saw at least ten armed knights riding towards them down the main street and calling to them to surrender or be slain. The three replied that surrender was unthought of.

'Then you are done for!' shouted the others, and gave their horses their heads.

The companions, who stood in little awe of them for all they were more numerous, and mounted too while they themselves were on foot, flashed out their swords; and Perceval struck one down from his horse, and caught the animal and mounted, to see that Galahad had done the same. As soon as both were horsed, they lost no time in felling and killing their attackers, and furnished Bors too with a mount. When their enemies found themselves being trounced, they turned and fled, and with the companions on their heels they thundered into the keep.

When they debouched into the hall above they found knights and sergeants arming, alerted by the clamour that had resounded through the castle. The three companions (who had dashed into the castle on horseback after the fugitives) rushed with drawn swords at these men whom they saw preparing for combat, and set about cutting them down like so many dumb beasts. The others defended their lives as best they could, but were forced in the end to turn tail, for Galahad gave such a display of strength and skill and slew so huge a count that he seemed to them no normal man but a fiend burst in among them to destroy them all. And at the last, when they saw there was no salvation, they took to their heels, the lucky by way of the door, while the rest leaped from the windows, breaking necks and legs and arms.

When the three companions saw the palace delivered, they looked at the bodies they had robbed of life and held themselves for sinners, saying it was an evil work to massacre so many.

'In truth,' said Bors, 'it is my firm belief Our Lord cannot have loved these men, for them to be thus slaughtered. It may be they were miscreants and apostates, men who had so sinned against Our Lord that He did not want them to remain alive; and so He sent us hither to destroy them.'

'That is a most inadequate explanation,' answered Galahad. 'If they sinned against Our Lord, the vengeance was not ours to take but His who holds His hand till the sinner repent. Wherefore I swear to you that I shall not rest easy until I learn, God willing, the truth about the work we have done this day.'

While they were talking thus, a white-robed priest came into the hall from an adjoining room, bearing the Lord's Body in a chalice. Catching sight of the dead bodies lying there he gaped in horror and drew back, clearly unnerved by the sight of such a carnage. Galahad, who had observed what he was bearing, removed his helm out of respect, realizing that the priest had suffered a shock. He signed to the others to be still, and going up to the good man, said to him:

'Sir, why have you halted? You need have no fear of us.'

'Who are you?' asked the other.

Galahad answered that they were men of King Arthur's household. These tidings were enough to cure the good man of his fright, and having composed himself he asked Galahad to tell him how the knights had met their death. Galahad recounted to him how he and his friends, all three companions of the Quest, had arrived at the castle, how they had been attacked, and how the tide had gone against their assailants, as was plain to see. When the priest heard this account, he said:

'Believe me, Sir, never did knights labour to better purpose; if you lived until the end of time I do not think you could perform a work of mercy to compare with this. I know for certain it was Our Lord who sent you here to do this work, for nowhere in the world were men who hated Him as much as the three brothers who were masters of this castle. In their great wickedness they had so suborned the inmates of this place that they were grown worse than infidels and did nothing but what affronted God and Holy Church.'

'Sir,' said Galahad, 'I was bitterly repenting having gone so far as to kill them, on account of their being Christians.'

'Have no regrets, but on the contrary rejoice in what is done. For I tell you truly that Our Lord is beholden to you for slaying them, for they were no Christians, but the most arrant scoundrels that I ever set eyes on; and I will tell you how it is I know.

'A year ago this castle had for lord one Count Ernol. He had three sons, all skilled in arms, and a daughter, who was by common consent the fairest maiden in this land. The love which the three brothers bore their sister was of such a carnal nature that, burning with ungovernable lust, they lay with her and robbed her of her maidenhead; and because she had spirit enough to dare appeal against them to her father, they killed her. When the count saw this turpitude he wanted to drive them out of his house, but they would have none of it; instead they seized their father and cast him into prison, inflicting grievous injuries on him, and would have killed him had not one of his brothers come to his aid. Having done these things they went on to commit every outrage under heaven, murdering clerks and priests, monks and abbots, and razing both the chapels that stood here. The list of their crimes is so long it is a wonder they were not consumed long since. But this morning it happened that their father, lying here ill and close, as I think, to death, sent for me to come and visit him, clad as you see me in the armour of God. I came with a willing step, as to one who in the past had always loved me well. But as soon as I entered these precincts I was subjected to worse indignities than I should have to suffer were I a captive of the Sarracens themselves. All this I endured most willingly for the love of that Lord in whose despite they did it. And when I was come to the dungeon where the count was held and had told him of my treatment, he replied: "Be not disturbed: my shame and yours shall be revenged by three servants of Jesus Christ; for thus did the Master send me word." You can rest assured on this testimony that Our Lord will bear no grudge for what was done; be it rather known to you that He sent you here for the purpose of overthrowing these men and making an end of them. And this day will furnish you with further proof, more palpable than any you have had as yet.'

Then Galahad called his companions over and repeated to

them the information given him by the priest, to wit that those whom they had slain were the most infamous band of men on earth; he told them, too, the story of the count, their father, whom they held prisoner, and why. When Bors had heard this tale he said:

'My lord Galahad, did I not say to you that Our Lord had sent us here so that we might take vengeance on them for their crimes? For without a doubt, if it were not His will, the three of us could never have killed so many in so short a time.'[64]

Next they went to the dungeon to release Count Ernol; and when they had carried him up into the palace and laid him in the great hall they saw that he was at the point of death. Nevertheless, as soon as he set eyes on Galahad he knew him, not because he had seen him previously, but empowered thereto by God. He began to weep then from the fullness of his heart, and said:

'Sir, we have waited long for your coming, till at last, thanks be to God, we have you with us. Now, for the love of God, hold me close against you, so that my soul may rejoice at the body's dying in the arms of so noble a man as you.'

With all his heart Galahad did as he was asked; and when he had laid him on his breast the count bowed his head like a man in mortal travail and said:

'Blessed Father in heaven, into Thy hands I commend my spirit.'*

Then his head fell forward and he lay so long in that position without moving that they thought him dead. However, he spoke again after a time and said:

'Galahad, the Master sends you word that you have wreaked such revenge upon His enemies this day on His behalf that the hosts of heaven rejoice. Now you must go to the Maimed King as soon as you are able, so that he may receive the healing he has waited for so long, for it is your coming that shall bring it to him. And separate directly an adventure comes your way.'

With that he fell silent for ever, for in that moment his soul took leave of his body. When such of the defenders of the castle as were left alive saw that the count was dead they broke into

* Cf. Luke 24, 46, also Psalm 31, 5.

mourning and lamentation in keeping with the great love they had borne him. Having arrayed the body for burial with all the splendour befitting a man of his rank they gave out the news of his death; and all the survivors who were roundabout returned to escort the body to its burial at a hermitage.

Next day the three companions left the castle and took to the road again, with Perceval's sister riding still beside them. They rode on their way until they came to the Waste Forest. When they had entered its shade they espied ahead and moving across their path the White Hart with its four attendant lions, the same that Perceval had seen on a former occasion.

'Galahad,' exclaimed Perceval, 'now you can witness a true marvel: for upon my oath I never saw a stranger or more wonderful adventure. I truly believe that those lions are guarding the Hart; and until I discover the truth I shall never know full contentment.'

'In God's name,' answered Galahad, 'I am most eager to find out myself. So let us go after it and follow it until we come upon its covert. For I think that this adventure is from God.'

The others were quick to agree, and they all set off on the tracks of the Hart and followed it until they came to a valley. Looking ahead they saw a hermitage set in a little coppice, the dwelling of an old and venerable anchorite. The Hart went in and so did the lions, and the knights who were in pursuit dismounted on approaching the building. They turned in to the chapel and saw the hermit arrayed in the armour of Our Lord and about to begin the mass of the Holy Ghost. At this sight the companions declared that they had chosen their moment well, and they went forward to hear the mass that the good man had just intoned. When he came to the consecration they had cause for yet greater wonderment and awe. For it seemed to them that before their eyes the Hart became a very man, and sat on the altar in a seat of the greatest beauty and magnificence; and the lions too were changed as they watched, the first assuming the shape of a man, the second that of an eagle, while the third became a lion-like beast and the fourth took the shape of a calf.[65] In this wise were the four lions transformed, and they had wings with which they might have flown had it so pleased Our Lord. They took hold of the seat where the Hart was sitting, two to its feet and two to the head, and it was like a throne; and they went out through a window in the chapel, in such a manner that the glass was still entire and perfect after their passing. And when they were gone and lost to the sight of those within, a voice from above made itself heard among the watchers, saying:

'In like manner did the Son of God enter the Virgin Mary, so that her virginity was left entire and perfect.'

At the sound of these words the companions fell prostrate to the ground. For the voice was accompanied by such a brilliant light and so deafening a thunderclap that they thought that the chapel had collapsed about them. When they had recovered their strength and faculties they saw that the priest was disrobing, as one whose mass was sung. So they went up to him and begged him to tell them the meaning of what they had seen.

'What was it, then, that you saw?' he asked.

'We saw a Hart take human shape and become a man, and lions translated into divers beasts.'

When the good man heard their reply he said to them:

'Welcome, Sirs, indeed! Your words are proof to me that you are of that band of godly men, of true and faithful knights, who shall see the Quest of the Holy Grail through to its ending, enduring and suffering much. For to you has Our Lord revealed His secrets and His hidden mysteries, in part indeed today; for in changing the Hart into a heavenly being, in no way mortal, He showed the transmutation that He underwent upon the Cross: cloaked there in the mortal garment of this human flesh, dying, He conquered death, and recovered for us eternal life. This is most aptly figured by the Hart. For just as the Hart rejuvenates itself by shedding part of its hide and coat, so did Our Lord return from death to life when He cast off his mortal hide, which was the human flesh He took in the Blessed Virgin's womb. And because the Blessed Virgin was ever free from sin, her Son appeared in the guise of a White Hart without spot. By the beasts attending Him you are to understand the four Evangelists, thrice-blessed men who left a written witness to many of the works of Jesus Christ, performed while He lived among us as a mortal man. Be it known to you also that no knight was ever able to penetrate this mystery or know what it could mean. And yet the blessed and the most high Lord has shown Himself in this and many other lands to good men and to knights in the same likeness of a Hart and escorted by the same four lions, so that those who saw might draw a lesson from it. Be assured, though, that from this day on none shall see Him in that guise again.'[66]

These words made the companions weep for joy and render thanks to Our Lord for allowing them to see His truth unveiled. When they had heard mass the following morning and were on the point of leaving, Perceval took the sword that Galahad had discarded and said that he would wear it from then on; and he left his own at the hermitage.

They took their leave and rode till past mid-day, when they found themselves approaching a well-positioned and well-defended castle. They did not enter, however, for their road bore off in another direction. Some little distance from the main gate they were overtaken by a knight who said to them:

'Sirs, is this maiden who rides with you a virgin?'

'Upon my faith,' swore Bors, 'she is, make no mistake.'

Hearing this reply the other, with a brusque gesture, seized her horse by the bridle, saying:

'By Holy Cross, you shall not give me the slip until you have complied with the custom of this castle.'

Perceval's anger rose at the sight of the knight restraining his sister in such a manner, and he said to him:

'Sir Knight, you are foolish to speak thus. For a maiden, wherever she goes, is not bound by any customs, above all so noble a maiden as this, the daughter of a king and queen.'

While they were speaking, ten armed knights came riding out of the castle, accompanied by a young woman who carried a silver dish in her hand. The new arrivals said to the three companions:

'Good Sirs, the maiden whom you are escorting will be compelled by force of arms to observe the custom of this castle.'

Galahad asked what the custom was.

'Sir,' said one of the knights, 'every maiden who passes this road must fill this dish brimful with blood from her right arm, and none goes by here without complying with this demand.'

'A curse upon the false knight who instituted this custom!'

said Galahad, 'for in truth it is an infamous and shameful one. And as God is my help, you have missed your mark this once; for while I have vigour and she trusts in me, this maiden will not cede you what you ask.'

'So help me God,' added Perceval, 'I would sooner be killed.'

'And so would I,' said Bors.

'By my faith,' said the knight, 'in that case you will die all three; for were you the best knights in the world you could not stand against us.'

At that each party charged the other, and it happened that the three companions unhorsed the ten knights before they had even broken their lances. Then they took hold of their swords and went about killing and felling them like beasts at the slaughter. And they would have despatched them easily enough had not some sixty armed knights come galloping out of the castle to reinforce their comrades. At their head rode an old man who addressed the companions, saying:

'Good Sirs, take pity on yourselves and save your lives, it would be a sorry business if you were killed, for you are men of the highest stamp and valour, and this being so we would beg of you to yield us what we ask.'

'In truth,' replied Galahad, 'further talk on your part would be pointless. Your request will never be complied with while the maiden trusts in me.'

'What,' said the other, 'are you bent on dying?'

'It is not come to that,' retorted Galahad. 'But certainly we would rather die than tolerate so great an infamy as you demand.'

Thereupon the fighting broke loose and the affray was fierce and furious, with the companions attacked from every quarter. But Galahad, wielding the Sword of the Strange Belt, smote to right and to left, dealing death at every stroke and performed such feats that all who saw him thought him no mere mortal but a monster of some sort. And he pressed relentlessly forward, never turning back, but gradually winning ground from his foes. He had, too, the advantage of his two companions helping him on either flank and thus preventing any from approaching save head on.

The battle raged until past the hour of none without the

three companions ever being outmatched or yielding any terrain. They stood their ground till night's black shadows falling had forced the warriors to disengage and the watchers in the castle to direct that the combat must be broken off. The old man who had spoken to them earlier returned again to say:

'Sirs, we beg you, in love and in courtesy, to come and lodge with us this night, and we pledge you in good faith that tomorrow we will return you to that state and place which you are in at present. Do you know why I make this offer? I am positive that as soon as you learn the reason for our request you will freely consent to the maiden's granting it.'

'Go with them, sirs,' said the maiden, 'since they beg it of you.'

The three assented, and a truce was accorded by both parties who then rode into the castle together. Never was there a more joyful welcome given than that extended to the three companions by their hosts, who proceeded to help them down from their horses and had them unarmed. Later, when they had eaten, they enquired about the custom of the castle, how and wherefore it had been established. One of the knights of the place replied at once:

'We will gladly tell you that.' Continuing, he said: 'Truth to tell, there is a maiden living here whose men we are, as are all the knights around; she is the lady of this castle and of many more besides. Some two years since, God willing, she fell ill. When she had been ailing some time we looked for the cause of her sickness and discovered that she was ravaged by the malady that goes by the name of leprosy. Seeing this, we sent for every physician far and near, but there was none who could advise us how to treat her sickness. Finally a wise man told us that if we could obtain a basin filled with the blood of a maiden who was a virgin both in fact and in intent, still more if she were the daughter of a king and queen and sister to Perceval the chaste, and if we anointed our mistress with it she would be speedily cured. On hearing these tidings we decreed that no maid should pass this way again, and she a virgin, without our procuring a dishful of her blood, and we placed guards at the castle gates to stop all those that passed. Now you have heard,' he finished, 'how the custom you encountered came to be established in this castle; and you will take what action you deem fitting.'

Thereupon the maiden called the three companions together and said to them:

'Sirs, you see that this maiden is ill, and that it lies with me to heal her or condemn. Tell me then what I should do.'

'Upon God's name,' said Galahad, 'if you do this thing, being young and tender, you will not come out of it alive.'

'In faith,' she answered, 'should I die to give her healing, honour would accrue to me and mine. Indeed I must perform this act, in part for them, in part also for you. For if you join battle tomorrow as you have done today, there will perforce be far worse losses than my death. This is why I must do as they enjoin, and thus this strife will be averted. I pray you therefore, for God's sake, to give me your consent.'

This, most regretfully, they did.

Then the maiden called to those of the castle and said to them:

'Be happy and rejoice! For there will be no battle tomorrow: and I promise you that tomorrow I will acquit myself in the manner prescribed.'

When the others heard what she said they thanked her with full hearts, and resumed their feasting with redoubled zest. They spared no pains in attending to the companions' wants, and bedded them as sumptuously as they were able. That night the three companions lay in comfort, and might have known still greater ease had they been willing to accept all that was offered them.

When they had all heard mass the following morning, Perceval's sister entered the palace and asked that the ailing lady whom her blood should heal be brought before her. Her people expressed their readiness and went to fetch her from the chamber where she was. When the companions set eyes on her they were aghast, for her face was so unsightly and pustulous and so disfigured by the leprosy that it was a wonder she could live in such affliction.[67] As she approached they rose to greet her and made her sit down with them; straight away she asked Perceval's sister to make good her promise to her;

the maiden agreed without demur, and asking for a basin to be brought she held out her arm and let them open the vein with a little blade as keen and sharp as a razor. The blood spurted out at once, and she blessed herself and commended herself to Our Lord before turning to the lady and saying:

'Madam, to give you healing I am come to the point of death. For God's sake, pray for my soul, for my life is at its end.'

As she spoke these words she fainted from loss of blood, for the basin was already full. The companions ran to hold her up and staunched the bleeding. It was a long while before she revived enough to speak, and then she said to Perceval:

'Ah! Perceval, my sweet brother, I am dying so that this lady may have health. I beg you not to have my body buried in this country, but as soon as life is gone, place me in a boat at the first port you come to: and let me go where chance shall carry me. I tell you moreover that whatever haste you make to the city of Sarras, where you will have to go in the wake of the Holy Grail, you will find me there before you, lying below the tower. And bury my body for mine and honour's sake within the spiritual palace. Do you know why I ask you this? Because Galahad is to lie there and you beside him.'

Perceval, weeping, granted her request and said that he would gladly carry out her wishes. Then she said again:

'Disperse tomorrow and go your separate ways till fortune reunite you in the house of the Maimed King. For such is the Master's will and that is His command to you through me.'

Again they affirmed that they would do as she said. She asked them then to have her Saviour brought to her, and they sent to a godly hermit who dwelt in a wood not far from the castle gate. He did not delay in coming since he sensed that the need was pressing. He hurried in to the maiden and when she saw him approaching she stretched out her hands towards her Saviour and received Him most devoutly. Thereupon she departed this world to the great grief of the companions, who despaired of any easy consolation for her loss.

The lady was restored to health that very day. For as soon as she was washed in the blood of the holy maid she was cleansed and healed of her leprosy and her flesh that had been blackened and hideous to look on recovered all its bloom, to the joy of her own people and of the companions too. As for the body of Perceval's sister, they did with it as she herself had asked, first taking out the entrails and such parts as must be removed, and then embalming it with as many costly spices as if it had been the body of the emperor himself. They had a boat built which they furnished with an awning of the finest silk and a couch of passing beauty. And when they had decked out the boat as splendidly as they knew how, they laid the maiden's body in it and pushed it out to sea. Bors remarked to Perceval that it worried him to think there was no letter with the body which would tell who the maiden was and how she came to die.

'I tell you,' said Perceval, 'that I have laid a letter by her head describing her ancestry, the manner of her death and all the adventures which she helped to carry through. So if some person in a foreign land should find her body, he will know all about her.'

Galahad said it was well done. 'For it may be,' he added, 'that he who finds the body will treat it with greater honour than he would have done had he not known her life and history.'

For as long as the denizens of the castle were able to see the boat they stayed on the shore, the majority weeping with emotion, for the maiden had acted with a most noble generosity in laying down her life to heal a lady of a foreign country; and never, so they said, had a maiden acted thus. When the boat had slipped out of sight they returned to the castle; the companions, however, declared that they would never set foot in it again for love of the maiden they had lost there in that fashion. So they waited outside, bidding the others bring them their arms, which they did forthwith.

The three companions had mounted and were about to ride away, when they noticed the sky growing very dark and big black rainclouds gathering, so they made towards a chapel which stood by the side of the road. They went in, stabling their mounts outside in a penthouse, and remarked that the weather meanwhile had got very much worse. At that moment it started to thunder and lighten and thunderbolts fell upon the castle in a serried rain. The storm raged all that day, wreaking its fearful havoc on the castle, so that half at least of the walls were shattered and left in ruins, to the stupefaction of the watchers who would not have believed it possible for the castle to be destroyed by a whole year's battering of such a storm as this, from what they saw of it from their retreat.*

When evening came and the sky had cleared again, the companions saw a short way off a sorely wounded knight fleeing across their path and crying out repeatedly:

'Ah! God, come to my aid in my hour of need!'

He was pursued at some little distance by another knight and a dwarf who were both shouting to him:

'You are dead, and no escaping!'

And the first knight stretched out his hands towards heaven, crying:

'Gracious Lord God, come to my aid and let me not die in this extremity, that I may not end my days in such great tribulation as besets me now.'

The sight of this knight crying out to God in his distress moved the companions to pity, and Galahad said that he would go to help him.

'Sir,' said Bors, 'not you, but I: for it is quite unnecessary that you bestir yourself for but one knight.'

The other replied that he consented since it was Bors' wish, and Bors went and saddled his horse and said to them:

'Good Sirs, if I do not come back, by no means abandon your quest on that account, but leave in the morning each by a different route, and go your ways till such time as Our Lord grant that the three of us meet again at the Maimed King's house.'

They bade him go in Our Lord's safekeeping, and said they two would separate next morning. And Bors set off at once in pursuit of the knights, for the purpose of helping the one who in his distress was calling piteously on Our Lord as he rode. But the tale speaks no more of him for the nonce, returning to the two companions who stayed behind in the chapel.

* Cf. The destruction of Sodom and Gomorrah, Genesis 19, 24–5.

Parting

Now the story relates that Galahad and Perceval remained together in the chapel all that night, and besought Our Lord most earnestly to be Bors' ward and guard wherever he might go. When light returned next morning, and the passing of the storm had left the sky calm and bright, they mounted their horses and headed towards the castle to ascertain the fate of those within. When they arrived at the gate they found it burnt to the ground and the walls in ruins. They made their way inside where the spectacle that met their eyes left them even more dumbfounded than before, for they found neither man nor woman left alive there. They went searching high and low, deploring such destruction and such terrible loss of life. When they came to the main palace they found that the outer and inner walls had fallen in, while the bodies of the knights lay strewn about where Our Lord had struck them down and blasted them for the wickedness of the life they had lived in common. When the companions saw what had befallen them, they said that it was surely the vengeance of heaven, adding that such a thing could only have come about by the working out of the Creator's wrath. While they were engaged in these reflections they heard a voice say to them:

'This is the vengeance taken for the blood of the innocent maidens which was spilled here for the earthly weal of a wicked and sinful woman.'

Upon hearing these words the companions said that the vengeance of Our Lord was wonderful indeed, and that he was worse than a fool who flouted His laws, whether moved by hope of life or fear of death.[68]

When the two companions had wandered around some time taking stock of the terrible slaughter, they came on a burialground at the farther end of a chapel, all green with grass and shrubs in leaf, and filled with fine tombstones, some sixty altogether. It was such a pretty and pleasant place that it seemed as though no storm had touched it. Nor had it, for in that plot lay the bodies of the maidens who had been put to death for love of the lady. When Perceval and Galahad, still on horseback, had entered the graveyard, they approached the tombs and found that each one bore the name of her who lay beneath. They went about reading the inscriptions till they had discovered that twelve kings' daughters of the highest ancestry lay in that place. This caused them to upbraid the people of the castle for maintaining a most base and wicked custom, and those of the country round for putting up with it so long, for many a great family had been brought low, and even blotted out, through the maidens' deaths who lay there underground.

When the two companions had lingered there till the hour of prime, they left the castle and wended their way to a forest. There, on its verge, Perceval said to Galahad:

'Sir, today is the day that we must part and go our different ways. I commend you to Our Lord: may He grant that our separation be a short one, for I never found a man in whose company I took such pleasure and delight as yours, which makes this parting much more painful to me than you could guess. However, it must be, since such is Our Lord's pleasure.'

With that he took off his helm and Galahad did the same: and they embraced on parting, for the love that they bore one another ran deep, as was well proven in their death, for the one did not survive the other long. So it was that the two companions parted on the edge of a forest known to the local inhabitants by the name of Aube, and each set out upon his solitary way. And now the tale speaks no more of them, but returns to Lancelot, for it is long since he was mentioned last.

[14]

Lancelot at Corbenic

Now the story relates that when Lancelot had come to the Median River he found himself hemmed in by three things, none of which offered him much comfort. On the one hand stretched the forest, vast and tortuous and mazy, on the other rose the great primeval rocks, while in front of him the deep, dark river flowed. It was these three hazards that made him decide to stay where he was and to wait on Our Lord's mercy: so there he remained until nightfall. When darkness was fast mingling with the ebbing day, Lancelot took off his armour, and lying down beside it commended himself to God, beseeching Our Lord, in the manner he had learned, to be ever mindful of him and to send him such relief for soul and body as He knew to be needful. His prayer ended, he fell asleep in a state of mind where his thoughts were more directed to Our Lord than to material things. As he lay sleeping, a voice made itself heard to him, saying:

'Lancelot, rise and take thine arms and enter into the first boat thou shalt find.'

He started at these words, and opened his eyes, and saw so bright a radiance round about that he thought it was broad daylight: but within a few moments it had faded away without his knowing how or why. He raised his hand and blessed himself, and taking up his arms he commended himself to Our Lord before donning his harness. When he was fully equipped and had belted on his sword, he looked towards the river's bank and saw a boat with neither sail nor oar; and he walked across to it and stepped inside. As soon as he entered the boat it seemed to him that the air he breathed was sweet with every fragrance earth can offer, and that he was filled with all the choicest viands that had ever pleased man's palate. Then was his happiness increased an hundredfold, for now he had, as it seemed to him, all he could ever wish for in this life. For this he gave thanks to Our Lord, kneeling there in the boat and saying:

'Gracious Lord Jesus Christ, I do not know whence this can come if it be not from Thee. For my heart is so transported with delight and rapture that I know not whether I am on earth or in the Earthly Paradise.'

Thereupon he propped himself against the side of the boat and fell asleep in this beatitude.

Lancelot passed that night in a state of such tranquility and bliss that he fancied he was not his wonted self, but a man transformed. Next morning on awaking he looked about him and observed amidships a rich and beautiful couch. In the middle of that couch lay the body of a maiden, swathed, but for the face, from head to foot. When Lancelot saw the maiden he approached, making the sign of the cross and thanking Our Lord for having provided him with such company. He stepped quite close, being curious to learn her land of origin and her descent. He hunted around so diligently that at last his eyes lit on a letter beneath her head. He put out his hand and took it, and on unfolding it he read the following words: 'This maiden was sister to Perceval of Wales, and was ever a virgin in fact and in intent. It is she who changed the belt on the Sword of the Strange Belt which Galahad now wears.' Reading further he learned from the letter how she had lived and died, and how the three companions, Galahad and Bors and Perceval, shrouded her in those burial clothes and placed her in the boat at the behest of the voice from heaven. When Lancelot learned the truth of the matter his happiness attained its zenith, for it gave him great joy to know that Bors and Galahad were together. He replaced the letter and went back to the side of the boat to pray to Our Lord that it be granted to him, before the con-summation of this Quest, to find his son Galahad, that he might see and speak with him and show him joy.

While Lancelot was making his petition, he glanced up to see the boat glide in beside a rocky outcrop worn by time; close by the rock where the boat drew in he spied a little chapel with an old man, hoary of head, sitting in front of the door. As soon as Lancelot came within earshot he saluted him, and the other returned his greeting with a deal more vigour than Lancelot had given him credit for. He rose from where he was sitting and came to the boat's side, where he sat himself on a hummock and asked Lancelot what adventure had brought him there. The knight explained his situation and told him how chance had brought him to this spot where, to the best of his knowledge, he had never been before. Next the good man asked him who he was and Lancelot named himself. On discovering that his visitor was Lancelot of the Lake, the other wondered, not without surprise, how he came to find himself in the boat, and he asked him who was with him.

'Sir,' said Lancelot, 'come and see, if you will.'

The old man stepped aboard at once and found the maiden and the letter. When he had read the script from start to finish, including the reference to the Sword of the Strange Belt, he exclaimed:

'Ah! Lancelot, I had never thought to see the day when I should learn the name of this sword. Now in all truth can you call yourself ill-fated when you were absent at the culmination of this high adventure, and those three knights were there, who once were held of lesser worth than you. Now, however, it is known and proven that they have been more constant and more valiant in God's service than have you. But whatever you did in the past, I do believe that if from now on you kept from mortal sin and from transgressing your Maker's law, you could still find compassion and mercy in Him who is the source of all compassion and who has already called you back into the path of truth. However, tell me now how you came to enter this boat.'

Lancelot told his story and the good man wept as he replied:

'Lancelot, know that Our Lord has shown you great goodwill in placing you in the company of so noble and holy a maid. See to it that you remain chaste in thought and deed from this time forth, so that your chastity accord with her virginity. And thus shall your companionship endure.'

Lancelot gave a frank and forthright promise that he would never wittingly offend his Maker.

'Go then, you have no cause to tarry longer, for, please God, in the fullness of time, you shall come to the house of your heart's desire.'

'And you, Sir,' asked Lancelot, 'will you stay here?'

'Yes,' he answered, 'for that is how it must be.'

The wind cut short their conversation, bearing down on the boat and driving it away from the rock; and when they found that they were drawing apart, they commended one another to God, and the old man made his way back to his chapel. But before he left the shore he shouted out:

'Ah! Lancelot, servant of Jesus Christ, for the love of God forget me not, but ask the true knight, Galahad, who will in the course of time be your companion, to pray to Our Lord that He of His sweet compassion have mercy on me!'[69]

This was his parting cry, and its message that Galahad was soon to join him made Lancelot a happy man indeed. Prostrating himself on knees and elbows at the ship's side, he asked Our Lord in prayer to guide him there where he might do His will.

So it was that Lancelot spent a month and more in the bark and never left it once. And to any who might ask what he lived on during that time, since he had found no stores on board, the story replies that the Almighty Lord who fed the Israelites with manna in the desert and brought water out of the rock for them to drink, sustained this knight in the following manner: each morning, as soon as he had said his prayers and called upon the Most High, begging Him to be mindful of his needs and to send him his daily bread, as is a father's part, each time, I say, that Lancelot prayed thus, he found himself so filled and sated, so suffused with the grace of the Holy Ghost, that it seemed to him that he had partaken of every delicacy earth could offer.

Lancelot had been a long time drifting without once setting foot on land when, in the dead of night, he beached where a forest ran down close to the shore. There fell on his listening ears the sound of a knight approaching on horseback, crashing noisily through the wood. When the rider came into the open and caught sight of the boat, he got off his horse and unsaddled it, turning it loose to wander where it would. Then he walked up to the boat and crossing himself, he stepped aboard in full accoutrements.

At the knight's approach Lancelot made no hurried move to snatch up his arms, persuaded that this was the fulfilment of the old man's promise that Galahad should be with him and keep him company a while. So he rose to his feet and said:

'Sir Knight, I wish you welcome.'

The greeting startled Galahad, who had believed the bark empty, and he replied in some astonishment:

'Sir, good fortune be yours; and now for God's love, if so be you may, tell me who you are, for I would dearly like to know.'

So Lancelot named himself, and said that he was Lancelot of the Lake.

'Truly, Sir,' said the newcomer, 'I wish you welcome too. Upon God's name I have desired to see and be with you beyond all men alive. And it is only natural that I should, for in you is my beginning.'

With that the knight removed his helm and placed it in the bottom of the boat, and Lancelot asked:

'Ah! Galahad, is it you?'

'Yes, Sir, in truth it is I.'

When Lancelot heard the answer he hastened to him with arms outstretched and the two embraced and kissed with a jubilation that defies description.

Then each asked the other how it went with him, and each in turn gave an exact account of the adventures that had befallen him since leaving court. They talked and talked till morning lightened and the sun had risen on another day; and when faces showed familiar in broad daylight they embraced again with deep and newfound joy. Directly Galahad caught sight of the maiden whose body lay in the boat he recognized her for Perceval's sister and asked Lancelot if he knew who she was.

'Yes,' replied the other, 'I am well aware: the letter by her head sets out her story. Tell me though, in God's name, whether success was yours in the adventure of the Sword of the Strange Belt.'

'Sir,' he replied, 'it was. And here is the sword, if perchance you never saw it before.'

When Lancelot had looked at the sword he did not doubt its provenance; he took it by the hilt and kissed in turn the pommel and scabbard and blade. Then he pressed Galahad to tell him how and where he had found it. So Galahad told him all about the ship that Solomon's wife had built in days gone by, and about the three posts and the planting by our mother Eve of the first tree which had endowed the posts with their intrinsic tints of white and green and red. After hearing the description of the ship and of all they had found written there, Lancelot said to Galahad that this was a more sublime adventure than ever fell to the lot of mortal knight.

Lancelot and Galahad abode in this boat for more than half a year, living a life wholeheartedly vowed to the service of Our Lord. Many a time they put in to islands far removed from human haunts, where none but wild beasts dwelled and where they met with strange adventures, triumphing always, whether through strength and skill, or by the grace of the Holy Ghost, who was their constant aid and succour. However, the story of the Holy Grail omits these tales, for it would take far too long to set forth everything that happened to these two.

After Easter, at the season of rebirth which clothes all things in green and sets the birds singing their sweet songs throughout the woodland to greet the coming of the warmer weather, the season of joy's zenith everywhere, it fell one day at noon that Lancelot and Galahad arrived beneath a cross that stood on the verge of the forest. At the same moment they saw a knight in white armour come riding out of the wood. His mount was richly caparisoned and at his right hand he was leading a snow-white horse. When he saw the boat hove to, he spurred towards it as fast as he could and greeting the two knights in the Master's name he addressed himself to Galahad:

'Sir Knight, you have been a long while with your father. Leave the boat now and mount this horse, which is as beautiful as it is white, and go where chance shall take you, seeking out and terminating once for all the adventures of the kingdom of Logres.'

When Galahad heard these words he moved quickly across to his father, and kissed him lovingly, weeping as he said to him:

'Most sweet, dear father, I know not whether we shall meet again. I commend you to the person of Jesus Christ, may He keep you ever in His service.'

Both wept, and wept again; and when Galahad had left the boat and mounted, a voice rent the space between them, saying:

'Henceforth let each bestir himself to virtue, for neither one shall see the other more until the dread and awful day when Our Lord shall render unto each his due: that is until the Day of Judgment.'

These words brought fresh tears to Lancelot's eyes as he said to Galahad:

'Son, since it is for ever that I leave you, do you beseech the Master in my name not to let me quit His service, but so to keep me close that I may be His servant in this life and the next.'

And Galahad answered him:

'Sir, there is no prayer so efficacious as your own. Be therefore mindful of yourself.'[70]

They parted forthwith and Galahad thrust into the forest,

while a strong and rushing wind bore down on the boat and carried Lancelot swiftly away from the shore.

So Lancelot was alone in the bark again, save for the body of the maiden. He drifted a whole month long at sea, during which time he slept but little, keeping vigil instead, and entreating Our Lord with earnest tears to lead him to a place where he might have some partial vision of the Holy Grail.

One night around midnight it so happened that he found himself in the lee of a great castle, nobly built and sited; in the rear wall was a gate which opened to seaward and was never shut by day or night. Nor did the inmates keep any watch on that side, for the entrance was always guarded by two lions standing face to face, so that anyone who sought to enter by that door was forced to pass between them. At the hour when Lancelot's boat came in, bright moonlight lit the landscape near and far and just then Lancelot heard a voice say to him:

'Lancelot, leave the boat and enter this castle, where thou shalt find in part the object of thy search and of thy deepest longings.'

At this command he hurriedly snatched up his arms, leaving nothing that he had brought with him behind. When he had stepped ashore and walked up to the gate he discovered the two lions, and fully expected to have to fight his way out. So he clapped his hand to his sword and prepared to defend himself. No sooner had he drawn his sword than glancing up he saw a flaming hand plunge earthwards, which struck him so hard on the arm that the sword flew out of his grip. At the same time he heard a voice proclaim:

'O man of little faith and most infirm belief, why placest thou greater trust in thine own arm than in thy Maker? Thou art but a sorry wretch to hold that He whom thou didst choose to serve can stand thee in no better stead than shield and sword!'*

This reproof and the blow from the hand so astounded Lancelot that he fell down dazed and in a state of such confusion that he knew not whether it were night or day. After a pause, however, he rose to his feet and said:

'Ah! gracious Lord Jesus Christ, I thank Thee and adore Thee for deigning to rebuke me for my offences. Now I see truly that

* Cf. Psalm 44, 3.

Thou dost hold me for Thy servant, when Thou showest me a sign of my want of faith.'

Thereupon he picked up his sword and sheathed it, swearing that he would not draw it again that day, but would trust instead in the mercy of Our Lord:

'And if it be His pleasure that I die, the body's death will be the soul's salvation; and if I am to come through this alive, it will be a mark of honour and renown.'

So saying, he made the sign of the cross on his forehead and commended himself to Our Lord before walking up to the lions. At his approach they both sat down and showed no sign of wanting to harm him, and he passed between them without their touching him. He pursued his course along the main street, going ever on and up till he came to the central fortress. By then it must have been midnight and all the inhabitants of the castle were already abed. Lancelot came to the steps and made his way up till he stood in all his armour within the great hall. Having come that far he looked all around but saw not a soul, to his astonishment, for he had not thought that so grand a palace and so fine a hall as met his gaze would be unoccupied. So he walked straight through, intending to go on till he found someone who could tell him where he was come to, for he did not know what country he was in.

Lancelot pursued his exploration till he came to a room with door closed fast. He pushed against it, thinking to open it, but could not; he tried again and again but nothing he did could gain him entry. Then there fell on his ear a strain so sweet that it seemed no mortal voice could utter it. In it he fancied he discerned the words: 'Glory and praise and honour be Thine, Father of heaven!'* When Lancelot heard what the voice was singing he knelt down with a swelling heart outside the chamber, convinced that the Holy Grail was present there. And as he knelt, he wept, and said:

'Most sweet Lord Jesus Christ, if ever I did anything that pleased Thee, then of Thy pity, gracious Lord, spurn me not now, denying me all sight of that which I have been seeking.'

Directly he had made this plea, Lancelot raised his eyes and

* Cf. Revelation 7, 12.

saw the door of the chamber standing wide and a great light flooding through the opening, as if the sun had its abode within. The brightness that came pouring out of the room illumined the whole palace till one would have thought that all the candles on earth were burning there. At this sight Lancelot's joy and his desire to see the source of the light grew so intense that he forgot everything beside. He went to the door and was on the point of entering when a voice said to him:

'Step back, Lancelot! On no account must thou enter here, it is forbidden thee. And if thou fly in the face of this proscription, thou shalt repent it.'

When Lancelot heard this warning, he stepped back sorrowing: a man most eager to enter, yet obedient to the order barring him.

So he let his gaze run round the room and observed the Holy Vessel standing beneath a cloth of bright red samite upon a silver table. And all around were ministering angels, some swinging silver censers, others holding lighted candles, crosses and other altar furnishings, each and every one intent upon some service. Before the Holy Vessel was an aged man in priestly vestments, engaged to all appearance in the consecration of the mass. When he came to elevate the host, Lancelot thought he saw, above his outstretched hands, three men, two of whom were placing the youngest in the hands of the priest who raised him aloft as though he were showing him to the people.[71]

Lancelot was more than a little amazed at what he saw; for he noticed that the celebrant was so weighed down by the figure he was holding that he seemed about to fall beneath the burden. Seeing this, he had a wish to go to his assistance, for he felt sure that none of those who were with him intended helping him. He was filled with such burning zeal that he quite forgot he had been forbidden to set foot there, and hastening to the door he said:

'Ah! gracious Lord Jesus Christ, let not my going to help this priest, who stands in need of aid, be a cause to me of hurt or of damnation.'

With that he crossed the threshold and made towards the silver table. As he drew near he felt a puff of wind which seemed to him shot through with flame, so hot it was, and as it fanned his features with its scorching breath he thought his face was burned.[72] He stood rooted to the ground like a man paralysed, bereft of sight and hearing and powerless in every limb. Then he felt himself seized by many hands and carried away. And when they had grabbed him by the arms and legs they pitched him out and left him where he fell.[73]

Next morning when bright daylight had returned and the inmates of the castle were about again, they found Lancelot lying in front of the door of the room and wondered greatly at the sight. They bade him rise, but he neither moved nor gave a sign that he had even heard them. Seeing this, they said he must be dead, and hurriedly unarmed him there and then and examined him all over to find out whether there was any life in him; however, he was powerless to speak or utter a word, and lay as inert as a clod. So they lifted him bodily and carried him in their arms to a secluded room in the castle and laid him in a richly furnished bed, where no noise could disturb him. They did all that they could for him, staying by him all that day, and addressing him often to see whether he could speak; but he answered not a word, nor gave any indication that he had ever spoken. They felt his pulse and examined his veins and exclaimed in astonishment at this knight who was certainly alive, yet could not speak to them; and some said that they knew not what the cause could be, unless it were some punishment or sign from God.

The inmates stayed throughout that day by Lancelot's bedside, and it was the same on the third day and the fourth. Some said he was dead, others averred he lived.

'In God's name,' said an old man of the house, who had a great knowledge of physic, 'I tell you truly that he is not dead at all, but as full of life as the most robust among us; I therefore recommend that he be well and handsomely looked after, until such time as Our Lord restores him to the health he once enjoyed; then shall we learn the truth about him, who he is and whence he hails. And believe you me, as I have some little knowledge, this man has been one of the foremost knights in the world, and shall be again one day, so it please Our Lord: for as I see it he is as yet in no danger of death, though I do not deny that he may yet languish long in his present state.'

The good man's view of Lancelot proved him uncommonly wise. Indeed he never said a thing about him that was not true to the last particular. For it turned out that they were watching over him for four and twenty days and four and twenty nights without his ever eating or drinking, or uttering a single word; nor did he move hand or foot or any member, or give any outward sign of life at all. None the less each time they scrutinized him closely it was plain to them that he lived. There was no one, man or woman, who was not sorry for him, and those who saw him would exclaim:

'God! What a shame it is about this knight who seems to have been a fine and valiant man, and was amazingly handsome, and now God has straitened him in this infirmity!'

Such sentiments were often on their lips, and tears, too, in their eyes; but for all they searched their memories they failed to recognize him for Lancelot, although the household counted many knights who had seen him so often that they should have known him.

Lancelot lay four and twenty days in a state that left his hosts foreseeing no outcome other than his death. It was around noon on the twenty-fourth day that he opened his eyes. At the sight of the people gathered round he set up a great lamentation, crying:

'Ah! God, why didst Thou waken me so soon? I was far happier now than ever I shall be again! Ah! gracious Lord Jesus Christ, where dwells the man so blessed by fortune and above reproach that he could contemplate Thy glorious mysteries and set his gaze there where my sinful sight was darkened and my eyes blinded, that had been sullied by looking on the midden of this world?'

The watchers round the bed rejoiced to hear him speak, and asked him what he had seen.

'I have seen,' he said, 'such glories and felicity that my tongue could never reveal their magnitude, nor could my heart conceive it. For this was no earthly but a spiritual vision. And but for my grievous sins and my most evil plight I should have seen still more, had I not lost the sight of my eyes and all power over my body, on account of the infamy that God had seen in me.'

Then Lancelot addressed his hosts and said:

'Good Sirs, I am at a loss to know why I am here, for I have no recollection of how I came to be placed here, nor in what circumstances.'

The others told him all they had seen, and explained how he had lain among them for twenty-four days without their knowing whether he was alive or dead. When Lancelot heard all this he began to wonder what meaning attached to the duration of his plight. At length he bethought himself that he had served the enemy for a space of twenty-four years, and that Our Lord, by way of penance for this sin, had deprived him four and twenty days of all his bodily faculties. Then Lancelot, looking up, caught sight of the hair-shirt he had worn for nearly half a year, and of which he saw himself now divested. The discovery grieved him, for it seemed to him that he had broken his vow in this regard. Those with him asked him how he felt, and he replied that he was fit and well, thanks be to God.

'But for the love of God,' he added, 'tell me where I am.'

'In the Castle of Corbenic,' came the reply.

A maiden came to Lancelot next, bringing him a fresh, new linen gown; but he would not put it on, taking the hair-shirt in its stead. Marking his gesture, the bystanders said to him:

'Sir Knight, you can leave off the hair-shirt now, for your quest is ended; there is no use your striving any longer to seek the Holy Grail; for you should know that you will not see more of it than you have seen. May God now bring us those who are to see that more.'

These words could not sway Lancelot's resolve: he took the hair-shirt and put it on, slipping on next the linen gown, and finally a gown of scarlet cloth that was brought him. When he was dressed and arrayed, all the members of the household came to see him, and viewed with wonder all that God had done for him. Hardly had they looked him up and down than they recognized him and cried:

'What! my lord Lancelot, is it you?'[74]

He said it was indeed. This was the sign for wondrous great rejoicing throughout the palace. The word sped so fast from mouth to mouth that at last it was brought to the ear of King Pellés himself by a knight who said to him:

'Sir, I have strange and wonderful news to tell you.'

'What is it?' asked the king.

'By my faith, that knight who was lying here as dead is risen fit and well, and he is none other than Sir Lancelot of the Lake!'

The king was happy indeed to hear these tidings and went to visit his guest. When Lancelot saw him coming he rose to greet him and wish him welcome, and received him with great joy. The king acquainted him with the death of his beautiful daughter, she on whom Galahad had been begotten; and Lancelot was very grieved, for she was a most noble lady and born of an exalted line.

Lancelot stayed four days in the palace, to the great delight of the king who had long desired his company. On the fifth day it happened as they sat down to dinner that the Holy Grail had already loaded the tables with such a wealth of dishes that a more plenteous spread were past imagining. During the meal they witnessed an adventure that appeared wonderful to everyone; for they saw quite clearly, and with profound amazement, the doors of the palace close of themselves. Thereupon a knight in all his armour and mounted on a great war-horse rode up to the main door and began to shout:

'Open up! Open up!'

Those of the household were reluctant to unbar the door to him. But he went on shouting and pestered them so much that the king himself rose from the table and went to one of the windows of the palace that overlooked the door. He peered out, and, seeing the knight waiting at the gate, he said:

'Sir Knight, you shall not enter; no man so proudly mounted as yourself shall enter here so long as the Holy Grail is within. Go back to your own country, for you are surely no companion of the Quest, but rather one of those who have quit the service of Jesus Christ to become the liegemen of the enemy.'

These words were bitter to the waiting knight and filled him with such chagrin that he knew not what to do. He had turned to go when the king called him back again and said to him:

'Sir Knight, since it is the case that you have come here, I pray you, tell me who you are.'

'Sir,' he replied, 'I am from the kingdom of Logres, my name is Hector of the Marsh and I am brother to Sir Lancelot of the Lake.'

'In God's name,' said the king, 'I recognize you now; and now I have fresh cause for sorrow, for I cared but little before, but now I do care, for the love I bear your brother who is within.'

When Hector heard that his brother was there, the man of whom he stood most in awe by reason of the great love he bore him, he said:

'Ah! God, now is my shame redoubled and grows greater every minute! Now I shall never dare to face my brother, since I have failed where others shall not fail, the worthy men and true knights of Our Lord. In verity the hermit on the hilltop spoke me true when he explained to me and Sir Gawain the meaning of our dreams!'

With that Hector left the courtyard and galloped out through the castle at the greatest speed he could screw from his horse. When the inhabitants saw him fleeing at such a pace, they all shouted after him, hooting and cursing the hour he was born, and calling him a scurvy knight and a coward; and he was so mortified that he wished he were dead. He pursued his headlong flight till he galloped out of the castle and dashed into the forest there where he saw it thickest. King Pellés meanwhile returned to Lancelot and told him the news about his brother, which distressed him beyond bearing. However he strove to hide his feelings he could not prevent his hosts from seeing the tears that were running down his face. The king was consumed with regret for what he had said to him; for he would not have said it for the world had he known that it would pain him to that extent.

When they had eaten, Lancelot asked the king to have his arms brought to him, for he wanted to return to the kingdom of Logres, from which he had been absent for more than a year.[75]

'Sir,' said the king, 'I pray you, forgive me what I said to you about your brother.'

Lancelot said that he forgave him with all his heart. The king then ordered his arms to be brought to him, and he armed himself as soon as they were fetched. When he was all accoutred and it remained but for him to mount, the king had a swift and powerful charger led into the courtyard, and bade Lancelot mount it, which he did. And when he was horsed and had taken leave of all the inmates of the palace, he went on his way and rode many a long day's journey through alien lands.

One evening Lancelot chanced to stop for the night at an abbey of white monks, where the brethren showed him every honour on account of his being a wandering knight. In the morning, when he had heard mass and was about to leave the church, he glanced to his right and noticed a tomb of great and splendid beauty, which gave the appearance of being newly hewn and carved. He turned aside to see what it was; a closer look at the exquisite workmanship convinced him that some great prince must lie beneath. Turning then to the head he saw an inscription, which read: HERE LIES KING BAUDEMAGUS OF GORRE, SLAIN BY GAWAIN, THE NEPHEW OF KING ARTHUR. This information grieved him not a little, for he had loved King Baudemagus deeply, and had his slayer been any other than Sir Gawain he would not have escaped with his life. Lancelot wept bitter tears for his friend, mourning him forlornly and bewailing a loss so grievous to those of King Arthur's household and many a good man else.

Lancelot remained there all that day in sorrow and vexation of spirit for love of the worthy king who had often honoured him. Next morning, when he was armed, he mounted his horse and, commending the monks to God's keeping, took to the road again. His journeyings, which followed no set course, brought him one day to the tombs which stand within their palisade of swords. As soon as he saw this prodigy he rode straight in without dismounting and looked at the tombs.[77] Then departing again he pursued his wanderings till he came at last to King Arthur's court, where the first glimpse of him was hailed with the greatest joy by all and sundry, who were waiting impatiently for his return and that of the other companions, few indeed of whom were yet come back. And those that had come back had accomplished nothing in the Quest, to their undying shame. And here the tale leaves them all and returns to Galahad, the son of Lancelot of the Lake.

The Holy Grail

Now the story relates that after leaving Lancelot, Galahad spent many days riding as chance led him, now forward and now back on his tracks, till he came at last to the abbey where King Mordrain was lying; and on hearing the story of how the king was waiting for the Good Knight, he thought he would go to see him. So the following morning directly after mass he went to the chapel where the king was lodged. As soon as the knight drew near him, King Mordrain, who by the will of God had long since lost his sight and bodily powers, was able to see plain. He raised himself up at the instant and said to Galahad:

'Galahad, servant of God, true knight whose coming I have so long awaited, take me in your arms and let me lie on your breast so that I may die in your embrace, for you are as pure and virginal compared to other knights as the lily flower, the symbol of virginity, is white beyond all other. You are the lily of purity, you are the true rose, the flower of strength and healing with the tint of fire: for the fire of the Holy Ghost burns in you so brightly that my flesh which was withered and dead is now made young and strong again.'

When Galahad heard these words he sat down at the head of the king's bed and embraced him and laid him against his breast, since that was where he wanted to repose. And the king leaned over towards him and clasped him in his arms, straining him close and saying:

'Blessed Lord Jesus Christ, now have I my heart's desire. I beseech Thee now to come to fetch me in this my present state, for I could not die in any spot so pleasant and delightful as is the one in which I find myself. For this bliss which I have yearned after so long is all composed of lilies and of roses.'*

Proof that Our Lord had heard his prayer followed at once on this request, for in the next moment he rendered up his spirit

*Cf. Song of Songs 2, 1.

to Him whom he had served so long, dying in Galahad's arms. When the brethren heard the news they came to attend to the body and found that the wounds he had suffered from for so many years were healed; and they held it for a great marvel. The body was buried afterwards in the abbey with all the honours that are due to a king.

Galahad tarried there two days. On the third he left, and after many a long day's journey he came to the Perilous Forest where he found the spring which seethed with giant bubbles, as was described in an earlier part of the story. No sooner had he plunged his hand into the water than the heat and fury went out of it, because there was no fever of lust in him. The inhabitants of the country received the news that the water was cooled with awe and wonderment. It was then that the spring lost the name it had always had and was known from then on as Galahad's Fount.

When he had put an end to this phenomenon his wanderings took him into the land of Gorre, and on until he came to the abbey which Lancelot had once visited, and where he had found the tomb of Galahad, king of Hosselice and son of Joseph of Arimathea,[78] together with that of Simeon, and where he had met with failure. When Galahad arrived he looked down into the crypt that lay under the church, and noticing the tomb which was burning with so strange and fierce a flame, he asked the brethren what it was.

'Sir,' they said, 'this fire is of so wonderful a nature that it will only be quenched by one who shall surpass in virtue and knightly skill all the companions of the Round Table.'

'If you please,' he said, 'I wish you would take me to the door which leads to it.'

They agreed readily to that, and conducted him to the door of the crypt. Galahad descended the steps, and as he approached the tomb the fire died down and the flame, which had burned year in, year out, with a strange intensity, was suddenly quenched at the coming of him in whom no base fires burned. Then, going to the tomb, he raised the stone up on end, and saw inside the body of Simeon, who had died a violent death;[79] and directly the heat had abated a voice was heard to say:

'Galahad, Galahad, you should tender your heartfelt thanks

to Our Lord for granting you such a favour: for by the goodness of your life you can save souls from earthly suffering and open to them the joys of Paradise. I am your forebear, Simeon, who have dwelt three hundred and fifty years in the furnace you have just seen, to expiate a sin I once committed against Joseph of Arimathea. And besides the torments that I have endured I would have perished everlastingly. But by reason of your great humility, the Holy Ghost, who works more powerfully in you than do the interests of this world, looked with compassion on me, and translated me, all thanks to Him, from earthly anguish to the joys of heaven, whereto the grace of your coming was sufficient.'

The monks, who had followed him down as soon as the flame was extinguished, overheard these words and regarded the incident as a miracle. Galahad gathered up the body and lifting it out of the tomb he carried it up into the church itself. There the brethren took it and, having shrouded it in a manner befitting a knight (for such had Simeon been), they buried his remains in front of the high altar. Having completed their task they came to Galahad, and after paying him every honour they could think of, they enquired what land and lineage he came from, and he told them who he was.

Next morning, after hearing mass, Galahad took his leave, commending the brethren to God, and set out again on his travels, roaming the land for five whole years before he arrived at the house of the Maimed King.[80] During those five years Perceval kept him company wherever he went, and by the end of that time they had done so much towards resolving the strange phenomena of the kingdom of Logres, that one does not witness many nowadays, unless it be some miraculous intervention of Our Lord. Nor on any occasion were their adversaries, however great their numbers, ever able to discomfit or daunt them or unman them.

It fell one day that on emerging from a vast, impenetrable forest, they espied the lone figure of Bors crossing their path. It needs not asking whether they were overjoyed on discovering who it was, for the parting had been a long one and they craved his company. So they made a great fuss of him, and wished him honour and good fortune, as did he to them. Then they asked him how he had fared, and he told them in reply of everything that had befallen him since leaving them, adding that in all of five years he had not slept four nights in a bed, nor in a human dwelling, but in outlandish brakes and inaccessible mountains where he would have succumbed a hundred times and more, had not the grace of the Holy Ghost been to him comfort, meat and drink in all his hardships.

'And did you ever find the thing we seek?' asked Perceval.

'No, indeed. But I think we shall not part again before concluding that for which this Quest was first begun.'

'God grant it may be so!' said Galahad. 'As for your arrival, as God is my help, nothing could make me happier: I longed for your presence, now I joy in it.'

Thus it was that the same hazard that had parted the three companions brought them together again. They kept company for a long time before their wanderings brought them one fine day to the Castle of Corbenic. When the king recognized his visitors a wave of jubilation was let loose, for it was well known that the coming of these three heralded the ending of these adventures which had been centred on the castle for so long. As the news of their advent spread to every corner, so did all the inhabitants come running out to see them. And King Pellés wept over his grandson Galahad, as did all the others who had known him as a child.

When the three had unarmed, King Pellés' son, Elyezer, carried in the Broken Sword which the tale has already mentioned, the same with which Joseph of Arimathea was wounded in the thigh.*When Elyezer had drawn it from the scabbard and described to them how it had come to be broken, Bors took it to try whether he could knit the pieces, but in vain. In view of his failure, he handed it to Perceval, saying:

'Sir, see whether you can be the one to perform this feat.'

'Gladly,' replied the other.

So Perceval took the broken sword and placed the two pieces end to end; but he could not make them knit at all. Seeing this, he turned to Galahad and said:

'Sir, our attempts have met with failure. Now it is for you to

---

* Cf. Sommer, Vol. I, pp. 252–6, and Vol. IV, pp. 323–8.

try your hand, and if you fail, I am sure no man of flesh and blood will ever bring off this feat.'

Then Galahad took the two parts of the sword and joined the severed edges, and at once the sections knit so perfectly that it was beyond the power of the human eye to discern the place of fracture, or even suspect that the sword had once been broken.

The companions, seeing this, declared that God had granted them to make a good beginning, and that since they had met with success in the first, the other adventures should be easily compassed. As for the people of the place, they rejoiced beyond measure to see the adventure of the sword brought to its close; they gave the weapon to Bors, saying that it could not have a better master, since he was a man of sterling worth and valour.

When the hour of vespers came, the sky began to grow dark and stormy, and an unearthly wind got up, which whistled through the palace: such heat was in its blast that many expected to be burned and some fell fainting from terror; and they heard in the same moment a voice, which said:

'Let those who are not to sit at the table of Jesus Christ take their departure, for now is the time when the true knights shall be fed with the food of heaven.'

At these words the entire company vacated the hall, with the exception of King Pellés, a man of great probity and godly life, his son Elyezer and a niece of the king's, the most devout and saintly creature then to grace the earth. And with these three there stayed the three companions, to see what sign Our Lord would favour them with. When they had waited a while, they saw nine armed knights come through the door, take off their helms and go up to Galahad, to whom they bowed and said:

'Sir, we have made great haste in order to sit down with you at the table where the heavenly food shall be dispensed.'

Galahad said in reply that they had come in good time, for they themselves had only just arrived. With that they all seated themselves in the middle of the hall, and Galahad asked the newcomers who they were. Three of them said that they were from Gaul, and three that they came from Ireland, while the other three said that they were from Denmark.[81]

T–L

During this exchange of greetings they noticed four maidens bearing in a wooden bed from a neighbouring room, and in this bed lay a man, apparently infirm, who had a gold crown on his head. When the maidens arrived in the centre of the hall they set the bed down and went back whence they had come, while he that lay there raised his head and spoke to Galahad, saying:

'Welcome, Sir! I have desired so much to see you and have waited on your coming for so long, in pain and torment such as another could not long have borne. But now, please God, the hour is come when my suffering shall find relief and I shall leave this world as was promised me long ago.'

As he finished speaking, a voice made itself heard among them, saying:

'Let him who has not been a companion of the Quest of the Holy Grail depart this place: for it is not right that any such should stay here longer.'

Directly after this pronouncement King Pellés, his son Elyezer and the maiden all went out. And when the hall stood empty except for those who felt themselves to be indeed companions of the Quest, to these, then, that remained, it seemed that a man came down from heaven garbed in a bishop's robes, and with a crozier in his hand and a mitre on his head; four angels bore him on a glorious throne, which they set down next to the table supporting the Holy Grail. This visitor, who had come among them in the guise of a bishop, had an inscription on his brow which read: THIS IS JOSEPHUS, THE FIRST CHRISTIAN BISHOP, THE SAME WHO WAS CONSECRATED BY OUR LORD IN SARRAS, IN THE SPIRITUAL PALACE. The knights could read the writing well enough, but its meaning left them agape with wonderment, for the Josephus whom the words referred to had departed this world more than three hundred years before. Now he spoke to them, saying:

'Ah! knights of God, servants of Jesus Christ, be not amazed if you see me before you conjointly with this Holy Vessel, for that same service I performed on earth I still discharge in heaven.'

Having said this, he approached the silver table and prostrated himself on hands and knees before the altar; after a lengthy interval the sound of the chamber door flying suddenly open burst upon his ear. He turned his head towards it, as did the others too, to see the angels who had borne him thither proceeding from the room; two had candles in their hands, the third bore a cloth of red samite, the fourth a lance which bled so freely that the drops were falling into a container which the angel held in his other hand. The first two placed the candles on the table, and the third laid the cloth beside the Holy Vessel; the fourth held the lance upright over the Vessel so that the blood running down the shaft was caught therein. As soon as these motions had been carried out, Josephus rose and lifted the lance a little higher above the Holy Vessel, which he then covered with the cloth.

Next Josephus acted as though he were entering on the consecration of the mass. After pausing a moment quietly, he took from the Vessel a host made in the likeness of bread. As he raised it aloft there descended from above a figure like to a child, whose countenance glowed and blazed as bright as fire; and he entered into the bread, which quite distinctly took on human form before the eyes of those assembled there. When Josephus had stood for some while holding his burden up to view, he replaced it in the Holy Vessel.[82]

Having discharged the functions of a priest as it might be at the office of the mass, Josephus went up to Galahad and kissed him, bidding him kiss his brethren likewise, which he did. Next he addressed them, saying:

'Servants of Jesus Christ, who have suffered and struggled and striven for some glimpse of the mysteries of the Holy Grail, be seated before this table and you shall be filled with the most sublime and glorious food that ever knights have tasted, and this at your Saviour's hand. You can justly claim to have laboured manfully, for you shall reap this day the highest recompense that ever knights received.'

When he had spoken thus, Josephus vanished from their midst, without their ever knowing what became of him. Fearfully they took their seats at the Table, their faces wet with tears of awe and love.

Then the companions, raising their eyes, saw the figure of a man appear from out of the Holy Vessel, unclothed, and bleeding from his hands and feet and side; and he said to them:

'My knights, my servants and my faithful sons who have attained to the spiritual life whilst in the flesh, you who have sought me so diligently that I can hide myself from you no longer, it is right you should see some part of my secrets and my mysteries, for your labours have won a place for you at my table, where no knight has eaten since the days of Joseph of Arimathea. As for the rest, they have had the servant's due: which means that the knights of this castle and many more beside have been filled with the grace of the Holy Vessel, but never face to face as you are now. Take now and eat of the precious food that you have craved so long and for which you have endured so many trials.'

Then he took the Holy Vessel in his hands, and going to Galahad, who knelt at his approach, he gave his Saviour to him. And Galahad, with both hands joined in homage, received with an overflowing heart. So too did the others, and to every one it seemed that the host placed on his tongue was made of bread. When they had all received the holy food, which they found so honeyed and delectable that it seemed as though the essence of all sweetness was housed within their bodies, he who had fed them said to Galahad:

'Son, who art as cleansed and free from stain as any may be in this life, knowst thou what I am holding?'

'No,' replied Galahad, 'unless thou tell it me.'

'It is,' he answered, 'the platter in which Jesus Christ partook of the paschal lamb with His disciples. It is the platter which has shown itself agreeable to those whom I have found my faithful servants, the same whose sight has ever been most hurtful to the faithless. And because it has shown itself agreeable to all my people it is called most properly the Holy Grail.[83] Now hast thou seen the object of thy heart's most fervent longing; yet shalt thou see it plainer still one day. Knowst thou where this shall be? In the city of Sarras, in the spiritual palace; and to this end it is imperative thou leave this place and escort the sacred Vessel on its way, for it is to leave the kingdom of Logres this same night and neither it nor the adventures it gave rise to shall ever more be seen there. Knowst thou the reason for its leaving? The inhabitants of this country neither serve nor honour it as is its due. They have lapsed into dissolute and worldly ways, despite the fact that they have ever been sustained by the grace of the Holy Vessel. And forasmuch as they have made such poor return I strip them of the honour I had granted them. This is why I would have thee go tomorrow morning to the sea, where thou shalt find the ship whence thou didst take the Sword of the Strange Belt. And so that thou shouldst not ride alone, I wish thee to take Bors and Perceval to keep thee company. However, since I would not have thee leave this place without the Maimed King's being healed, thou shalt take first some blood of this lance and anoint his legs with it: for this and this alone can bring him back to health.'

'Ah, Lord,' said Galahad, 'why wilt thou not allow them all to come with me?'

'Such is not my wish,' he answered, 'rather are you to figure my apostles. For as they ate with me at the Last Supper, even so did you eat with me now at the table of the Holy Grail. And you are twelve, as they too numbered twelve, and I the thirteenth over and above you, to be your shepherd and your master. And even as I dispersed them and sent them throughout the world to preach the true law, so do I send you too, some one way, some another.'

With that he gave them his blessing and vanished in such a manner that they knew not what became of him, save that they saw him rising heavenwards.

Then Galahad went to the lance which lay across the table, and touching the blood with his fingers, he walked across to the Maimed King and anointed his legs with it where the steel had pierced him. And immediately the king put on a gown, and springing hale and sound from his bed, he offered thanks to Our Lord for looking so graciously upon him. He lived for a long time after, but not in the world, however, for he left at once to enter a monastery of white monks, where Our Lord for love of him performed in after days many notable miracles, which are not mentioned in this story since they are not essential to its purpose.

Around midnight, after a long time spent imploring Our Lord of His mercy to keep their souls in safety wherever they might go, they heard the sound of a voice among them, saying:

'My sons, in name and nature both, my friends, no foes to me, depart from here, and go where you think you will be best employed and where adventure leads you.'

To this command they answered with one voice:

'Father of heaven, blessed be Thou who deignest to consider us Thy sons and friends!* Now do we see that our labours were not vain.'

With that they left the palace and went down into the courtyard below where they found arms and horses. They equipped themselves without delay, and as soon as all were mounted they rode out of the castle. Asking one another whence they came, the better to be acquainted, they discovered that one of the knights from Gaul was Claudin, son of King Claudas,[84] while the other two, whichever countries they hailed from, were men of gentle birth and high descent. When the time came for parting, they kissed one another like brothers, shedding fond tears, and saying to Galahad with one accord:

'Know, Sir, in very truth, that we never tasted joy so full as at the hour when we first learned that we were to bear you company, nor ever grief so sharp as we now feel at leaving you so soon. We see, though, that this parting is pleasing to Our Lord, and it behoves us therefore to part without repining.'

'Fair Sirs,' said Galahad, 'if you had a liking for my company, yours was as dear to me. But you see that our continuing together cannot be. So I commend you all to God, and beg of you, should you come to King Arthur's court, to greet my father Sir Lancelot and all those of the Round Table on my behalf.'

The others replied that if they went that way they would not forget his charge.

With that they took their leave of one another. Galahad rode off with his companions and the three of them covered so much country that they came to the sea in less than four days' riding. They would have got there sooner still save that, being strangers to those parts, they did not take by any means the shortest route.

When they came to the sea, lying close inshore they found the ship which had harboured the Sword of the Strange Belt, and saw again the inscription on the hull which said that none

* Cf. John 15, 15.

should enter unless he firmly believed in Jesus Christ. Standing at the ship's side and looking down into it, they spied the silver table last seen in the Maimed King's palace, and resting now on the bed which had been set up in the ship. On it stood the Holy Grail, beneath a piece of bright red samite in the form of a chalice veil. The companions drew one another's attention to this wonder, acclaiming their good fortune at having that which above all else they loved and longed to see, to keep them company till their journey's end. Then, making the sign of the cross, they commended themselves to Our Lord and entered the ship. Directly they had stepped aboard, the wind which earlier had been hushed and still came whistling into the sail with frightening force, driving the ship from the shore and speeding it towards the open sea, where its ever-growing strength sent the bark scudding faster and faster over the waves.

They spent many weeks at sea without knowing whither God was guiding them. Each night when Galahad lay down to sleep and every morning when he rose he besought Our Lord that at the hour of his asking, He would grant him release from this life. He prayed so sedulously night and morning that at last the divine voice said to him:

'Be not down-hearted, Galahad, for Our Lord will do thy pleasure in this matter: at whatever hour thou shalt ask to die in the body it shall be granted thee, and thou shalt live in the spirit and have joy everlasting.'

This request, that Galahad had made so often, was overheard by Perceval, to the latter's great bewilderment; he begged him, by their friendship and the faith they owed each other, to confide in him the reason for his asking such a thing.

'I will tell you that with pleasure,' said Galahad. 'The other day, when we saw in part the wonders of the Holy Grail which Our Lord of His gracious mercy deigned to show us, as I was looking on the hidden mysteries that are not disclosed to common view, but only to them that wait on Jesus Christ, in the moment that revealed to me those things that the heart of mortal man cannot conceive nor tongue relate, my heart was ravished with such joy and bliss, that had I died forthwith I know that no man ever breathed his last in such beatitude as then was mine. For so great a host of angels was before me and such a multitude of heavenly beings, that I was translated in that moment from the earthly plane to the celestial, to the joy of the glorious martyrs and the beloved of Our Lord. And because I hope to be again as favourably placed as I was then, or better still, to contemplate this bliss, therefore I made the plea you overheard. And thus I trust that I shall depart this life, by God's goodwill, while looking on the glories of the Holy Grail.'

So it was that Galahad announced to Perceval his coming death, as he himself had learnt it in the reply vouchsafed from heaven. And so too, in the manner I have related, did the people of Logres through their sinfulness forfeit the presence of the Holy Grail, which had fed and nourished them so often with unstinted measure. And just as Our Lord had sent the Holy Vessel to Galahad and Josephus and their posterity because of the goodness that he found in them, so did he divest the sinful heirs on account of their turpitude and wicked ways. Thus it is plain to see that the wicked descendants lost through evil-doing what the upright had retained through righteousness.

One day, when the companions had been long at sea, Bors and Perceval said to Galahad:

'Sir, you have never slept in this bed which, according to what we have read, was made and prepared for you, and this is something you ought to do, for the letter said you would rest there.'

Galahad declared himself willing and, lying down in the bed, slept long and deep; and when he awoke, he looked ahead and beheld the city of Sarras.[85] Just then a voice made itself heard to the three companions, saying:

'Leave the ship, ye knights of Jesus Christ, and take this silver table with its burden, and carry it between you into the city, without once setting it down until you find yourselves in the spiritual palace, where Josephus was first consecrated bishop by Our Lord.'

As they set about taking the table out of the ship, they glanced across the water and saw the bark come gliding in, in which they had laid Perceval's sister many weeks before. The sight of it led them to exclaim to one another:

'In God's name, this maiden has kept faith with us right well, to follow us thus far.'

Then they took up the silver table and carried it ashore.

With Bors and Perceval in front and Galahad to the rear they moved off in the direction of the city. By the time they came to the gate, Galahad was flagging under the table's heavy weight. He noticed a man on crutches sitting beneath the archway in the hope of receiving alms from the passers-by, who often gave to him for love of Jesus Christ. As he drew near him Galahad called to the man and said:

'Come here, good friend, and help me carry this table up yonder into the palace.'

'Ah! Sir, for the love of God,' exclaimed the other, 'what is it you are saying? It is more than ten years since last I walked unaided.'

'Be not concerned,' said Galahad, 'rise to your feet and doubt not, for you are healed.'

Galahad had hardly finished speaking when the man made a tentative effort to get up, and discovered himself in the trying to be as fit and strong as if he had never known a day's infirmity. Running to the table, he took the corner next to Galahad, and as he entered the city he told everyone he met of the miracle that God had performed for him.

When they had made their way up into the palace, they beheld the throne which Our Lord had prepared for Josephus to sit on long ago. They were followed at once by a crowd of citizens, hastening in amazement to see the cripple who had just regained the use of his limbs. Having carried out their instructions, the companions went down again to the harbour and stepped into the boat where Perceval's sister lay. Between them they lifted the bed and carried her on it up into the palace, where they buried her with such ceremony as befitted a king's daughter.

When the king of that city, one Escorant by name, first saw the three companions, he asked them where they came from and what it was they had brought with them on the silver table. To all his questions they gave truthful answers, and told him of the wondrous nature of the Grail and of the power with which God had invested it. But he was a cruel and perfidious man, taking as he did his whole descent from the accursed pagan breed. He believed not a word they said, but declared them to be base impostors. He bided his time till he saw them weaponless, and then had them seized by his men and thrown into his dungeon where he held them for a year in strict incarceration. For them this proved a source of good, inasmuch as Our Lord did not forget His servants, but sent the Holy Grail, from the first day of their imprisonment, to visit and abide with them, and to fill them daily with its grace as long as they lay captive.

When the year had passed, Galahad happened one day to make his plaint to Our Lord, saying:

'Lord, it seems to me that I have been long enough in this world: grant me, if it please Thee, prompt deliverance.'

The same day, as it chanced, King Escorant was lying ill on his death-bed. He summoned the three before him and asked their pardon for having wrongfully ill-treated them. The companions forgave him from their hearts, and he died directly after.

Once he was buried, the citizens were seized with consternation, for they did not know whom to have for king. They consulted long together, and while they were still in council they heard a voice declare:

'Take the youngest of the three companions to your king: he will protect you well and be your counsellor as long as he lives among you.'

They did as the voice commanded, taking Galahad and making him king, whether he would or no, and setting the crown on his head. All this displeased him greatly, but seeing that needs must (for they would have killed him else), he acceded to their desire.[86]

When Galahad found himself the lord of a domain, he had an ark of gold and precious stones built over the silver table to house the Holy Vessel. And every morning, directly he had risen, he and his two companions presented themselves before the Holy Vessel and there recited their prayers and orisons.

When the year was up and the self-same day that had seen Galahad crowned came round again, the three companions rose at crack of dawn and went up to the palace which men termed spiritual. Looking towards the Holy Vessel they saw a noble-looking man in the vestments of a bishop kneeling before the table reciting the Confiteor. After a long moment he rose from his knees and intoned the mass of the glorious Mother of God. When he came to the solemn part of the mass and had taken the paten off the sacred Vessel, he called Galahad over with the words:

'Come forward, servant of Jesus Christ, and look on that which you have so ardently desired to see.'

Galahad drew near and looked into the Holy Vessel. He had but glanced within when a violent trembling seized his mortal flesh at the contemplation of the spiritual mysteries. Then lifting up his hands to heaven, he said:

'Lord, I worship Thee and give Thee thanks that Thou hast granted my desire, for now I see revealed what tongue could not relate nor heart conceive. Here is the source of valour undismayed, the spring-head of endeavour; here I see the wonder that passes every other! And since, sweet Lord, Thou hast fulfilled my wish to let me see what I have ever craved, I pray Thee now that in this state Thou suffer me to pass from earthly life to life eternal.'[87]

As soon as Galahad had made his petition to Our Lord, the venerable man who stood in bishop's robes before the altar took the Lord's Body from the table, and tendered it to Galahad who received it humbly and with great devotion. When he had received it, the man of God said to him:

'Do you know who I am?'

'No, Sir, unless you tell me.'

'Learn then,' he said, 'that I am Josephus, son of Joseph of Arimathea, whom Our Lord has sent you for companion. And do you know why he has sent me rather than another? Because you have resembled me in two particulars: in that you have contemplated the mysteries of the Holy Grail, as I did too, and in that you are a virgin like myself; wherefore it is most fitting that I should keep my fellow company.'

When Josephus had finished speaking, Galahad went to Perceval and kissed him, and then to Bors and said to him:

'Bors, as soon as you see Sir Lancelot, my father, greet him from me.'

Returning then to the table he prostrated himself on hands and knees before it; and it was not long before he fell face downwards on the flagged floor of the palace, for his soul had already fled its house of flesh and was borne to heaven by angels making jubilation and blessing the name of Our Lord.

A great marvel followed immediately on Galahad's death: the two remaining companions saw quite plainly a hand come down from heaven, but not the body it belonged to. It proceeded straight to the Holy Vessel and took both it and the lance, and carried them up to heaven, to the end that no man since has ever dared to say he saw the Holy Grail.

When Bors and Perceval saw that Galahad was dead they plumbed the very depths of grief. And had they not been men of the greatest godliness of life and character, they might have fallen into despair on account of the great love they had borne him. And the people of the country, too, mourned him with heavy hearts.

There where he died they dug his grave; and as soon as he had been buried Perceval left for a hermitage outside the city walls and took the religious habit. Bors kept him company, but never quitted his secular dress, for it was still his ambition to return to King Arthur's court. Perceval abode in the hermitage for a year and three days and then departed this life; and Bors had him buried in the spiritual palace where his sister and Galahad lay.

Finding himself left all alone in this far-distant land on Egypt's confines, Bors put on all his armour and, leaving Sarras, went down to the sea where he boarded a ship. Circumstances favoured him, and after a short voyage he arrived in the kingdom of Logres. After landing there he journeyed on horseback as far as Camelot where he found king and court. Never was there such exultation as greeted his arrival, for they thought to have lost him for ever, since he had been so long abroad.

When they had dined King Arthur summoned his clerks who were keeping a record of all the adventures undergone by the knights of his household. When Bors had related to them the adventures of the Holy Grail as witnessed by himself, they were written down and the record kept in the library at Salisbury, whence Master Walter Map extracted them in order to make his book of the Holy Grail for love of his lord King Henry, who had the story translated from Latin into French. And with that the tale falls silent and has no more to say about the Adventures of the Holy Grail.

Notes

1. (p. 31) The medieval day was marked off into three-hourly sections which corresponded to the canonical hours of the Breviary. The first, prime, was normally fixed at 6 a.m., the second, terce, corresponded to 9 a.m., sext to midday, none to 3 o'clock in the afternoon, vespers to 6 p.m., while compline was the office sung before retiring. It is only the hours of prime, none and vespers that figure regularly in this book.

2. (p. 36) It is his respect for feudal loyalty that determines Gawain's action. The claims of courtesy, if not simple prudence (for there is nothing to show he sets much store by Lancelot's warning), would have held him back, but overriding all are the faith and obedience that he owes his liege-lord. This was the very pivot of feudal society, yet the author affirms that it constitutes no defence against the demands of a higher imperative.

3. (p. 37) A reference to St John, chapter 20, verse 19: 'When the doors were shut where the disciples were assembled for fear of the Jews, came Jesus and stood in the midst, and saith unto them, Peace be unto you.' Cf. also John 20, 26.

4. (p. 37) Red and white are the colours symbolically associated with Christ. Bors will put on a coarse white garment and a scarlet gown before his solemn communion, and the reader will find many other examples of colours used symbolically in the text.

5. (p. 37) The Celtic sources would seem to have had originally but one Grail Keeper, the god-king who was wounded with his own sacred weapon, lance or sword. As time went by this figure split into two or three who occasionally converge again. In the *Quest* the Maimed King, called in one episode King Parlan, is the father of the Rich Fisher King. The name Fisher King is itself something of a mystery. Robert de Boron has one Bron catching fish for the table of the Grail and thus acquiring the title; at the same time he makes the connexion with the Ichthus, the symbol of Christ. In the *Estoire del Graal* the first Fisher King's name is Alain, but the explanation is substantially the same. At a more primitive level, water is the principle and symbol of fertility and the sea-god was the king of the Other World. From Ireland too comes the legend of the salmon of wisdom which it is tempting to connect with Chrétien's strange statement that the Grail was a large

platter such as might contain a salmon or a lamprey. Perhaps it is wise to remember that symbols can work on many levels and be integrated into systems with no common origin. In the *Quest* there is some confusion concerning the identities of the Fisher King and King Pellés, lord of the Grail castle. Usually they appear to be one and the same person, and this is the most logical view. Here, however, as the result of some slip, whether of author or scribe, they are differentiated.

6. (p. 39) A reference to the episode of Galahad's conception related in Sommer, vol. v. pp. 105–12. The daughter of the Fisher King falls providentially in love with Lancelot who, as a result of a machination contrived by her lady-in-waiting, Brisane, lies with her under the impression that she is Guinevere. Not one of the most convincing passages, it has, besides, the unfortunate effect of tarring Galahad with the brush of bastardy. Since, however, the Perfect Knight had to stem from the line of the Fisher Kings and also from Lancelot, the fallen hero, the author was caught in a cleft stick.

7. (p. 43) The allusions to the descent of the Holy Ghost on the apostles, as described in Acts 2, 1–4, are here quite plain. The clap of thunder patently represents that 'sudden noise from heaven', just as the sunbeam reproduces the tongues of fire. The author then transcribes almost word for word the verse 'and they were all filled with the grace of the Holy Ghost'. Next, however, there is a significant divergence, for instead of 'speaking with other tongues' like the apostles, the knights of the Round Table could not even utter a word in their own language: sin had deprived them of speech. It is worth noting in passing that the Old French has, literally, 'and they were struck dumb, great and small', which may well be a reference to Genesis 19, 11, where the angels guarding Lot's house against the Sodomites 'smote the men that were at the door with blindness, both small and great'.

8. (p. 44) Welsh legend has a dish among whose properties was the dispensation to each guest of the food of his choice. On the other hand St Bernard, in the sermon on the Song of Songs quoted by Gilson in his article on the *Quest*, speaks of the sweet savour of the Divine Presence pleasing the soul's palate in different ways. This is perhaps another example of the fusing of different traditions and of a legendary seed springing to a new life in alien soil. It may equally well be coincidental, since there are a limited number of symbols in which man's experience can find expression.

9. (p. 47) The Old French word 'serjant' presents the translator with an almost insoluble problem. Should it be rendered 'soldier' or

'servant'? In an age when soldiers served and servants commonly fought it obviously had a double connotation. The author uses it in the parable of the talents where the English has 'servant'. Partly for that reason, and partly because it is usually coupled with the term 'chevaliers Jesuchrist', which embodies the military overtones, I have opted for 'servant' throughout.

10. (p. 47) The author repeatedly returns to these words of St Paul, I Corinthians 2, 9–10, (quoting in his turn Isaiah 64, 4) when describing the purpose and goal of the Quest. They form almost a *leitmotif* and obviously represent the essence of his conception of the Holy Grail.

11. (p. 59) Nascien was the brother-in-law of King Evalach. His name before baptism was Seraph, a derivative of the Arabic El-Ashraf, and he is occasionally referred to by his pagan name.

12. (p. 59) The name taken in baptism by King Evalach and frequently used to describe him, particularly in the latter part of the book.

13. (p. 60) For the list of Nascien's descendants, culminating in Galahad, see the dream of King Mordrain, pp. 151–2.

14. (p. 64) No one verse of the Psalms seems to lie at the source of these words; on the other hand they echo the theme of solitude and abandonment that runs through the great prophetical psalms which are generally considered to prefigure the Passion, notably Psalms 21, 37, 68 and 87 in the Authorized Version.

15. (p. 78) Gawain has already taken the wrong path in killing the seven brothers, as will shortly be pointed out to him. It is therefore no coincidence that he takes the wrong direction here and loses track of Galahad.

16. (p. 80) Lancelot, hitherto invincible, is unhorsed by Galahad, the knight who is to replace and supersede him. Perceval and Lancelot fail to recognize him not on the material plane alone, but because Galahad's arms are the arms of Christ. Lancelot through sin and Perceval through the arrogance of his class are both incapable of discerning the Redeemer.

17. (p 87) The false simoniac is presumably a reference to Simon the magician, who offered money to the apostles in exchange for the power of conferring the Holy Ghost through the laying-on of hands. Cf. Acts 8, 9–24.

18. (p. 87) I have not been able to find any trace of this expression in Scripture, nor am I inclined to believe that it comes from either the Old or the New Testament. The metaphorical uses of fire and related words in the Bible fall into two classes: either they are connected in the more moralizing books (Prov. Eccli., Sap., etc.) with the lusts of the flesh, or in the Prophets they are

associated with the power and particularly with the word of God, nowhere with divine love. This is true of the only N.T. example in any way germane to the issue (cf. Luke 24, 32). The association of fire and love would therefore seem to postdate Pentecost and the writings of St John. Thus it seems likely that the author is referring unwittingly to some saying of the Fathers or catch-phrase popular among preachers, for which Scripture may well have provided some such pattern as is found in Eccli. 8, 10: 'Kindle not the coals of a sinner, lest thou be burned with the flame of his fire' (Vulgate 8, 13).

19. (p. 92) Cf. Numbers, 20, 10. Even as the manna prefigured the Eucharistic Bread, so was the water struck from the rock equated with the fountain of life; see 1 Cor. 10, 4 '. . . for they drank of that Spiritual Rock that followed them: and that Rock was Christ'.

20. (p. 96) Although there are three chosen knights who are destined to pursue the quest of the Holy Grail to its ending, although the coming of Galahad has been ordained and prepared since the days of Solomon, there is no question of predestination in a calvinistic sense. Man's free will is entire, if not to good at any rate to evil, and he can always reject God's grace and the joys in store for him. A little later we see a hermit assuring Lancelot that if Galahad were to fall into mortal sin he would get no further in the quest than any other knight. Cf. p. 134.

21. (p. 98) This episode embodies a three-fold reminiscence: firstly of the manna distributed to the Israelites in the desert, secondly of the multiplication of the loaves and fishes, and thirdly of the Last Supper, thus clearly linking the Old and the New Testaments in the concept of the bread which sustains both body and soul.

22. (p. 99) The Ptolemaic system of astronomy conceived the earth as a fixed point around which rotated a series of transparent and concentric spheres carrying the planets and fixed stars. A very clear description of the system will be found in Dorothy Sayers's notes to her translation of the *Divine Comedy*, Vol. 1, in the Penguin Classics. For a discussion of the meaning of the three tables see A. Micha, 'La Table Ronde chez Robert de Boron et dans la Queste del Saint Graal', *Colloques Internationales du CNRS*, III, Paris, 1956.

23. (p. 99) Luke 18, 29 speaks of leaving 'house, or parents, or brethren, or wife, or children, for the kingdom of God's sake'. This, together with the mention of the fraternal love that binds the companions, makes it plain that the Round Table was another figuration of the eucharistic meal. The chain will be completed at Corbenic with the twelve knights representing the apostles and Christ himself present as priest and victim.

24. (p. 115) The lion in medieval bestiaries and iconography is commonly a figure of Christ; the equation doubtless takes its origin from Revelations 5, 5: 'behold, the Lion of the tribe of Judah'.

25. (p. 119) This ship is the first of several to play an important part in the *Quest*. As a symbol it had a rich heritage to draw on, at once in classical literature, as a symbol of the Church as will be apparent later on, and more immediately in Celtic myth where the rudderless ship, to which the hero entrusts himself, transparently denotes the acceptance of life's adventure and its concomitant perils and rewards. The ship, too, offers passage to the Other World, and is noteworthy that in the *Quest* these craft either ferry the emissaries of heaven or hell, or carry the chosen knights on voyages of spiritual discovery.

26. (p. 122) An allusion at once to the Old Testament record of the translation of Enoch and Elijah (for the first, see Genesis 5, 24, for the second 2 Kings 2, 1–11), and to the Gospel of Nicodemus, which relates how these two, who 'did not see death' (see Hebrews 11, 5), were to return to earth in the last days to fight in Jerusalem with Antichrist, who would make them both 'martyrs' to God, before being finally crushed by a thunderbolt hurled from heaven by an angel (cf. *Trois versions rimées de l'Evangile de Nicodème*, éd. G. Paris et A. Bos, SATF. Paris, 1885). One suspects the early Christians to have felt that the exceptional fate reserved to Enoch and Elijah was a trifle unfair, and diminished in some degree the uniqueness of Christ's Ascension and the Assumption of Our Lady. Antichrist provided a providential means of dispatching the champions and ensuring that they did not escape the common human lot.

27. (p. 122) The opposition of the Old Law and the New has of course its basis in Scripture. St Paul speaks of the two sons of Abraham, the one by a bondmaid, the other by a freewoman, 'which things are an allegory' (Galatians 4, 22–6). Margaret Schlauch, in a study of Church and Synagogue in the *Perlesvaus*, writes of 'the close connexion between this literary motif and an important body of Church literature on Synagogue and Church, which although originating with the Fathers, received particularly elaborate and frequent treatment about 1200 AD'. She cites the great number of disputations between Synagogue and Church, or between Jew and Christian, composed about this time, mostly in Latin but some in the vernacular (M. Schlauch, 'The Allegory of Church and Synagogue', in *Speculum*, 1939, pp. 448–64). For examples in the plastic arts and the symbolical interpretation of the Crucifixion one can consult E. Mâle, *L'Art religieux du XIII siècle en France*, pp. 225–31. It is worth noting that the author of

the *Quest* does not make use of the traditional representation
of the Synagogue as a blind woman. The idea of the Synagogue as mounted on the serpent and shown thereby to be in
league with Satan does not of course refer to the old dispensation, when the Law symbolized God's covenant with man. It is
only since the Crucifixion that the Synagogue has become the
devil's creature, symbolizing the rejection of Christ and His saving
power, the cleaving to sin and the refusal of the New Covenant
embodied in the Church. Bors in his turn will become em-
broiled in the struggle between Church and Synagogue which is
represented as a fight to the end of time for the hearts of men, the
tide of battle now ebbing, now advancing according to the loyalty of the Church's sons. Cf. pp. 181–7 and 197.

The scriptural theme of the Covenant between God and man is
indeed central to the entire *Quest* – witness the number and
importance of the references to the Pentateuch and to all the
texts touching the Eucharist, as also the symbolism surrounding
the Grail itself: the table, the six-branched candelabra, and the
ark which Galahad finally builds to house it, which patently hark
back to the Mosaic prescriptions enshrined in chapters 25 and 37
of Exodus.

28. (p. 126) Perceval's temptress is here obviously attacking the principle of total self-abandonment to God. Possibly the adage that
'God helps those who help themselves' is an expression of the
well-known English tendency to Pelagianism!

29. (p. 126) A reference to the saying in Deuteronomy 8, 3, that
'man doth not live by bread only, but by every word that pro-
ceedeth out of the mouth of the Lord doth man live', which
Christ quoted against Satan in the desert (cf. Matt. 4, 4 and Luke
4, 4); it is developed further in the 6th chapter of St John's Gospel where Our Lord foreshadows the doctrine of the
Eucharist, particularly in verse 35: 'I am the bread of life: he
that cometh to me shall never hunger and he that believeth
on me shall never thirst.'

30. (p. 126) It is not self-interest, but interest in others, compassion
for the oppressed, that leads Perceval into mortal danger, thereby
illustrating the importance of prudence in the face of appeals to
the emotions. Perceval is singularly deficient in this gift of the
Holy Ghost, a fact that his temptress is quick to seize upon, for
noting his immediate and unconsidered response, she adds fuel
to the fire by reminding him of his oath to succour damsels in
distress.

31. (p. 128) It is unarmed that Perceval enters the tent. The maiden
takes care first to have his helm and hauberk and sword removed:

surely the 'helmet of salvation', the 'breastplate of righteousness'
and the 'sword of the spirit' which St Paul details in Eph. 6, 11–17
as being part of that armour of God that is needed to withstand
the wiles of the devil. It is worth noting that the heroes of the
Quest frequently spend the hours of darkness with their heads
resting on their shields (the 'shield of faith') or hauberks (cf.
Lancelot, p. 82 Perceval, p. 130. The green grass of humility
and patience is also favoured (cf. Lancelot, p. 155, Bors, p. 179,
Galahad, p. 209). They habitually spend much of the night in
prayer (cf. Perceval, p. 114, Lancelot, p. 160, Perceval and
Galahad, p. 252). In contrast we find Gawain and Hector, after
taking refuge in an abandoned chapel and saying a modicum of
prayers, lying down to sleep 'where best they could' (p. 164).

32. (p. 129) It has been suggested that Perceval's escape from sin has
been in some sense 'rigged' by the author. Why should he so con-
veniently catch sight of the cross on his sword-hilt at the crucial
moment? Is not this a clumsy and unwarrantable device on the
author's part to save his hero's chastity? To argue thus is to
misunderstand grievously the providential nature of Perceval's
escape and to underestimate the author's powers. He himself has
deliberately underlined the role of providence by the repetition
of such expressions as 'by chance', 'he happened', etc. Yet this is
not an example of God loading the dice in the hero's favour. The
episode is perfectly prepared and motivated on the spiritual plane.
Perceval has not left himself completely unguarded. He has kept
his sword by him. Divine providence, symbolized by the fortui-
tous element in human actions, intervenes, not haphazardly, but
as the counterweight to Perceval's innocence, his 'sancta simplicitas'. Because he has placed his whole trust in God, God in His
mercy saves him from the consequences of his human imperfec-
tions. It is an illustration of the Psalmist's assurance: 'He shall
give his angels charge over thee lest thou dash thy foot against a
stone.'

33. (p. 132) Cf. John 9, 4–5 '... the night cometh, when no man can
work. As long as I am in the world, I am the light of the world.'

34. (p. 133) Cf. John 6, 51. It is significant that Perceval, who invari-
ably fails to pierce the devil's disguises, instinctively recognizes
Christ. One is reminded of John 10, 14, 'I know my sheep and am
known of mine'. Indeed this chapter of the *Quest* constantly
draws its imagery from St John's Gospel, which is one long hymn
to the Son's knowledge of the Father, to the Father's love for the
Son, each term throwing a deeper light on the other, which brings
us back to the Cistercian equation of knowledge and love underlined by Gilson (see Introduction, p. 20).

35. (p. 136) This slighting of Guinevere to the lover who but a few days earlier was giving her the credit for all he had and was, is perhaps the most dramatic reversal the *Quest* has to offer. Now he is told that her love for him, that love he had lived by for so many years, was poor and paltry, since it went against his true interests. Human love seeks its own and not the loved one's good. Lancelot's awakening to a new set of values is measured by his silence in the face of these taunts. The courtly code would have demanded an immediate avenging of his lady's honour.

36. (p. 141) A reference on the one hand to John 14, 23, '... and we will come unto him and make our abode with him', and on the other to the unclean spirit returning to the house and finding it 'swept and garnished' (Luke 11, 25).

37. (p. 141) The earlier books tell us that Lancelot was baptized Lancelot-Galahad. This fact was only revealed to him later and he loses through sin his right to his second baptismal name (see Sommer, vols. IV, 176 and V, 114). Thus it is plain that from the outset the plan contained the bold conception of Lancelot-Adam, father of Galahad-Christ. Both were perfectly endowed by nature, but only in the second was that perfection sustained and brought to its final flowering by grace.

38. (p. 143) Finally we learn that not only has Lancelot's adulterous love debarred him from the mystical vision of the Holy Grail, it did not even enable him, as he believed, to scale the heights of knightly prowess. His worldly attainments were themselves attributable to the remnants of those gifts once vested in him by God and so misused. The cult of the lady has been stripped of its last support.

39. (p. 151) An allusion to Galahad's bastardy.

40. (p. 151) One is tempted to see an echo of Peter's plea to Christ: 'Lord, not my feet only, but also my hands and my head' (John 13, 9).

41. (p. 152) A previous episode relates how Lancelot finds his grandfather's grave in the Perilous Forest and kills the two lions guarding it, but stands helpless before the boiling spring into which his grandfather's head had been thrown. His burning passion renders him powerless to quench its heat and the loosing of the spell must wait the coming of Galahad (cf. Sommer, vol. V, pp. 243–8, and *infra*, p. 270).

42. (p. 154) This passage touches on many aspects of doctrine, none of which is expounded fully. Firstly, it must be stressed that the author is not denying human participation in original sin, but merely affirming that each individual is wholly responsible for the sins he personally commits, and that at the last day God will

'reward every man according to his works'. Neither can it be said, for later passages disprove it, that he is rejecting the communion of saints and the value of intercession. What he is attempting to bring out is that each man must work out his own salvation with the help of Christ, the perfect Mediator. It is no use Lancelot's relying on the sanctity of others to haul him into heaven by his bootstraps while he renounces all personal effort. God's answer to Lancelot is the same as he gave Paul: 'My grace is sufficient for thee: for my strength is made perfect in weakness.'

43. (p. 160) There is a certain mystery about the name of the river which bars Lancelot's advance. The author calls it 'l'eau Marcoise', which might mean boundary, as in 'march', or alternatively marshy. Either would fit the theme, the first in the sense of the point of no return, the second in that of Bunyan's Slough of Despond. I have opted for the first in rendering it by Median River, because the author says plainly that it divided the forest in two. Certainly his arrival at the river marks a crucial stage in Lancelot's pilgrimage. Like Perceval, he has come to the end of his own possibilities. Once again afoot, without a war-horse, the proud caste-mark of the knight, hemmed in by physical obstacles symbolizing the spiritual impasse in which he finds himself, he can go no further unaided along the road he has chosen. Faced with the temptation of despair, he has no other choice but to 'sit still, his peace in God's will'. And so we leave him, wondering whether he will ever cross to the spiritual uplands on the other side.

44. (p. 162) This term 'adventure' that occurs on almost every page raises problems at once linguistic and interpretive. If I have not discussed it until now it is because I have preferred to let the context speak for itself. The arthurian romances and the 'matière de Bretagne' in general are based on the concept of the *aventure*, which word has a much wider connotation than its modern English equivalent. To render it 'adventure' is misleading, and yet there is no other alternative; one needs must let the context supply what is lacking. In a general way the adventure represents the random, the gratuitous, the unpredictable element in life; often it is the challenge which causes a man to measure himself against standards more than human, to gamble life for honour or both for love. To this the author of the *Quest* adds a further dimension. For him the adventure is above all God working and manifesting Himself in the physical world. To accept an adventure is to accept an encounter with a force which is in the proper sense of the word supernatural, an encounter which is always perilous for the sinner or the man of little faith and much presumption.

To the faithful it implies submission to God's providence. On two occasions Christ says specifically: 'Go where adventure leads you,' once to Perceval (p. 133) and once to the twelve knights whom he sends abroad in a repetition of the dispersion of the apostles (p. 278). Providence is 'safe' only to those whose wills are aligned with the divine purpose. Gawain's failure to meet with any adventure springs from his spiritual blindness, his inability to discern the divine element in human life.

I think it is true to say that the author of the *Quest* uses the concept of the *aventure* as a symbol of providence just as precisely and consistently as he uses the Holy Grail as a symbol of mystical experience. Unfortunately the equivalent English word has become so contracted in its meaning that it is often impossible to render one by the other. While recognizing that it is most unsatisfactory to have half a dozen words symbolizing a concept so vital to the central theme, I have frequently been compelled by the demands of clarity and usage to substitute for 'adventure' such terms as 'chance', 'fortune', 'phenomenon', etc. I feel therefore doubly bound to stress that beneath the multiplicity of terms there runs through the story like an unbroken thread the idea of providential guidance which man can either accept, refuse or simply fail to see.

45. (p. 163) Gawain is always ready to give praise where it is due. His is a real generosity of mind, and the tears he sheds over his murdered companions are wholly genuine. The author constantly underlines his human qualities in order to bring out the more poignantly the inadequacy of the courtly ideal.

46. (p. 164) An allusion to the internecine strife that will decimate the Round Table in the *Mort le Roi Artu*, the last book of the cycle.

47. (p. 170) Compare the emerald green of constancy and long-suffering, p. 141.

48. (p. 178) The author returns to the question of personal responsibility of which a previous hermit had discoursed to Lancelot (see p. 154 and Note 42). Initially Bors' companion appears to be a trifle muddled, since the parable of the tree and its fruits refers to the works produced in the soul by grace and not to heredity (cf. Matt. 17, 7). Perhaps his remark is more in the manner of a well-turned compliment. At all events it enables Bors to show off his knowledge and at the same time to be corrected on a subtle point of theology; for man's liberty is partial rather than entire, in that he needs grace to will the good as well as to accomplish it. For the image of ship and helm, cf. James 3, 4.

49. (p. 179) Presumably a garment of coarse material such as was

worn by the Cistercians, who were forbidden the use of fine, soft shirts (see *supra*, p. 138).

50. (p. 181) A twelfth-century Latin bestiary, translated and edited by T. H. White, gives this version of the widely held belief concerning the habits of the pelican:

'The Pelican is excessively devoted to its children. But when these have been born and begin to grow up, they flap their parents in the face with their wings, and the parents striking back kill them. Three days afterwards the mother pierces her breast, opens her side, and lays herself across her young, pouring out her blood over the dead bodies. This brings them to life again.

'In the same way, Our Lord Jesus Christ, who is the originator and maker of all created things, begets us and calls us into being out of nothing. We, on the contrary, strike him in the face. As the prophet Isaiah says: "I have borne children and exalted them and truly they have scorned me." We have struck him in the face by devoting ourselves to the creation rather than the creator.

'That was why he ascended into the height of the cross, and, his side having been pierced, there came from it blood and water for our salvation and eternal life.'

The author of the *Quest* provides a very similar gloss on p. 196.

51. (p. 194) The argument of the end and the means is carried here to its logical conclusion. It is commonplace nowadays to decry the preoccupation with personal salvation, considered to be a form of selfishness. The Church, however, teaches that a man's first duty is to his own soul. This is not a question of selfishness but of efficacy: the salvation of others cannot after all be bought at the price of one's own damnation, since sin is of its essence negative.

52. (p. 198) Perceval's temptation was that of a straight appeal to the senses, reasons having been dulled by wine. With the stolider and more thoughtful Bors the assault is on the mind, and on the substance of belief which in turn is the motive force determining or rejecting each particular act. Unreason, error, was to lead Bors to doubt God's providence, thence to despair, and thence again to sin, since not only would the bridle of faith no longer have held him in check, but the brutal destruction of all that he had lived by must have unbalanced his whole personality.

53. (p. 201) From the very outset of the *Quest* we find Bors and Lionel together. Theirs are the first familiar faces that Lancelot sees after leaving Camelot on his mysterious mission, and he finds them 'lying asleep in two beds'. Much stress is laid on the mutual joy of this encounter. It is they, too, who are the first,

with Lancelot, to set eyes on Galahad, though Lionel, signifi-
cantly, plays no part in knighting him. Together with Lancelot
they make the discovery of the inscription on the Seat of Danger. It is obvious that they habitually went about together, since
the companions of the Round Table give them a particular welcome after their long absence. Lionel's violent attack on his
brother is thus totally unprepared, and its significance lies in this
very factor. It is to be understood in the light of Our Lord's saying: 'I come not to bring peace, but a sword'; the fulfilment of the
prophecy that His coming was to set sons against their fathers
and divide families against one another. The quest for truth is
double-edged, and once the courtly veneer is peeled off by ex-
posure to a brighter light Lionel is seen for what he is.

54. (p. 208) Gawain is the first to ride on Galahad's heels and lament
the fact of always arriving too late to catch his quarry. Now by a
supreme irony, having confined his quest to ever more pointless killings, he finds himself on the wrong side and is struck
down by the knight whom he had sought so zealously.

55. (p. 208) Galahad's frequent disappearances call to mind Christ's
habit of withdrawing unseen from the midst of those seeking to
follow or seize Him.

56. (p. 213) This ship, which is to play an important part in the
story from now on, and whose history will gradually be unfolded, has been generally taken to represent the Church. The
symbolism is self-evident. The Church has traditionally been
likened to a ship and one often finds it referred to as the Bark of
Peter. None the less the inscription would appear to cast doubt
on so straightforward an interpretation. This is certainly not the
Church as an institution, the Church on earth, refuge and mother
of sinners. Perhaps the difficulty lessens if we take the ship as
representing the Church as seen through the Song of Songs, the
Church as the mystical bride of Christ. Then the inscription may
be read as a warning against the dangers of ill-considered ven-
tures into mysticism, a warning which the Church herself has
repeatedly issued down the centuries.

57. (p. 214) The exact significance of this sword has puzzled scholars.
Pauphilet probably lit on the truth in affirming that this must
be the 'sword of the Spirit, which is the word of God'. St Paul
compares the word of God on another occasion to a two-edged
sword (Hebrews 4, 12), and we find the same image in Revelation 1, 10 and in Psalm 149, 6. The author reveals later that the
blade was taken from the sword of David, the greatest perhaps of
the Old Testament figures of Christ. The fact that the hilt serves
as a protection against heat may or may not be an allusion to the

saving of Shadrach, Meshach and Abednego in the fiery furnace, or it may be that the author has in mind God's promise to Israel: '... when thou walkest through the fire, thou shalt not be burned: neither shall the flame kindle upon thee' (Isaiah 43, 2). Juridical ordeal by fire was in any case a common touchstone for truth in the Middle Ages. Perhaps more significant is the single-mindedness with which its wielder is instantly invested. Undoubtedly the spiritual symbolism has, as will shortly appear, been somewhat overlaid by surviving elements of Celtic myth which render interpretation at best tentative.

58. (p. 216) It may be helpful at this point to say a word about the theme of the Waste Land and the fatal or grievous sword-stroke. The Celtic legend follows a set pattern. A hero sets out for the Other World in response to an appeal or challenge from its sovereign or his messenger. The king of the Other World has been wounded, or crippled, or sometimes killed by a blow from one of his magic weapons, the sword or the javelin-like lance, which has usually been taken from him by stealth or treachery. From the moment of his death or wounding, his kingdom becomes barren, and as a result of the interdependence of the worlds of gods and men, analogous disasters visit earth, while the sword, after delivering the fatal blow, habitually snaps in two and can only be knit by the hero who redeems the land. Most of these elements have been incorporated in the *Quest* in a series of interconnected episodes. In this, the first of the three, the theme of the Waste Land makes its initial appearance and will subsequently be linked to the story of Genesis. Presumably King Varlan is shown as a Christian in order to accentuate the gravity of the sin, which thereby takes on a fratricidal note echoing the slaying of Abel by Cain.

59. (p. 221) The theme of the 'fatal blow' has furnished the author of the *Quest* with three episodes, each containing elements figuring in Celtic legends: the blow itself with the resulting devastation of the kingdom, the sword which snaps in two, and the flying lance or spear which wounds, presumably in the genitals, the father of the Fisher King. Obviously these motifs make uneasy bedfellows with the Christian symbolism which the author is attempting to superimpose on the older material. Conscious perhaps of a certain awkwardness, he has avoided specifying whether the lance that wounds King Parlan is identical with the bleeding lance of Longinus; instead he has contented himself with trying to bring these pagan elements within a Christian framework by representing in each case the injuries as a punishment for the sin of presumption.

60. (p. 229) This paraphrase of the story of Genesis is an adaptation of the ancient legend of the Cross, which enjoyed widespread popularity in the Middle Ages and of which there were several differing versions. Any reader who might wish to study the question in greater detail will find much valuable information in Pauphilet, *Études sur la Queste del Saint Graal*, pp. 144–56, and E. Mâle *L'Art religieux du XIII siècle en France*, vol. IV, ch. I. It was no doubt natural curiosity in part that built up a body of apocryphal literature around the lives of Adam and Eve and their children, but more immediately responsible was the tendency to see the whole of the Old Testament as an allegorical prefiguration of the New. The medieval love of symmetry and parallelism looked naturally for a link between the tree which caused the Fall and that other tree which bore mankind's Redemption. The version given here, as far as the death of Abel, while it follows the general lines laid down by tradition, is, as far as is known, unique in a number of details. Firstly in the importance of the role accorded to Eve. Whereas in the common version Seth, at Adam's behest, returns to the Garden of Eden, where an angel shows him in the topmost branches of the Tree of Knowledge the Babe who is to redeem his father's race, and hands him three seeds to place in Adam's mouth at his death, from which will spring the three trees, cedar, cyprus and pine, which will provide the wood of the cross, in the *Quest* it is Eve who carries, unconsciously, a twig of the tree of Paradise in her hand, and plants it in remembrance of her lost happiness; thus she who had been responsible for sin entering the world unknowingly prepares the world's redemption. Thus, too, there is in the beginning but one tree, symbolizing in its changing colours – the white of purity, the green of piety, the red of sacrifice – the three essential facets of Christ's life on earth.

The theme of the Waste Land is reintroduced through the cursing of the earth after the murder of Abel, and again after the devastation of the Flood, thereby giving a new and deeper meaning to the Celtic myth.

61. (p. 234) After Abel's death the author of the *Quest* parts company with the legend of the Cross. Having introduced into his work much of the allegorical material traditionally associated with the coming of Christ, he now has to find some means of fitting it, without the result appearing sacrilegious, to his new hero, Galahad. As with the couple Adam and Eve he magnifies the woman's role, so he proceeds in the same manner with Solomon and his wife. Solomon's wife stands midway between Eve and Mary. In her feminine guile, in her addiction to deceit,

she looks backward towards Eve, symbolizing the medieval obsession with woman as the author of man's downfall; in the part she plays, half-consciously, in preparing the way for the fulfilment of the prophecies, she prefigures the Virgin Mary. She represents the Old Testament, at once in its greatness and its limitations: a storehouse of wisdom, as yet imperfectly understood, since only the coming of Christ and the gift of the Spirit can make all things plain.

62. (p. 237) Perceval's sister, who remains throughout strangely anonymous, consummates what Solomon's wife left uncompleted. She is the New Testament, which gives to the Old its full meaning. Like a nun at her profession, she shaves her hair, her 'crowning glory', thereby consecrating her virginity to Christ, the Divine Bridegroom. It is she who provides the link between the first and second parts of the *Quest*, the preparation and the apotheosis, she who calls Galahad and leads him to the ship, she who will later reunite Lancelot with Galahad and bring him finally to Corbenic.

63. (p. 237) There are four couples in the *Quest*, two drawn from Scripture or para-scriptural tradition (Adam and Eve, Solomon and his wife), and two belonging to the *Quest* proper. Between these four the contrasts, parallels and cross-references are multiplied. Much has been made of the anti-feminism of the *Quest*. Given, however, the monastic slant of the text, and the traditional attitude of the medieval Church to women, reinforced no doubt by the prejudices of a celibate clergy, a good case can be made for the moderation of our author in this respect. Both Eve and Guinevere are represented in the part of the eternal temptress; in respect of Eve there was of course good authority, and her role has simply been transferred to Guinevere, who offers the forbidden fruit to the new Lancelot-Adam. There is however little overt condemnation of Guinevere, and as for Eve, we are told with perfect logic that she, being subject to Adam, and the weaker sex, was held less responsible by God than he. Only with reference to Solomon's wife does the author allow himself a broadside, and it must be admitted that Proverbs and Ecclesiastes furnished him with ample material. Conversely he always assigns to his women a positive part in the redemption of mankind. Eve carried the sacred branch out of Paradise, Solomon's wife prepares the ship with the wooden frame above the bed symbolizing the Cross, and the sword of David at its foot, and finally in Perceval's sister we have the figure of woman redeemed and in her turn redeeming. The very concept of courtly love is presented purified and sublimated; the scene where Galahad

accepts the sword from the hand of Perceval's sister is a pendant to that earlier scene where Lancelot received his knighthood at the hands of Guinevere.

64. (p. 242) The events of Castle Carcelois stand in contraposition, both as regards their meaning and the episode's placing in the story, to those enacted at the Castle of the Maidens. In the first instance Galahad contents himself with routing the wicked brothers and re-establishing the rule of right, in a demonstration of God's mercy towards sinners. In the later the crimes, though of the same order, are infinitely greater in degree:- to rape is added incest, to injustice sacrilege, murders are multiplied and sin and crime become the way of life of an entire community. This enables the author to counterbalance God's twin prerogatives of mercy and justice, this time bringing the scales down on the side of justice. Galahad, who has never until now deprived an adversary of the life that, while it lasts, holds the promise of repentance, has difficulty in accepting his role of divine avenger, and requires the reassurance of a priest to convince him.

65. (p. 243) The four beasts of the Apocalypse (Rev. 6, 6–9), popularly represented as figuring the four evangelists. The same beasts first appear in the vision of Ezechiel (ch. 1), and in both books they are depicted as beneath or around a throne which bears one 'in the likeness of a man.'

66. (p. 245) This vision, the last vouchsafed to the companions before the three-fold revelation of the Grail at Corbenic and Sarras, enfolds the central doctrines of the Christian faith: Incarnation, Passion and Resurrection. The transparency of glass to light was a favourite figure for the Virgin Birth. The redemption of mankind is symbolized by the metamorphosis of the four evangelists.

67. (p. 248) Leprosy is a traditional symbol of sin, and the *Quest* alludes more than once to the external manifestations of grace or sin in the soul; first in the repeated insistence on Galahad's physical beauty, and secondly in Gawain's vision, where the companions of the Round Table appear as bulls, dappled and spotted, because 'their guilt could not stay hidden in the inner man but must affect the outer' (p. 170). Perceval's sister, through her offering of her life-blood, freely made, redeems the figure of sinful Eve.

68. (p. 252) Here too, divine judgement follows on the murder of the innocent; it is not, as is made clear, a punishment for the death of Perceval's sister, whose sacrifice was wholly voluntary.

69. (p. 256) It is during this voyage that for the first time Lancelot is termed 'servant of Jesus Christ', an epithet hitherto reserved to the three heroes.

70. (p. 259) Again the theme of personal responsibility, once again in the context of the relationship between Lancelot and Galahad, and clearly linked here to the question of intercession. Once before Lancelot has been told that Galahad's merits will not ensure his salvation, this time Galahad himself repeats the warning. He does not say that he will not pray for his father, indeed one must assume from knowledge of his role and character that he will; he merely stresses that no prayers will have the value of Lancelot's own. This is certainly not to be interpreted, as Pauphilet seems to have thought, as an attack on the value of intercessory prayer – there is evidence enough to the contrary. When Lancelot leaves his first hermit host he asks him for his prayers, and the other promises to pray for him (p. 135). Bors does the same and receives a similar assurance (p. 180). The hermit on the rock begs Lancelot to ask for Galahad's intercession on his behalf. Most significant of all, the abbot asks Bors to pray for him, thinking that God will listen more readily to Bors than to himself (cf. James 5, 16, 'The effectual fervent prayer of a righteous man availeth much'). Therefore if Lancelot is twice adjured in terms almost harsh to count only on himself and his Saviour, it is because of an essential weakness in his nature which can only be overcome by unremitting effort.

71. (p. 262) The Three Persons of the Trinity are shown as participating in the Son's sacrifice.

72. (p. 263) The Old Testament is full of these burning winds, 'ventus urens' in the Vulgate. It is this wind that brings the plague of locusts on Egypt (Exodus 10, 13) and divides the Red Sea (Exodus 14, 21). In the Prophets it is the symbol of the power and more frequently of the wrath of God (cf. Jer. 4, 11; 18, 17, and Hos. 13, 15, Jonah 4, 8, Hag. 2, 8, Amos 4, 9 and Hab. 1, 9). The Authorized Version translates it as an 'east wind', but the author of the *Quest* would have had the Vulgate in mind and it is surely to these Old Testament images of the terrible power of God's judgement that he is referring here. Similarly the Castle of Corbenic is swept by a burning wind which is the signal for the departure of all those who are unworthy to assist at the mass of the Holy Grail. (Cf. p. 273.)

73. (p. 263) It may seem hard that Lancelot's good intentions should earn him such harsh treatment, but the very nature of his gesture serves to measure his progress in the spiritual life. He is indeed 'purblind' as he himself recognized earlier: at the culmination of his quest he is still so lacking in spiritual insight that he interprets in physical terms an experience purely mystical. The entire passage brings to mind the parable of the marriage feast

quoted, no doubt prophetically, to Lancelot by the hermit
whose companion he had helped to bury. Surely his forcible
removal from the spiritual banquet is a deliberate echo of Matt.
22, 13: 'Then said the king to the servants, bind him hand and
foot, and take him away, and cast him into outer darkness'. For
Lancelot there was no weeping and gnashing of teeth – that was
reserved for Hector. Both brothers aspire to be guests at the selfsame feast; one is utterly rejected, the one without a wedding
garment; the other, who has made some preparation, first pays
the penalty of its deficiency and is then admitted to that degree
of participation that his imperfect spirituality allows.

The punishment inflicted on Lancelot for presuming to approach the holy of holies is also surely linked with the blindness
which struck King Mordrain in similar circumstances (see p. 106),
and both passages would seem to hark back to the nineteenth
chapter of Exodus, where God forbids the children of Israel to
approach Mount Sinai (cf. verses 12 and especially 21): 'And the
Lord said unto Moses, go down, charge the people, lest they
break through unto the Lord to gaze, and many of them perish'.

74. (p. 265) One may well wonder why the inhabitants of Corbenic
failed to recognize Lancelot earlier. By underlining the point the
author presumably meant to emphasize the spiritual nature of
his ecstasy. One is reminded of St Paul speaking of the man caught
up to the third heaven, 'whether in the body, I cannot tell; or
whether out of the body, I cannot tell; God knoweth'. (2 Cor. 12,
2.) Lancelot is transformed outwardly by the inward grace of the
Holy Ghost. Only when he returns to the world, symbolized by
the gown of scarlet cloth, do the bystanders know him for
the Lancelot they had often met before.

75. (p. 267) It is human love that precipitates Lancelot's departure
from Corbenic, a foretaste of the love for Guinevere that will
catch him in its toils again in the *Mort Artu*, before his final
renunciation and redemption.

76. (p. 268) The slaying off-stage of good King Baudemagus, friend of
Lancelot and Arthur, marks Gawain's final 'non-appearance' in
the tale. It is an apt touch that the knight whose contribution
to the quest has been negative from start to finish, should consummate his failure *in absentia*.

77. (p. 268) A reference to an earlier episode in which Chanaan, one of
the followers of Joseph of Arimathea, killed his twelve brothers
while they slept. The following day their swords were found upright like a hedge about their graves (cf. Sommer, 1, pp. 266–8).
Gawain and Hector, coming by chance on the graves, find an inscription warning them that the adventure was to be Lancelot's

(cf. Sommer, IV, pp. 339–41). The exact nature of the adventure remains obscure. It presumably consisted in Lancelot's riding through the impenetrable sword-hedge, but the explanation appears somewhat inadequate and one feels that the author only included the episode in order to tie up a loose end, and did not wish to waste more time on Lancelot now that his quest was over.

78. (p. 270) Wales, if we are to believe the 'Lancelot-Grail', was originally known as Hosselice and acquired the names of Galles (Wales) from its first Christian king, Galahad of Galefort.

79. (p. 270) Simeon had attempted to kill his cousin, Peter, in a fit of jealousy (cf. Sommer, I, pp. 265–6).

80. (p. 271) There is an apparent lacuna in the manuscript at this point. F. Lot surmises that the missing passage related, among other matters, the reunion of Galahad and Perceval (cf. Lot, op. cit., p. 253).

81. (p. 273) It is obvious that the nine strange knights have been introduced only to complete the apostolic count.

82. (p. 275) The twelfth century had seen a controversy over the exact moment when transubstantiation took place. One Pierre le Chantre affirmed that it only occurred after the consecration of both bread and wine. The author of the *Quest* comes down on the side of orthodoxy. The eucharistic mystery is twice described in the *Quest* and each time it is plain that Christ is bodily present from the moment of the major elevation when the priest pronounces the words: *Hic est enim corpus meum*. For further discussion of the eucharistic tradition in the Grail romances, see Roach, *Zeitschrift für romanische Philologie* LIX, 1939, pp. 10–56.

83. (p. 276) This fanciful etymology of the word Grail (in the Old French: Graal < gré) is first found in Robert de Boron's poem which predates the *Quest* by some thirty years. It doubtless owes its repetition to the regrettable medieval predilection for such things.

84. (p. 278) A character who plays a minor part in a previous episode (cf. Sommer, V., pp. 340–75).

85. (p. 280) It is here that the symbolism of the bed becomes finally clear. Plainly it derives from the Song of Songs 2, 6–7, 'Who is this that cometh out of the wilderness like pillars of smoke, perfumed with myrrh and frankincense, with all the perfumes of the merchant. Behold his bed, which is Solomon's'. Pauphilet has suggested that the bed symbolizes the perfect repose of death, which is to say Christ's death on the Cross; therefore the bed is the altar on which that sacrifice is re-enacted (cf. Pauphilet,

Études, p. 151). No doubt this interpretation can validly be placed on it. But in the light of Galahad's long sleep from which he awakes to see the city of Sarras, the Heavenly Jerusalem, we might seem to be closer to the author's meaning in accepting Gilson's theory, based on St Bernard's writings, that Solomon's bed is the symbol of the ecstatic vision.

86. (p. 282) This last chapter in the life of Galahad shows the Perfect Knight undergoing two years of purification through suffering, first in prison and then weighed down by the yoke of worldly honour, before his final apotheosis.

87. (p. 283) It is here above all that Gilson's equation of the Grail with the grace of God appears inadequate. It is inconceivable that a writer as conscious both of his art and of his aims as the author of the *Quest* should end his book on an anti-climax. The three manifestations of the secrets of the Grail must follow an ascending curve. It 'appears' to Lancelot that he sees the Trinity made manifest at the elevation of the Host; this is properly a visionary experience. At the re-enacting of the Last Supper Christ emerges bodily from the chalice and Himself communicates His new apostles. What then is left for Galahad, who has expressly stated his hopes of greater bliss? It could but be what Lancelot had seen 'in semblance', the contemplation 'face to face' of the triune Godhead, that which had been refused to Moses: 'Thou canst not see my face, for there shall no man see me and live'. Exodus 33, 20. The meaning is made doubly plain by Galahad's death immediately following.